Hedge Witch

The Cloven Land Trilogy, Book 1

Simon Kewin

Hedge Witch – The Cloven Land Trilogy, Book 1

Copyright © Simon Kewin 2014

STORM
CROW
BOOKS

ISBN: 978-1-9993395-2-4

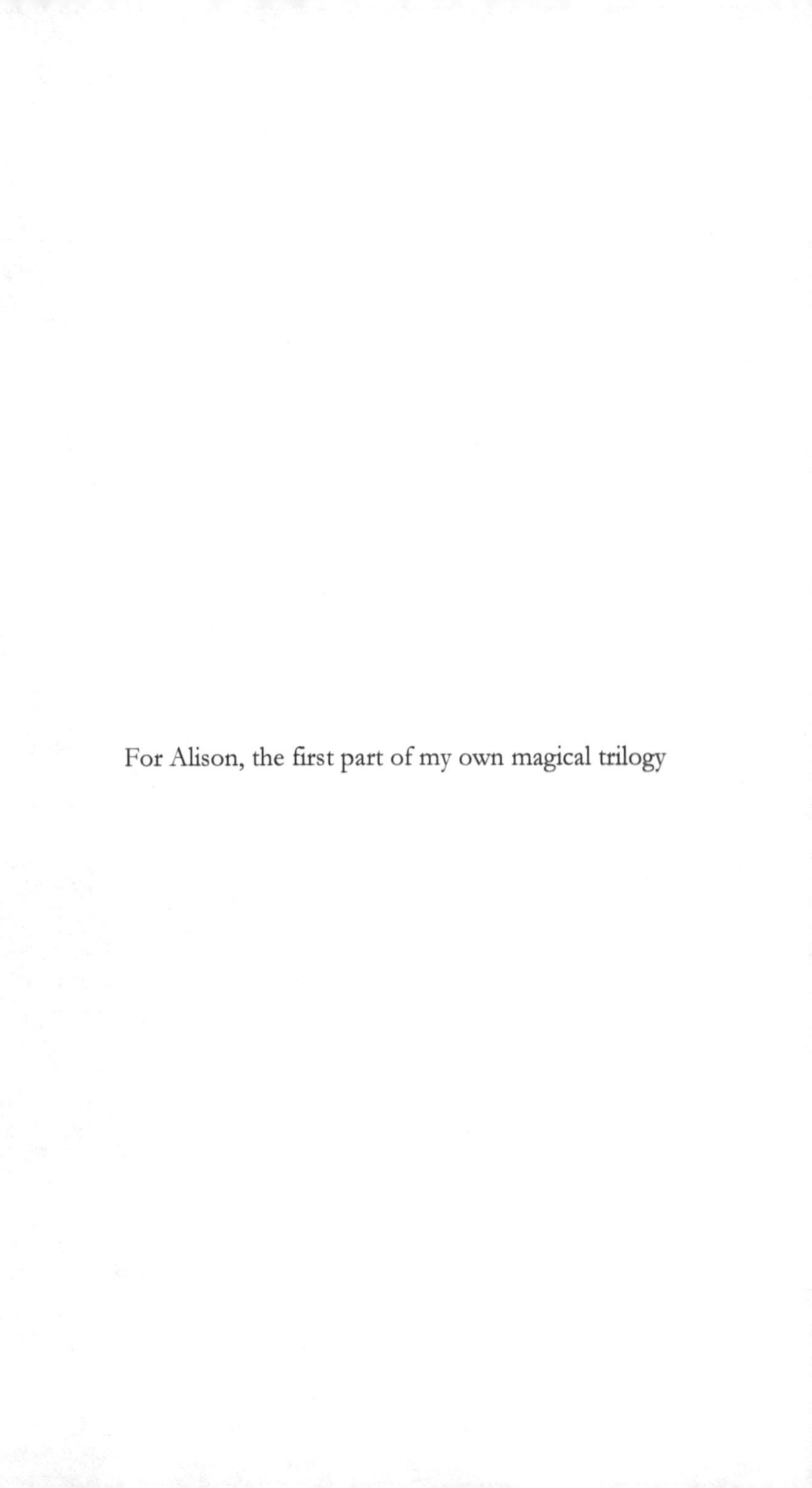

For Alison, the first part of my own magical trilogy

CONTENTS

		Page
1	Cait	1
2	Forbidden Books	7
3	Wild Hunt	17
4	Grimoire	23
5	Fer	33
6	Undain	41
7	Islagray Wycka	53
8	Coven	61
9	Snow on the Northern Hills	73
10	Archaeon	89
11	Tanglewood	99
12	Broken	111
13	Fires	123
14	Death on the Ring Road	133
15	Empire Towers	157
16	Returning	175
17	Aethernal	189
18	Witch-Marks	199
19	The Golden Palace	213
20	Extraction Engine Nmbr 1	225
21	Screaming Machinery	235
22	Hedge Witch	255
23	A Parliament of Owls	267
24	Shadow Paths	283
25	Night Fall	297

1 - CAIT

Manchester, England

Cait pushed her way through the crowded tram and just made it to the doors before they slid shut. Outside, she stood for a moment and breathed. Her eyes had closed more than once on the journey into Manchester, the result of a long, hot day at school and the rocking of the carriage as it rattled into the city. A breeze blew down Mosley Street but it did little to lift the oppressive weight of the air. The weather forecast had predicted thunderstorms. There was no sign of them yet.

The street was busy: office workers sweating in their suits and ties, shoppers burdened with purchases, rowdy children clouting each other with their backpacks. Beyond them all rose the grey, curving walls of the Central Library, like a round fortress built in the heart of the city.

She sighed. She'd promised herself she wouldn't get off here. She thought about Devi, Rachel, Val and Jen, the friends she'd promised to meet one stop up the line at the Arndale Shopping Centre. She watched the tram thundering off that way, ploughing through the traffic toward Piccadilly

Square. They'd be there already, cruising through the crowds, laughing and shouting, never bothering to move out of anyone's way. As a group they were invincible. She imagined them veering from shop window to shop window, shouting their disgust at this, their burning desire for that. And no one, no grown-up, no security guard, would dare confront them.

She loved them all, but in her mind she saw herself at the back of the group, saying nothing, not involved. It was like that some days. She would look at them from a distance, marvelling at how they all talked at once but still seemed to hear what each other said. Other times, without really knowing how, she was a part of that. But not today. She couldn't face them today.

She looked down the tracks the way the tram had come. The rails gleamed in the sun, running past the oblong bulk of the war memorial and out of the city, south toward the suburbs.

Her mother would be getting home about now. Cait imagined her switching on the television, pulling steaming food from the microwave. She should be there, too. Another promise. But she couldn't face going home either. She'd left a message, done the right thing. She'd go back later.

She sighed again. The tram had vanished and she hadn't moved. She couldn't just stand there, people would stare. *Come on, Cait. Back to the real world.*

She thought about last Saturday, her disastrous attempt to secure a weekend job at *Bling Thing*. He'd said that, the manager, as he explained to her why she was so unsuitable for the role.

"Look, love. You have to live in the real world. You have to smile, be happy to serve the customers. Be enthusiastic about the products. Be excited by them."

His words had amused her, then annoyed her. He'd wanted her to be something she wasn't. She'd felt trapped, had to fight down the urge to flee. It was all so mundane.

Where was the beauty in it? Where was the magic? She'd imagined the man would be old but he was in his twenties or something. He was smartly dressed, polite, but his staring eyes, the way he droned on about *retailing*, made her shudder and say little.

His office was a square, shabby room at the back of the store, its walls concrete blocks painted lime-green. On the floor, a kettle and a jar of instant coffee sat on a tray. Boxes of stock were strewn all around, in contrast to the manicured layout of the shop. When he took off his jacket, she saw the sweat-rings creeping around his armpits, circles widening toward the white stains of past sweat-rings. She thought of herself still at *Bling Thing* in five, ten years' time. Interviewing some other poor soul for a job. Would she sound like him by then?

A poster on the wall, the blu-tac holding it up visible as dark smudges in each corner, said *Smile - it costs nothing*. It wasn't true. Right then, a smile would have cost her more than she could give. And what she actually said to him was, "Hmm."

And so she hadn't got the job. She was a failure, it was clear. She was no good at school. She tried, she really did, but she always ended up antagonizing her teachers for some reason. Now she couldn't even cut it as a Saturday girl in *Bling Thing*. She was a failure, going nowhere. Already her life was over.

She threw her rucksack over one shoulder and set off, a small pile of text books cradled in one arm. How she hated her black school uniform. She'd tried to subvert it with blue in her hair and piercings that contravened all the rules. None of it helped. She hated how she looked. She scowled as she walked, warning everyone not to bother her.

Slumped against the grey stone wall of the library, out of the way of hurrying feet and the light of the sun, a man sat on a piece of tatty cardboard. A threadbare blanket was wrapped around his shoulders. On the ground before him lay a hat containing a paltry four or five coins, all coppers.

He held a sign in his hands that said simply, *Please*. The rest of the message, whatever he was begging for, had been torn away. He was asleep, his head nodding forward, long, matted hair covering his face. The crowd ignored him, probably didn't even see him.

She wondered who he was, where he'd come from, what his story was. Perhaps he was one of the few who'd escaped the fire: the factory blaze that had killed her father. This man had limped out, choking, his clothes smoking, his skin burned. He was disfigured now, unable to work, unable to do anything but sit and beg. The formless pleading of that single word on his sign.

She wanted to go to him, sit with him, talk to him. She felt suddenly closer to him than all the people around her. They had so much in common, this shared bond of not belonging to the crowd. She stopped walking. A woman dressed in a smart blue business-suit, her gold necklace expensive, white earphones in her ears, *tutted* loudly at Cait for being in the way.

A flap of the beggar's cardboard seat caught the breeze and she saw the words *This Way Up* in red letters. Underneath, smaller, the name of some company.

The man looked up sharply at her. Or rather, *through* her to something beyond, as if he couldn't focus his eyes properly. He was young. He couldn't possibly have worked with her father. Of course. His skin was unscarred, his features thin and pale. Anger flashed through her, an anger that was part adrenaline. The stupid ideas she had. What was she thinking?

"The hunt! The hunt is coming! Monsters! Run and hide, run and hide!" the man shouted. No one paid him any attention. "They'll chase you down, corner you. You'll see! Sleep safe in your beds, that's when they come. The dead of night, down these streets, knives flashing. Run and hide, run and hide …" He trailed off, his head lolling again as if he was a toy whose battery had run down.

Cait stood for a moment, feeling ridiculous. He was just

some loser, disgusting, probably mad.

Then he looked up, this time directly at her, focusing on her. A look of surprise filled his face.

"You?" he said, not shouting now, but still speaking loudly. "Here?"

Concern, then fear, then amusement flashed across his features. He started shouting again, pointing at her.

"They will hunt *you*! Once they find you, who you are and what you are, they will come! Day or night! You … here all along! All along!"

He started to laugh. A crazy, utterly uninhibited sound. He flicked his head from side to side, expecting everyone to see the joke.

It was too much for Cait. She turned and ran for the library, eyes down, shutting out the beggar, his words knives in her mind.

Simon Kewin

2 – FORBIDDEN BOOKS

A line of pillars guarded the entrance to the library, like a great, gap-toothed mouth. Cait hurried through. She breathed deeply, her heart thundering in her chest. She glanced over her shoulder, expecting the crazy tramp to be following her like a zombie in some ridiculous horror movie. But there was no one. She was safe.

A security guard eyed her. He was tall and heavily built, but with more fat than muscle. He looked like an ex-soldier past his prime. He kept his hair closely cropped but there was a sadness in his eyes, as if he couldn't believe how his life had worked out. His uniform was shabby, the trousers a slightly different shade of blue to his tunic, his cuffs and the peak of his cap threadbare. He said nothing, not moving. She sometimes thought they were all asleep, slumbering away the long, poorly-paid hours with their eyes open. She smiled at him as reassuringly as she could, holding up her textbooks to make it clear she belonged in a library.

The large, circular reading-room that took up most of the ground-floor was a maze of desks and shelves. If you knew the path, the dead-ends to avoid, you could reach the sanctuary of the middle, the island of desks where the librarians stamped and piled books. If not, you could get lost and wind up in the dead-end of Ancient History, the wastelands of Chemistry.

Cait relished the familiar, busy hush. The sound of people concentrating, turning pages, scribbling. It was cooler in here. Controlled. She loved the aroma of the books, of all that paper and leather. She started to relax.

She looked for her gran and spotted her across the floor, her head appearing above a high bookcase as if she were a giant the library employed to reach the top shelves.

Cait set off across the great circle, between huge tables carpeted with open newspapers. She walked along passageways, between high walls of books, wondering what they all said. So much knowledge, how could she ever hope to make sense of things? She couldn't read a thousandth of what was written here.

She weaved her way through the labyrinth until she reached the foot of the step-ladders where her gran perched.

"Hi," said Cait.

Her grandmother was always pleased to see her. Always had time for her. Still, she managed to make it quite clear when Cait had done something she disapproved of. It was never anything she said; she just made her eyes glint in a certain way. How did she do that? The look was there now as she peered down at Cait through her gold-rimmed glasses.

"Cait, love. I didn't expect to see you." She stepped down holding three large, dusty books in one arm. Her pendant earrings, tear-shaped gold mesh clasping nuggets of polished amber, swayed in time with each tread. "Are you all right?"

"I'm fine. Just wanted to drop by. You know."

"Weren't you going shopping with your friends?"

"Oh, couldn't stand the politics."

"The politics?"

"Oh, Jen has stopped seeing Ed; Devi texted CJ to say that she was going out with Peter after all and yada yada yada."

Her gran smiled. Her hair was grey. It always surprised Cait that her hair was grey.

"Dear me. If you're not going to give me your daily updates I'll have to go back to watching the soaps," said her gran.

Cait offered her gran a hand as she landed on the ground. "Sorry."

"Well, it's not that bad yet. Come on, I have to take these books down to the vault. Walk with me and tell me the real problem."

"Let me carry the books," said Cait.

"OK, love. Let me just tell someone where I'm going."

They walked to the centre of the circle, where her gran conversed with her friend Jane. She was odd, Jane: perfectly nice, but very, very quiet. She was from Eastern Europe, or somewhere. The simplest things left her genuinely amazed, while big things or scary things didn't bother her in the least. Last week a man had got angry about something, shouting and swearing at her, jabbing at her with his finger. She'd smiled as if he were a foolish boy and waved him away while the security guards converged. She was cool, really.

Her gran finished her conversation and returned to Cait. They walked to a pair of grey lift doors. A sign in faded blue said *Staff Only*. Her gran took a set of keys from her pocket and used one in the keyhole where the buttons would normally be to summon the lift. Inside, the paint was scratched, the wooden floor scuffed. They descended slowly, the lift clanking and jerking as if reluctant to descend.

Cait's mobile chimed to say a text had arrived. She read it, still holding the books in one arm, then put the phone away without replying.

"Yada yada?" asked her gran.

"Yada yada."

There was silence for a few moments more. The lift went past the public basement and down to a deeper level.

"And what about Danny?" asked her gran. "Aren't you going to see him?"

The lift stopped. There was a pause while the doors

realised they could open.

"He's not my boyfriend, gran. He's just a mate. We like the same bands, that's all."

It was dark down here, and distinctly cold. They stepped out. Cait waited while her gran found the light switch.

"Ah yes, of course. Let me see. *Screaming Machinery*. I remember that tee-shirt of his. The one you were wearing. Very colourful."

"It was just a tee-shirt."

"I'm very disappointed in you about that, Cait."

"We're the only ones into them, that's all. There's nothing more to it. He's even got one of their guitar picks from that concert we went to at the G-Mex."

The lights came on. There was her gran, closer than Cait had expected, smiling broadly.

"I mean about the compilation you promised me. I still don't have it."

"I thought you were joking."

"You thought I was too old, you mean. I know how much you love them so I want to hear them."

"But …"

"You're afraid I'll be shocked or deafened. Is that it?"

Cait smiled. Even when her gran was cross with her she was fun.

"OK," said Cait. "I really promise now."

Ahead of them, a straight, concrete corridor led into the gloom. A string of lights provided occasional clearings in the darkness. Old, wispy cobwebs, with no evidence of any actual spiders, hung in the high corners.

"Anyway," said her gran, "I liked him. I thought he was polite. Made a nice cup of tea."

"Yeah."

"So where is he then?"

"How should I know?"

Her gran looked at her and said exactly nothing.

"OK, he's at home," said Cait. "Revising."

"Ah, yes. I was coming to that."

"I thought you might. It's ages until the exams, gran."

"Three weeks. And I didn't mean that. I meant going home. Your mother will be missing you."

They walked down the corridor. At regular intervals they passed locked, metal doors, as if the basement were some sort of dungeon. The place the librarians imprisoned troublesome borrowers.

"What is all this down here?" asked Cait. Her voice boomed in the confined space. It didn't sound like her speaking at all.

"Book storage. We only have a small percentage of the volumes on display upstairs, you know. The rest are down here, carefully catalogued and protected."

"It's huge. There must be hundreds of doors."

"It's much bigger than the library upstairs. Not many people know this level is even here. It extends a long way under the streets. I like to think this part of the city is built on a foundation of books. It's pleasant down here, so peaceful …" She was half talking to herself. It was something she did. "I like the feeling of the ground all around me. The depths of time. Who knows what's about us in the earth? Victorian coffins. Roman temples. Celtic roundhouses."

"And … all these doors?"

"In case of fire. To stop flames spreading."

Her gran glanced at her, concern clear on her face. The mention of fire, the mere suggestion of the building burning. Cait smiled reassurance back at her.

Her gran stopped walking. "She will miss you, you know, your mum. You're all she's got."

"She's got the television."

"She wants you."

Cait shrugged. She could never get a word out of her mother. She would ask her how her day had been, and *fine* was the best she could hope for. Wasn't it supposed to be the other way around? The mad thing was, they only talked, had something approaching a conversation, when they watched television together.

The problem was they liked different things. Cait wanted to watch programmes that told her something, showed her something, gave her new ideas. Her mother liked to watch the same safe, comforting drivel over and over. Talent shows and soaps. But sometimes they would sit together and watch a programme acceptable to both. A film maybe. Then one of them would speak, saying something critical. The other would agree or disagree. And so it would go, in a companionable sort of way. They conversed about the people on the screen, never really about themselves, but it was something. It was as if the television was a translator, allowing them to exchange a few broken, half-understood words in each other's language. It wasn't much, but it was something Cait always looked forward to.

"I know, gran," she said. In the gloom, the quiet, she found she could speak more easily. "Look, I know what she is. She's still your little girl and she's still my mum. But she's given in. She's given up on herself and given up on me. She's a loser. And she thinks I'm a loser, too."

Her gran put her hands onto Cait's shoulders, then all the way around her.

"If she thinks that it's because she has lost a lot, Cait."

"I know she has." Unexpectedly, Cait was crying. The tears were cool on her cheeks. "We all miss Dad. But she's been stuck in limbo for two years now."

Her gran smiled. She actually smiled. "You know, she used to be just like you. So lively. So strong-minded. So hard to please. Give her time, Cait. However long it takes, she'll come back to us. OK?"

"I'll try, gran. I do try. I just wish she would, too."

"Well. Anyway. Let's go in." She nodded to the door behind Cait. "This is us."

Cait turned to look at the door. The words *Vault 23* were stencilled onto it. She stepped aside while her gran took out her key ring.

The room inside was plain, square and surprisingly large.

Its floor and ceiling were concrete. More shelves - metal here rather than wood - lined the walls. Labelled cardboard boxes filled them, each full of books. A kick-stool sat in the middle of the room.

"Right, I'll just put these in their proper place," said her gran as she wrote something on a clipboard that hung from a hook. Cait handed the books over, then wandered across to one of the shelves, thinking about her mother, her father.

She had the urge to pick a book at random, pick one of the pages in the book, and read a sentence, just to see what it was. See if it was some great pearl of wisdom, some advice to give her guidance in life. But she didn't want to upset the filing system.

"Gran," she said. "These boxes. I've seen one of them today. Just outside the library. A beggar sat on one. I mean, a flattened one. He was pretty mad actually. Started shouting all sorts of weird stuff at me. It was a bit scary."

Her gran spoke with her back to Cait as she put the books into their correct places. "Young Tom you mean? Oh, he's harmless, love. We've tried to help him, find him somewhere to stay, but he keeps coming back."

"He seemed to recognize me. Said mad things."

Her gran turned to her, not smiling, a very direct look on her face. "He's nothing to worry about. Mild schizophrenia and a hard life on the streets. What did he say exactly?"

"Something about *if they knew who I really was, if they knew I'd been here all along, they'd come for me.*"

"He said that?" She was silent for a moment, her eyes still intent on Cait, sharp as knitting-needles. "Well, as I say, he's not well. But the only person he'd harm is himself."

Cait nodded. She paced around the room, touching each box with the tip of her finger. In one corner a part of the shelf was sectioned off with strong metal grilling, a large padlock securing a hatchway in it. Several old books were inside, placed carefully onto the shelf so they weren't touching each other.

"So … why are these books locked away when they're in a room that's already locked?"

"Oh they're valuable," said her gran, turning to face her again. "We sometimes look after books for other people. They have to be well protected for insurance. Some of them have been here for years." She looked thoughtful for a moment.

"I wonder what's in these," said Cait.

"Come on. We'd better go. They'll be wondering what's happened to me."

They locked the door to Vault 23 and retraced their steps to the lift, which still waited with its door open, held by the key. Her gran switched off the lights in the basement as they stepped inside. Cait had the distinct feeling of all the books settling back down to sleep in the darkness, like disappointed dogs in a rescue home.

The old lift doors clanked together. Cait was about to ask her gran whom the locked-away books belonged to when there was suddenly more light in the basement. Flickering, yellow-green beams lit up the walls of the corridor they had walked down.

Cait looked at her gran to ask her what it was, but stopped when she saw her look of terror, saw her step backward from the door as if they were in danger.

The doors juddered slowly together. They heard rapid footsteps then, becoming louder: someone running toward them, although limping slightly, the rhythm uneven. Through the narrowing crack, Cait could see the indistinct shape of someone against the green light, a child-sized silhouette.

Whoever it was reached them as the doors touched together. A ferocious banging rattled the lift doors, the metal denting with each blow. Cait found she had stepped backward, too. She was next to her gran. They were holding hands. There was a faint, sickly smell of burning metal. She imagined motors overheating, cables smoking and snapping, fire in the lift-shaft. Were they trapped down here?

Then slowly, like some creaking, steam-powered space-rocket, the lift began to rise. The pounding on the doors slipped away, fading as Cait and her gran crept upward, back to the light.

3 – WILD HUNT

Nox smiled, revving his Harley-Davison V-Rod. They had good prey today. The lad was cunning. Brave, too. But the end was near now. They had him trapped on a footbridge that arched over the motorway, both ends blocked by Nox's men. No escape. So often they ended up hunting some low-life waster who barely knew what was going on. It was too easy then, the fun all over in a couple of minutes. But this was more like it. They'd flushed him out of a Salford doorway two hours ago, waking him from his slumber amid stinking blankets. He'd given them good sport ever since.

Nox turned to look at the phalanx of bodyguards waiting patiently behind him. His glance told them to be ready. Their motorcycles gleamed silver in the bright sun. Each wore a helmet so it was impossible to see their face, but they all nodded, awaiting his command. Nox rode with no helmet, preferring to feel the wind in his hair, hear the shouts and screams. He loved everything about this. The throb and roar of the bikes. The sweet smell of burning fuel. The thrill of the chase. The kill.

He pulled the baton from its holster on the bike: a long, elegant bar of brushed steel, its tip decorated with a spiral pattern of conical spikes. It felt good to hold it in his hand. He practised a few strokes. It was an intimate weapon, preferable to the sleek little gun he carried strapped to his thigh. The gun was reliable; its intelligent sighting and ballistic control system meant he couldn't really miss his target. But that made it too easy. The baton gave the prey a fighting chance.

He climbed off his bike and walked forward. The lad backed away, panic clear on his filthy face. Nox practised a few more strokes. He would take this slowly. Savour it. There was no hurry.

"You've done well," called Nox. "Really, you have. But now it's over."

The lad froze, wild eyes darting. Then, once again, he did something unexpected. He clambered over the fencing that lined the walkway to perch with shaking legs on the footbridge's struts, thirty feet above the motorway. The traffic thundered beneath him, the roar and rush filling the air. He stopped there, grasping the rail behind him, looking down in terror. He had only to let go to plunge to his death.

Nox charged. He wouldn't be denied now. One blow at least, that was all he asked. The prey glanced up, looking Nox straight in the eye. Then back at the traffic. He let go even as Nox swung.

The baton caught empty air. Cursing, Nox peered over the rail. He expected to see the prey's mangled body on the carriageway. Cars swerving to avoid it. But there was nothing. How could that be? He turned to the other side of the bridge. A container lorry thundered away up the road. And there, perching on top, sat the prey.

The lad waved. He actually waved.

Nox struck the railing with his hand in frustration. Then he ran to his bike. The chase was still on. He'd been away from the office too long, but he pushed the thought aside. He wasn't going to give up now. And when they did finally catch this one it would be all the sweeter.

As he mounted his bike he barked out orders to his men, arranging them into a pursuit pattern.

They caught up with the prey an hour later. They'd

followed him all across the city as he hopped from vehicle to vehicle. But they had him now. Nowhere left to run. The side-street upon which they waited was a narrow, dusty dead-end. On one side was the gable end of a house, a triangle on top of a square, everything made from red bricks the colour of dried blood. On the other side lay a rectangle of derelict land, as if the house there had simply disappeared one night. Scrubby, stunted bushes grew in the space, decorated with rustling plastic bags, the toxic fruit of this small urban orchard.

Nox turned his attention to the dots on his military-grade GPS, each representing one of his men as they moved through the maze of streets. Here in the badlands of Longsight it was impossible to track any other way. Row after row of the same houses, thousands of them packed together in bland, ugly estates. How did people even manage to find their own homes? Really, it was remarkable. Caution was essential. There were too many dead-ends and cul-de-sacs. Ginnels too narrow for a bike to get down. Walls a desperate man could scale. They weren't going to lose him again.

The dots formed a circle around the prey. Nox watched as they followed the pattern he'd dictated. So much of his life was spent doing this. Directing things from afar. Manipulating figures on screens. Subtly influencing events. Which he was very good at. Still, he often resented the remoteness of it. Another reason he loved the hunt. It was good to get your hands dirty from time to time.

The circle shrank, a noose tightening around the prey. Excellent. Not long now. He readied his gun. No time to use the baton. He'd already been away far too long. He resisted the temptation to check in with Central Control, make sure everything was running smoothly. Of course it was. He was just nervous because of the imminent arrival of their visitor.

He tried to put that out of his mind, too. Everything was in place. It wasn't unknown for such visits to happen.

There'd been several over the centuries. And there could be many reasons for one now. Certainly his performance couldn't be called into question. Genera had met and surpassed all its targets. Profits were vast, for all that mattered. Raw tonnage was high and rising. And the refinery piped huge amounts of Spirit. Attention to detail, that was what he brought to the table. He'd given them reliability. No. There could be no possible problem.

The more he thought about it, the more likely reason for the visit was a reward. Recognition. Perhaps he would be offered the promotion, the *ascension* he so craved. At long last. It would explain the personal visit. His masters had to be careful, of course. Had to protect themselves. He would be grilled to ensure this was what he really wanted, that he was ready, that he was right. There was no doubt in his mind he was.

A call interrupted these delicious thoughts, the bike relaying it to the tiny transceiver he wore as a silver stud in his ear. This would be it; the men had spotted the prey. He revved his engine, savouring the great growl of the machine through his body like the deep laughter of a demon. Behind him, one of his men's horns blared, a hunting call over the rush of the cars on the nearby main road.

"Do you have him?" he asked.

But it was Central Control, not one of his men.

"I have a message for you, Mr. Nox."

He scowled. It had better be something important. He'd left strict instructions. "What is it? Has our visitor arrived early?"

"No, sir. But one of the monitors has detected an electromagnetic anomaly."

"Where?"

"In Manchester. The Central Library."

"You're sure?"

"Yes, sir. The readings are quite clear. Something came through 30 seconds ago."

Damn. He couldn't ignore this. He'd prepared too long

for this. Those old fragments of paper had hinted there was an *archive* of some sort at both ends of the pathway between the worlds. He'd always suspected it would be a library. They watched them the world over, of course, but Manchester especially, after everything that had happened here.

"How many came through?"

"Just one."

Nox calculated, gunning his engine again in frustration. They'd have to abandon the hunt, that was clear. And he *hated* to be beaten. But there was no choice. And this could work out very well. Their visitor due in a few days, and now this. Yes. It could work out very well indeed.

"Very well. Make sure you capture CCTV. And send soldiers. A lot of them. I'll go there myself."

Without looking back he dropped his bike into gear and roared off toward the city centre, moving through traffic as if it wasn't there, his bodyguards filing in around him.

Somewhere behind them, at the end of an alley, a young man crouched in a wheelie-bin rank with the smell of old milk and rotting vegetables. Shaking, eyes wide, breathing panicky, he listened to the sound of engines as they faded into the distance.

Simon Kewin

4 – GRIMOIRE

"Wait here. Hold the lift. Make sure *no one* uses it," said her gran once they'd creaked up to the ground floor. She slipped sideways through the reluctant doors when they were only half-open and walked briskly into the library.

Cait stood by the open lift, feeling that everyone was looking at her. She tried to breathe deeply, slowly, in, out. She'd read in a magazine that it calmed the nerves. It didn't seem to be helping. A churning sickness filled her stomach. She waited, afraid, useless. Her gran and Jane were talking, their heads close. Her gran pointed toward the lift. They bustled over together.

"Who was that in the basement gran?" asked Cait. "Where did they come from?"

"We have to hurry," said Jane, ignoring Cait. The urgency was clear in her voice despite her accent. "Cait can stay up here. You and I must do this."

"Do you think she'll be safer up here?" asked her gran. A stern look replaced her usual smile. It was unsettling, as if all her normal warmth was a front. "Tom recognized her. Others could, too."

"She's just a girl," said Jane.

Her gran's features were taut with tension. Underneath, Cait could tell she was weary. Sometimes, when she had been working too hard, or when she'd been ill, she did look old after all.

"Look, whatever's going on here, I want to come with you," said Cait. "I can't just leave you." She was speaking in a sort of whispered shout. Readers at nearby tables frowned at her. She stepped into the lift.

The two women exchanged glances then followed her inside. Her gran smiled, but the expression melted into anxiety almost immediately. Jane pressed the button to descend. Cait hooked her arm through her gran's, as she had done so many times.

"Who is it down there, gran?" she asked. "What is going on?"

The lift began to shudder and clank. Her gran squeezed her arm. Her voice was thin as she spoke. "We only have a few moments, love. Listen carefully, all right? I'll try to explain. And Cait, when we get to the basement, do what I say for once?"

Cait nodded.

"OK," said her gran. "The truth is, there's something down there. In the basement. Something that shouldn't be there. Something that shouldn't even *be*."

"Oh, come on."

"Cait, listen to me. This thing is extremely dangerous and, I'm not going to lie to you, extremely frightening. It's come from another world in search of something. A book. And we must stop that from happening, at whatever cost. Do you understand?"

She didn't in the least, but she nodded again.

"We thought, we'd hoped, this would never happen," her gran continued. "But it has and there's only us here to stop it. So that's what we're going to do."

They were nearly at the bottom, the lift slowing as it reached the basement. Jane was breathing quickly, clearly afraid. Cait felt suddenly claustrophobic, enclosed in the tiny square lift. Her heart raced, surely too rapidly. She could do nothing but nod again, unable to think of anything to say.

She had come to protect her gran, but really, what good would she be? She was useless. She couldn't do anything.

They heard three great booms from outside, as if someone were striking a huge drum. The whole lift shook with each concussion.

"Were you able to tell what it is?" Jane asked quietly.

"Not really," said her gran. "Just this great emptiness, sucking in the light. One of the higher nobility, maybe. Perhaps one of the Elder Dukes or even a Prince."

Jane nodded. "Well. We must do what we can."

Her gran put on her glasses. As they waited for the doors to jerk open, she turned to Cait. She tried to look reassuring despite the fear in her eyes.

"Stay close, love," she said. "And … I'm sorry."

The doors opened.

Cait's first impression was of snow. It drifted in the air, thick as a winter's storm. But it was black snow. She saw what it really was: charred scraps of paper. The air hung heavy with ash and smoke, sharp at the back of her throat.

Another great boom echoed down the corridor. Moments later, a great flurry of shredded, blackened tatters bloomed into the air, as though carried on a strong northern wind.

Jane and her gran strode forward. Cait followed, wading through mounds of ash and paper scraps like fallen leaves.

They reached the first metal fire-door. It bent inward as though struck by a huge force. It stood like a ship's sail in a high wind, hanging on by its hinges. All around lay great drifts of tattered and burned pages. To Cait it seemed like someone had started with a chainsaw, then set the whole lot on fire. How was that possible? They'd only been gone for a minute or two. The ash in the air grew thicker, the smell of smouldering paper stronger, making Cait cough and retch. Why hadn't the sprinklers and alarms come on? It wasn't supposed to be possible for fires to just burn like this.

They continued down the corridor, stepping around larger piles of shredded paper, until sudden footsteps galloped toward them.

They stopped. Cait wanted to turn and run for the lift after all: get away, get up and out into the fresh air. She wanted to be back in that crowd on the streets of Manchester. She would have run, too, but her legs wouldn't obey. Her whole body shook and it was all she could do to remain standing.

Something hurtled around the corner. It ran like a dog, but larger, perhaps as tall as Cait. Its hairless body was the colour of wax. Its head was completely featureless: a bone battering ram that it used to smash down the metal doors. It bound up to them and stopped. A mouth appeared, a great wide crack full of needle teeth splitting its head.

"Three more witches," it said, its voice strangely soft. "I will eat you alive."

"No," replied her gran. "You will not."

The creature snarled, its mouth gaping as it did so. "You are powerless and you know it. Tell me where the Grimoire is. I grow impatient. It is here somewhere, I can smell it. Tell me!"

Jane stepped forward. She held her palm forward, as if that would be enough to stop the creature. "Yes, the book is here. But it is protected by many Forbidding Wards. You will have to kill me to remove them, undain."

"Jane, no," said her gran, alarm clear in her voice. "Don't do this!"

"I must," said Jane, not looking at her gran, not taking her eyes off the monster. "For Andar, or whatever is left of it. For this world. I must. There is no other way."

"No!"

"I'm sorry."

The creature snarled and leaped. It ran up one of the walls and slammed down onto Jane, taking her whole arm into its mouth. Jane screamed and staggered backward. But somehow she stayed upright. Through clenched teeth she spoke words in a language Cait didn't recognize.

The creature roared and began to change shape. Its

mouth shrank and lengthened. A tongue became an arm, Jane's hand grasped in its fist. Cait could see something, an energy, flowing down Jane's arm. The creature howled in agony, but didn't let go. Perhaps it couldn't. It fought back with a burning fire of its own.

Her gran stepped forward, her own hand outstretched. Seeing her, the creature grew another limb with astonishing speed. An arm ending in a great club lashed out and knocked her gran flying, slamming her against a wall. She sank to the floor, her eyes closed.

Cait found she could move then. Anger filled her, overcoming her terror. She charged at the creature. She still carried her school textbooks. Uselessly, not really knowing what she was doing, she tried to batter the monster with *English Literature*.

The creature swung its club arm at Cait, intending to swat her aside as it had her gran. Cait flinched. But as the blow was about to land, the creature stopped. Eyes swivelled on the side of its head, tiny like a whale's, little flecks of red clear as if it burned on the inside. It seemed to be studying her.

"But ..." it said.

At that moment Jane screamed, her voice a mixture of determined fury and pain. The creature's whole arm glowed white. Jane's arm also burned, brighter and brighter. Cait stepped backward. What was happening? She shaded her eyes, the heat alarming on her face. Jane and the creature became indistinct shapes in the gathering fury of the light.

The explosion hurled Cait down the corridor. She expected pain as she struck a wall or the floor. Instead, she landed in one of the drifts of tattered pages and disappeared.

For a moment, everything was quiet. She was tempted to lie there, hidden, out of sight. But she knew she couldn't.

She pushed her way out, spitting dry paper from her mouth, and peered down the corridor. The monster, Jane and her gran lay unmoving on the floor, a neat triangle of bodies.

She went to her gran first. She was breathing, her limbs twisted at odd angles, like a broken doll. She opened her eyes as Cait stroked her face.

"Hello, love," said her gran. She peered over at Jane and the monster. "Cait. You must hurry. Take Jane's key. It's around her neck. Go get the book. It's in a cage like the ones you were asking about. Vault 42."

"But, gran."

"Please, Cait."

"OK."

Cait's stomach heaved as she lifted the key from Jane's neck. The smell of burning flesh made her retch. She expected the key to be burning hot but it was cold metal.

"Good," her gran whispered. "Go now. Be quick."

Cait ran. Vault 42 was nearby. The door had been smashed like the others and the books inside shredded. But the locked cage in the corner was intact, as if the monster hadn't noticed it.

She waded through a sea of paper tatters, of scattered words, to get to the far corner of the vault. A single book waited inside the cage, its leather cover a rich, mottled red. She slipped the key into the large padlock. It turned with a series of gentle clicks.

She reached inside, expecting something to happen as she touched the book. Nothing did. Etched into the leather was the sketch of a skull and symbols or letters she didn't recognize. A complete skeleton stretched the length of the book's spine. Cait put the book under her arm, turned, and ran back to her gran.

"Well done, love. Now get out of here. Others will be coming. This evil thing has friends. Take the book and destroy it. Burn it. Burn every page. Not a word must survive. When you've burned it, shred the ashes, too." She lay back, her eyes shut.

"Gran I … I can't do this," said Cait. "I can't do any of this. I don't know what's going on, and I don't want to."

"I know, love," said her gran, her eyes closed. "I know.

But we do what must be done. And you … you always underestimate yourself."

"But I can't just leave you and Jane with this … this thing."

"Cait, Jane is dead. She always said it was hard to craft here. She used up all her strength to stun it. But it won't be out for long. It's too strong, much too strong. Don't waste her sacrifice. Go and do what I said."

"To mum?"

"No. They will expect that. Go to …" She winced as some agony cut through her. "Go to Danny. I liked him. Destroy the book together."

"But what about you? I can't leave you here."

"You must. I'll be fine, Cait. Go on."

"But …"

"Go, Cait. Please."

The world blurring through the tears in her eyes, Cait picked up her school books and placed them around the old tome to conceal it. She looked down at the creature lying on the floor.

"It wouldn't attack me," she said. "Why wouldn't it attack me? It seemed like it recognized me."

"No time now," said her gran. "Remember what I said. Off you go, love." Her voice was barely audible.

Cait nodded and tore herself away, a sob rising in her throat.

Back upstairs, security guards crowded the library. These were not like the shabby man she'd seen earlier. These wore black riot-gear and had helmets with visors covering their faces. They cradled guns in their arms and had an array of batons, side-arms and unidentifiable electronic gear hanging at their belts. They wore no insignia, or anything to identify who they were. They moved methodically amongst the shelves as if they were clearing the streets of some invaded city.

Luckily for Cait no one noticed her arrival. A man with thin, grey hair was arguing with two of the guards, shouting about having fought in the war. For a moment, all eyes looked that way. Cait slipped out of the lift and darted into a deserted aisle between two shelves.

She stopped for a moment to consider her options. The guards had formed a ring around everyone in the library and were corralling them to the doors, gradually tightening the circle. Perhaps, if she was quick, she could sneak through the cordon and escape.

She sprinted between the bookshelves toward a bank of desks. She stopped at an intersection. The desks were a few metres away. She might easily be seen if she continued. But time was short. She had no choice. She ran to the desks, sat down and opened one of her books half-way though, her hands shaking. She expected to hear shouts or the sound of boots stomping toward her. She pulled her iPod from her pocket with trembling fingers, put in her earphones, and buried herself in the text.

Moments later someone nudged her roughly on the shoulder. One of the guards stood behind her, pushing at her with the butt of his rifle. She did her best to look shocked and frightened, which wasn't that difficult.

"Who ... what?" She gabbled, half shouting, as if she had loud music playing in her head.

The guard said nothing for a moment, then he nodded to the main library doors and spoke in a dead, mechanical voice. "Leave."

Quickly, Cait picked up her books, taking care to keep the old leather tome as well-hidden as possible, and trotted toward the doors. She was the last person to reach them.

Outside the library stood a handsome man next to a powerful-looking, silver motor-bike. He wore expensive sunglasses, a black leather jacket and steel-capped, black leather boots. He was mid-thirties maybe, and looked like something from a glossy advert for expensive watches. He observed everything taking place, all the while talking, apparently to himself.

She felt suddenly self-conscious under his gaze. Not

daring to look at him directly she walked past, sure he would stop her and take the book. All of her fear and uncertainty returned.

She slipped on the step and fell, scattering her books onto the ground at the man's feet. The red leather book was clearly visible, right by his boot.

She glanced up into his face. He looked at her, assessing her. He reached down and picked something out of her hair. A scrap of paper from the basement.

He inspected it carefully. He was about to say something when one of the guards, a woman this time, hoisted Cait up. The guard nodded her head toward the street. Cait scrabbled her books together and, not daring to look back, ran toward the crowd of people being herded away from the library.

She pushed through the throng, all the time expecting more shouts, the sound of pursuit. For once, a tram waited at the stop. It was going the wrong way, up into the city centre, but she pushed inside anyway just as the doors swept shut.

She managed to find a seat at the far end of the carriage. She held the books tightly to her chest, trying to make herself small and insignificant. She peeped out of the window. The man in the leather jacket remained by the library doors. He stared directly at the tram. Directly, it seemed, at her. Even as they moved off she could see his mouth moving, giving orders to his troops.

Surely they would pursue her, especially when they went to the basement and saw what was there. The bodies and the book gone. What chance did she have? Still, she had to try. It was tempting to give up, let them catch her, not shoulder the responsibility. But she thought of her gran, and of Jane. She thought, for some reason, of her Dad and what had happened to him. She would do what her gran had asked. Try at least. It was little enough.

She'd change trams a few times, get a bus, walk through the crowds to put them off her scent. Like they did in the movies. The soldiers, or whatever they were, would be able to track her. CCTV cameras perhaps. But it would take time. Time enough, perhaps, to destroy the book.

She reached into her pocket and switched off her mobile. At least they wouldn't be able to find her from that. Next, she fished her iPod out and, this time, switched it on for real.

Familiar soaring melodies and crashing guitars filled her. She felt instantly strengthened and reassured. A few minutes later, still clutching the books, she left the tram at Piccadilly Gardens and disappeared into the crowds.

5 - FER

The Witches' Isle, Andar

Four days earlier

Hellen Meggenwar, eldest of Islagray, awoke to the clanging of bells.

She sat up, gasping for air. She had been running from a booming, metallic voice that made her insides liquid with terror. It was glorious to find she was safe in her own room, the familiar bed beneath her old back. The watchtower bell tolled. A nightmare, nothing more than that.

Except, she knew, that was no more than a comforting lie. The time was coming. Strange how, despite the long years of planning, she felt so unprepared.

From outside came the clatter of running footsteps, voices calling, as the others headed for the shore. She sighed and touched the star-shaped lamp that hung by a silver chain from the oak beam above her bed. She worked the simple magic to bring it to life. The gentle tug, a pinch within her stomach, was welcome, almost enjoyable. The familiarity, reassuring. The flame bobbed, wavered, then settled down, tinting the darkness yellow.

The tolling of the bell ceased. She reached into the night to borrow the eyes and ears of those already at the lake's edge. There was nothing on the dark waters, but she could make out a splashing sound, distant but clear. Oars dipping into the water, no rhythm to them. Someone unaccustomed to rowing, or someone hurt, was crossing the Silverwater to the island.

Hellen opened her own eyes. Attracted by the light, a moth the size of her hand had blundered through an open window. It was a Death's Head, the white and black markings on its back a little picture of a skull. Its tiny, rapid mind flitted around the room, the sound of its wings like paper being ruffled. It skipped across the books lying open upon her desk, touching the paper as if frantically seeking the answer to some puzzle. Then it gave up and flew out of another window, its mind fading into the night.

Hellen rose, groaning at her aching joints. She pulled a black ankle-length robe over her head and sheaved her hair into some sort of order with a scrap of purple cloth. She hauled on her boots and holding a shawl around her shoulders, went out into the darkness, too.

Twenty or thirty witches stood at the quay. Familiar faces cast worried glances toward her. She picked her way to the front and stood next to Ariane. The two old friends said nothing as they peered out over the water, their breath billowing in a faint mist. The torches set along the water's edge hissed and crackled, filling the air with scents of honey and beeswax. Hellen glanced at her friend. Wrinkles lined her chestnut-brown face. Ariane, too, had dressed hurriedly. Her feet were bare.

"So, who comes to this dreadful place at the dead of night?" asked Hellen.

"According to the shore bell, a man bringing a witch," said Ariane.

"Alive?"

"Perhaps."

Down a shifting pathway of gold light a figure rowed toward them. His exhaustion was clear. He stopped every few strokes, glancing over his shoulder to see how far remained. Then he dropped the blades of his oars back into the water and, with a great effort, hauled on them to nudge himself a little nearer.

When he was close enough a rope was thrown, vanishing into the night before reappearing with a heavy splash beside the boat. The man shipped his oars, grasped the rope, made it fast, then slumped forward, shoulders heaving.

As they drew him alongside, Hellen saw that a woman lay inside the small boat, furs covering her body. She looked young. Her hair was dark, black or deep brown, but her face, even in the yellow light of the torches, seemed pale. She wore knotted silver jewellery through her earlobes and eyebrows. One hand was visible, clutching the edge of the fur. For a moment, with the shadows playing about her knuckles, Hellen saw the moth there, before she blinked and it was the girl's hand again.

They pulled the man ashore. He was maybe forty-years old, round in the belly, hair thinning. Lines of fatigue marked his face. He panted, unused to such exertions. Certainly he was no warrior. He wore a fine cloak of brown wool with delicate whorls of embroidery decorating the cuffs and collar. A merchant, she guessed. She could feel the fear consuming him, coming off him like heat.

"Welcome to Islagray, friend," she said. "We are grateful to you."

The man bowed nervously, clearly unsure how to act.

Meanwhile, two witches lifted the girl from the boat. Ariane kneeled down and put her ear to the girl's mouth, touching her with two fingers on her forehead, neck, and breast. She took each of the girl's hands and examined them before gently releasing them. Then she looked up at those around her.

"Her name is Fer. A hedge witch. She is uninjured. She worked some terrible magic and the pain threw her into this stupor. In time she will recover."

Hellen turned to the man. She read relief and weariness on his face. He still had not spoken.

"Will you tell us what happened?" she asked.

He spoke in a rush, a speech prepared and rehearsed for some time. "Lady, we travelled north together up the coast road toward Forness. Very glad of her company I was, too; the wilds round there are terrible. We were talking away when she stopped suddenly and looked toward the river, all alarmed. *Stay here* she says, and marches into the trees that line the road there. I stood for a while, the light fading, not knowing what to do. Then I heard two screams. One hers. Terrible it was. Another from something else. I … I didn't know what to do."

"You considered running away," prompted Hellen. "Who would not?"

The man looked uncomfortable. "My mother's sister was a witch. A good woman. I had to help. I made my way through the trees and found Fer unconscious in a small clearing next to the water, her feet actually in the An. The other creature was sprawled next to her, dead. Don't know what she did to it. Don't want to know. Only bones and tattered flesh were left of it. I tried to rouse her but couldn't. So I dragged her to the road, threw the goods off my cart, put her on and turned back south. I came as fast as I could. Oakleaf, my horse, is half-dead from the effort. And Fer has barely stirred all the way here. Lady, my name is Merdoc. I am a simple trader in spices."

Hellen smiled, placed a hand on his arm. "You have done all you could, Merdoc. Rest here as long as you wish."

"She is trying to speak," said Ariane, still bending over the young witch.

Hellen kneeled as well. The girl's chalky face was more animated now, exertion lining her features. Her lips opened and closed as if she was trying to utter words too big for her mouth. Finally she managed a whisper.

"Undain."

A memory of a dream flashed into Hellen's mind. She flew over Andar. The rolling patchwork of greens and yellows, forests and fields, stretched beneath her like a rumpled blanket. But the great river An ran red instead of blue. A thick, sluggish red. Shapeless objects floated in its current like clots. Not clumps of Floatweed and Swimming Jacaranda; even from this distance she knew these were bodies. A flood of bodies.

She met Ariane's eyes. A look of shock, as if she had been struck, pinched her friend's face.

"Merdoc," said Hellen, standing up, first to one leg and then, after a pause, the other. "The place where you found her. Has it a name?"

"We were passing through the Crow Woods, a place called Gorse Point or Goose Point by those living nearby."

"Very well. Come inside and rest now."

Four of them carried the girl on a makeshift litter toward the stone buildings of Islagray Wycka. Hellen walked between Ariane and Merdoc. For a while, no one spoke. Worry glowed in Merdoc's mind as he fretted over what might happen to him.

"Tell me, Merdoc," said Hellen. "What spices do you trade?"

"I carry chalce, bittersweet, lemane, red fireseed, black fireseed, lovespice, snakeroot – all manner of precious delicacies, borne thousands of miles up the Spice Route along the An. Through war and desert, over mountain and plain. From Azandia, Endest and even the distant lands of the Pirate Kings." He sounded more sure of himself as he slipped into his merchant's patter.

"A cart load of such spices must have been a great loss to you," said Hellen.

"They were my goods for the whole year. I trade them in the midwinter markets along the An. The farther north, the better the price. They say there will be an Ice Fair at Guilden this year. It would have been a good year for spice."

"You were heading for Guilden?" asked Hellen.

"Every winter for twelve years now."

"Tell me, is your quality good?"

"The best."

"What of your prices?"

"My customers always come back to me."

"Very well, Merdoc. We will repay you as best we can. And if you come east to Islagray each year we will happily trade. We have need for spice. We can pay well, in gold and in other ways."

Merdoc smiled, looking relieved. "I am honoured, Lady."

"And no doubt it will make a good line at the markets, yes? Merdoc, supplier of spices to the Witches' Isle?"

His grin widened and he nodded.

"Very well," said Hellen. "And we will do what we can for the brave Oakleaf."

If her worst fears came true, they might not be here in a year's time. But for now, life marched on. This simple act of gratitude was the right thing to do.

A young witch whose name she couldn't recall took Merdoc to a bed. When he was gone, she and Ariane moved on slowly, letting the other witches outpace them.

"You heard what she said?" asked Ariane.

"I did," said Hellen.

"Can it be true? Is such a thing possible?"

"You know what I believe. But perhaps her mind is lost in some nightmare and she was attacked by a pack of wolves."

Ariane snorted. "I don't believe that and neither do you, old fool. Why would a wolf pack attack her? And if they did, they'd be no match. She nearly killed herself with the magic she worked."

Hellen stopped walking. Away from the torches the stars shone cold and hard in the black sky. She shivered, the skin on her arms prickling with goose bumps. She tightened her shawl around her shoulders.

"Yes. There is something very wrong here," she said. "Our brave trader said only bones were left of whatever the girl fought." She peered upward, as if seeking for answers. "And I know of no magic that can strip a creature to its skeleton."

"Something summoned or crafted," said Ariane. "Some horror. The impossible has happened. This Fer simply spoke what she saw. An undain has come across the An and we are no longer safe."

"We must be sure," said Hellen. "I will go and see for myself. Once we know the truth we will meet, the whole coven."

They resumed their plodding pace, neither speaking. They should send word to the other world, thought Hellen. Tell Jaiin. These events concerned her, too. She and the others there. But the aether had been so disrupted of late. Hellen hadn't been able to speak to them for months. Was Jaiin even still alive? Or had the undain of that confusing, cacophonous world found her after all this time?

More and more, Hellen regretted not telling the other witches everything she had done.

"Hedge witch, eh?" she said at last. "She's in for a surprise when she awakens."

"I seem to recall another girl about her age," said Ariane. "Muttering about covens and rules as though she wanted nothing to do with the place."

"And she hasn't stopped muttering," said Hellen. "Still plenty of time to give all this up. Take to the road and do some real good."

They both smiled. It was an old conversation. A comfort.

"Something else in Merdoc's story troubles me," said Hellen. "He said Forness can be *terrible*. It's nothing of the sort. This time of year the valleys are beautiful as the mists drift through them. The air is rich with autumn jasmine. Something strikes a wrong note there."

"He is a man of towns and cities. He fears the wilds, fears the dark."

"Perhaps."

They made their way in silence after that. From beneath the Wycka, they began to hear the Song. To Hellen's ear, there were notes of sadness in it of late: lamentation, perhaps, for the fading beauty of summer. The sound swelled as they approached the main doors of the building. The singing was more subdued at night. But in the brittle darkness the discord to it was clear. The sound of something vast and unsettling approaching. It made her think of swarming bees or rumbles of distant thunder. She tried to follow the rhythm, but could not.

Back in her room she undressed. She washed with a bowl of water warmed on her smouldering fire, then found clothes for the journey. Stout boots, a thick serge cloak. She paused for a moment to think. She took a small leather pouch from a hook by her bed and tied it to her belt by its drawstrings. Then she made her bed, blew out the lamp and left.

Away in the east the sky lightened, the tops of the trees becoming visible against a purple backdrop. She turned away and stepped into the air, as if climbing an invisible staircase.

Hellen rose rapidly and floated over the buildings of Islagray, westward into the dark.

6 – UNDAIN

An unnatural emptiness shrouded the remains of the undain, fogging Hellen's mind. She had spent her whole life aware of the teem and rush of life. To stand here, in this muffled hush, unnerved her.

She could sense living creatures all around her, but they were pale ghosts of themselves. Only if she closed her eyes and reached with her whole mind could she feel the slow, sombre rhythm of the trees; the rapid, chattering life of woodland creatures; the panicky flight of birds. Some carnivore was there too, hiding and full of hunger, but she couldn't put her finger on where or what it was.

Far out in the unfathomable depths of the An she felt the ferocious, towering minds of the river serpents. She caught glimpses in her mind, creatures as large as a town, the bulk of their vast coils rolling in the water, a flash of a tooth longer than her own body. She gazed into the distance, as if she might see them.

Mists covered the An, as they did most days. A crisp chill floated off the water, like cold breath. North of her, up the coast, the spire of Caer L'dun peeked out, the sun's rays glinting off its high windows. From there the dragonriders waited and watched for attack from Angere. A watch they'd kept for nearly five hundred years. Although, if you listened to the muttering of tavern drunks, the dragonriders waited to welcome the undain, not fight them. But there. You could tell people the truth all you liked, but you couldn't always make them believe it.

Above the misty waters a transparent moon hung low, little more than tatters of lace with the bright blue sky visible through it. Everything was beautiful, peaceful. It was hard to believe that on that other shore, only a hundred miles or so, Angere actually existed. The Lost Land. The Lands of the Dead. It would be a surprise to many in Andar to learn the place was real and not some child's fairy story.

She'd seen it once, many years ago, as it stepped forward into the real world from the shadows of myth. One summer's evening some way north of here. She was young, barely a woman. She dangled her feet in the river, enjoying the cool water around her toes after trudging through the heat. She tossed stones out just to hear them splash. She thought about her mother, a hedge witch herself. Hellen planned to follow the same road. Islagray was a temptation but she'd decided she could do more good if she travelled around, helping where she could. With each woman she assisted in childbirth, each sheep or cow she healed, she would make the world a better place.

She'd looked out over the river, thinking about the An's eternal flow, from no known source to no known end. And suddenly they were there, distant but clear on the far shore, as if the two banks had crept closer together. Or as if the mists were a veil that had momentarily parted for her. Towers, domes and palaces, all sparkling in the evening light, stretching up and down the other shore as far as the eye could see. The white city of the undain. It was a moment of clarity for her in more ways than one. Her mind was suddenly made up. She would go to Islagray after all.

She kneeled, now, to examine the remains of the broken undain. The creature was, as Merdoc had said, little more than bone. A few tatters of flesh remained here and there. The undain was clearly sorcerous in nature, something that should never have lived. Bone and feather lashed together in roughly the right shape and only able to fly because of the death magic that filled it. Hellen retched from the rotting smell.

Worse than the stench was how the skeleton had been cut. Human bones sawn up and mixed with those of animals or some giant bird. She could not imagine what ritual had been involved in the creation of this flying creature. How long the ordeal must have lasted for the victims.

Something has begun. And yet this was no invasion. Was it a test flight? Were they being spied upon? She stayed on her knees for long moments, as if she could read meaning from the scattered bones.

She became aware of the attack a moment before it happened. The muffling fog that surrounded the undain burst and the familiar rush of life came roaring back. It was no mere carnivore that lurked in the trees. A vivid image of the five warriors flashed into her mind. For a moment she caught a glimpse of the scene through the eyes of the nearest one. The slender, silvery boughs of the trees like the limbs of a crowd of graceful giants. The serpentine blade he held in his hand. Autumn leaves, lemon yellow, blood red, whirling to the ground. The old woman, small and frail, kneeling by the river, seemingly oblivious.

For all her skill she was a weather-worker at heart. When pressed, it was to this art she turned. Magic flared within her, drawn in from her surroundings. It was easy here, the air thick with the rushing energy of the An. The pain would be bearable. Words of power burned the back of her throat, pleading to be spoken.

She paused, forcing herself to breathe as an older, wiser voice within her took control. No. This was no enemy. To harm him would be unspeakable.

She made no movement other than to lift her head toward her attacker, a warm smile on her face. "Ah, excellent. A young dragonrider to give me a hand up."

The effect on him was immediate. He stopped as if struck, then sank to one knee and laid his sword at his feet, his head bowed.

"Forgive me, my Lady. I thought …"

"That I was undain, like this abomination. I may be old but there's still a little life left in me yet. And less of the *Lady*. My name is Hellen."

He looked up at her, his eyes sharp. "I am Beltaine. And I know your name, Hellen Meggenwar. Forgive me. I know you are a friend."

She held out her hand to touch him on the shoulder. "Really? And how do you know that?"

He rose to his feet, leaving his sword on the ground, and offered a hand to her. He was tall, his grip strong. He moved with the controlled grace of all dragonriders. Leather armour covered his torso, legs and arms, but she could see the tattoos on his head and hands, red as blood, the intricate whorls and spirals that would cover his whole body. His hair was shaved short. In his left ear were three silver studs to denote his rank. Around his neck, the gold chain studded with its string of small red gems. Penitence Stones. His eyes were a rich brown. If he wasn't so sombre he'd be quite handsome. Ah, if only she was one hundred and thirty years younger …

"Borrn spoke of you. How you aided him once," said Beltaine.

"Hah! That was twenty years ago. And we helped each other."

"Even so, we do not forget. We have few friends in Andar."

"Anyone hostile to you has forgotten the stories they were told as children. Or they were never told them in the first place."

He shrugged. "No matter."

"Maybe. But I have often thought it's time you stopped feeling so guilty for the mistakes of your grandparents' grandparents." She glanced at the broken bones around her. "But there, perhaps you'll get the chance to make amends very soon."

"Perhaps. Something stirs. This is not the first flight across the An we have heard of."

"That's news. How many others?"

"Two. Further north."

Was it possible the armies of the Witch King were gathering, only a hundred miles from where they stood? Even she, after all these years, found it hard to believe. The waters of the An looked so peaceful.

"Tell me," she said. "Why have you been waiting here?"

"In case the other undain returns."

Her stomach went cold for a moment, as if the river's chill had crept into her.

"The *other* undain?"

"The rider. Small, skulking creature. Its tracks led south, following the cart."

"You are sure?"

"We are."

She should have realised. Ariane was right; she was an old fool. But what did it mean? To make this miraculous flight across the An and land next to a witch. Was that bad luck or good luck?

"I must return to Islagray," she said.

"The cart went there?"

"It came in the middle of the night."

He nodded, his expression still dour. "We will stay here. The rider may still return."

"If it does, can you defeat it?" asked Hellen.

"Perhaps."

"Then I wish you luck. Send word to Islagray if you learn anything more. Or if you need our help."

"I will."

"In what is coming, we will all have to learn to work together, I think," said Hellen.

"Then let me help now," he said. "Three of us followed the cart and rider. A day behind, but if they are still alive they should be at Islagray by now. Ran leads them. Say to him *Dethnior unthwai sen thain* and he will know he can trust you. If you have need of him he will help."

She smiled in acknowledgement. "I shall do so."

She turned to go. But another matter came to mind: unimportant, perhaps, in the scheme of things, but a thing she could put right.

"Tell me," she said. "Were there any sacks of spice lying round here when you arrived?"

"By the road. We stacked them out of sight."

She unstrung the leather pouch from her belt and held it up. "Then before I leave, could you possibly pop them into this?"

Beltaine looked at the small bag. He nearly objected, but then chose to say nothing. He made some intricate gestures in the air, speaking their hand-language. Two of the hidden dragonriders, a woman and a man, materialised from the trees and strode to him. He spoke brief, quiet orders. They took the pouch and hurried off through the trees.

Hellen turned back to gaze out over the An. The water sparkled and danced in the brightening sun. The mists had lifted a little, but it wasn't possible to see even the middle of the river. Beltaine stood next to her. He watched the haze over the river with suspicion, as if he expected an army to loom out at any moment.

She saw the suggestion of a dragon in the tattoos about his neck and head: a shimmering creature of fire woven from lines of red. Borrn had been the same. It was as if the dragon was there, living beneath his skin. In Angere, five hundred years ago, they'd ridden dragons. Were the tattoos merely a memory, a mark of that? Borrn had said they were an armour, but against what she didn't know.

She wondered where Borrn was now, what had happened to him in the wilds of the north. There'd been no word from him for a long time. Both of them caught up in their own lives.

A fish leaped from the river, catching a fly. The waters swallowed it with a wet gulp, leaving a widening set of rings on the surface. A frown on the face of the An.

"You know," she said. "I believe you're only the second person ever to have charged at me wielding a sword."

"What befell the other?"

"Oh, you know, within a year or two he was good as new."

He almost smiled. She was about to speak again, to tell him the old tale, try and coax that smile out onto his face, when she felt a new presence, distant but clear.

Beltaine's eyes narrowed, questioning her.

"More vultures circling the corpse," she said. "Someone comes. Someone on the river."

"*On* the river?" Even as Beltaine spoke he was signalling to the remaining two waiting out of sight. "Who?"

"I don't know," said Hellen. "It is strange. There is a man, certainly, but he seems to be asleep. His dreams are outlandish, vast buildings and great machines. Very loud noise. There is another mind there, too. Something magical, the work of mancers."

Beltaine reached for his sword once more.

"Wait," said Hellen, placing a hand on his arm. "I don't think you'll need that. See."

Upstream, the shore became lost in shadows. Old, twisted willow trees dipped long branches into the river as if sipping from the water. In the shifting, dappled light it was hard to make out detail. Hellen and Beltaine stood in silence, peering through the branches, waiting for the newcomer.

The prow of a small boat peeked through the trees. It drifted toward the bank without oar or sail. A clear wake fanned out behind it.

The craft was perhaps five yards long, a housing taking up its forward half and an open space the rear. A small, golden figurehead in the shape of a man adorned its prow, leaning as if in flight. The figurehead's eyes flicked left and right and she knew, then, this was the magical presence she had sensed. The boat itself. It was painted all over with a glossy tangle of vines and rambling brambles. Tiny painted flowers, purple and yellow and red, as well as iridescent butterflies, were dotted here and there. Hellen found herself smiling at the shining beauty of it, so unexpected there on the waters of the river.

Inside lay a man. His wide-brimmed, floppy hat covered his face as he slept. He looked tall, and was dressed in colourful clothes, a tattered patchwork of greens and gold.

Another body in another boat. Strange how these patterns form.

The boat touched its port side to the bank near the remains of the undain. The eyes of the figurehead closed. A few moments later, awoken by the lack of motion, or as if he could only wake when the boat slept, the man inside stirred.

He lifted his hat from his eyes, squinting up at the two of them. Then he sat up sharply and, all wiry energy, hopped to his feet. He was young, tall and thin, with a good-natured face, a wide smile. His hair was long and ragged. His eyes sparkled. He could have been a scarecrow taken from some sunny field and brought to life.

"A witch and a wyrm lord stood by the An," he said, grinning. "Hey, a good first line for a song. Or perhaps an amusing story."

"You are a singer?" asked Hellen.

"I am. A wandering minstrel. A bard, a busker, a jongleur. Dances, banquets and parties a speciality. Songs written to order to suit any occasion. Jokes told and magic performed. Fire-eating and juggling with knives. My name is Johnny. Johnny Electric." He bowed low, theatrically, the boat swaying beneath him.

"A strange name," said Hellen. "It suits you."

The man smiled.

"This magic," said Beltaine, his mind cold suspicion. "You are a mancer?"

"Mere tricks, my friend: simple entertainments for children and grown-ups alike."

"The boat is not your own creation?"

"*Smoke on the Water?* No. A … gift from a grateful fan."

"A *fan*? I do not understand."

"Someone who liked my singing."

"They must have liked it a lot," said Hellen.

"I try, my Lady, I try." He sat back down. "Truth is, *Smoke on the Water* is more my companion than my possession."

"What brings you here?" asked Beltaine. Hellen could feel his mistrust although he kept his voice neutral.

"Nothing other than the wide, slow An *brings* me here. I don't even know where *here* is. I'm sailing south from Guilden. As I see it, I am bound to pass every point along the bank. *Smoke on the Water* saw you and, being friendly, pulled in to say hi."

Guilden again, too. She hadn't heard the place mentioned for months and now two strangers had talked of it on the same day. Two strangers in two boats.

"The mancer who made it was powerful," said Beltaine.

Johnny lay back down with his hands behind his head and grinned up at them, as if this was all a fine joke. The rocking of the boat swayed him gently. "Don't worry, no humans or animals were harmed in the making of this boat. If you must know, if it will persuade you not to slice me into pieces with that sword of yours, he was powerful, yes. But also old and broken with disease. He couldn't even walk. And yet he longed to travel the world. See the things he had neglected to see. So he came up with this." He patted the boat a few times. The eyes of the figurehead flickered open briefly.

"Then … the boat *is* the mancer?" asked Hellen. "He transformed himself into this?"

"Sure. And now he takes me about, I sing to him, and we see the world together. *Smoke on the Water* is, you understand, just my name for him."

He wasn't lying, she could tell. He seemed relaxed, completely self-assured. She felt no malice in either him or the boat. And although she disliked the unnatural arts of the mancers, she had to admit she sympathised with what this one had done. Was it really so different from the witches? All those bent old trees in the orchard back on Islagray?

Beltaine, however, remained unconvinced. "And this boat, it can …"

"He," cut in Johnny.

"*He* can sail on the An safely? Can he fight serpents, too?"

"No, no. Nothing like that. He can avoid rocks and banks under the water. He can feel the currents and ride them. But as for serpents, probably not. He knows when they're coming and we make a dash for the shore."

"Serpents aren't the only danger," said Hellen.

"What else is there to fear in this wide and beautiful land?"

Hellen said nothing, but nodded at the bones on the bank.

The man kneeled up to see where she pointed. He was silent for a while.

"What was it?" he said, quietly.

There, no doubt about it. A foggy, looming fear she had sensed in him had come sharply into focus. His merry exterior was genuine enough but he was also afraid of something. Something from which he fled.

"An undain. From over the An," said Hellen.

He fell silent again. The urgency rose within him. But very little surprise. He did not seem shocked at what she had told him.

"I must be on my way," he said simply.

"You sail away from Guilden?" said Hellen. "Now that is strange. I would have thought you should be sailing *to* Guilden. The midwinter festivals will be rich with paying customers."

"My lady, you are right. But I have decided to sail south. Sail all the way out of Andar. See if this river really does have an end." There it was again, the fear in him clear.

"You flee from something."

"No. Not really. Lady, the story is long and time is short.

But I – we – have decided to leave."

There was a part of the puzzle here, she was sure. There were things she needed to know about. Not just what he fled from, but who he was. He spoke like no one else she had ever met. She had never heard of anyone with the family name *Electric*. But her time was short, too. She had to return to Islagray to warn them about the undain rider.

"You know, it would be a shame to leave without ever hearing the Song," she said.

He was silent for a moment. He was tempted, no doubt about it.

"It really exists?"

"Of course. Sung unceasingly at Islagray for years uncounted. Andar itself given voice. The spirit of the land. The beauty of it, the life and death of it."

"I would be allowed to hear?"

"Oh, we aren't nearly so terrible as you have heard. And you have a story to tell, young man. A story I would like to hear."

His grin returned. "I would like to hear the Song. I think I maybe heard an echo of it once. But winter is coming on. I'll consider it, OK?"

"Very well. I can ask no more," said Hellen. "Half a day south of here the Gleaming joins the An. A further half day up there and you reach the Silverwater and the island of the witches. Come if you can. You would be welcome, Johnny Electric."

He nodded. At the same time, the eyes on the figurehead reopened, as if, between them, they had decided to move.

Hellen turned to Beltaine. "Well then. Let us all hope to meet again soon."

Beltaine handed her the pouch, filled now with all the sacks of spices. It was no larger or heavier.

She took it, nodded at both of them, then stepped into the air, climbing up over the trees.

As she flew away, she slipped lightly into Beltaine's mind for a moment, curious about both of them.

Beltaine said nothing, simply stooping to pick up his sword. Johnny stood gazing upward, watching her disappear into the sky.

"Cool," he said. He nodded to Beltaine, then cast his gaze downriver as *Smoke on the Water* moved off.

Hellen, leaving the dragonrider's mind, looked onward, toward the east.

7 – ISLAGRAY WYCKA

From afar, Islagray looked peaceful. The Silverwater filled the world below her, shining all the way to its distant banks. The moon shone solid again now, hanging low over the land. In the middle of the lake, directly ahead, lay the island of the witches. Trees covered its slopes so that it resembled a clump of moss there on the water. Around it, darkness gathered.

Hellen flew downward. She ached with weariness. Flying over water always exhausted her. The cold made her cheeks hurt sharply. She began to hear the raucous calling of the island's crows, louder and louder, as if they were becoming more and more angry. The spire of Islagray Wycka jutted out from the tree-tops. She would soon be home.

Thoughts jostled in her mind, so many that she couldn't focus on any one of them before another distracted her. She had so much to do. She kept returning to the same nagging worry. Was she ready for all this? After all this time, could she face it? Did she have the strength to even try? Beyond the Wycka, atop a small rise in the land, an open space appeared, dotted with small black trees, each bent and crooked as if growing in the teeth of a fierce gale. The Orchard of Witches.

Some day soon, she thought. *Some day soon.*

But then a wave of panic and fear washed through her.

It rose off the island like an invisible hand seizing hold of her insides. Three hundred witches united in their pain. Something was terribly wrong on Islagray. She sought out Ariane among the hubbub of voices and found her standing among the trees. Hellen spoke to her from afar, mind to mind.

"Ariane."

"Hellen. You are safe. Thank the stars. We were afraid for you." Ariane's relief was clear, as was her distress.

"Tell me what has happened."

"Something is on the island. Two witches were attacked a few hours after you left. Both were killed. More than just killed, Hellen. Sucked dry. There is an undain here."

"Who were they?"

"Shireen and Diane."

"Ah. Both so young." She was close now. Individuals hurried to-and-fro on the ground.

"The hedge witch," continued Hellen. "Fer. Is she safe?"

"She is," replied Ariane. "And the merchant. Neither has stirred."

"That is good. She may be very important in all this. Perhaps the key to it."

Hellen landed, stepping lightly onto the ground outside the main door of Islagray Wycka. A small clearing lay in the trees there, with paths leading off in all directions, including the one they had walked along from the quay early that morning. Ariane emerged at a run from the nearby oaks, her face drawn into hard lines. She continued the conversation out loud, as if they had been walking side-by-side all along.

"We thought about waking them. We thought perhaps it was one of them. Their souls wandering. Something possessing them."

"Tell me how the two died," said Hellen.

"Shireen was killed near here. We thought she must have been in the way of something trying to get out. Then we heard Diane screaming from inside. We were there in moments but it was no use."

Hellen put her arms around Ariane and they held each other for a moment, eyes shut.

"An undain," said Ariane, the shock clear in her voice. "Here, of all places."

"It flew across the An, travelled here in Merdoc's cart," said Hellen. "The one the merchant saw was just its mount. It was the rider Fer tried to warn us about. A powerful undain lord."

"It must have been there with us this morning," said Ariane. "Close to us all and we didn't know."

"And now it is inside," said Hellen. "We must hurry to the archive."

Hellen strode up the steps toward the open doorway. But Ariane did not move.

"The archive? Surely it is the Songroom that matters? That is where we have been gathering, not down amongst the old books. We must protect the singers." The slightest note of anger sounded in Ariane's voice. It had been a long day. Even so, it was something that perhaps only Hellen would have noticed. She stopped and turned back.

"There is no time for this now, Ariane. I know what you think, what you all think. Let me say it out loud, eh? Mad old Hellen is too much the mancer, dabbling in sorcery down there among the spell books."

"Hellen, no …"

"Witches should be out doing things, not sitting in the dark and scribbling. That's it, eh?"

She took a step down the worn stairs toward Ariane. She tried to keep the anger from her own voice.

"Well, maybe you're right. And maybe you're not. But I promise you, this thing has not come to kill the Singers, or any of us, unless we get in the way. It has come for a book. Just a book. Witches may not care for written incantations, but mancers do. Especially necromancers. And that's what this thing is."

Neither spoke for a moment, staring into each other's eyes. They had been friends for one hundred and fifty-three years. It was Hellen that broke the silence.

"Please trust me. The archive is where this abomination has gone. And that's where I'm going. But I'd feel a lot happier if you were with me, Ariane."

She turned around and walked into Islagray Wycka. Behind her, Ariane paused for a moment, smiled a private grin to herself, then walked up the steps to follow Hellen inside.

Candles in sconces sent dancing lights up the sloping sides of the Wycka's great hollow chimney. It was deserted for the moment: the others were either scouring the island or huddled underground in the Songroom. Hellen could feel the thrumming of the voices in her bones. She heard a clear wrongness in them now: notes of pain, harsh discords. It felt like walking across sharp stones.

She didn't stop, her tiredness forgotten. Half-way across the floor, near the well the rainwater drained into, a dark patch stained the stones. Diane's blood. She had no time to stop. The rain would wash it away eventually. She hurried on to a wooden door between the widdershins and sunwise staircases.

A moment later, Ariane caught up.

"Hellen, we couldn't feel it," said Ariane. "That was almost the worst of it. We knew it was here but we couldn't see it. We refreshed all the cobweb spells. We set beetles and crows on its path. We crafted black dogs to track it down. But we felt nothing. It was there and yet … not there. How can this be?"

"Black Meg, who lived at the time of the schism between Andar and Angere, said the mind of the undain is a patch of deeper darkness at night," said Hellen. "Seeing them with the inner eye is like looking for the absence of something. It's a skill we need to start learning. Now, come."

Hellen pushed at the door, taking two heaves to budge it from its frame. Inside, a stifling silence waited for them. They stood for a moment. Five passageways led off like the fingers of a hand, each hewn from the rock and sloping into the ground at different angles. Torches here and there showed many doorways in the walls of each passageway, leading to more caverns. Four of the five tunnels eventually disappeared around bends but the fifth, the central one, seemed to go straight down forever.

"I'd forgotten the size of these caves," said Ariane.

"They fill the ground beneath Islagray as the roots of a tree," said Hellen.

She turned to a wooden desk, set into an alcove next to the door. A large, tattered book lay upon it, the open page full of scribbled letters in a variety of hands. The borrowers' book. A pool of ink, spilled from a small metal flask that had overturned, spread slowly across the desk. On the floor, a white quill lay in an inky pool. She was more certain than ever the undain had come this way. Thena, the current Storyteller, must have gone after it, or been taken by it. They had to hurry.

She turned to a large, iron cage that hung from a hook in the wall behind the door. Inside was a dark, rustling mass of leaves and cobwebs. She reached through the grating of the cage and pulled out something black, cupping it in her hand.

"Here," she said to Ariane.

She opened her hand to reveal a large furry spider, bright purple bands on its legs and body. She held it close to Ariane's hair and the spider stepped across, feeling its way with its long legs, nestling into its new home.

"Why do I need that?"

"It really has been a long time, hasn't it? The spiders lived here long before we did. They know these caves and they know how to get out. When you want to return, look for the spider's shimmering thread. It will be faint but you can catch it in the torch light. Follow that and it will bring you out."

"But surely you won't get lost? You've spent years of your life down here."

"Yes, but what if I don't come back, Ariane? If you end

up alone you *would* get lost."

"And if we find this thing. Or it finds us. What is your plan then?" asked Ariane.

"We do what we can to put an end to it," said Hellen.

Ariane said nothing for a moment, doubt clear on her face.

"Enough," said Hellen. "There is no time. Let us go!"

They set off down one of the side passageways. It sloped, then twisted in a spiral so it was soon impossible to know which direction they faced, where the moon sat in the sky above their heads.

The air smelled of earth and paper, with the faintest tang of honey as they passed each sputtering torch. It was, as ever, cool and dry on Hellen's face - which helped, along with the spells the witches crafted, to make the caves so perfect for preserving all the ancient parchment.

The reverberations from the Songroom became gradually fainter, as did her sense of the others above them. She tried to put everything out of her mind, tried to reach out and feel for the undain, see the shadow hiding in the darkness as they walked down and down into the earth.

Above each doorway a sigil had been carved into the rock. Here they passed a curving lizard on a leafy branch, there a representation of the sun with rays coming from it like a fiery crown. The archive had been meticulously organized over the centuries by the Storytellers of Islagray: the sigils identifying, to them at least, what books and scrolls lay inside each room.

Hellen couldn't help glancing inside as they passed. One or two she knew well. Some she had visited occasionally. Many she had never yet set foot inside. So many voices waited down here. She fancied she could hear them calling to her as they hurried by, words of warning or fear in the still air. In the shadows she imagined glimpses of long-dead witches and warlocks. Women and men who had walked the land as she now did, people who had laughed and cried and learned, all waiting down here to be heard.

They walked briskly for perhaps half an hour, Hellen leading, passing through doorways that sometimes opened into large halls, sometimes into further small, twisting passageways. Through doors marked with an eye, a flame, a heart, a bird. Always, they headed downward.

After a while, the torches in the walls became fewer and fewer, before stopping completely. Darkness huddled there beyond the last light, waiting to swallow them. Hellen took a torch from its holder and carried it into the darkness. Monstrous, shifting shadows accompanied them.

Finally, they stopped before a doorway, half way along a passage that appeared identical to all the others they had walked down. Above this door, a skull had been carved into the rock.

Hellen pointed into the room to tell Ariane this was the place, then closed her eyes and listened hard. Her heart thudded in her chest, partly from the long walk, mostly from fear. If the undain was still in there, they could both die.

She felt *something* through the doorway. A foggy hint of fear and pain, but very indistinct. It made Hellen shiver just to touch it with her mind. Was that what necromancers immersed themselves in? Setting aside her discomfort, refusing to be afraid, she reached out again. She crafted strong magic in her mind, steeling her body for the searing pain. She would destroy this thing, whatever the cost to herself. Behind her, Ariane prepared to do the same.

A faint smell came to her then. She paused for a moment, thinking. Something she had read in another of the old books. She turned to Ariane.

"Can you smell burning metal?" she asked out loud.

Ariane looked surprised but said nothing. After a few moments, she nodded.

"Very well," said Hellen. She marched through the doorway.

Inside was the simple, round room she remembered, with no other doorways. It was a natural cave; great stalactites hung from the ceiling above stalagmites on the floor. The more ancient ones had met, fingers touching to form solid pillars. The walls had the pink-red tinge of ochre. It was hard to escape the impression they stood inside some giant mouth full of jagged teeth.

There were no sconces around the walls of this room. But in its centre stood a low, stone plinth, large enough to hold a book. It was empty. On the floor next to it lay the body of Thena, the eighty-seventh Storyteller of Islagray. Her face was grey, shrunken to bone as if she had died long ago.

Nothing attacked them. The undain, like the book it had come for, was gone.

8 – COVEN

Six of them met in the orchard. The sun shone hot, although hulking clouds drifting from the west cast them repeatedly into shadow. It was two days after the death of three witches and the loss of the book. The undain that had stalked the island had not been found.

Hellen had insisted they wait until Fer was with them again. The young hedge witch sat opposite Hellen now, very pale, her gaze cast on the ground. She looked exhausted. She panted slightly as if she had been running. She had said little since waking up and could remember nothing of her struggle on the banks of the An. It was often the way with strong magic, of course: her mind sparing her the memory of overwhelming pain. But eventually they would need to know.

She wore the simple, white gown from the infirmary. Her hair, rich chestnut brown, flowed to the middle of her back. Occasionally she glanced around, her silver jewellery glinting in the sun, a glimmer of fierce defiance in her. Her teeth were gritted as if she looked at the world through veils of pain. Hellen hadn't spoken to her yet, but she found herself liking the girl's spirit. Many would have been in bed for a week or more. It was a good sign. Much still lay ahead of the young witch.

Next to her sat Ariane, who had tended to Fer almost

without rest and who had offered her support for the short walk to the orchard. Fer and Ariane had smiled at each other as they approached. That was promising, too. Fer would be wary of them and it was vital they gained her trust.

On the other side of Fer sat Seleena, a young witch of Islagray who knew Fer distantly. Hellen had seen them together about the infirmary. The beginnings of a friendship grew there by the look of it. Seleena sat very still, staring into the middle of the circle, her arms crossed firmly across her chest. She wore her hair shaved. Her silver jewellery resembled Fer's a little: lines of delicate, silver stars connecting her ears and eyebrows.

Between Seleena and Hellen sat Ran, the dragonrider. The day before, Hellen had rowed a boat across the Silverwater, stood on the wooden quay next to the watch tower and shouted the words *Dethnior unthwai sen thain* into the trees. The dragonrider had emerged immediately, dropping from a branch to stand before her. His two companions had appeared from behind large boughs. Once again, she hadn't been able to feel the presence of any of them until they showed themselves.

Ran was younger than Beltaine but he had the same sombre expression. He wore identical clothes and carried the same serpentine sword at his side. He had only one silver stud in his ear. The tattoos on his body were a deep blue where Beltaine's had been red. His hair was long rather than close shaven and bound in a tightly knotted sheaf that reached half way down his back. It lashed to-and-fro as he walked like a spitting snake. He stood slightly shorter than Beltaine but looked physically stronger, his arms and legs thick with muscles.

A shame. She much preferred them lithe and willowy. A memory came to her of Borrn, the moonlight on his tall, pale body, smooth as the boughs of a coppiced tree, the feeling of his arms around her. Strange. She hadn't thought of him for many years. Still, this young dragonrider was handsome enough, his movements flowing and graceful despite his strength.

"My Lady," he'd said. "We will help you if we may."

"Then please accompany me across the water to Islagray. There is much to talk about. Your companions may return to Beltaine."

At Ran's nod the other two turned to disappear into the shadows of the trees.

Part way across the lake, Ran, rowing, paused for a moment.

"My Lady, no dragonrider has ever been to Islagray."

"You won't be the last. And it's Hellen."

He nodded at that and continued rowing. Since then he hadn't spoken another word. When they reached Islagray he left his sword in the skiff, where it still lay.

On the other side of Hellen, lying on the grass between her and Ariane, sat Johnny. He seemed to be asleep once again. He arrived early that morning, *Smoke on the Water* drifting slowly up from the outlet of the Gleaming in defiance of all the currents. He had taken his time; she'd been sure he'd decided not to come. Then they spotted his dazzling boat in the distance. *Smoke on the Water* came close enough to let Johnny hop out before drifting away to lie some way off the island.

Hellen had shown Johnny around, taken him to hear the Song. He sat for three hours on the stone floor of the echoing, round chamber, saying nothing, his eyes shut. In the end, she had to rouse him, touch his shoulder to invite him upstairs for food. He simply smiled his thanks and came away with her, unusually silent. By then, Fer was awake and able to walk.

Now they sat, six in the circle, but with all the inhabitants of Islagray listening and watching through the eyes of one of the three island witches. When decisions needed to be made, they would all have their say.

Hellen looked up past the waiting faces to the winding, gnarled boughs of the ancient trees. They grasped at the sky like skeletal hands: apple, crab-apple, damson, wytch hazel, blackthorn and hawthorn. She could feel their presence. Some were so old the life in them was a mere whisper. Others, those that had more recently walked the land, were alert, watching, talking. The air buzzed with thoughts of the dead witches of Islagray, hanging like a scent or a mist you could taste. It was a place she often came to sit and think. She drew in a deep breath before beginning.

"I will speak first," she said. "I will tell you of my journey to and from the An, two days since."

After she had finished, there was a thoughtful silence. She expected Ariane to say something but it was Johnny who spoke, sitting up suddenly.

"So, OK, you're saying this thing meant to come here, yeah? It flew across the An, this impossible flight, just to get to Islagray?"

"I believe so," replied Hellen. "Somehow it used Fer, flew to her like a moth to a light. I think it found her in order to find us."

Fer said nothing. Her gaze remained locked on the grass at her bare feet.

"But what about the An?" said Johnny. "The undain can't cross running water. Everyone knows that. There are loads of songs about it. You know, *Only the soul or a swan may cross the An* and all that."

"It's a myth," said Hellen. "A story we tell ourselves to feel safer. We pretend that Angere is where bad people go when they die and by doing so we make the distance seem greater. We pretend it is spiritual and not just a matter of miles. But you saw the creature on the river bank. Flying over water is hard but the undain are as capable of doing it as we are. They can't cross the An for the same reasons we can't. The serpents devour any ship that tries and it is too far to fly by magic. Or so we thought."

"Great," said Johnny. His fear flared again, his urge to flee. "But all that just for some old book? What's that all about?"

"A good question. It might help if we all knew

something of its history." She turned to look at Ran.

The dragonrider held her gaze for a moment, then sprang to his feet. He looked around the circle, making sure he had their full attention.

"What part would you see?" he asked.

The shame burned in him. And the intense desire to spell out what the dragonriders had done all those years ago. The longing for penance. They were too proud, too hard on themselves. But there was no stopping them.

"Just the battle at the golden doors for now, I think."

"I will need the fire."

Borrn had used their campfire to show her, one cold night in the northern wilds when they'd travelled together. The sky had lightened in the east, she remembered, before she witnessed the whole story. For now, the small pile of twigs she gathered would suffice. Twigs dropped from the trees of the Orchard.

She reached out with her hand and touched a spark to the kindling, ignoring the brief, sharp stitch of pain in her stomach. The kindling sent curls of smoke into the air, then orange flame. Soon the twigs burned.

Ran took the gold chain from around his neck and slid off the small red gems strung upon it, counting them as he did so. He took the seventh and held it over the fire.

"Witness the shame of the dragonriders," he said, as if they were the words of some ceremony, and dropped the gem into the flames.

In the shifting air above the fire, an image formed. It was indistinct at first, mere shapes in the smoke, but it rapidly solidified, hard edges and details becoming clear. At the same time, it expanded outward so it appeared the images held within the gemstone were all around them.

There stood the huge pair of golden doors she remembered so clearly. They were the height of three people and ornately decorated with jewels laid out in snaking patterns.

Five figures stood guard in front of the doors,

dragonriders, three men and two women. They had the same tattoos as Ran and Beltaine, similar armour and swords, but no gold chains around their necks.

She smelled the decay she remembered so clearly from last time, making her stomach clench. Such horror within such dazzling splendour. She knew if she stood up and walked away from the fire the vision would fade. But the least she could do was sit and watch the terrible events again.

Screams echoed down the long, marble hallway that led up to the gates. A dozen or so young men and women were pulled in chains by five more dragonriders. Some of the victims were unconscious, dragged by their arms like rag-dolls. Others were awake, frantic, trying to break free from their shackles. The dragonriders forced them all forward, hauling them, jabbing at them with their swords.

The guards at the door parted to let them through. Hellen saw one, the nearest, tighten her grip on her sword, her knuckles white. This was Dervil. Glances passed between the dragonriders, an unspoken conversation. It was clear how uneasy they were. Sworn to obey their King, sworn to protect him, they were already lost. Finally, one turned and pounded on the doors with the pommel of his serpentine sword.

Footsteps came nearer and a man heaved open one of the doors. If she had met him in other circumstances she would have thought him unremarkable. He was short and bald. She might have mistaken him for a landlord in some quiet, wayside inn. A joyless, resentful landlord. But his eyes were flared wide, like an injured rabbit cornered in the woods and blood was splattered all over him. Some belonged to him, from a series of knife-cuts on his forearms, runes carved out in deep scarlet gashes.

Ilminion the necromancer shouted harsh, incomprehensible words, urging the dragonriders to bring the victims through. Over his shoulder, Hellen could see glimpses of the King's chamber. There was Menhroth himself, lying prone inside the ritual circle. He was alive again by now, his body twitching and bucking. He lay naked, his body purple-blue like a new-born baby. Near his head stood a golden lectern in the shape of an eagle, its wings outstretched, holding the open book. All around, in the ruined splendour of his throne-room, stood great iron cauldrons, and from each were thin tubes leading directly into his body.

She heard more screaming from the prisoners, an edge of panic to their cries. She had to remind herself these were old wrongs. Five hundred years later, there was nothing she could do to help.

More shouts came from the hallway, this time roars of fury rather than fear. A group of warriors, swords held before them, ran toward the doors. There were perhaps thirty of them, all wounded as if they had fought through much to make it this far.

The dragonriders moved quickly in front of the prisoners, allowing them to be hauled through the open golden door while forming a line to protect the King's chamber.

Hellen finally closed her eyes. There was nothing to be gained from watching this part again. But she was unable to block out the sounds. For long moments she listened, flinching, to the clang of metal upon metal, the screams of the attackers as they fell and the muffled cries of the prisoners from inside the chamber.

Eventually, silence returned. She opened her eyes. Bodies lay everywhere. Only the five dragonriders still stood. They were out of breath at least. They looked at each other, a wariness clear in their eyes. Guilt.

Ilminion reappeared at the doors, fresh blood on his face. He began to shout, exhaustion making his voice ragged. Hellen knew from Borrn what his words meant. The ritual was not yet finished. He needed more victims, the life of one more along with his own blood, to seal the magic.

Here at last was the moment the fate of Angere and Andar, and other worlds too, was decided. Here was the turning point.

Hellen's gaze moved to Dervil. She stood uninjured. Around her feet lay the bodies of perhaps seven attackers, as if she had built herself a nest.

Ilminion stepped through the doorway and began to kick each of the bodies on the ground. Most were dead but one groaned and tried to defend himself, arms held uselessly over his face. Despite the deep cuts to his body and neck, he lived. Hellen caught glimpses of his face. He was very young, his eyes wide with horror. He resembled Dervil a little: black hair and rich, golden-brown skin. Someone from the same part of Angere, perhaps. Ilminion dragged him into the chamber, calling to the dragonriders to help.

It was this, finally, that was too much for Dervil. Hellen could sense nothing of her mind, the stones only relaying sights, sounds and smells. Dervil's expression didn't change. The dragonriders were trained never to reveal their intentions in battle. But she turned with a dancer's elegance, her sword held out horizontally, and sliced the necromancer's head cleanly from his shoulders. In a single blow she achieved what an entire army had failed to do in weeks of fighting. The sight was horrific but also strangely comic, the headless body standing there for a moment as if confused, before crumpling to the marble floor.

The other dragonriders flinched, their hands going back to their swords. But they didn't stop Dervil as she marched into the King's chamber, her serpentine sword before her. She walked up to the prone King, who bellowed helplessly, without the strength to rise. Dervil stopped before him. What ran through her mind? Did it occur to her to slay the king? And if she had done so, what would the world be like now?

They would never know. Dervil lowered her sword and bowed deeply to the king, the man she had sworn to protect. Then she walked to the lectern, took the book and marched out of the chamber and down the hall, not looking backward.

The vision faded. As it wavered and collapsed back into the flames of the twig fire, most of the dragonriders at the doors followed Dervil, leaving their king, although a few stayed where they were to guard the doors.

Sunlight burst through the scene, dissipating it like early morning mist. They were back in the orchard. The sweet tang of the grass came to her. The only sound was the hissing of the small fire and a lark, twittering and twittering high up in the blue sky.

She looked around the circle. Ran was stony-faced, still standing. Fer looked weaker again and close to tears. Seleena shook her head slightly as if attempting to dislodge the sights she had just witnessed. Ariane simply looked sad, while Johnny's face was wide-eyed with shock.

"Holy hell," he said.

"I am sorry for having to show you," said Hellen.

"So that was the necromancer? The one in all the stories?" asked Johnny.

"Ilminion, yes," replied Hellen. "And in the chamber, undergoing the ritual, that was Menhroth himself. The Witch King as he now calls himself."

"So the dragonriders were like, the king's guard?" asked Johnny. He looked up at Ran, who met his gaze. The dragonrider was like someone standing outside in the rain, enjoying the sensation of it lashing against his face. He wanted their condemnation, welcomed their scorn for everything that had been done by his ancestors.

"They were," said Hellen. "They followed their orders and allowed Ilminion to work his necromancy. It is said that over a thousand people died within the chamber as Menhroth was ritually killed and brought back as undain."

"Yet the rite was not completed," Ariane said quietly. "We saw. That dragonrider killed the necromancer before his work was complete. She did that at least."

"True," said Hellen. "And that was something. Not enough to stop Menhroth, but still."

"So he is vulnerable," said Fer, speaking for the first

time, looking not at any of them but gazing into the distance. "It is an incomplete circle. However small, the gap must still be there."

She was clever too, no doubt about it. She had seen it.

"Which is why the undain came here after all this time," said Hellen.

"The book in the vision," said Ariane. "It came for that? It is here?"

"It is. Or it was. That was the Grimoire. The book in which Ilminion detailed all the arts of his death magic."

"All this trouble over a book written so long ago," said Ariane.

"A book whose magic allowed Menhroth to become what he is," said Hellen. "Allowed him, in turn, to create all the undain, all of Angere as we now know it. Everything comes back to the sorcery in it."

"Why now though?" said Fer, still looking away, as if she was thinking out loud rather than talking. "Why have they come now?"

"Perhaps they only just found out how to work the magic to cross so much water," said Hellen.

The girl looked unconvinced. As was Hellen come to that. *Why now* was a very good question indeed. She glanced at Johnny, who still sat upright, as if ready to make a run for it there and then. He fidgeted with his fingers, plucking at the strings of an imaginary instrument.

"Not everyone in Angere accepted what the king was doing," said Ariane. She was angry, the wrinkles around her eyes deepening as she frowned. "We saw. Some tried to stop him."

"Not enough," said Hellen. "The necromancer was no fool. He chose his victims for his early experiments carefully: those that people didn't care much about, thieves and pirates and beggars. Then he set the simple beings he created to work, doing all the dangerous and dirty jobs no one else wanted to do, labouring without rest. Seeing that, the people allowed him to continue."

"But the Witch King is no *simple being*," said Ariane. "In Angere he is considered a god, all-powerful."

"Over long years, Ilminion perfected the Ritual of the Seven Ascensions, as he named it," said Hellen. "It is described in the books. He offered Menhroth eternal life and inhuman power. Offered him all the powers of necromancy, too."

"Still, to let yourself be killed," said Ariane. "To let yourself become what he is, that abomination. It's unthinkable."

"Is it?" asked Hellen. "The king was old and afraid of dying. Many people would have been tempted, I dare say."

"Look, what does it matter?" said Johnny, half-shouting, his agitation finally boiling over. "What does any of it matter? They have the book now. They can finish the hocus-pocus. They can do whatever they want! When the war comes, they'll be unstoppable. Andar - everything - will fall. Don't you see?"

There it was. The great weight of dread she had sensed on the banks of the An. She had shocked it out of him, brought it to the surface like poison drawn from a wound. Now things might become clearer.

There was silence in the circle. Everyone there, everyone in the coven, watched him.

"War?" said Hellen. "An interesting word, Johnny Electric. That is the first time anyone has talked of *war*."

9 – SNOW ON THE NORTHERN HILLS

Hellen searched into Johnny's mind. But it was hard to see anything through the fog of his fear.

"I just thought that … well, an invasion's bound to happen isn't it?" he said. "I mean, like, sooner or later?"

"You have forgotten the An," said Ariane. "It has kept us safe for many hundreds of years. A single miraculous flight is one thing, an invasion quite another."

He opened his mouth. He prepared to speak, but he stopped himself.

"You have heard the Song," Hellen said to him. "You have heard the beauty of it."

He looked haunted. "I have."

"The song is the land," said Hellen. "The land is the song. There is no difference. They are like the sound of the river and the river itself. You heard the discord in it?"

He looked down. "Yes."

"Sometimes there are breaks in the rhythm, complete pauses in the music. One day soon, if we don't act, perhaps the singing will stop completely."

He said nothing.

"Johnny Electric, I think you should tell us your story," said Hellen. "Before you leave Andar, tell us what you are running from."

He was silent for a moment more, staring into the sky.

High above, the lark still hovered, warbling its long, beautiful song to the world.

"Then I can go?" he asked.

"Then you can leave Andar, yes," said Hellen.

He sighed. "OK."

He scratched his chin where a thin beard grew. He folded his legs, glancing at each of them.

"I was in Guilden for the Proclamation two weeks ago," Johnny began. "The talk in the taverns was all of the Ice Fair. Everyone said there would be one this winter. The place was buzzing. Minstrels and mummers and acrobats juggling fire on every corner. All sorts of weird stuff going on. And all this just for the *announcement* about the Ice Fair, yeah?

"The three mancers that make the observations had returned from the far north the day before, all their arcane calculations complete. They appeared on this ornate balcony overlooking the Golden Square bang in the centre of Guilden. The place was full from first light. It was heaving. I didn't know there *were* so many people in Andar. So, they make the Proclamation through these great brass megaphones. When the voice of the oldest guy boomed out there would be an Ice Fair, the place exploded. The sound of the crowd cheering and shouting was amazing. It was like … well, it was *really* loud.

"But I happened to know the youngest of the three. I met him at the court of the Doge of Guilden a few times. He wasn't on the balcony. I came across him later that day in a quiet back street. He was plainly dressed, no flashy purple robes or regalia, upon a horse-drawn wagon that was well laden.

"I asked him where he was going, what with all the partying and excitement. He looked troubled. I think he just needed to tell someone what had happened. Seems there'd been arguments amongst the three of them. He said the observations they made had been strange. *Extreme* was the word he used. He told me how the first snow normally appears on the distant peak of Howl Hill around the autumn equinox, how they chart its progress over two weeks to predict the winter. This year, when they got there, the entire slope was covered. Howl Hill and all the northern peaks. The three of them couldn't agree what this meant. The young mancer foresaw things the others did not. In the end, the other two overruled him and simply announced there would be an Ice Fair, nothing more. But he was leaving Guilden, heading south, because of what he said was coming."

Johnny stopped speaking, looking back up into the sky.

"And what was that?" asked Hellen. "Didn't this young mancer think there would be an Ice Fair, too?" Across the circle, she saw, Ariane scowled slightly, mistrustful of the wisdom of mancers.

"Oh yeah," said Johnny. "No problem there. He told me there was definitely a cold winter coming. But a really, really cold winter: worse, he said, than any in the records. Andar will be locked in ice and the An ..."

He stopped again. Hellen wondered who the young mancer from Guilden was. She had an inkling about that, too. But all in good time.

"Go on," she said.

"He said the An will freeze. I mean, freeze *right over*. Bank to bank. Not just the little area in the bay near Guilden, but the whole thing."

"No!" said Ariane.

"Yeah. No doubt about it. The An is going to freeze over. The undain army can just march across the ice and destroy us all. And there's not a damn thing we can do."

There. That was it. Now it all made sense. There was the great mass of fear that drove him from Andar. It made many things clear. Things really were moving at last. It explained the book. It explained all the little coincidences. It explained the Song.

Perhaps, she thought, it even explained why Merdoc had found Forness so terrible in winter, a detail that had been troubling her. Forness was the closest point to Angere, south of Guilden. Had the undain been amassing across the wide waters? Waiting for the winter? Had some whisper come across the river on the wind to haunt the nights of those that lived there?

She looked around her. It was strange how beautiful the day remained. It seemed as if nothing had changed. The blue sky, the skylark singing. But the air of the orchard murmured, now, with the troubled thoughts of the trees. In truth, everything had changed. Most of all, Hellen felt relief. Now, at least, they could act.

"Well," she said, looking at each of them in turn. "We are getting somewhere. That is some good news at least."

"What?" said Johnny, genuine shock on his face. "Good news? How can any of that be good news? Are you mad? Didn't you hear what I said?"

He turned to the others in disbelief. Fer stared at the ground, her body slumped. Seleena and Ariane watched Hellen, uncomprehending. Only Ran met Johnny's gaze, his expression unchanged.

Hellen felt their despair. In truth, it was difficult to feel anything else. But she smiled at each of them.

"Consider this," she said. "They have shown their hand. They want the book. Perhaps they need it for the completion of their plans. Perhaps it is a danger to them. They could have destroyed their half and removed that threat. By coming here they have told us they haven't done so."

"But they are going to invade!" said Johnny, agitated now, half-shouting. "An army of undead supermen is going to waltz across the ice this winter and kill us all. Turn us into zombies. Slaughter us in terrible rites, yeah? I mean, it's the whole Dark Lord trip."

"Yes, yes," said Hellen. "Of course. That's all been obvious for years. But they need the book, don't you see? I couldn't be sure. The question is *why*. If they are going to cross the An this winter, why go to all this trouble?" She indicated Islagray with a wave of her hand.

"OK then," said Johnny. "Why?"

"I think they're planning ahead. They want to be sure we don't destroy our half of the book when we see them coming. Maybe they have plans beyond Andar and there is magic in it they need. Or, then again, maybe they need it in order to attack us at all. To cross the An. Something in the necromancy we don't understand."

"Half the book," Ariane interjected. "You keep saying half the book. That makes no sense. You told us it was here, now you're saying only part of it was."

She was angry at being left out of all these secrets. Really, it was understandable.

"Ran," said Hellen. "Could you bear to show us the vision of another of your penance stones? The cleaving of the book?"

The dragonrider sprang to his feet, fingers counting the red stones like someone working an abacus. Hellen turned her attention to the smouldering fire. With a stick she poked the first jewel onto the grass. It was cold as she picked it up and handed it to Ran. Then she rearranged the twigs and, adding some more kindling, blew on the glow to bring it back into life. When there were flames once more, Ran dropped in the second stone.

Again, an image formed in the rising smoke and wavering air of the fire. They saw a wood upon a hilltop, full of shadows and flickering half-light from branches blowing in a wind they did not feel. Beneath the hill a green plain stretched into the distance. The land could have been Andar, divided up into its hotchpotch pattern of fields. Beyond lay a great stretch of blue water, shimmering in the hazy distance. The An, seen from the other side.

The wind ruffled the hair of seven figures. Dervil stood there, Ilminion's red-leather tome cradled in her arms. Two other dragonriders stood next to her. All three looked badly wounded.

They faced three other warriors, all also bearing signs of

recent fighting. Each had the symbol of a stone bridge engraved upon dented breastplates. Next to them stood a fourth person, older and uninjured, not wearing armour, his hair long and grey. His beard had been carefully woven into plaits, with strips of leather twined into it. This was Akbar, mancer of the failed Angere rebellion.

The two groups of people faced each other warily. They had clearly been arguing. Hellen wanted the coven to understand what they were saying. She worked the necessary magic, a spell of tongues she had used many times as she strove to understand some scrap of writing. It invariably gave her a throbbing headache, sometimes a megrim bad enough to pin her to her bed for hours on end. But it had to be done. As she completed the spell, the words of the people in the vision became suddenly understandable.

"… not your enemies," said Dervil.

"We have fought you in battle after battle," one of the bridge warriors said. "Now you are our friends?" Hellen couldn't recall the warrior's name, or anything about him. He had a bad scar on his cheek, livid red, a recent slash from a sword. It made him look cruel, but without it he would have been handsome. He stood tall and powerful, like a village blacksmith. His curly, black hair turned to silver at his temples. Who was he when he wasn't in his armour? Had he a woman? Children? She would never know.

"We fight you no more," one of the other dragonriders said. "Now we are the hunted. We have left our dragons behind. This, who you doubt killed Ilminion just six days ago. This is Dervil. She carries the book of necromancy she took from him."

"Let me see," said Akbar. Dervil handed him the book. The mancer opened it at random and read, turning over a few pages, frowning as he went.

"Well?" the unknown warrior asked. "Is it what they say?" His voice quavered with anger. He had seen too much, been through too much.

Akbar still studied the book, his gaze darting over the

pages. "It is hard to follow. The hand is difficult. And of course, I have no knowledge of necromancy. No one apart from Menhroth now does. But yes, I do believe they speak the truth."

"Then let us destroy it," the warrior said. "Before we are caught by the King's armies. At least we can keep it out of his claws." He reached to take the book.

"Wait," said Dervil. "I ask you to wait."

"Oh, you do?" The warrior's hand went to the pommel of his sword. Another turning point. They could all so easily have been killed here.

"We may be able to make use of it," said Dervil. Hellen found herself mouthing the words as she heard them again. She had thought them over long and hard since first hearing them with Borrn. "The necromancer's magic is all there. How it works, how it may be broken. The book may be our only hope for stopping them. We must not destroy it."

The warrior's weariness was clear in his voice. "We are surrounded by their armies. Your friends and their dragons are destroying us minute by minute. How exactly did you plan to keep this cursed book from them?"

"By taking it to Andar," said Dervil. "By crossing the great bridge with it."

"You will never get there. None of us will ever get there now. We are overrun. They will find us, take the book and kill us all. At least, they will kill *us*. I am not sure about you."

"Then we have little to lose, do we?" said Akbar. "The dragonrider's plan makes sense. But it is my opinion we should divide the book into two. Dervil can take one half and we the other. That way, there is less chance of the King being able to retrieve the complete article. They would need to find both of us."

"I don't need you to cut a book in two, Akbar," the warrior said. "I can do it with my sword."

"Yes, yes, but you do not know if the important magic is in the one half. No one does. But I can divide it so that neither part is usable without the other. They would need both halves to make any use of the book."

"As would we," the warrior said. "How does that help?"

"It means they have less chance of reclaiming the complete thing whilst still giving us a chance - a very slim chance - to do so."

A series of calls came through the trees, followed by the sound of someone running. Another warrior crashed into the glade, out of breath from sprinting in full armour. He held his sword and shield in his hands.

"They are coming," he said. "The King's dragons, searing the land. Their riders direct the army toward us."

"Be ready to retreat," the warrior shouted . He turned to Akbar. "It is a pointless task, but do as you like. We will try to fight our way down the Meltwater valley to the bridgehead."

Akbar looked at Dervil, who nodded her head. The mancer placed the book on the ground. He took some small vials from a pouch at his belt and poured a fine dust onto it, followed by a drop of some blue liquid. His hands trembled. He mumbled the words of a spell, too quiet to hear. There was a flash and two books, identical, lay on the ground.

Akbar picked up one of them. Dervil stooped to take the other.

The warrior had already turned to leave. Dervil shouted to him. "We are sorry for what we have done. We are sorry for everything."

The warrior glanced back at her for a moment. Then, saying nothing, he walked away.

As he disappeared into the trees' shadows, the vision faded. In moments, they were back in the orchard. Ran sat once more, watching them, his face expressionless.

"Two or three hundred dragonriders came across the bridge with Dervil, carrying half of the book," said Hellen. "The so-called left-hand half. It was brought here to Islagray for safekeeping. Nothing was ever seen of the others. A week later the bridgehead was overrun. The witches of the time unleashed the flood that swept away the ancient bridge and Andar and Angere were divided. Until now."

"And now they have our half of the book, they will be able to reunite the Grimoire," said Ariane, her fear clear. "Johnny is right. Nothing can stop them. Not the mancers, not the dragonriders, not all the witches of Islagray."

Hellen smiled calmly at her old friend. "They do not have the book."

"What? What do you mean? We both saw it was gone."

"Yes, it was not there. But it has not been there for twenty years."

"Twenty years!" said Ariane. There was a pause. No one spoke. Even the lark seemed to be cowed. Ariane stared at her. This went close to the heart of their long friendship.

"I think it is time you told us more of this, Hellen Meggenwar," said Ariane.

"You remember that I was unwell? Twenty years ago or so?"

"We thought you were for the orchard. You were at death's door for a whole month. We thought the canker ate you away."

"I wasn't ill. I was craft-burned. I was working magic – strong, gruelling magic – all that time. Yes it did, in fact, nearly finish me. But I did it."

"Did what?"

"I opened a gateway, a shadow path to another world, and sent the book through for safekeeping."

"You did all this but told no one?" Ariane's voice was low, level.

"There was Jaiin," said Hellen.

"The previous Storyteller? She who left at about the time … ah, I see."

"Jaiin took the book. She was odd like me, Ariane of the Smiling Eyes. She loved the old wisdom, all the voices returning to life from the ancient paper. The other end of the path is an archive, too. She wanted to go through, see what was to be learned there."

"But, you reopened one of the three gateways into

Andar, sealed since the days of the schism. You let Jaiin walk through, taking the book out of our hands. You nearly killed yourself. And you did all this without telling anyone? Without telling me?"

Hellen said nothing for a moment. Everyone was looking at her, waiting for her reply. There was anger in Ariane, of course, but also sadness.

"It was wrong of me," Hellen said, quietly. "Too wrapped up in my plots and plans. Isn't that what you use to say? Pots and pans before plots and plans. You were right. You were always right. I am sorry."

"Being eldest does not make you a leader," Ariane said, not finished yet. "We're witches not mancers. It's supposed to mean you're the wisest, that's all."

"No. I know. It should have been a matter for the whole coven. But there is no time for argument now. What's done is done. We must act and, yes, despite everything I've done, we must act together. Please."

Ariane smiled, actually smiled, as she shook her head. "Old fool."

"Quite possibly," said Hellen. "But you should know that Jaiin wanted to go through. It was her idea. And I did little to endanger Andar. It was safe to open the gateway and safe to send the book. Until now, anyway. The book is protected and watched. We have friends in that other world as well as enemies."

"Friend? What friends?" asked Ariane.

"Others like us. Others that care for the world and value life. Others that see both the great cycles and the little rhythms. Witches, in their own way."

"Who? Who are these people? How can you talk to them?"

"It's all in the old books, Ariane. There are many means of talking through the aether. Reflections in water, shapes in fire. When this is over, if we're both still alive, I'll happily show you."

"Woah, woah, woah," Johnny said, interrupting,

"Rewind. You said the book was safe *until now*. You're talking about that undain aren't you?"

She turned to address him, stretching and rearranging her legs to ease the ache in them. Her head throbbed from the magic she had worked.

"I am. It will have gone through the gateway. Opened it back up to go in search of the missing half of the book. You remember the smell of burning metal, Ariane?"

"Burning metal?" She looked confused for a moment. "Yes. In the archive."

"I smelled the same thing when I originally opened the path. Some effect of the magic. The undain would have found the gateway easily, which I left only lightly sealed. It would have noticed straight away the book in the archive was a fake. Something, I may say, no witch has spotted in two decades."

"So it's there now. It may have already got its hands – if, like, it has hands – on the book," said Johnny.

"I don't think so," replied Hellen. "As we speak it is hunting for it, but it has not found it yet. I put a little protection of my own on the path. We have a little time left. But we have to act. We have to go there. To this other world. We have to retrieve the book before the undain does."

"I don't see the sudden urgency," said Ariane, "From everything we've heard, we're lost anyway."

"No," said Hellen. "No, we are not! Not yet, anyways. Don't you see? There is still time. Sending the book to the other world twenty years ago has saved us for now. They assumed we'd keep it here. And now, as we know they want the book, we can find it and destroy it and foil whatever plans they have. Or we can bring it back here and try and use it in the war that is coming. You heard what that dragonrider said. I think she and Akbar were right."

"But we need both halves," said Johnny. "Same as they do, yeah?"

"Yes, yes," said Hellen. "Well. We'll cross that bridge

when we come to it. Small steps. For now we must at least make sure they do not retrieve the left-hand."

"So that's your plan?" said Ariane. "You want to go to this other world, find the book and, while you're there, defeat the undain. Then somehow retrieve the other half from Angere, all so we can create an Ilminion of our own? In the hope we can then defeat the undying hordes that will be pouring across the ice in a few months' time?"

"No," said Fer, looking up at the group. "Don't you see? She doesn't plan to do that at all. She plans for *me* to do that. She waited for me to awake so I could go through the gateway. Isn't that your scheme, Hellen Meggenwar?"

"Of course it isn't," said Ariane, "You can barely walk. Don't be ridiculous, girl. Tell her Hellen."

Ariane turned to face her and, as Hellen said nothing, a look of doubt then shock moved across her face.

"Oh, no, Hellen. No. That can't be right. She needs weeks of rest yet. Probably months. And this is difficult work. It needs someone experienced, a wise head, someone like you."

"I'm too old Ariane," said Hellen. "We're too old. This has gone beyond us."

"But why her?"

"You're unhappy because she's a hedge witch? Untamed, untrained, not one of us?"

"Of course not," said Ariane. "It isn't that at all. She's just so young, so weak."

She paused for a moment to choose her words carefully. The rest of the coven would consent if she could persuade Ariane. "Fer is at the heart of this. She can't recall how she defeated that undain on the banks of the An, but that's what she did: the only witch to have ever done so. She must be the one to go."

"No," said Ariane. "It is madness."

"Yes," said Hellen. "It is the only way."

"Don't you think you should ask *my* opinion?" said Fer. "I'm not your chess piece to instruct. You squabble as if I wasn't even here. I can do whatever I like, no matter what the great witches of Islagray say."

Hellen kept her face grave as she replied, but inwardly she felt delighted at the girl's anger, her fire. Perhaps she really would do, after all. "Then I'll ask you now," she said. "Will you do this? Go to the other world?"

"It is madness," Fer replied, her expression fierce. "Tell me, Hellen Meggenwar, Eldest of Andar, if someone had asked you to attempt it when you were my age, what would you have said?"

Hellen knew perfectly well. She'd have told them it was impossible. And then, when they weren't looking, gone anyway. But of course she couldn't say that just now.

"I'm sure I would have done the wise thing, the right thing, too."

Fer studied her for a moment, trying to discern the true meaning of her words. Finally she shook her head. "Tell me, is this how covens always work? By clever words and double meanings? By this influence and manipulation?"

"Quite often, yes." said Hellen. "Although I would use other words myself. Agreement, perhaps. Decisions shared."

"You must do as you see fit, Fer," said Ariane.

"Oh, I will," said Fer. "Because it's obvious what I have to do, isn't it? Go to the other world. At least try and put this right."

Hellen maintained her expressionless face carefully. The girl's spirit couldn't be doubted. But did she have wisdom with it? If she insisted on travelling alone she would have little chance of surviving.

"Very well. But if you'll allow, it might be best to travel with companions. You don't have to face this on your own."

Fer considered for a moment. "Which companions?"

"Well, I had some in mind, but it is up to you, of course. And to them."

"Tell me who."

"I thought five of you. A pentad, a good number." She

turned to Ran and raised an eyebrow, throwing the question at him. If he agreed, Ran would be invaluable. He'd fight to the end to protect them.

"Ran? Would you take this chance to assuage some of the guilt you insist on being burdened with?"

Ran, saying nothing, simply nodded.

Hellen turned back to Fer, raising a questioning eyebrow to her as well. After a moment the girl nodded.

"Excellent. Seleena? Are you willing to go too?" Fer would need someone she could talk to, someone she could confide it.

Fer and Seleena glanced at each other before Seleena looked back at Hellen.

"I will."

"Thank you. One of the five is not here so we can come to them later. But the fourth is."

"And who is this to be?" asked Ariane. "One of the trees?"

"Old fool yourself, Ariane. The other world is not like here. Everything is mixed together. There is no river separating an Andar from an Angere. The world is both at the same time. Ugliness and beauty, death and life. We need someone who understands that."

She turned to Johnny. "So, we shall need a guide. Are you willing?"

"Me? No!" said Johnny.

"You. Yes. This is your world we're talking about isn't it? Where you're really from. How you got here I don't know. But I have seen your dreams and I have seen glimpses of that world. They are the same."

"Didn't I tell you? *Smoke on the Water* and I are sailing south, out of Andar."

"And you think you'll be safe then? You think they'll stop at Andar? No, they'll keep going. They don't know how to stop. And you'll spend the rest of your days trying to stay ahead of them."

No one spoke for a second. The sweet smell of the grass

came to her as a slight breeze blew through the orchard. Fer studied Johnny, awaiting his answer.

"So?" said Hellen.

Johnny lay down on the ground and threw his hat over his face.

"Ah, bugger," he said.

Simon Kewin

10 – ARCHAEON

Fer drew deep breaths as she stood in the shadows of Islagray Wycka. Pain stabbed in her chest, as if she had run across the hills rather than walked from the infirmary.

She sat on the stone ground, feeling the resonance of the song through her whole body, letting it fill her. The aches in her muscles were duller today. Already her body healed itself from the effort and pain of her ordeal on the banks of the An.

She tried, once again, to recall what had happened there, how she had destroyed the winged undain. Whether she had seen the rider. But her memories remained closed. She recalled walking the coast road with Merdoc, then the sudden sense of *wrongness* looming over the waters of the An, coming fast at her. Then she remembered nothing until she woke at Islagray, except for a confused image of jostling along in the back of the cart, the tang of fireseed in her nose and the stars dancing above her.

She looked around, thinking how strange it was she should be here. The one place in all of Andar she thought she'd never see. She'd shunned covens all her life, hating the thought of being controlled. And Islagray was the greatest, most powerful coven of them all. How did any of them live with that? How did they allow themselves to be subsumed?

She seethed at the way Hellen had manipulated her, manipulated them all, to get what she wanted. The old witch had done much good in her life, no doubt, but that didn't mean she could order them around. More than once over the past day, Fer had decided to leave. The problem was, Hellen's plans made sense. They were the right thing to do. She reassured herself, once again, that she was only going along with those plans because *she*, not Hellen, thought they were for the best.

She sat alone in the Wycka. She had come up early, conscious of how slowly she still walked. She studied the area while she waited. She'd expected the great stone building to oppress her, weigh down on her, hold her in. But she liked that there were no closed doors or windows. Songbirds flittered above her head. The wind scattered armfuls of leaves around her. The first drops of rain pattered on her upturned face. Despite herself, she felt a thrilling sense of being at the centre of things. The resonance of the song soothed her muscles, as if someone gently rubbed them. She shut her eyes to enjoy it all, knowing it wouldn't last long.

The others soon arrived. Ran came into the hall first. At Johnny's insistence, he had swapped his armour for simple cotton clothes, grey shirt and trousers, an off-white woollen tunic. He'd kept his stout leather boots but left behind the Penitence Stones. His hair fell loosely around his shoulders, covering up much of his tattooing. She'd been worried that Ran's skin, and indeed her and Seleena's jewellery, might mark them as strangers in the other world. But Johnny assured them no one would notice.

They'd talked about Ran's sword for some time. Johnny insisted it could not be carried, at least not openly. It seemed strange that in a world where the war was already being fought, swords and other weapons were not commonplace. In the end, they decided to hide the sword in Johnny's instrument case. Ran carried this across his back now. If it wasn't for the agile, feline way he moved, the calculating look in his eye, he might have been just another wandering minstrel.

She tried to gently touch his mind and gauge his feelings, little more intrusive than reading the expression on his face. She discerned nothing. What they said about the dragonriders' immunity to magic appeared to be true. Fer nodded to him as he padded up to her and he, towering over her, nodded silently in reply.

Johnny came next. He ambled toward them, paying more attention to the ancient walls of the hall and the birds. He wore plain, tight blue trousers, although his shirt was the same hotchpotch of golds and greens. *Smoke on the Water*, she knew, lay somewhere out on the lake, awaiting his return.

Johnny's mind, by contrast to Ran's, was easy to read. She saw his nervousness at what they were about to attempt, his white-hot fear of Angere. But also, in the front of his mind, his pleasure at the Song and the sights of Islagray. He was easy-going, good-natured and probably useless in a fight. Still, they would need him.

Finally, Seleena arrived, walking between Hellen and Ariane. Seleena wore clothes similar to Fer's own: boots, a black skirt, a long, black woollen tunic. Sensible travelling garb. Hellen and Ariane had not changed. Interesting. So it was true neither of the old witches was to be the mysterious fifth companion. She didn't attempt to peer into any of their minds, futile and impolite as it would be.

She knew Seleena distantly; she'd grown up in a neighbouring valley. Seleena's mother was a witch too, the fire-keeper of her village. They'd talked together recently, only a few months back, when Seleena had decided to come to Islagray. She was witty and friendly, once you got to know her. But, of course, all too ready to submit to the ways of the witches' isle.

Fer stood, pulling herself up on the arm Ran offered her. She picked up her small leather backpack. Johnny ambled over to stand with them. Seleena's face was a blank as she approached. Ariane frowned and Hellen smiled broadly. No doubt the old witch had more secret plans for them all.

"So," said Hellen. "Here we are. Now we must go into the archive to find our fifth and then we will be ready."

"The archive?" said Ariane. "One of those spiders, is it?" The two old friends argued constantly. But it was the gentle disagreement of two people used to each other, like a loving old couple. Fer could see there was nothing vindictive in their exasperation. The problem was, of course, Hellen got her own way eventually, even with Ariane.

"No," said Hellen. "The spiders would be completely useless outside of the caves, wouldn't they? I have in mind a different inhabitant, quite a rare one. Let us see if we can track one down." She turned and walked toward the archive door.

Inside it was cool and quiet. A muffled sense of age filled the ancient caves. Fer liked the idea of all this writing down here, the wisdom of the dead, preserved. Hedge witches such as herself usually shunned written knowledge, passing on what they knew in song or verse, but this had always seemed an unreliable approach. Songs changed in the singing, tales in the telling. When she was no more, it would be good to know her thoughts, her ideas, were stored here for others to unearth.

Hellen led the way down the middle of the five passageways that fanned out beneath the Wycka. Fer caught up with her, walked alongside her, limping slightly and trying not to wince at the pains in her legs and stomach muscles as she kept pace with the old witch.

"Here," said Hellen, glancing across at her. "A gift." She handed her an ancient, battered book, pocket-sized but thick and bound in black leather. Fer took it and opened it to a random page. Dense, neat script in an alphabet she didn't recognize filled the page, interspersed with hand-drawn maps and diagrams involving spheres, triangles and arrows. She flicked to a few other pages and found more of the same, a table of figures next to a sketch of an iron doorway. Rough notes in several hands had been scribbled here and there in the pages' margins.

"You must know I am unable to read this," said Fer.

"Oh, no matter. It's just an old book of mine. It should be of sufficient interest to suit our purposes."

"Purposes? What exactly are your purposes? Who is this mysterious fifth?"

"Hush, best be quiet now. We don't want to alarm it, do we?"

Hellen ducked through a low doorway to her left, the symbol of an oak tree carved into the stone above it. Fer, pausing for a moment, gritting her teeth, followed.

Inside, she found a long, oblong room with several rows of leather-bound tomes set in sconces around the walls. There were hundreds of books here: their covers browny-red like dried blood, yellowy-green like fallen leaves, blue like deep water.

Hellen placed a finger over her lips to tell everyone to be silent. Then, closing her eyes, she made her way around the edge of the room, one hand held out toward the books as if trying to feel something invisible. She completed the circuit five or six times. Fer glanced at Seleena and Ariane, but they watched only Hellen.

Finally, the old witch stopped and put her hand on a red book from a shelf at shoulder-height. She pulled it out as if it were delicate and carried it carefully toward the table that stood in the centre of the room. She set it down, unopened.

"Fer, may I have that little book I gave you please?"

She thought about refusing until Hellen explained what, exactly, was going on. But clearly this was a delicate operation. She stepped forward and placed the small black book next to the larger red one. Hellen opened them both, the black book at the first page, the red book somewhere in its middle. Carefully, she began to turn pages as if looking for a particular passage. The ancient calf-skin crackled. Fer could see each leaf was beautifully illustrated with intricate drawings that glowed gold, red and purple. Columns of neat, black writing wound between the drawings. She found herself wanting to look closer, to stroke a hand over the ancient pages, even though she wouldn't be able to decipher the words. What wonders were written about there? What secrets? And who had gone to these extraordinary lengths to create such a beautiful book? What love had driven them on?

Hellen stopped at a particular page. The representation of a small dragon, its body all curving, intertwined lines like the knotted shoots of a bramble, or the silverwork of a master jeweller, filled half of a page. It had been painted with breath-taking care, each tiny scale painted in gold or silver. Its eyes were shut, as if asleep, but the features on its face were so vivid it could have been alive. It curved around the words as if guarding treasure.

Hellen placed the black book directly next to the picture, then passed a hand across the dragon, touching it gently. The drawing moved. The creature opened one eye, seeming to lift its head off the page. Fer could see its tiny gilded rib cage moving in and out as it breathed. It looked around at them, sniffing in the air with its long, gold and red snout. It stopped when it saw the black book. Slowly, it uncurled itself.

It was incredible to see. She knew it was merely a drawing, however exquisite. Just paint and ink on the pages of a book. At the same time, its legs moved as it walked, the words visible through its body. The illuminated dragon flowed across the gap to the black book. It shrank in size as it crossed onto the smaller pages. It stopped, turned around once, then burrowed down *through* the pages into its new home. In a moment, it was gone.

Hellen carefully closed both books and handed the black one back to Fer.

"There. Now we are ready," she whispered, half to herself, a slight smile on her wrinkled face. She turned to walk past them, through the doorway.

Fer caught up with her, holding the black book more

carefully now.

"What was that?"

"An archaeon. A bookwyrm, if you prefer. Very rare. Very ancient. There are a few still inhabiting the archive."

"I have never heard of such a being."

"They are creatures of spirit, of thought. Not flesh and blood. They eat and sleep ideas. They don't really live in our world at all. What few there are have found their way to libraries like ours. They love words; it's the perfect habitat for them. This one will have been roaming around in our scrolls and tomes for centuries."

"So we need it because of what it knows?"

The old witch nodded, smiling appreciatively as if Fer were a bright child.

"I've read perhaps a hundredth of what is written down here. I remember perhaps a hundredth of what I've read. The archaeon, on the other hand, will be able to recall almost every word of every work. Its knowledge is vast. Maybe you won't need it, but we don't know what you're going to face. It seemed a good idea to invite it along."

"It was hardly invited."

"True. You'll have to explain to it what is happening. Placate it as best you can, Fer. I'm sure you'll find a way."

"Oh, you are?"

"I have every confidence in you. But, be polite with it. Respectful, yes? It won't like to be bothered and the very old are often irritable. Or so I'm told."

"And how do I do that? What tongue does it speak?"

"It speaks *all* of them, of course. Ah, we're here."

They reached another doorway, this one marked with a skull. This had to be the room where the Grimoire had been kept. The room where the undain had slain Thena before walking the shadow path to the other world.

"Are you frightened?" asked Hellen, staring at her, the words quiet, intended only for Fer.

She thought about denying it, but refused to play any of the old witch's games.

"I am," said Fer.

"That's good," replied Hellen. "So am I. I don't need to tell you what we face. Andar's long summer is coming to an end. We can only hope there is a spring to follow the winter."

"Spring always follows winter," said Fer.

"True. But the winter doesn't care who lives through it and who dies."

Inside, apart from the low plinth upon which the book must have rested, the room was bare. She had expected something sinister, a pool of blood perhaps, but there were only stalactites and stalagmites and the muddy red of the walls.

"There is one more thing to tell you before you go," said Hellen, loudly now so everyone could hear. She closed her eyes for a moment and held out her left arm. The wince of pain on her face was brief but clear. A bat flitted down from somewhere on the roof and flew around Hellen several times, closer and closer on each circuit. Fer could hear its high-pitched *chirp*. It landed on Hellen and hung upside-down from her outstretched wrist, instantly asleep. The smell of burning metal, faint but distinct, came to her.

"This is the gateway," said Hellen. "Let it bite you and you will leave Andar. But the way no longer leads directly to the other world. For anyone to pass between the worlds they also must find a way through the Tanglewood I set upon the shadow path twenty years ago. I will tell you the secret of how to do this now."

"A Tanglewood from twenty years ago?" said Ariane. "This can not be."

Fer knew the Tanglewood spell well. She had crafted one on several occasions, when being pursued by some large wild beast she did not wish to confront. It made a small section of woodland confusing, its paths knotty and impossible to follow, making you walk in circles or reach dead ends. It was easier with some woods than others: there were ancient places near where she had grown up that were more or less like that already. If you didn't know their ways, you could wander around all day in them, never knowing where you were going.

"I made a permanent one," said Hellen.

"Such a thing isn't possible," said Ariane.

"That's what I thought until I tried. It was a lot of work, but easier in the spaces between the worlds than it would have been here."

The display of artistry and strength was considerable. Fer was, briefly, impressed. But more than that, it worried her. Great displays of power were an imbalance. There was always a price to pay: something lost, perhaps, or some greater power needed to counteract what had been done. Still, again, she could see the sense in Hellen's actions. It was what had to be done. And perhaps she had paid the price already, twenty years ago when she'd nearly died with the effort of it.

"By now the wood will have grown," continued Hellen. "You will become lost easily unless you know the secret. Be very careful. The undain will probably be lurking in there. Or it may have found the path out. I do not know.

"But look for a great oak: tall, ancient, as wide as this room but lightning-blasted, its centre hollow and black. Climb inside it and you will find an opening at the top. Go out and there will be two great boughs. One, the left, goes over a small pool. Walk along this until you get to a knot in the wood that looks like the face of an owl. Jump into the pool and you will land in the other world. To come back here, take the other bough and find the knot that looks like the crescent moon. From there jump into a patch of thistles, nettles and brambles. You will return here."

She held out the arm from which the bat dangled.

"That is all the help I can give. Find the book. Bring it here if you can. Destroy it if you have to. Luck be with you."

They said no more. Ran went first. He took his sword from the case on his back and stepped toward Hellen, his spare hand stretched toward the bat. The creature looked up, sniffed the air with its tiny, whiffling nose, then sank its teeth into Ran's wrist. The dragonrider disappeared instantly. Johnny shrugged and went next, followed by Seleena.

Fer looked at Hellen one more time, questions she could not quite identify filling her mind, anger at everything that had happened still burning. The old witch simply smiled. Fer, too, stepped forward, clutching the black book in one hand, holding her free wrist out to the bat.

She felt the briefest spike of pain and Islagray disappeared.

11 – TANGLEWOOD

The Aether

They stood in a small clearing. Fer saw no sign of the gateway they had come through. Dew pearled the grass under their feet; the air smelled rich and earthy. Trees huge and apparently ancient, great broadleaves, surrounded them. Their leaves glowed green in the clear sunlight, but darkness gathered underneath them, as though they carried great bundles of it under their outstretched arms.

Fer reached with her mind but felt nothing; an utter lack of life save for Seleena, Ran and Johnny. The wood was clearly unnatural. And silent, apart from the gentle roar of countless leaves brushing together in the breeze.

Paths led in all directions. They reminded her of the carved sun above one of the doors in the archive: the central circle, the rays winding off that seemed, through some artifice of the carver, to move as you walked by. The paths too, when you turned back to them, had shifted. They had disappeared completely, or led uphill instead of down, or divided into two paths.

Which way should they go? It probably didn't matter.

Johnny gazed around, admiring the scene, sucking in deep breaths of air. Seleena and Ran both stared at her. Ran, especially, seemed to expect her to make a decision. She found it uncomfortable. Of course, the dragonriders were utterly devoted to protecting Andar and its people. And so Ran had chosen to throw himself into this quest, to follow and protect them. But this appeared to mean specifically *her*. It was understandable, she supposed, but she didn't relish the idea. It felt too much like subservience. Many mistrusted the dragonriders, calling them *wyrm lords* and muttering about their ancient ties to Angere. She didn't believe any of that for a moment. But she'd find them easier to deal with if they were a little less fanatical in their defence of Andar.

"Let's go that way," she said, pointing to one of the paths. She had no reason to choose it over the others; it only mattered that they move.

She headed forward. Ran, his body all wary tension, his sword still drawn, pushed ahead of her to the front. Seleena walked behind her and Johnny, pottering along, brought up the rear.

They soon became lost. Leaving the clearing felt like diving into a shifting, green pool of shadows and half-glimpsed shapes. The paths wound around and around through the trees. Fer was sure they travelled in circles, although the scene changed constantly. Always they saw different gnarled tree trunks with different toadstool villages growing about their roots.

Here and there, boulders the size of a house heaved from the ground. Some seemed to have trees growing out of them, their roots writhing across the surface of the rock in search of soil. Sometimes the path wound behind the boulders and sometimes it passed between two of them, trapping them briefly between high, stone walls.

They hiked upward and downward and upward again, but found no sign of the blasted oak.

Fer's mind wandered. Seleena walked ahead of her now. The ground was flat. The trees rose high here, their branches leaving great vaults of space on the ground. Beams of sunlight shone through the canopy, illuminating great swathes of bluebells, glowing like the sky at sunrise, their smell like butter. There were many stands of ferns too, their fronds unfurled like the keels and prows of boats.

Had they been this way before? It was a meaningless question: in a Tanglewood, words like *here* and *there* meant little.

A rook or a raven, pure black against the light through the leaves, watched them from a branch that crossed far above the path. As they passed underneath, it hopped around in a half-circle to watch them leave, head cocked on one side. Fer reached to it with her mind but felt nothing. The creature was as conjured as the rest of the place.

Perhaps it was time to try and talk with the archaeon she carried with her. She was unsure how to go about it. She focused her thoughts on the old black book she carried in her backpack, trying to delve inside it.

At first there was no hint of anything alive. But she persisted and caught a distant echo of the creature: breaths, slow and sonorous, like the wind between mountaintops.

She pushed deeper, moving toward the sound. She lost it for a moment, then found it again. It was louder, nearer. She felt a sense, a scent perhaps, of great age. A rush of ideas and feelings swept over her, like standing in a roaring gale of half-heard words. She kept pushing, and had the sensation of tumbling down a long, cobweb-filled tunnel, deep into the ground, the stream of words and thoughts battering against her.

She focused all her mind on the effort of working her way forward. She emerged, suddenly, into a great open space, still underground but brilliantly lit. Red fires glowed all around. Light sparkled from the walls. She caught glimpses of symbols reflected in them: runes that shifted and swirled as she tried to identify them. A bitter, sulphurous smell clogged the air.

She still had her eyes open; the Tanglewood rose around her if she concentrated. But also, clear in her mind, she saw the archaeon. It filled most of the vast cavern, curled up like a cat, its eyes closed. This must be how it saw itself. It was as colourful as before, its body a patchwork of brilliant purples, vermilions and gold. But now she saw it clearly as a creature of flesh and blood, not line and ink. Its great sides heaved as it breathed. Its breath on her face was hot like the wind from the southern deserts.

She wondered how to address it. The creature must be aware of her presence.

"I am Fer," she said.

The great beast opened one of its eyes and regarded her, saying nothing for long moments.

"And I am thinking," it said at last, its voice a rumble. "What is it witch?" Its teeth were brilliant white, the longest as big as she was.

"We must talk. There are things you should know."

"Is that so?" It seemed amused. It closed its eyes again. She thought it had gone back to sleep, but then it spoke.

"In that case, let us talk. There are things *you* should know. Tell me first, are you related to Fer the witch of An? She that was called Fleetfoot?"

"I … yes, she was my great, great grandmother. I was named after her. You knew her?"

"Of her. There is much written in the journals. Interesting." It lifted its head from the ground and turned to regard her. Its hot breath made her skin feel like old parchment stretched across her bones. "So, tell me where it is we are going, little witch."

"You are aware we're moving?"

"Do you even know what book this is I am in?"

"No. Some old book of her own, Hellen said. Nothing important."

"Ah, the wily old Hellen Meggenwar. Of course. Then let me tell you, little witch, this old book is probably the most important in the library of Islagray. After the Grimoire."

"Then what is it? Little archaeon."

"This old book that she *happened* to give you is a map of all the shadow paths connecting the worlds. I have never seen it before. Read about it of course. It isn't kept in the archive."

"Then … I suppose it's no coincidence she gave it to me."

"It has been passed from witch to mancer to witch for centuries and centuries. It has been fought over, killed for, stolen. It is unique, so far as we know, in all of An. The writing is in silver-rune: crafted, not mere ink. It is almost alive. The words shift depending on where you are. It cannot be copied. Coincidence? There are very few of them where *she* is concerned. The fact is we are travelling somewhere, to another world I would say, and Hellen Meggenwar wanted to be sure you could find your way home."

"We've just passed through the Islagray gateway," said Fer. "We intend to return the same way. We won't need a map for that."

The archaeon looked amused again, a glint shining in its great eye. Fer's face reflected there, small and distant.

"Little witch, I am sure you are right. She gave you this book, along with an ancient and wise archaeon to interpret it, just so you would not be bored on your short journey."

"You think she lied?"

"What do you think?" The archaeon closed its eyes again, as if settling down to a pleasant sleep. "But at least you can console yourself with the fact that *you* knew you were coming."

"Yes. Hellen did say I might need to persuade you to help."

"And this is you being persuasive?"

"No. This is me trying to be friendly. I asked for none of this myself. But, you might like to know, the place we travel to in the other world is also a library. I've been thinking about that. I wonder how many books there are you haven't even heard of?"

The archaeon lay unmoving for several moments. "Interesting. The truth is I have been a long time at Islagray, little witch. Well, we shall see. Now, if you will excuse me, I have a book to read. We may soon need to know what it has to say."

"But …"

"Good bye."

The image of the shining cavern faded in her mind. She had the sensation of being blown back up to ground-level. For a moment, she felt disorientated to find she was still walking through the cool air of the Tanglewood.

She had obviously been moving slowly while she conversed with the archaeon. Johnny still ambled behind her, humming a tune to himself she didn't recognize. But Seleena and Ran walked some distance ahead.

"Wait!" she shouted. She still felt so weak. She couldn't walk at Ran's pace all day. When she wasn't willing herself on she moved so slowly. And talking with the archaeon had drained her further. "We can't get separated! We might never find each other in here."

Seleena and Ran turned and waited for her and Johnny. They stood for a few minutes, sipping water from leather bottles.

"No sign of the oak tree," said Seleena.

"Well," said Fer, slightly out of breath, "we need to keep going. Sooner or later we'll find it. But stay close or we'll be wandering down different paths. And remember, this is a Tanglewood. It barely matters how fast we walk."

Ran, looking at her for a moment, nodded. She felt like she'd given him an order. Just as Hellen had given them all orders not so long ago. She frowned at the thought.

They marched on. The sun stayed high in the sky; clearly day did not progress here. It became impossible to judge the passage of time. It felt as though they had always been here. Fer's mind wandered again. Weariness weighed her down. Ran and Seleena would spot the tree; she didn't need to look for it, too.

She thought about the archaeon. It appeared to be familiar with the Grimoire; perhaps it had occupied it at some point. Had it made any sense of what it found? It was dangerous to dabble in such things, of course, but perhaps the creature had unearthed some clue in the book about how she had defeated the winged undain.

And what did the archaeon know about her great, great grandmother? And why, exactly, had it said Fer's identity was *interesting*? She had to converse with it again. This time she'd be more prepared, not so tongue-tied. She'd ask it all the questions crowding her mind. The creature was as bad as Hellen, the way it played games with her. She'd had enough of them.

But, try as she might, she could not reach the cavern again. She sensed the creature, but couldn't find the cobwebbed tunnel to its lair. It appeared the archaeon did not wish to be interrupted. She tried and tried but it was no use. Her questions would have to wait.

A scream rang through the quiet trees, jarring her from her thoughts. The raw, ragged sound was alarming after so long in the unnatural hush of the wood. As it died she heard the splash of something heavy falling into water.

Her full attention snapped to the woods, her heart hammering. They'd become separated after all. Seleena and Ran had walked ahead of her and she'd been too lost in her thoughts to notice. The woods grew thick here: great bramble castles lined the path so it was impossible to see very far.

She broke into a run, limping painfully, aware of Johnny coming up just behind her. What terrible scene would greet her? Hideous images filled her mind. The undain must still be here with them.

Seleena came into view. She stood staring out over a small lake. At the same moment as Fer saw her, Ran appeared around another bend beyond Seleena. He held his sword forward, ready to fight.

Seleena never tore her gaze from the lake, her body stone-still. Walking now, her heartbeat slowing, Fer approached. She glanced nervously at the lake.

"It was there. I saw it," said Seleena. She shook visibly.

"What did you see?" asked Fer.

"The undain. It was terrible. In the water. It came at me. I screamed and it disappeared."

"What did it look like?"

"A monster. Huge. All teeth and dead eyes. Like something that chases you in a nightmare." She sounded numbed, cold, shocked by what she had seen.

"So it is trapped in the Tanglewood, too," said Fer. "And it can change shape. It was small when it came to Islagray." She turned to Ran and Johnny. "It will follow us, of course, and try to discover the doorway. It must know by now we're its only hope. It'll be desperate."

"Great," said Johnny. "You know, I really am enjoying this more and more."

"We must move away from here," continued Fer. "But we should camp soon. I can't walk much farther. One more hour. Perhaps we'll see the tree. If not, we'll try again tomorrow."

"If there is a tomorrow," said Johnny. He smiled but the strain was clear on his face. Seleena took no notice; she watched the small lake, seemingly reliving what she had seen. Ran said nothing. He nodded, turned and set off.

They sipped more water and ate bread and meat from their backpacks. Fer peered into the shadows between the trees as they went, expecting to see a glimpse of the undain. Exhaustion crept over her, spreading through her limbs like frost. Each footfall felt heavier and heavier. Judging by how much they'd eaten they'd been travelling for the most of the day. They really had to stop soon. But she had to keep going a little longer. In the magical wood it made no sense to attempt to get away from the lake where Seleena had seen the undain. But still, she wanted to try.

"Hey, there's the tree," said Johnny. "Weird eh? It must have appeared after we walked past."

He'd stopped and was looking behind them. A great oak stood a short way into the undergrowth, its huge trunk like a crooked little house, wide branches reaching into the woods. A pond lay to one side, the tree's lower beams hanging over it.

"Keep your eyes on it," said Fer. "We don't want to lose it."

"You think it might run off?" said Johnny.

Ran took the lead again, striding toward the tree with his sword drawn, as if he intended to fight it. As they walked closer, Fer saw it had been struck by lightning. It was a familiar enough sight. At home they sometimes called the oak the *lightning tree* as it was always the first to be hit in a storm. This one had a great, blackened scar down its side as though it was burned inside. At its base stood an opening, large enough for them to pass through if they crouched.

"I will go last," said Ran, standing at the trunk as if guarding a royal palace.

"Very well," said Fer. "Let's go before the undain comes. Remember what Hellen said. The left branch. Jump off at the knot that resembles an owl."

Seleena crouched and wriggled into the opening. For a moment she was stuck, her hips too wide. As Fer watched, it seemed that Seleena's body became momentarily snake-like and slithered through the hole.

Was she exhausted, imagining things? She reached with her mind to check that Seleena was well, the faintest inklings of dread creeping over her.

The young witch wasn't there. There was no one there. Fer saw one of Seleena's feet, but sensed only emptiness where the witch's mind should be.

"Ran!" she shouted, stepping back. "It's here! It's Seleena!"

The dragonrider whirled and struck so rapidly his sword was a silver blur. He hacked at Seleena's foot within the tree.

A howl boomed, muffled by the tree but clearly inhuman. Fire seared Fer's mind. Ran pulled back and struck again, but this time made no contact. The undain climbed, its foot disappearing from sight. It scuffled and scrabbled up the inside of the hollow tree.

She'd reminded them how to find the doorway. In doing so, she had told the undain, too. The realisation hit her like a punch to the stomach. Then she thought of Seleena. The scream they'd heard, the splash of something heavy falling into the water.

Behind her, Johnny panicked, shuffling forward and backward, unable to decide what to do. "This is not good! This is not good!"

Ran, meanwhile, acted. He squeezed inside the oak tree, then hauled himself upward and out of view.

Fer stepped aside. At the same moment, the undain appeared above her. Two great branches, wide enough to walk along, reached across the pond, just as Hellen had described. The creature took the left one. Already it changed. It still partly resembled Seleena, but it shrank, warped, became something altogether different. Its flesh was red now, raw as though flayed. For a moment, the creature balanced on the oak tree's great bough with Seleena's features half-visible on its face.

Then Seleena disappeared altogether. The undain was no longer blood-red, but a sallow, sickly colour, like something made from tallow wax or old bones. Its shape writhed and warped. For a moment, Fer saw a great walking mass of maggots up there. It had two, tiny red circles for eyes, as though she glimpsed its raw, molten insides through them.

It stopped and turned as Ran emerged onto the branch, his sword before him, already charging.

She heard another howl from the creature, angrier sounding. She expected it to attack Ran, but instead it reached down and touched the wood of the tree at its feet. Magic surged from it: raw, ragged power with no attempt at harmony. Even as Ran surged toward the creature, rot bloomed in the wood where the undain stood. The branch turned grey and lifeless, the life sucked out of it.

In a moment it could no longer support the undain's weight. The bough sagged and, in a great puff of sawdust, broke from the tree. The undain fell toward the pool and, when it was just above the water, vanished.

Ran fell too, but he hit the water with a wet smack. Other splashes followed as more and more of the tree's limbs rotted and fell. Fer and Johnny had to run to stop themselves being buried under falling beams.

She turned to watch the tree crumble to pieces. There was nothing she could do. Even if magic could help, she had no strength left to wield it. Soon, there was little left of the oak but a rotting stump, looking as if it had been dead for years and years.

Fer buried her face in her hands as the truth of their situation struck her. Seleena was dead, the undain had escaped into the other world and she, Ran and Johnny were now trapped, forever, inside the Tanglewood.

And all of it, all of it was her fault. She had failed them all.

12 – BROKEN

The Witches' Isle, Andar

Hellen watched *Smoke on the Water* bob in the distance on the shining Silverwater. Two swans flew in low, wide circles, never quite catching each other, their white so brilliant they glowed.

She pulled her gaze away. She had work to do. She'd tried and failed for a day to see across the aether into the other world.

She closed her eyes and reached out, once more, to seek Jaiin. Still Hellen found no sign of her. She ignored the obvious reason. It must be the troubled aether, that and the draining effect of the other world. For reasons they didn't understand, working magic there was hard, required more effort, brought with it more pain. Even talking between the worlds involved great effort on both sides. It felt always like a tarnished pane of glass lay between them, keeping them apart.

She decided to try a different approach. If not Jaiin then perhaps Fer. The girl was inexperienced and weak, but no fool. She might be able to work the magic. Hellen quested for her, eyes open but no longer seeing the lake. She searched for long minutes, deeper and deeper into the grey, the tearing pain in her gut mounting with the effort of it.

Nothing. She returned to herself with a gasp. She sat down on the bank, chest heaving, waiting for her strength to return. Perhaps both Jaiin and Fer were dead.

There was one other she could try. She had spoken to the woman of that world, Catherine, Jaiin's friend in the library, on more than one occasion over the years. Catherine's magic was weak, but there was no one else. Two years ago, Fiona, Catherine's daughter, would have been the obvious choice. Fiona's strength was considerable. For a witch of that world, remarkable. Hellen had once been convinced Fiona was the one they'd waited for. But events of two years ago had broken the woman's spirit and the magic had fled her. No, it had to be Catherine. In any case, she should be there at the library. She would know who or what had come down the shadow path from Andar.

Summoning her strength, Hellen sought into the aether a final time.

After long, long minutes she found the particular smudge of light she searched for. It flickered like a distant candle glimpsed through shifting trees in the night. She pulled herself toward it, reeling it in like a fish on a line. It slipped away several times, as indistinct as a twist of smoke, but each time she plunged after it, refusing to lose it. Her connection to Islagray, to Andar, stretched thinner and thinner behind her. If she went too far the line would break and her mind would be adrift in the aether, forever lost. But she had to reach further, just a little further. The pains through her stomach were sharp, now, but distant also. Such was the danger of traversing the void.

Finally she caught up with the light. It skipped and skittered like a panicky insect, nearly fading completely before flaring again. Hellen cradled it, protected it, a candle-flame in the wind. It was a projection, a reflection of Catherine's mind and through it lay the whole world Fer had gone to. With a final effort Hellen flew into the light, letting herself be absorbed by it.

She could tell, immediately, something was wrong. Pain

flooded through the other woman's body. Something, perhaps several things, were broken. The sickening smell of burning flesh filled the air. For a moment, her mind sinking too deeply, the pain and stench merged and she couldn't tell which sensation was which. She panicked, floundering in stormy waters. Unconsciousness threatened to suck Catherine - and Hellen with her - into the depths.

"Catherine? Can you hear me?"

"Hellen?"

"I'm here. What has happened?"

Hellen steadied herself, her control of the connection improving, keeping herself distinct from, but overlapping with, the other woman. Keeping them both afloat amid that sea of pain.

Hellen looked out through Catherine's eyes. She appeared to be lying on the stone ground of some cavern. At first she thought it was snowing, but then she saw singed scraps of paper filling the air, drifting down. Two bodies lay nearby. One was Jaiin, undoubtedly dead. Next to her, still living, but not moving, the undain.

"I tried to protect her from it," said Catherine, speaking out loud. "Tried to keep her safe. But I couldn't, Hellen. I had to get her involved. She's taken the book."

Hellen spoke to the other woman in her mind. "Who, Catherine? Who has taken the book?"

"Cait. My darling granddaughter Cait. She's just a girl. I tried to keep her out of it, but I had no choice."

"Did anyone else come down the shadow path apart from the undain?"

"No. No one."

So. In all likelihood, Fer and the others were dead, too. Hellen tried to think, tried to calm her mind. Across the cavern the undain stirred. Its friends in that world would be arriving soon. Nox himself, no doubt. A man almost worse than the creatures of Angere. And the Grimoire in the hands of a weak and ignorant girl. Cait wouldn't last long on her own. All Hellen's careful plans were unravelling and there was little she could do.

They should have put a stop to Nox years ago. But they'd never been strong enough.

"Can you stand, Catherine?"

"No. My legs don't seem to work. I'm sorry."

"We will try and help," said Hellen. "Stay with me, hold on to me."

She withdrew from Catherine's mind as far as she dared and let a part of herself flee back along the thread that anchored her to her own body. She ignored the unpleasant sensation of being torn in two. As she neared Andar she called out with her mind for Ariane. There was no response, her call too weak.

She tried again, letting herself slip further from Catherine's mind, terrified of losing her completely. This time she found her old friend, collecting firewood for the infirmary in the woods of Islagray.

"Hurry, Ariane. Come quickly. I need you."

At the same time she heard Catherine in the distance.

"Hurry, Hellen. The undain is waking."

The two scenes, the ruined library and the trees of Islagray, overlaid each other in Hellen's vision. She struggled to maintain her connection with both. She was stretched too thin. Her mind could be cloven in two at any moment.

Ariane arrived at a run, her face all alarm, her arms still cradling the sticks she had found.

"Ariane," said Hellen. "Hurry. Help me heal this woman. She is across the aether, in the other world."

"She's *where*?"

"Just help me. You can tell me how foolish I am later."

Hellen flew back down the shifting pathway. Now the familiar, reassuring presence of Ariane was with her. Together they set about using their strength to heal the woman lying there on that distant, cold floor. Hellen saw better, now, what Catherine's injuries were. Her pelvis, right arm and three ribs were broken. They concentrated on these, ignoring all the bruises and cuts.

Hellen heard a distinct *clack* as they worked the long bones of an arm together. She heard Catherine cry out with pain, felt a jarring echo of it in her own mind. They didn't stop. Normally they would put the injured person into a deep sleep, keep them there with magic and herbs while they worked slow, careful healing. They had no time for that now. They laboured on, the two of them, despite the cramping and bruising of their own bodies back in Andar, despite the repeated cries from the other world. They closed up the long, thin crack in Catherine's pelvis and knitted her broken ribs back together as best they could. They healed torn muscles and staunched flows of blood.

When they finished, their exhausted minds fled the other world, returning to the haven of their own bodies. Hellen had sunk to her knees by the Silverwater. She sucked in lungfuls of air. Beside her, her sticks dropped and scattered, Ariane lay curled on the ground, barely conscious from the effort.

Another witch, thought Hellen, broken beside the water.

"Catherine?" she said, her voice hoarse, speaking out loud as well as down the shadow path. "Is it enough?"

There was silence for a moment. Then the reply came along the slender thread connecting them.

"I think ... I think I can stand now," said Catherine.

"Catherine. The book. Destroy it if you must, but we may need it yet. It is a terrible weapon. Better burned than used against us but better still if we can use it."

"We'll do what we can. Tell me, is Andar overrun?"

"No. Not yet. But the time draws near. Events move quickly. There is much to tell you and no time to do it. But one thing. Another young witch – Fer – went there to retrieve the book. She may be dead already but ... she met and defeated an undain here. She, I'm not sure, she may be of the blood, too."

"I understand," said Catherine.

"I will stay with you as long as I can," said Hellen. "Offer you what strength I have. But I am nearly spent. It is up to you now."

"Thank you."

Hellen closed her eyes and saw, distantly, what the woman from the other world saw, heard what she heard. But the connection between them was fading, flickering. In truth, she could do nothing to help. She could only look on until the line between them snapped.

She watched Catherine stand, swaying on wobbly legs. On the ground nearby, the undain writhed through a series of shapes as if trying to escape a sheet it had become entangled in. Lights came on, and she heard the whirr of machinery. Someone was coming. Hellen clearly felt Catherine's alarm. The woman set off, limping from the lights. She passed a series of metal doors, all of them staved in by a massive force. Scattered books and torn paper lay everywhere.

Three times as she walked Catherine stopped, briefly, to touch the wall with her finger, drawing an invisible pattern. Hellen smiled. The charms were a small thing, probably pointless, but they might do some good. At least they meant she wasn't fleeing helplessly.

The woman arrived at a square, metal grille set in the floor of an alcove. A heavy iron padlock secured it. She fished keys from her pocket. They must have kept the padlock well-oiled as it opened easily. An iron bar leaning against the wall nearby allowed her to lever up the grille. She switched on a tiny flameless light attached to some keys and shone it down into the shaft. Iron steps led down into the darkness. Hellen felt, briefly, the sensation of cold air on her face, a foul smell.

Catherine began to descend, the metal torch held in her mouth, keys dangling against her chin. Hellen caught glimpses of her fear, her barely-controlled panic. She was being pursued; the forces of Angere were close. For a moment Catherine talked to herself, reassuring herself. *You can do this. You can do this.* The woman's face was level with the ground when movement appeared up the corridor. Running boots, many pairs, coming for her. Hellen was about to shout a warning when the connection through the aether finally snapped.

Catherine felt the Andar witch fleeing her mind. Well, she would have to manage on her own. Her pursuers were near. Soldiers, bristling with weapons and high-tech gadgetry, surged down the corridor.

She reached up to a handle that protruded from the underside of the grille. She braced herself on the ladder and pulled hard, grunting with the effort, sharp pains blazing across her shoulders. After a moment when it seemed nothing was happening, the grille crashed down into place above her head with a resonating clang.

She paused to calm herself. *Think. Remember the plan.* She fumbled for the padlock in her pocket then looked up to point the spot of yellow light from the torch onto the grille. A strong iron latch protruded from the wall near her head. A large eye, fastened underneath the grid, fitted through it. Terrified that she might drop the padlock, she reached up to thread it through the eye. She missed the first time, the light from the torch dim, her fingers shaking. Then she managed to hook it through. With a click, she had the padlock shut. It wouldn't stop them for long but it would give her a few extra moments.

She set off down the iron ladder. There were thirteen steps. As she felt her way down each rung, the muscles in her legs and back complained, stretched too far. She counted as she went, trying not to think of what pursued her from above.

At the bottom she paused for a moment to catch her breath. She and Jane had studied all the old municipal maps of the maze of tunnels that spread beneath the streets of

Manchester. There were a great many of them, some in use, some long-abandoned. There were old mine workings, natural caves, Victorian sewers, wartime air-raid shelters and quite a few whose origins were unclear. But they all interconnected.

Together they had plotted the best escape route. They had imagined themselves fleeing down here with the book, pursued by someone or something from Angere. As it was she was alone and didn't have the book but still, the plan was the same.

She had the layout of the tunnels carefully memorized. An old Victorian sewer tunnel, now used to capture storm run-off, led toward Piccadilly Gardens. It was tall enough to walk in if you stooped. It was completely circular in cross-section, built from countless thousands of red bricks.

She moved as quickly as she could, against the flow, the trickle of water deep enough to cover her ankles even in summer. Her feet were soon numb from the cold. The smell was vile but she consoled herself it might help put her pursuers off her scent. The light from the torch was fading already. She shone it to her right, counting the side-tunnels. If she missed one and became lost she would be trapped down here. She could have crafted a light, but using the torch meant she conserved her strength. And she had precious little left.

She had two possible escape routes. The nearer one was a grid that emerged in a quiet corner of the Piccadilly Gardens bus terminal. But it was quite possible that it would be blocked by a bus parked on top of it. The other was farther, an opening in the basement of a disused mill in Ancoats. This was sure to be open, but there was a good chance she wouldn't be able to make it that far without being caught.

Her neck and shoulders complained at the unnatural posture she had to adopt. Her breath came rapid and shallow. The temptation was always to straighten up and relieve her muscles, but she had to concentrate, to repeatedly remind herself she would bash her head on the low brick roof if she did. She counted two tunnels leading off to the right and then a third. There would be two more, then she would take the one after that. *Nearly there*, she told herself again and again. *You can do it.* Despite her desperate hurry, she still stopped at each junction to draw her mark upon the sewer wall.

She heard deep, muffled rumbles through the stone and earth as buses and trams passed somewhere overhead. Occasionally, her torchlight picked up twin sparks in the darkness, or the flick of a whipped tail. There were plenty of rats living down here. She found the thought comforting. Rats were fine, they were natural, she could understand them. It was the things chasing her that frightened her.

A loud *boom* reverberated from behind her. They must have smashed through the grille. The undain probably. She ran harder, breath panicky now, past another side-entrance and then another. The turning was next. The torch picked out more and more brick. It felt as if she wasn't actually moving forward at all. Shouldn't she be there by now? Perhaps she'd missed it, or miscounted. If she had, she was lost; they would hunt her down easily. She heard calls and splashes echoing up the tunnel, clear in the still, cold air. It sounded as if they were just behind her. She expected to feel a blow to the back of her head at any moment.

She almost ran past the side-passage. It sloped upward, smooth concrete rather than brick, square rather than round. A slight but steady breeze breathed down it. She switched off the torch and saw, faintly, a thinning of the darkness ahead.

She was tired now, very tired. Cycling in to work every day had paid off, but she couldn't go much farther. She wouldn't make it to Ancoats. She'd done well to get this far. She suddenly wasn't even sure she could make it to the street grid. She had the perverse desire to stop and wait for them to reach her, to put an end to her struggle.

But no, Cait needed her. She drew another invisible mark

on the wall, four quick lines, and set off up the side-passage as quickly as she could manage. It was definitely getting lighter. There was no water now, but she stepped on leaves and litter that had blown down from above, the crunching noise echoing in the enclosed space.

This tunnel was lower than the Victorian one, so she had to shuffle along like an ape, sharp pains in her lower-back. Fortunately it didn't take long to reach the grid. She paused for a few breaths. This was her only chance. If she couldn't get out here, she was trapped.

There was a cantilever mechanism beneath the grid that meant it should be easy to push open from below without needing a key. She simply had to flip a lever then lift with her shoulders. She braced herself and heaved. Nothing happened. The grid refused to budge. Something was on top of it.

She glanced down the tunnel. Her pursuers sounded as if they were at the turning. She thought of the people walking around above her head, oblivious to the slaughter about to occur.

She had a little craft. Nothing compared to the others. She lacked the raw talent of her daughter and she lacked the history, the centuries of wisdom and folklore passed from witch to witch in Andar. In this world, so much was lost or broken. But she would do what she could. She had some small ability with the elements. She could perhaps bring up a fire. She knew it wouldn't be enough.

She looked at the grid again, using her torch to check she had switched the lever properly. She hadn't. It was jammed half-way across. Desperately she tugged at it, skinning her knuckles in the process. The blood on her fingers was warm.

She braced against the grid and pushed with all her strength. This time it moved. A line of daylight flared around its edge. She couldn't hold it; it fell back into place with an alarming bang.

She had to get out. She bent her knees, crouched down, and raised her arms straight above her head. Locking her elbows, she tried to straighten up, using the strength of her legs to push. She caught a glimpse of something large moving toward her, a deeper shadow in the gloom. She closed her eyes and put everything she had into the effort. Her muscles felt as though they were tearing in two. The grid gave with a metallic screech, swinging up and round onto the ground.

The light blinded her as she stood. The ground level was at chest-height. The city bustled all around her; shops and people and buses. She must look ridiculous. Desperately she hauled herself onto the pavement. Something grabbed at her foot, pulling her back down. She kicked and her shoe came off, held by her pursuer. Her favourite shoes, too. She hauled herself to her feet and kicked the grid back into place.

Nearby, a bus stood with its engine running. It said *Out Of Service* on its sign. The driver, a young man, his tie askew, sat in his cab reading a tabloid newspaper spread out over the steering-wheel. He watched her in some amazement. If he had parked his bus just a little farther forward she would have been trapped.

She hurried to the driver's window, trying not to think about how she must look. She calmed her breathing while smoothing her hair into place. She knocked on the glass, smiling warmly.

"Hello."

The driver's instinctive politeness overrode his astonishment. "All right love?"

"Much better now, thank you. I wonder if I could ask you a favour?"

He looked at her for a moment, clearly afraid of what she was going to ask. She could feel something of his inner turmoil. He wondered if she was mad. But she could have been his own grandmother, or a teacher, or any one of a range of fearsome women he had known in his life. He looked at her severe, grey dress, her grey hair, her hard eyes and was powerless to refuse her anything.

"What is it?"

"Do you think you could drive your bus forward a little so that one wheel is resting on that grid?"

"The grid you just came up?"

"Yes, that's the one."

He wanted to ask why, ask what she'd been doing down there. But her smile sweetened and instead he shrugged.

"All right, love."

Without moving the newspaper he adjusted a lever on his dashboard. The bus juddered forward until one wheel rested on the grid.

"Thank you so very much," she said.

"You're welcome, love. But …"

"Yes?"

"Oh. Nothing."

The driver returned to his newspaper, shaking his head as if he'd seen everything now.

Catherine walked to the concrete wall of a nearby building and drew one final invisible mark, placing it among rival graffiti about Manchester United and Manchester City. This sketch took a little longer than the others, its message more complicated.

Then she walked away, limping more now with only the one shoe. At a safe distance she turned to look backward. The bus was still there but she could distinctly see it being jerked up and down as the undain tried to force the grid upward. So far it wasn't succeeding.

So. She had to get away from the library. She had to phone her daughter and let her know Cait was going to Danny's. And then she had to help Cait destroy or somehow hide the book while staying away from the undain and the forces of Genera.

There was much to do. But, before any of it, what she really needed was a sit down and a nice cup of tea.

13 – FIRES

Manchester, England

“Hi, Danny.”

“Cait! Hi. Come in.”

Two of the family's dogs barked around her legs, a lively white puppy, all ears and tail, and an older, lumbering Labrador. She was never entirely clear how many dogs lived there let alone what they were called. But she loved coming to Danny's house. This explosion of noise and excitement always greeted her. The whole place was a jumble of people, dogs and clutter. At the same time she could always find a quiet corner to sit and talk. Not like back home. There, Cait and her mother just got in each other's way. They only had the living room, where the TV stood, and you either watched that or tried to talk over it.

She liked Danny's kitchen best. It was always busy: one of his parents cooking, one or more of his sisters eating, someone she didn't even recognise dashing through saying *hi* or *good bye*.

Danny's mother peered around the kitchen door to see who it was. She waved with hands covered in flour. She wore her smartest work clothes, austere blacks and greys, the effect lessened by her apron, which had the picture of an unclothed and curvaceous woman across it.

They shouted a conversation over the din of the dogs.

"Hello, Cait. Cup of tea?"

"Lovely, thanks."

"How's your mum doing?"

"She's, you know, the same really."

"Well. Go on upstairs and I'll bring your tea."

"Thanks, Mrs. G."

Cait and Danny headed upstairs while the dogs, three of them now, dashed to some other part of the house, careering along like a single creature with multiple heads.

In his room, Danny sat at the little desk next to his bed. He wore jeans and a crumpled tee-shirt, his feet bare and his hair tousled as if he'd been holding his head in his hands. He'd been working: textbooks, paper and pens lay strewn all over his desk and on the floor. Screwed-up paper formed a mountain in his bin. Cait sat on the unmade bed and studied his posters. She particularly coveted the *Screaming Machinery* one with the original line-up. For the first time since the library she felt a little safer.

"How's it going?" she asked, nodding her head toward his desk.

He grinned and sat back, his hands behind his head. "Oh, it'll all come together eventually. You?"

"Don't ask."

Danny's dad came in carrying a mug of tea for each of them, and a plate of chocolate biscuits and some home-made fairy cakes.

"These should help with the revision. Give us a shout if you need anything."

"Thanks, Dad."

"Maths getting you down again is it?" asked Danny when his father had gone.

He could tell she was upset. Was it so obvious?

"No, it's not that," she said. "I mean, yeah, that's going badly, but there's something else."

She hesitated. The whole thing seemed suddenly ridiculous.

"Go on. Tell me about it," said Danny.

"Well, I went to the library after school to see my gran. Something pretty messed-up happened."

She sipped at her tea and examined her mug for a moment, tracing the intricate knotwork pattern upon it with a peacock-blue fingernail.

"What?"

She sighed. He'd think she was completely crazy. Perhaps she was. "Sure you want to know?"

"Course."

"OK. We were down in the basement …"

"So, pretty crazy, eh?" she said when she'd finished, trying to make it all sound like a bit of a joke.

He sat quietly for a moment, watching her. He was going to look away, the light gone from his eyes, make some excuse about having to get back to his work. It was ridiculous, the whole thing. What the hell must he think of her?

But instead he laughed, gleefully, as if he'd just been given some good news. "This is great! I mean, not Jane, obviously. But it all makes sense. I knew it! Hey, you have the book with you? That's it there?"

"You believe me?" she asked.

"Well, *yeah*. You've seen all those web-sites I've shown you, all the crazy theories. I've spent long enough trying to persuade you to take them seriously. There's this blog I read that talks all about this stuff. It fits perfectly. This monster must have come from the other world. And the book. And Jane too, don't you see?"

"I still can't believe it happened. It's like something from a kid's story. Maybe I'm just having a nightmare."

"You're saying I'm the man of your dreams?"

"Ha ha."

"Look," said Danny, "This is real. Trust me. Pinch yourself and see if it hurts."

"But, I might just dream that it hurts."

"Are you serious?"

"Yeah. Being chased by monsters. People dying. That doesn't happen in real life."

"In that case, it won't do any harm to look at the book."

She clutched it under her arm, but placed it on the bed now. Danny came over and kneeled beside her.

It smelled old: paper, leather and dust. Danny ran his fingers over the embossed skull etched into the leather cover. It looked human, but proportioned differently, taller and slimmer, the eye-sockets unusually large. In the stronger light she could see it shone faintly reddish-gold, most of the colour long-faded. Near the letters underneath the skull she could see a dark, irregular stain, like the map of an unknown continent.

"Strange letters," said Danny. "I wonder what they say."

He turned the book around. The skeleton on the spine was arranged with its arms crossed over its chest. More letters or symbols ran around its edge. The back was blank apart from a single symbol, a double-star upon which the gold colouring gleamed.

Danny opened the book in the middle. There was writing on the left-hand side of the page but nothing on the right. The words were hand-written in tiny, cramped symbols, the ink purplish-red, with many additions and notes added here and there. It looked more like an exercise-book than a textbook.

Danny turned the page, the leathery, off-white paper crackling. They could see more of the closely-written script, but again only on the left-hand side. Sketches interspersed the text. A human body, showing marks where cuts should be made, like a medical diagram. A series of concentric circles with symbols at random points inside each ring, like something from a horoscope. Each drawing had scribbled notes surrounding it.

"What *is* this book?" said Danny.

"I don't know," said Cait. "But I can see why Gran wanted it destroyed. It gives me the creeps just looking at it."

"The people in the library, the ones you said were like the police. And that guy with the sunglasses. Do you think they were after this, too?"

"I suppose so, yeah," said Cait.

"Or maybe they'd come for the creature. They detected it and came to deal with it. Maybe they're the good guys."

"I don't think so. They didn't behave like good guys. Plus Gran said *this evil thing has friends here*. I think they're all on the same side. I think they're all trying to get this book. And Gran and Jane risked their lives to stop them."

"I wonder why," said Danny. He looked up at her, directly into her eyes. He had such nice brown eyes, visible through the strands of his long, untidy fringe. She saw anxiety in them now, though. It had dawned on him what she was getting him into. She smiled, trying to be reassuring, but all her own fears returned, an electric shock in her stomach.

He grinned back and slammed the book shut.

"Hey, let's see what they're saying about it on the news." He turned to the computer on his desk and browsed to the BBC. Underneath a red banner saying *Breaking News*, it read:

> Police have cordoned off the Central Library in Manchester following an incident inside the building. It is not yet known whether there are any casualties. Details are scarce, but there are unconfirmed reports of fires and a number of small explosions within the building.
>
> Police are keen to speak to anyone who was at the library at around 16:30 this afternoon. They are especially keen to speak to the people who were evacuated from the library when the attack occurred.
> More details soon.

"Hah, I bet they are," said Danny. "Looks like they've realised you slipped through the net."

Cait nodded, saying nothing. She felt sick. What had happened to her gran? And what chance did she have? She wasn't really safe here. They had changed the news, changed what had really happened. How could she possibly evade such people?

"We have to destroy the book, Danny," she said. "We have to destroy it now."

"I suppose," he replied. "Shame though. It looks cool. I'd love to know what it's about. I bet if we did some research on the net we could translate some of it."

"Danny, I mean it."

"OK, OK," he said. "I guess you're right." He looked thoughtful for a moment, gazing through his window. "Dad had a bonfire before. Let's go chuck it on there."

They walked through a soft, evening light that made the whole garden glow. A mound of hedge-trimmings crackled and burned at the far end of the lawn, sending a line of white smoke straight into the still evening air. The smell of smouldering wood and leaves filled the air. Danny took a stick and poked the fire, exposing the red glow at its core, exciting it back into flames.

"Go on then," he said. "Throw it on."

Cait paused for a moment. Was this the right thing to do? Should they just destroy this ancient book? But she thought of her gran, and Jane, and hurled the book into the centre of the fire. It opened mid-flight, pages flapping as if it was going to fly away to avoid the flames. But it landed with a gentle *wumph* in the middle, sending up clouds of sparks. They watched for a moment as the flames burned brighter.

"That's that then," said Danny. "Come on, let's go in and get some tea."

Thinking back later on, it seemed incredible to Cait they sat there in the kitchen eating cold, left-over pie, laughing about their teachers or the stupid things their friends did, as if all their troubles were over.

Nox strode to the small, square, mid-terrace house. Glancing around to ensure his men were in place behind him, he rapped on the grimy plastic door.

He heard shuffling inside, footsteps, then the door opened to reveal the drab, slow-eyed woman he had come to see. To think they had once suspected Fiona Weerd of being the one. She barely had a spark of life about her. Overweight, hair a mess, clothes chosen for comfort. Ten years ago he'd received a report this woman might be the most powerful witch in England. Laughable. She *was* a witch, of course, but only in name. Since the death of her husband, her power had withered away completely. Now she was little better than one of the healing-crystals-and-dreamcatchers brigade.

"Mrs. Weerd? I'd like to speak to your daughter."

For a moment he thought he saw a flicker of life in her eyes. He dismissed it. She couldn't possibly have duped them. They'd monitored all three of them for years, profiled them, graded them. Nothing. The daughter had no power at all, the mother and grandmother next to nothing. Still, the older hag *had* worked at Central Library. A connection they had failed to make, for which heads would roll. And the little rat of a daughter had been there too, had actually walked past him. And now both daughter and book had disappeared. All that took it beyond coincidence. No doubt the three of them were being directed by some unseen power, but for now his top priority was to track down Cait Weerd. No real damage had been done yet, but the imminent arrival of the delegation from Angere gave everything a sudden and unwelcome urgency. The current situation could not, and would not, be allowed to continue.

"My daughter? Why, what has she done? Is she all right?

Are you the police?"

She looked utterly resigned to her fate. If she was play-acting it was an incredible performance. He pushed past her and into the house. She simply stepped aside to let him and his two guards past.

"You can't come in without being asked. Who do you think you are?"

He ignored her mewling. "Your mother phoned you not long ago. Your daughter has gone to her boyfriend's. Where is that?"

"I … I don't know. We aren't as close as we should be. What is this all about?"

He strode into her cramped, rectangular living-room. The flat-screen television seemed to take up most of the space. She'd obviously been sorting out old photographs; they lay strewn over the floor, some in piles, others scattered at random. They looked like the tedious family snaps he would have expected. He trampled across them and turned to face her.

"The book of course. I have no time for games, Mrs. Weerd."

"Book? What book? I'm afraid I don't know what she gets up to. She's out of control. She doesn't listen to me any more. It's a different boyfriend every week. I don't know where she is."

Was she lying? Possibly. So far as he knew Cait Weerd *didn't* have a different boyfriend each week. Right now he didn't really care.

He picked up one of the photographs, a picture of Mike, her husband, standing on a pier somewhere, laughing as the wind blew his hair. Nox took a slim, silver cigarette lighter from his pocket. He held the photograph for her to see and clicked a button on the lighter, setting fire to a corner.

"A terrible tragedy what happened to your husband."

The burning picture held her gaze. "Yes."

The photograph burned right through leaving a crisp, blackened curl. He dropped it and picked up another, this time of Cait.

"And what a double tragedy it would be if lightning struck again."

"I don't know where she is. Who are you?"

"Imagine the misfortune of two of your family members dying such a terrible death, trapped screaming in a burning building. Or all of you. Tragedy repeating itself. The Daily Mail could make a nice headline of it."

"I don't know anything."

She looked agitated, cornered. Perhaps he could goad her into some action, make her reveal her true colours. If she had any.

He lit the corner of the picture of Cait. "I wonder if it was over quickly for him. Or did it take time? Did he feel the flames as he burned, do you think?"

She said nothing, her gaze flicking between him and the two guards.

"Very well. Since you don't know anything useful we might as well kill you." He inclined his head toward a guard. "Make sure it's quiet. I want it to look like a burglary. Afterwards …"

The stud in his ear tingled as a call came through. He turned away from the woman to answer it.

"Nox."

He listened as the voice on the other end filled him in on developments, then cut the connection.

"Well," he said. "It seems we have found your daughter without your help. Change of plan. I shall go and retrieve her and the book now. Then I'll return for you, Mrs. Weerd. You do, of course, work for our *competition*, so you must be dealt with. You and your mother."

He glanced at the guards. "Keep her here until I return. Kill her if necessary."

There was no reply. Both guards took out guns and held them across their chests in a co-ordinated movement, fingers on triggers.

"Until later," said Nox.

As he swept outside he wondered, again, whether he had misjudged this small, drab woman in her small, drab house. Would two guards be enough? He put those doubts out of his mind. He couldn't be mistaken. She was nothing. Only the book mattered.

He sparked his bike into life and roared off down the street.

They stood together in the fading light. The fire smouldered, lazy coils of smoke winding off into the air. Danny poked around in it with a stick.

Cait shivered and wrapped her arms around herself, thinking she should be getting home. "Did it all burn? We should set light to any scraps that are left. Gran said to make sure I destroyed every single word."

"Cait. Look." Danny turned. In his hands he held the book. He brushed grey ash off its red cover to reveal it was unharmed. He opened it and leafed through. "It's not even hot. How is that possible?"

Cait was about to speak when they heard a great roar from the street in front of the house. For a moment Cait thought the monster from the library had come for her.

"Motorbikes," said Danny. They ran toward the wooden fence that screened the back-garden off from the small driveway. They had to push their way through a large Fuchsia bush, smooth red flowers on it like thousands of tiny hearts. They peered through the gaps between the vertical slats.

Out on the street, five men climbed off large, silver motorcycles to stride toward the house.

"It's him," said Cait. "The man at the library. He's found me."

14 – DEATH ON THE RING ROAD

"Come on," said Danny. "Out the back way."
Holding the book, Cait extricated herself from the fuchsia, trying to make as little noise as possible, panic thumping through her. Danny followed.

Danny's parents wouldn't be able to stop this man. She thought, briefly, about going back inside the house anyway, not wanting to leave Mr. and Mrs. Greene to face her pursuers. But she couldn't risk *them* getting the book. She had no choice but to flee.

They ran across the lawn past the smouldering bonfire and around the old, sagging shed where Danny's family kept their bicycles and rust. A tall, wooden fence stood in their way. In it was a gate, lime-green with mildew.

Danny peered through a crack between the gate and fence. "Come on. There's no one there." He yanked on the handle, but the gate wouldn't budge. Age and damp had warped the wood, jamming it into its frame.

"Let me try," said Cait, her voice a panicky whisper. The gate still refused to open. They pulled together. After a few tugs it came free, the wood squeaking. It swung inward on creaky hinges and they hurried through, slamming it behind them.

They stood in a narrow back-lane, about the width of a single car, bordered on each side by a long line of fences and walls. The warm orange light that had suffused the garden was lost to the shadows here. Wheelie-bins stood scattered up and down the lane at random angles, as if they'd been dancing and froze when they saw people coming.

One end of the lane led onto a side-road, which joined the main street. The other end, closer to Cait and Danny, led to a patch of rough, overgrown ground where the ruins of an old house stood. They hesitated for a moment, unsure. A black cat, barely able to keep its eyes open, watched them from a nearby wall.

"Which way?" said Danny.

"Let's get away from the road," said Cait.

They ran toward the rough ground, their footsteps echoing off the high walls on either side of them. It was hard not to feel trapped in this narrow, urban canyon. If they could get to the ruined house they might have a chance. Paths led off in many different directions from there, most of them too small for a motorcycle.

They were half-way there when motorbikes roared behind them. Cait stopped and turned to see two riders at the far end of the lane. The bikes sped forward, two headlights on each like great eyes. They dodged around the wheelie-bins without slowing down.

The walls around her were high here, much higher than she could climb. On one side, jagged shards of glass had been cemented onto the top to deter intruders. A gate led into the back garden of one of Danny's neighbours, but it was sure to be locked.

She thought about throwing the book into one of the gardens in the hope the riders wouldn't see. But it seemed pointless. She glanced at Danny, standing a few metres behind her. He, too, had stopped running, transfixed by the sight of the motorcycles bearing down on them, alarm bright upon his face.

Cait shuffled backward, desperate to get away from the riders but unable to take her eyes off them.

The motorcycles had nearly reached Danny's house

when the black cat leaped into their path. She expected to see it run, alarmed by the noise of the two machines. Instead it sat nonchalantly in the middle of the lane, its back to the approaching riders. It began to clean its claws.

Cait was about to call out some warning, to try, uselessly, to frighten the cat out of harm's way. Instead she watched, open-mouthed, as something in the air near it shifted. The air there thickened, became a fog and then, rapidly, a cloud of blackness, like a fragment of night. It formed around the cat, obscuring it. She had the distinct impression of flesh, a texture of something shiny and leathery like a bat's wing or a beetle's carapace.

Then the fog thinned away and a spider's web was strung across the alleyway. A huge spider's web, its strands as thick as her leg.

The riders had no chance to stop. Smoke rose from their tyres as they braked hard, but they were travelling too quickly. They smashed into the huge web, which absorbed the impact as if they were insects. She half-expected to see them stuck, pinned helplessly like flies. Instead, riders and motorcycles crashed to the floor, the wheels of the bikes still spinning, their engines still roaring.

The cat still sat with its back to what was happening, indifferent to the whole thing. It stood, finally, stretched into an arc and walked away, ignoring the riders. It looked down the lane at Cait and Danny, blinked, then leaped effortlessly onto its wall, where it went back to sleep.

"Come on," said Cait. She ran toward Danny, who stood for a moment longer, amazement on his face. Then he, too, sprinted down the lane.

At the end, a single concrete bollard, cracked and canted at an angle, marked the point where the tarmac petered out and the wilderness began. They ran into the long grass without slowing, following a path worn by many pairs of feet that used the rough ground as a shortcut. Soon, they reached the old building.

It had once been a grand house, but it had lost its roof

years ago. Vandalism and the elements had slowly reduced it to rubble. Danny's dad had told her it was once a mansion, built when there were fields where Danny's estate now stood. Over the years it had been surrounded. Its gardens chipped away, triangle by triangle, until only this little, odd-shaped patch remained. People weren't allowed to build on it for some legal reason. It was an odd place; it always felt detached from the modern world, the city around it, as if lost in memories of its glory days. She liked it. Strange plants grew everywhere. Exotic trees that existed nowhere else in Manchester. Large shrubs with glossy, green leaves and vivid, sticky flowers that gave off a sickly smell in the summer warmth.

Whole walls of the house still stood, even with glass in some of the windows, but the building was an empty shell, as much vegetation growing inside as out. Nevertheless, it felt like the walls offered them protection. They dashed into a large, square room, hidden from view of the lane, both of them panting.

The room must once have been impressive. She could still see patches of ornate tile work on the floor. A blackened circle, the remains of someone's fire, filled the centre of the room, several empty beer-cans scattered nearby. The place smelled of earth and decay.

Danny's chest heaved. He bent forward with his hands on his knees as he spoke. "What was that thing? That black cloud? The web?"

"Don't know. Something sent by Gran perhaps. But there's no time to think about it now. What are we going to do with the book?"

"Going to destroy it. Like you said."

"But where?"

"We need a hotter fire. Only one place round here I know of. The factory where your dad worked."

"The factory? No."

"It isn't that far. If we go cross-country we can be there in an hour."

"No, I mean I don't like the idea of it. I haven't been there since, you know ..."

He stood up straight and looked at her, his breathing becoming calmer. "It's the only place, Cait. I bet the book won't survive being thrown into a blast furnace."

It was the furnace that had gone wrong. Some monitoring systems had been poorly maintained, they'd said. It had overheated. There was an explosion and her dad had been standing nearby. *He probably died instantly*, the policewoman had said, trying to comfort her.

"I don't like it."

"Yeah, I know." He put his arm around her. "But it's our only chance. We can make it."

"We can't just walk in there."

He stood back from her, thinking. He glanced outside. "We'll tell them who you are. They're bound to let us in."

"Why?"

"We say you've come to see where your dad, you know, died. You've finally plucked up the courage, that sort of thing. There's no way they can refuse you. Then we ask someone to chuck the book in for us. Tell them ... tell them it has some special meaning for you, yeah?"

She tried to think of a different plan, something that didn't involve going to the factory. But she couldn't. Time was short and they had to keep moving. There would be other riders seeking them, perhaps surrounding them even now. She hated it, but he was right. Could she do it? If they went before she had chance to think about it, perhaps she could.

It was hard to read Danny's expression in the fading light but she thought she saw concern there, overlaying his usual easy-going expression.

"You know," she said, "This is not turning out to be a great day for me."

He smiled. "Yeah, I know what you mean."

"You don't have to do this."

He shrugged and said nothing. She leaned forward and

kissed him on the cheek.

"What was that for?" he asked.

It was her turn to smile. "Because. Come on, let's go. If we get across the canal we might be a bit safer. Maybe they can't cross running water."

"Yeah, right."

They ran from the old house, out of its long shadow and into bright sunlight as the low rays of the setting sun found them again. They followed a path through a small wood of spindly white saplings, the place where supermarket trolleys gathered to die.

On the other side of the trees a mud bank sloped onto the towpath of an old canal, cutting through the heart of the city. A road bridge spanned the canal farther down. A double-decker bus waited on it, internal lights on, probably stuck in traffic. High above it, a ragged flock of gulls wheeled and called, their voices rough and raucous even from this distance. A single crow flapped through the scene.

"Let's go the other way," said Danny. "There's a footbridge."

They set off, walking quickly rather than running. The waters of the canal to her right stood still, so that it was impossible to tell which way they flowed. Buildings on the far bank reflected darkly in the opaque, brown surface. Here and there tree branches dipped into the water, as if they bore weights too great for them.

They came to the bridge. It was, in fact, just a large, iron pipe that crossed the canal. The pipe erupted from the bank, rose vertically for a couple of metres, spanned the water then dropped into the ground on the other side, like the loop of a huge metal serpent. A simple plank was bolted on top of the pipe, with wires strung across on either side to hold on to. At each end, a fan-shaped gate, with barbed-wire wound all around it, had been padlocked on so no one could climb up. A sign at the foot of the ladder said, in faded red letters, *Danger. Keep Off.*

Danny climbed and, expertly, unhooked the gate on the

opposite side to the padlock. He stepped onto the plank, then reached down to Cait.

"Give me the book," he said.

She handed it to him and climbed the rusting rungs of the ladder.

"Done this before haven't you?" she said.

"Once or twice. Don't worry. The water's not really that deep."

"Oh, *great.*"

They stepped their way across the plank, each footstep a hollow clang. The wire railings were low, coming up to Cait's thighs. She held on with both hands and took it slow while Danny carried the book. Half-way across, he stopped.

"Look," he said.

On the road bridge, standing at its centre, a figure watched them, silhouetted against the sky. He or she gesticulated, as if directing someone they couldn't see. The gulls circled around in the air, mere flecks of black ink from this distance.

"That's them isn't it?" she said.

"I reckon," said Danny. "Come on."

Cait stood a moment longer, wondering who these people were, why they were so desperate for the book. The water below her lay in shadow, a path stretching up to the other bridge and the figure who stood watching her.

They regarded each other, as if they could make out each other's features. She had the weirdest feeling of the space between them shrinking, then, something drawing them together. She felt dizzy. Distantly, the wires cut into her where she grasped them. She found herself flying through the evening air, her body left behind on the little bridge, sweeping over the dark waters of the canal right up to the shadowy figure.

It was the man she'd seen at the library. He smiled as she came, as if enjoying himself, enjoying the hunt. But she could sense the surprise in him, too. It didn't register on his face but she could tell, without knowing how she did it. She understood then. He wasn't pulling her in; *she* was doing this. She could feel his anxiety, too. His fear of what would happen if she and Danny and the book slipped out of his hands. He would stop at nothing to get them.

Anger flared in her. Anger at being pursued, anger at what had been done to her, and to her gran and Jane. And to Danny and his parents, too. She wanted to shout at the man, attack him. She wanted to reach out and hurt him. She could do it. He was within her grasp. It would be so easy …

"Come on," called Danny from the other end of the bridge. "They know where we are now. We have to go."

A moment of dizzying disorientation and she stood, swaying, back on the bridge, the figure distant once more. She shook her head. She was tired. The whole day had been too mad.

Danny handed her the book and climbed down the ladder on the other side of the canal. She threw it to him and followed.

"We have to get across the motorway somehow," he said. "And they'll have the bridges watched. They must know which way we're going."

"We could run across. Wait for a gap in the traffic."

"You're crazy! There's no way we could make it." He looked horrified. "Besides, there are cameras everywhere. They're bound to see us."

"I guess."

He seemed thoughtful for a moment, while Cait glanced around for anyone approaching them.

"How about the footbridge?" he said.

"Which footbridge?"

"You know, it crosses at Wythenshawe. It's too narrow for a motorbike and it's hard to find anyway. You have to know the roads through the estate to get to it."

"Sounds good," she said. "Come on."

They made their way up the far bank, avoiding patches of nettles, to reach a tarmac path. This led between garden fences to another housing estate. They weren't too far from

Cait's own home, Northenden or Northern Moor maybe, everything vaguely familiar to her. The houses looked more or less the same as her own: square, semi-detached, unremarkable. But the layout of the streets confused her. To fit so many houses in, the streets wound around and around like a knot. She was soon disorientated.

Fortunately, Danny knew the area better. They walked along the pavement trying to be inconspicuous. She imagined eyes watching them from every house. Each time a car passed she looked for an escape route, a narrow path to run down if it stopped.

They moved in silence. The gardens were better tended here than back home. Each house had a small square of ground in front, most planted with flowers. Some were given over entirely to roses, heady smells drifting from huge flamboyant blooms on top of spiky, skeletal stems. Other gardens were laid out more intricately, with little pathways between carefully trimmed plants she didn't recognize.

She thought about what had happened on the bridge. Had she imagined flying out of her body? Some effect of the stress? It *felt* like she'd controlled it. How could that be? She couldn't do anything like that. It was good, though; she'd felt powerful. Assured. It wasn't like her. It was like finding a singing voice you didn't know you had. It felt right.

They reached the footbridge without further incident. It rose in a gentle arc over the M60, which ran through a cutting at this point. Cars and lorries streamed along the motorway in both directions, a river of oncoming white lights and receding red ones, their roar constant. Cait and Danny stood and watched, wary of stepping from the shelter of the houses. She was surprised at how quickly the cars travelled, how close together they were. It wouldn't take much - one mistake by one driver - for there to be a terrible pile-up.

Tall motorway lights, orange like clusters of small suns, shimmered above the carriageway, although the sunlight hadn't completely faded from the sky. The bridge rose higher than the lights but she and Danny would still be visible from down there, silhouetted against the deepening blue. Attached to some of the lights, cameras spied on the traffic, but they all pointed downward.

"Let's go," she said. She wanted to get this over with now. Get to the industrial estate where her dad had worked, not too far away in Stretford. Talk their way into the factory and destroy the book so this whole, crazy episode could be over.

The wind picked up as they crossed the bridge. She shivered. Neither of them were very well-prepared, still in thin summer clothing. She clutched the book to her chest as they walked.

They weren't even halfway across when silver bikes appeared on the motorway. There were three of them, riding in a V-shaped formation in the fast-lane. She tugged at Danny's arm and pointed. The riders raced toward them at high speed.

"They can't get to us," said Danny, raising his voice against the roar of the traffic. "We're quite safe." The wind ruffled his fringe as he looked down.

They stood still as the riders approached, afraid to move in case they caught the riders' attention. She felt exposed standing there. She tried to find the state of mind she'd slipped into at the canal, but it eluded her. Instead she heard Danny shout.

"They've seen us!"

Down on the motorway the riders braked hard, swerving across to the hard shoulder. She watched in horror as cars and lorries skidded to avoid them, the straight lines of traffic breaking down as vehicles veered out of their lanes. Brakes and tyres squealed. For a moment she thought they were going to avoid each other, but then a lorry jack-knifed, its cab slewing one way and the container it hauled going the other. The lorry ended up across two lanes before crashing onto its side.

A sickening series of collisions followed as cars, coaches

and lorries smashed into the blockage. The destruction radiated down the road with alarming speed as more vehicles piled in from behind.

"No!" was all she could say. "Oh no, no, no!"

Too busy watching the unfolding catastrophe, they didn't pay attention to the riders. Something banged against the railing near Danny's hand. He glanced at it absent-mindedly, not realising what was happening.

"They're shooting at us!" she shouted. "Come on, we have to go back!"

Down on the hard shoulder, ignoring the destruction they'd caused, the three riders calmly stopped their bikes and climbed up the motorway verge to avoid the wreckage and colliding cars. They stood with guns in hand, taking careful aim at her and Danny. Trying to duck below the level of the railing, she sprinted off the bridge, Danny close behind her. She heard more shots *ping* through the air behind her. They stopped when they reached the safety of the houses, out of sight of the motorway. The metallic *crump* of further collisions filled the air, along with the wail of alarms.

"They tried to kill us," said Danny, amazement rather than shock in his voice.

"They were only aiming at you," said Cait.

"Huh?"

"Didn't you notice? They fired at you, not me. It was the same in the Library; that thing wouldn't attack me, either. Why not? What's going on?"

"You'd prefer it if they *did* shoot at you?"

"No, but ... look, Danny, I think you should go home. Go and see if your parents are OK."

"What?"

"This is all insane; it's way too dangerous. Go home and I'll take the book. I can find the factory from here. I could, I don't know, just call a taxi or something."

"No way. You think they've got something pleasant lined up for you if they catch you? It's probably something,

I don't know, *worse* than being killed."

"Still, I should do this," she said. "It's sweet of you to help but I don't want you to get hurt because of me."

Danny shook his head and actually grinned. "It's either this or back to my homework. There's no contest."

"I'm serious Danny!"

"So am I! I'm not going to leave you here with armed lunatics chasing you about on motorbikes."

"You don't have to be a hero to impress me, Danny. This isn't some movie. I'd understand."

"I'm not leaving, Cait. Now stop trying to get rid of me and let's go. They know where we are and they'll be coming to find us."

It was a huge relief. The thought of doing this on her own filled her with dread. At the same time, she felt a burden of responsibility for Danny. If anything happened to him because of this ...

"OK," she said. "Are there any other bridges we could use?"

"Only where the roads cross. But they're a long way round and they're bound to be watched."

"So, maybe we could hitch a ride. Get away from here and try from a different direction."

"Maybe."

"We should move anyway. Even if we don't know where we're going, we shouldn't stay here."

"OK."

They set off into the housing estate that bordered the motorway behind high wooden fences. Without needing to discuss it, they moved in the direction that led from the crash scene. A small residential road ran parallel to the carriageway for a distance before curving away. When it did so, Danny cut down a path between two more houses onto an open area of grass between the estate and the motorway. The grass sloped into a valley here, too steep for houses. The carriageway went along an embankment, its walls running high above the little valley. Deepening shadows made it hard to see anything at the bottom of the slope.

"I used to cycle around here," said Danny. "There's a tunnel under the motorway ... Hey! Of course!"

"A tunnel?"

"Yeah! There was this old footpath to the woods and they had to build a tunnel for it when they built the motorway. It's not too far; we could be there in five minutes."

"It sounds dangerous. If we get trapped down there we've had it. No one will hear us."

"True, but it's dark and quiet. If they don't know about it we could be through and away while they're still looking for us over here."

She hesitated, trying to think of a better plan, trying to think clearly. The most important thing was to keep moving.

"OK, let's go. I guess."

They broke into a half-run, loping down the slope. She heard the wails of emergency vehicles, growing louder.

The marshy ground at the bottom slowed their progress. They leapt between tussocks of grass in an attempt to avoid muddy pools but, inevitably, both soon had wet feet. The icy water felt unpleasant as it squelched around in her shoes. Occasionally they had to climb over fences or battle through clumps of tough, whippy bushes that slapped her more than once. A particularly vicious one caught her across the face, cutting her cheek. Danny kept assuring her they were nearly there. Long after five minutes was up, they still hadn't reached the tunnel.

"Perhaps they sealed it up?" she said.

"Nah. It's here somewhere."

They almost missed it, hidden behind a large, ragged bush that grew out of the concrete foundations of the embankment. Only a large, evil-looking puddle at the entranceway revealed it to Danny.

"It's always like this," he said. "We're not far from the Mersey."

"I never liked these trainers much anyway."

The puddle was far too wide to jump. They edged around it, against the embankment wall, and even then they were paddling in shallow, cold water. The traffic on the motorway rumbled through her shoulders as she worked her way along.

They soon reached the entrance to the tunnel. It had straight sides and a rounded roof, like a miniature railway tunnel, just high enough for them to walk through without stooping. From the dim illumination of distant streetlights the floor seemed to be more mud, in which feet and bicycle tyres had worn a deep groove. Most of the path was lost in darkness but an arch-shaped patch of grey shone dimly at the other end. It seemed farther away than it should be. No one waited in the darkness for them, it seemed. She glanced up the cliff of the motorway embankment. Nobody in sight. If they were lucky, they could get through and be away without the riders knowing.

"Come on," she said, rubbing her stinging cheek. "It gets cold as soon as you stop moving."

It was black inside the tunnel. She held out her arms like a movie zombie to stop herself from walking into anything. The sound of the traffic came to them as muffled booms through the stone, like great drums being struck. Traffic still moved down one carriageway at least. They continued to hear emergency vehicles racing to the crash. How many people had been hurt? Killed? The whole thing was terrible, just terrible.

They'd nearly reached the far end of the tunnel when a figure appeared, silhouetted in the archway. It stood, unmoving, waiting for them. She stopped and Danny, walking behind her, put his hand on her shoulder.

She glanced the way they'd come. No one there at least. She was about to speak, suggest they run back, when the figure lit a torch, shining it in their eyes. The person laughed and strode toward them.

"Two little children out past their bedtimes. Shouldn't be down here, should you? Could be dangerous. All sorts of nutters around."

It didn't sound like the man from the Library. Danny's grip tightened on her shoulder. She was about to speak when he pushed past her, screamed and charged at the figure, blindly into the light. What the hell was he doing? Cait lunged after him, also shouting. She saw the glint of a knife, slashing from side to side in the beam of the torch. Then a scream as Danny crashed into the man, sending them both reeling to the ground. The torch fell also, to illuminate a small patch of grey stone wall while the two grunted and fought in the shadows. Danny screamed again, in pain this time.

Cait snatched up the torch and shone it on the scene. Danny and the man, a tall lad dressed in scruffy denim, grappled on the ground. Danny tried to grab the lad's knife, but blood on his hand from a cut made his grip slippery. She watched as Danny let go and the knife flew toward his chest.

"No!" she called. Anger rose in her again. And something else, too. A sense of power within her. Clear, calm knowledge of what she should do.

She thrust out her hands as if to knock someone over. Without touching him, she sent the man flying through the air, backward and head-first down the tunnel like a bullet from the barrel of a gun. He landed with a muffled thud just outside the entrance.

The sharp pain jarring through her shoulders made her gasp. She felt like something heavy had struck her. She ignored it and ran to Danny, who was lying on his back. She scrabbled up the torch and shone it over him, terrified of seeing a wound, a patch of blood. But there was nothing.

"I'm fine, don't worry. I just cut my hand."

"What the hell did you think you were doing?" She was angry at him, her voice booming in the enclosed space.

"Seemed like a good idea at the time."

"It was *incredibly* stupid. I thought he'd stabbed you!"

"He nearly did." Danny held up the book, cradled close to his chest. "He hit this instead. How about that, this thing saved my life."

She helped him to his feet, hoisting him up by the shoulder. "Yeah, everyone should carry around a book of evil magic in case they get jumped."

"What happened to him?"

"We'd better go see."

They made their way out of the tunnel. In the grey half-light their attacker lay unmoving. He looked younger now, sixteen maybe. His shaved head and his height had made him look more fearsome. Cait kneeled down to study him, afraid of what she'd done. It looked like he'd struck the back of his head on some stones strewn on the ground. She couldn't see any blood and he breathed peacefully, like he'd just lain down to sleep.

"What did you do?" asked Danny. "I didn't know you had secret ninja powers."

"Oh, you know. We're not supposed to let on."

"Seriously."

"Seriously, I don't know what I did, do I? It felt like the right thing to do. So I did it."

"Cool."

"I might have hurt him, Danny!"

"This guy who just attacked us with a knife."

"Even so." She stood, trying to decide what to do. Shouldn't they phone an ambulance or something? But if they did they'd be giving themselves away.

"It's strange," she said. "It made my shoulder hurt even though I didn't touch him."

"Is it OK now?"

"Fine. What about you? Your hand?"

"It stings a bit. It'll stop bleeding soon."

Cait held out a paper handkerchief. It was the best she could do. "Wrap this around it."

She looked back down at their attacker. He didn't look like one of *them*. He was just some idiot. She switched off the torch and left it next to his hand.

"We might need that," said Danny.

She shrugged, then winced at the sharp jolt of pain in her shoulder. "We'll manage. Come on, let's get away from here."

They stood in a small open space surrounded by a wood that stretched all along this side of the embankment. An unnatural orange light from the road above illuminated the scene, leeching it of all colour. It was difficult to judge how big the wood was. Underneath the canopy of leaves, darkness gathered.

Five different paths led from the tunnel. One in each direction along the embankment and three through the trees.

"Any idea which way?" asked Cait.

"Not really." Danny looked about for a moment, then pointed at the middle path. "I guess that one's more or less the right direction."

In the darkness it became tricky to follow the path as it twisted and turned through the trees. Several times they stumbled into patches of brambles or nettles. Cait's ankles were soon badly scratched and stung.

"If only we had, I don't know, a torch of some sort," muttered Danny, picking himself up after tripping over a tree-root.

She ignored him and pressed on. It was only the sound of the vehicles on the motorway which told her which way to walk. Soon even that was gone and it became impossible to tell if they were walking in a straight line or round in circles.

Their progress slowed as they took care not to lose the path. After a few minutes of silence, she stopped. "Are we lost?"

"These woods aren't *that* big."

"I'll take that as a yes."

The rattle of a helicopter came to them, hovering somewhere above the pile-up. It didn't sound very far, the noise becoming louder and quieter as the machine circled. Its searchlights flashed through the branches, then moved on.

"At least they won't be able to see us from up there," said Cait.

"Don't be so sure. They have infrared don't they? They could probably spot us."

"Let's keep going."

She was about to set off when she glimpsed another light, low behind them. It twinkled through the trees, impossible to tell how far away. A car on a road somewhere? Someone with a torch following them?

The light passed in front of a tree, a clear flash of silver bark. Whatever it might be, it was in the woods and coming closer.

"Danny." She put her hand on his shoulder to direct him. "Look."

She readied herself to fight as the light crept nearer. The odd thing was she couldn't hear footsteps, had no sense of anyone else in the woods with them. The smudge of silvery light, she saw now, was very close. It must be small, an insect or something. It wandered right up to them, bobbing as if carried by an invisible hand. It was small and round yet it flickered like a candle flame. It stopped briefly when it reached them, taking a look at them, then carried on through the trees.

"What is it?" whispered Danny.

As much as anything, it was the fact that it was so small and weak, such a feeble flame compared to the powerful lights of the motorcycles and the helicopter, that persuaded her.

"I think it's trying to guide us," said Cait. "I think we should follow it."

"This is another of your new superpowers is it? The ability to tell if strange, moving lights are friendly or not?"

"It's just obvious. If the riders knew where we were they wouldn't mess around with a light would they? They'd just come and get us. This must be someone trying to help us."

"Or some sort of elaborate trap."

"Maybe. But I think we should take the risk. We need all the help we can get." She looked at directly at him, although she couldn't see his face. "Are you coming?"

He sighed in an exaggerated way. "Yes. I'm coming."

The light moved at a quick walking pace. They had to hurry to stay near as it disappeared behind the boughs of trees ahead.

It soon led them out of the woods. They stood at the edge of an empty stretch of land, the ground ahead a great expanse of darkness. Some way off, civilisation started again, street-lights and houses twinkling in the twilight. Tower-blocks and factories, too, all lit up so they resembled patchworks of square lights rather than anything solid.

The werelight bobbed on without stopping, cutting across the waste ground, heading for the buildings.

"That's about the way we want to go," conceded Danny. "But it still could be a trap."

"It would have led us back through the woods to the motorway," said Cait.

"Ah, but we wouldn't have followed it then. Perhaps it's clever."

"I'm sure it's trying to help us."

"OK. But take it slowly. Let's make sure we're not so busy following the light that we walk straight into the Mersey."

The light turned abruptly ahead of them. They followed and found they were being led along the path beside the river. It wasn't like the canal; this water flowed strongly. It was too dark to see, but Cait heard it chopping and chortling close at hand. It sucked all the remaining warmth out of her. She shivered and clutched the book like a hot-water bottle as she strode along.

Fatigue and fear weighed her down. Her face stung and her shoulder throbbed. Her soaked trainers had warmed up a little, but they still felt horrible to walk in. She could feel the blisters forming. She was heading to the factory where her dad had died, pursued by crazy people with guns and worse. And there was nothing she could do but carry on. How had this all happened? She had gone to see her gran at the library, everything normal, and then suddenly all this. The whole thing was insane.

They came to a footbridge and, still led by the will o' the wisp, crossed over the river. Their footsteps clumped loudly on the bridge's wooden slats. On the other side, the light moved purposefully into the darkness, away from the river, always toward the buildings.

They went in silence. The path cut through a field of rough, hummocky grass. She couldn't see Danny any more, nor hear him on the soft ground.

"Danny?"

"Yeah?"

"I'm sorry about this. About all of this."

She heard the grin in his voice as he replied.

"It's fine. Really."

The helicopter's engine clattered in the clear air, circling towards them. Its searchlights pointed at the ground, as if they were the machine's spindly legs. It seemed to survey a wider and wider area, away from the distant ring-road.

"Is it looking for us do you think?" asked Danny without stopping.

"I think it might be, yeah."

"Who are these people?"

"Don't know. Don't want to know. Come on, let's hurry."

They broke into a jog, drawing level with the will o' the wisp and then overtaking it. It seemed to be aware of them. It sped up, too, moving a little way ahead of them.

The helicopter continued to circle in the dark sky. It turned toward the river, then shot back toward them, its blades making a loud *clumping* sound. It flew low to the ground. The downdraught buffeted her as the machine roared overhead. Her hair lashed around. She had to resist the urge to duck. Leaves and dust whipped into her face and eyes. The helicopter's lights raked across the ground nearby, two patches of daylight in the black. One flashed over them. She caught a glimpse of Danny's back.

"Run!" he shouted. She barely heard his voice over the racket.

The helicopter stopped flying in circles and hovered above their heads, its engine deafening. The light picked them out, tracking them as they ran. Cait expected a voice, or a gun-shot, at any moment. She was exhausted. She'd had enough. What chance did they have? She felt the ridiculous urge to stand and defy the great machine. Shout at it; perhaps try and knock it from the sky as she'd knocked over their attacker in the tunnel. She stopped and turned. She was pretty sure she was screaming, but she heard nothing over the sound of the machine.

"Come on!" Danny's mouth was right next to her ear. He pulled her by the arm. She refused to go.

"Cait!" He stood next to her in the spotlight.

The gale in her face made it hard to keep her eyes open. She imagined someone with a gun up there, taking aim. At him.

She wouldn't let them harm Danny. She ran, pulling him out of the light. Not far ahead, the rough ground ended and the city began again.

A car drove to the end of the nearest street, only a few metres away. It stopped at a bollard, as if the driver was surprised to find the road vanishing. Was it one of them? Were they trapped? Perhaps the helicopter was directing the driver to them. But the car turned around and sped into the night.

They sprinted onto the tarmac of the street. The will o' the wisp caught them up, overtook them again and bobbed down the pavement, moving more frantically now as if held by an invisible runner. The helicopter had to fly higher to avoid the buildings, but still it tracked them.

"What are they waiting for?" asked Danny, his voice ragged with the effort of running.

She didn't reply. She put all her effort into following the

bobbing light. The streetlights washed it out; they had to keep very close. It turned up a side-street, then cut into a cul-de-sac. At the end, a narrow footpath led through to a larger road, a dual-carriageway full of traffic.

They hit the pavement of the busy road. The light turned left and darted away, toward a large roundabout.

Cait was about to follow when she saw the riders. Two of them, coming down the opposite carriageway, their gleaming, silver motorcycles unmistakable. The helicopter flew high above, a distant roar above the traffic noise, watching the net being drawn.

The riders stared directly at them as they cruised by. They sped on, but only toward a gap in the fence between the two carriageways down the road. They would soon get through and return.

Cait and Danny ran from pure terror. It hurt to breathe, Cait's lungs prickling with heat. Her thigh muscles burned. The riders would reach them at any moment.

She'd lost the light somewhere up ahead. They reached the point where the road opened onto the roundabout when Cait caught a glimpse of it again, half-way across the lanes of traffic streaming around the island.

The large, irregular roundabout had five roads leading from it. A clump of trees covered it, some of them large, as if a wood had been left in the middle of the city and the roads built around it.

The light didn't stop. It sped into the trees, not bobbing now but moving in a fast, straight line, blurring like a shooting-star. Cait glanced at Danny. He shrugged, too out of breath to talk. The motorcycles rumbled nearer, their deep roars distinctive above the other noise.

Dodging between cars, horns blaring in their ears, they raced after the light, across the road and up a small grassy bank into the trees.

Darkness enfolded them. The noise of the traffic became muffled. Glancing backward, she saw two motorcycles, and then a third, the riders circling them.

They pressed on into the trees, the little light a distant smudge. The wood seemed larger than she would have thought possible. Surely they should have reached the other side by now? Still they walked on, into deeper and deeper darkness.

The light vanished altogether. She and Danny stopped, exhausted, not sure what to do next. Apart from their panicky breathing, the distant whoosh of the traffic was the only noise. Unseen leaves tickled her face.

Another light blinked. This time it was a match, then a candle, held by an indistinct figure, hard to see in the dim, shifting light.

Cait reached for Danny's hand and they stood together, waiting to see who this was, unable to run any farther.

A woman spoke.

"Cait, Love. Danny. You made it."

Cait fell forward and threw her arms around her gran.

15 – EMPIRE TOWERS

Cait didn't know if she was crying because she was safe or because her gran was safe.

"How did you get out of the library? I thought they'd got you. I thought … I might not see you again."

Her gran hugged her close, pressing Cait's face into the softness of her woollen shawl.

"Oh, don't worry about me. I called up a few friends for help."

"But that thing down there. All those soldiers."

"Jane and I had an escape route planned. I walked out the back door while they came in the front."

The thought of Jane and the way she'd died was, finally, too much. Everything came out in a confused flood of tears and words. "We've been chased across the city, Gran. Riders on motorcycles. And there was this terrible pile-up on the motorway. Then a helicopter chased us. And a guy attacked Danny with a knife. And they fired at us! They tried to kill us. I was so scared."

She could get no more words out for the moment. Her gran's hold on her tightened as she stroked Cait's hair, telling her it was all right. They stood like that for long moments.

It was warmer under the trees. Slowly her sobbing subsided. Danny sat down beside her. The traffic became a distant rush in the muffled darkness. From somewhere nearby, an owl made a gentle *hooing* noise, as though enquiring who she and Danny were.

Cait looked up in sudden alarm. "Gran, they were just behind us, out on the road. They'll find us here. We must get away."

"No, no," said her gran. "We're safe for a time here, Cait. This place will protect us."

"How?"

Her gran released her and stooped to pick up the candle she'd dropped when Cait rushed into her arms.

"Let's sit down and talk."

She lit the candle with a match, then used it to light others scattered around the grove. Cait and Danny huddled together on a log. Her gran picked up her battered, tartan flask and poured tea into plastic cups.

They sipped at the hot liquid, saying nothing. There were biscuits, too. Her gran had come prepared. The candles hissed and sputtered, enclosing them in a sphere of soft light. The spiny shadows of branches danced around them.

"That flame we followed. It was you bringing us here wasn't it?" said Cait.

"The fetch light, yes," replied her gran. "It was a brave thing you did, Cait, taking the book and running."

"We tried to destroy it like you said. But it wouldn't burn."

"Ah. I wondered about that."

Her gran turned to Danny, who sat quietly sipping his tea. "And you, too. You're a good friend to our Cait to come with her."

"Oh well, you know," replied Danny. "Not much on telly tonight."

Cait could hear the smile in his voice. Danny liked her gran. He actually flirted with her from time to time, pretended it was really her he had come to see. He could be such an embarrassment.

"Show me your hand," said her gran.

Danny unwrapped the paper handkerchief to show her the knife-cut. It had stopped bleeding. Her gran took a tube of ointment from one of her pockets and rubbed it on.

"Magic potion?" asked Danny.

"Antiseptic."

"Gran, that spider's web in the lane," said Cait. "That cat. That was you, too?"

"Spider's web? No. Tell me."

"Well, we saw this cat near Danny's house. Two of the bikers were chasing us and the cat created this great web across the lane. To stop them reaching us. It had to be you."

"Not me, love. I'm not capable of anything like that. Something so big while out of body, too."

"Who then?"

Her gran looked puzzled. "I really don't know. How intriguing."

"And this place," said Cait. "How can we be safe here? Why haven't they found us? They're just out there."

"Oh, this grove has been here hundreds of years. Thousands maybe. You can still find places like it here and there. Magic grows through the wood. There are rooks in these trees smarter than a lot of people I know. When the city reached this far they just built around it, without knowing why."

"So it's like Stonehenge or something?"

"Something like that. Not so impressive. But it'll keep us safe for a while."

"That thing in the library. I bet it could get us here," said Cait. "Or the man in charge of the riders."

"You met Mr. Nox?"

"Didn't hear his name. The guy telling everyone what to do."

"That's him. Nasty piece of work. He's hunted us for years, does terrible things to please his masters."

"His masters?"

Her gran went quiet for a moment, considering where to start a long story. "There's a lot to tell you, my love. A lot you should already have been told, maybe. And I'm not talking about the birds and the bees here."

"The birds and the bees I know," she said, ignoring Danny's suppressed snort of laughter. "Tell me who those people chasing us are. And what that creature is. And about this book. And … how you sent that little light to find us in the darkness."

"Well. The creature is called an *undain*. You remember I told you it's from the other world, yes? A world close to ours, similar in some ways, different in others?"

"The world Jane came from," said Danny.

Her gran laughed at that. "Very good. Where Jane came from, yes."

"And this book is, what, a spell book?" said Cait.

"Something like that. It's half a book that belonged to a sorcerer from the other world. He was a good man at the start, I dare say. Sought wisdom for its own sake. But power corrupted him."

"He discovered how to summon monsters like that thing in the library?" asked Cait. "That *undain*?"

"No, not that, love. Something much worse. He learned how to *make* monsters like that thing in the library. Make them out of normal, ordinary people. He discovered how a person like you or I could become like that."

"How?"

"It isn't something we talk about much. But it's important you understand. The book describes a ritual where a person gets killed, then resurrected. Only, others are slaughtered too, and their spirit used to fuel the person's return, make them a hundred, a thousand times stronger."

"So that creature was once a man or a woman?"

"Oh, yes. A long time ago I expect. Now it is an undain. And it has come for the book."

"Why?"

"I'll tell you the story as Jane told me."

The tale took ten minutes to recount. "So," said her gran when she'd finished, "the sorcerer died and the king survived, although the ritual bringing him back to life remained incomplete. I believe the plan was for the king to perform the rite on the sorcerer in turn, but that obviously never happened. And I've always thought there must have been some trickery or treachery involved, from one or both of them, but I don't know what."

"So the king learned how to do the necromancy," said Danny. "He used it to create the rest of the undain."

"That's it," said her gran. "He got it all from the necromancer. Used the knowledge to create a whole undain empire. But without the book they have to burn the lives of more and more victims to sustain themselves."

"So why wasn't the book destroyed long ago?" said Cait.

"There was an outside chance we could use it ourselves," said her gran. "Use it against them. It would be terribly dangerous, of course."

"So it was kept hidden all this time," said Danny.

"Hidden and watched. But now they've come for it and it's better we destroy it than risk them having it."

Cait stood. "Then we should get on and do it. Sitting here won't help."

"Where were you taking it?"

"The factory where Dad died. We thought we'd throw it in the furnace. If that doesn't destroy it, nothing will."

"Cait, love, are you sure about this?"

"No. But it's the best plan we could come up with. You'll come with us won't you?"

"Best I don't."

"But why?"

"Cait, I'm getting old. You'll go more quickly without me. And if I stay here I can keep them distracted for a while, create a few delusions in their minds while you slip away. I'd do anything to protect you, the both of you, but I think it's best you go alone."

"But we barely made it here, and that was with all the

weird lights and cats and stuff helping us. We need you, Gran."

Her gran stood to hold her tight. "Oh, Cait, love. I know. But this is the best way. Once the book is destroyed it will be different. We can sit down properly and talk about everything. I promise."

Cait simply nodded. If they destroyed the book would that really be an end to it? What of all the soldiers? The undain? The other world? She'd thought she'd be home for bedtime. Now that seemed unlikely. She said nothing and her gran, perhaps knowing what she felt, said nothing more either.

Danny stood up too. "Well, we should go. They'll be calling in reinforcements to surround us."

"I'll come with you to the edge of the grove," said her gran.

They picked their way along a different path, her gran going first with a candle. The roar from the traffic grew louder with each step.

"The factory is only twenty minutes from here," said her gran. "But the roads will be watched. I don't think they'll have guessed what you are up to, not yet. It might not even occur to them you plan to destroy the book, as it's so precious. If you can get past them you'll have a chance. There's a culvert that runs under the road. It's pretty dry this time of year. Take that and you'll be able to get away."

"After that we can take a shortcut through the abandoned tower blocks," said Danny.

"You mean Empire Towers?" said her gran.

"Yeah. A mate of mine used to live there before they boarded them all up."

"I don't like it," said her gran. "That's always been a bad place."

"Well, we'll make it somehow," said Cait, trying to at least sound brave. "If it means we can get to the factory unseen it's worth it. We did manage to look after ourselves under the motorway." She still hadn't told her gran exactly how they'd done that.

"Oh, it's not angry young men with knives I'm worried about," said her gran. "That place is … unquiet. Always has been. I remember the mill they demolished when they put up the towers. Such a vast, grim old building. When the wind howls there you can hear voices in it."

"You're saying the place is haunted?" asked Cait.

"Maybe. Some lingering anger or fear. Places often have a presence, an atmosphere. Like this grove. Not everyone is really aware of it. But that's the reason those tower blocks were closed. Oh, there was the damp and all the rest, but the fact is no one liked to live there. Without really knowing why."

"We'll slip quickly through," said Danny. "We'll be fine."

"And what about you, Gran?" asked Cait. "Will you be safe?"

"Oh, don't worry about me. A few simple tricks of light, illusions of you flitting through the shadows in the opposite direction, and they'll be fooled."

"They'll come for you eventually. The undain may come for you. You said it would be able to get in here."

They were nearly at the edge of the trees. The traffic roared louder. The riders circled, waiting for Cait and Danny to emerge. The growl of their motorcycles struck dread into her heart.

"Well," said her gran. "If it comes to it, we'll see how much of a match for me that thing is when I'm here. In any case, I can delay them long enough for you to get away. That's all that really matters, love."

"And these riders - and the man controlling them at the library - are they all more undain?" asked Cait.

"Some may be. They're from Genera Corporation. The multinational that is the front for Angere in our world."

Cait nodded, trying to take it all in.

"You should take this," said her gran. She put her hands behind her head, under her long, grey hair, to unclasp the necklace she wore. Cait had seen it often. The long silver chain held a green stone as large as a boiled sweet. Her gran fastened it around Cait's neck.

"It suits you. Not very *Bling Thing* I'm afraid."

"What is it?"

"You've heard of the evil eye?"

"I suppose."

"A silly myth. Witches casting malignant spells on people by looking at them. As if we haven't got better things to do. But maybe stones like this are the source for such stories."

"What does it do?"

"It's a seeing stone. You look through it and it helps you see what is really there."

"I don't understand."

"It's hard to explain. The stone is old and I don't know everything it does myself. But it helps you see beyond the surface of things, see through the material to what lies underneath. Strong witches don't need such toys; they can see with their eyes closed, with their inner eye."

"I still don't get it, Gran."

"Best you just try it."

Cait held it up to her left eye and, closing her right, looked around.

The woods they'd walked through had been dark, the cars' headlights from the road failing to penetrate. Now they teemed with light. Not just green, as she had expected, but many colours. She could see her gran clearly, glowing a hazy honey colour, her smile bright. Danny was next to her, primary colours compared to her gran's pastels, all red and blue. Beyond them, countless smaller lights: birds in the trees, small smudges on the ground or in mid-air that must be mammals or insects. She began to make them out properly, see the fluttering wings of moths, the scurrying blur of mice's legs.

Cait closed her left eye and opened the right. All was darkness under the trees again except for the guttering light of the candle. She looked toward the cars whizzing by, drivers invisible inside their vehicles. She switched back to her left eye and then she could see them, person-shaped lights glowing orange and purple and green. The vehicles, meanwhile, were dim and hard to discern. It was like watching sitting people flying through the air.

"Here comes a rider," said her gran. "Look at him."

Cait peered through the stone, but only the dimmest fleck of light drifted past.

"It's as if he isn't alive," she said.

"Very good," said her gran. "The stone helps you *see*. See the important things if you like. Use your own eyes, too, but the stone may help if danger threatens."

"Thank you."

Something still troubled Cait. She couldn't leave without asking. "Gran, it's magic though isn't it? And you said that magic corrupted that sorcerer. Yet you made that werelight for us. How was that any better?" She didn't mention the guilty thought that really concerned her. That she, too, had worked magic, without really knowing how. Had she done something wrong, forbidden? Was she tainted now?

"That's a question with a long answer, love. Tell me, have you ever made something happen you couldn't explain?"

She wanted to take the easy way out, say no. But she might not get another chance. "I … yes. The guy in the tunnel. I kind of sent him flying without touching him. And before that, when we were crossing the canal, I seemed to fly out of my body for a time."

"I thought as much. When you struck at your attacker. Did you notice any effect on yourself?"

"My shoulder. There was a sharp pain as if I'd been stabbed. It was *really* sore. I think it's bruised."

"Ah. And tell me, knowing it would hurt you this way, would you do the same again?"

"If I had to."

"And if you knew a way to work the magic without it hurting you?"

"That would be cool," said Danny enthusiastically. "Think what you could do. I mean it could be anything."

Cait thought about it for a moment. "It would be tempting, of course. But I think … I think it would be dangerous. Where would I stop?"

"That's it, love. That's it exactly. There's the difference between the magic we work and the magic of the undain. Magic should never be used lightly. It is a wonderful and terrible gift. And there is always a cost. What you send out comes back to you threefold. It's the way of nature, the way it should be. And we accept, welcome even, the price paid.

"But sorcery cheats. It wields power without paying the price. Alchemists who try to wring magic from the elements. Summoners who leech it from magical beings. And the undain. Their necromancy has its price just like ours. They just don't pay it themselves. Knowing that using magic will hurt you keeps you human, stops you becoming like *them*."

"So it hurts for you, too? When you worked that werelight?"

"The light was easy. It took concentration but no great strength. It was a bit uncomfortable. Mind you, sustaining it for so long … I'm glad I had my flask of tea with me."

"And it will always hurt?"

"Always. In fact, you're lucky to feel simple, physical pain. It's a constant reminder not to work magic lightly. That's often how it is for the strong ones. For others it's a slow-creeping depression fogging their minds, or apparent bad luck for years to come. I had a friend, Ada her name was, who aged each time she used the magic. You could tell she'd done something big; she looked suddenly older and weaker. As if years had passed rather than days. She's dead, now. But she never used magic lightly, you can be sure."

"But I could harm others, couldn't I?" said Cait. "Just because it hurts doesn't stop me doing bad things."

"That's true. And plenty of witches have done bad things. We're just people, love, trying to get by. But if you ignore the suffering of others, well, you're not far from the sorcerers are you?"

"So, what I did, was that wrong?"

"It's not really for me to say. But if it helps, I'd have done the same."

Cait nodded in the dark and said no more. It was a relief to hear her gran's words. There was much more she wanted to ask, but for now that was enough. She needed time to think, to try and understand everything that had happened.

"I'll show you that culvert," said her gran.

They circled a few metres around the edge of the grove, always keeping in the shadows of the trees. The riders cruised past among the cars. They obviously knew she and Danny were there.

"Here it is," said her gran.

Down a steep slope strewn with twigs and tree-roots, a round stone entrance led under the road. In the light from the candle, Cait could see a trickle of water running through it, sinking into the ground through a grid.

"This runs underground for some way," said her gran. "It takes you in the right direction. I think you'll be safe in there. Follow it as far as you can."

"Thanks, gran."

"Yeah, thanks," said Danny, peering into the tunnel.

Her gran gave her one final hug, holding her tight for a second, then shook Danny by the hand.

"Take care of yourselves," she whispered.

"And you."

This tunnel was perfectly round: a large, concrete pipe that carried the stream under the road. Cait led the way, holding a small torch that her gran had taken off her key-ring. Danny carried the book.

They had to crouch as they walked, making Cait's back ache. Thin, pallid stalactites, little bigger than fish-bones, grew where two of the pipe's sections met. Cait ducked rather than snap them off. The pain in her back became sharper. Fortunately, there was only the slightest trickle of water underfoot. For a time the sound of the traffic on the road above rumbled through the walls. But that faded until she could hear only their own footsteps echoing and the soft rush of their breathing.

She felt safe at first, knowing her gran was behind them in the darkness, a place they could retreat to. But with each step she became more uneasy. The tunnel snaked around several corners as it led away from the wood.

"You OK, Danny?" she said. He didn't like enclosed spaces, she knew. They'd been at the front of a concert a few months ago, the crowd pressing tightly around them, and it got to him after a while. They'd fought their way through the throng to watch the rest of the gig from the back.

"I'm fine," he replied, although a note of tension coloured his voice.

"I think I can see the end. It's not far."

The tunnel ended between two low, grassy banks, the stream's natural course. It was all-but dried up, strewn with cans and scraps of newspaper. A road ran nearby. From somewhere an alarm sounded, its morose tones rising and falling slowly as if its power was running down.

Cait peered out carefully, wary of ambush, ready to dart inside. But there was no one about. "Come on."

They scrambled up the bank to stand on a square of rough ground between a garage and a low, red-brick office block. There had clearly once been a building here; half-bricks and shards of glass carpeted the ground.

They made sure no motorcycles were in sight then walked onto the road. The garage was open, its garish neon lights bright after the darkness of the tunnel. Across the road, a high fence made from sheets of corrugated iron lined the pavement.

"The tower blocks are through here," said Danny. "Let's find a way in before we're seen."

"OK."

They hurried along the pavement next to the fence. Cars zoomed past and each time Cait's stomach fluttered. But none slowed. After a few yards they found a place where a corner of one of the sheets had been bent. There was enough room to squeeze through. They took turns holding the triangular flap of metal open but, even so, Cait gashed her shin on one of the sharp edges.

They crept toward the two tower blocks, great square bulks reaching into the night sky. They were identical and unlit save for a red light placed atop each to warn aircraft. Cait shivered and clutched her arms around herself. The ground underfoot was a patchwork of broken paving slabs, uneven, some cracked into pieces in shallow depressions, some heaving up in slight mounds.

The moon rose in the east, nearly full, looking huge as it drifted above the roofs of the city. Its features were crisp and clear, casting a white light across the whole scene, a light that brought more shadow than illumination. She could see where there'd once been a children's playground. A single remaining swing swayed in the wind, squeaking slightly. A gate stood at the playground's entrance but the iron railings had been flattened to the ground as if in some great stampede.

As they approached the towers, she saw the windows on the lowest three floors were boarded up. Great padlocked chains secured the doors. There was no one living there. She stopped for a moment, the towers looming over her, wondering about the people who had lived in those flats. What had become of them? Danny strode on ahead of her.

She thought she caught a glimpse, then, of something in the deeper darkness beside the nearer tower, a shifting in the shadows. She peered at it but it eluded her, staying in the shadows, reluctant.

She was imagining things. A cat or something. The place had spooked her. Everything that had happened today spooked her. She set off to catch up with Danny. She was between the two towers now. One of the windows remained miraculously unbroken. She glanced into it to see, in a field of black, her own, faint reflection. Then, quite clearly, something moved behind her, a flash of grey in the shadows.

She gasped and wheeled around. This time the shadow lingered. She could make it out against the black bulk of the building. It wasn't a cat. Too big. The shape flickered, its edges disappearing and reappearing. She stepped toward it, moving slowly, feeling that whatever it was, she didn't want to frighten it. She had the clear impression it wasn't anything dangerous. She sensed a tumult of different emotions, each very brief: bewilderment, curiosity, confusion, reticence. Who or what was this?

She held her hand in front of her, seeking the touch of the indistinct being. There were more flickers in the darkness, mere lines of grey, like pencil sketches on slate, drawn and disappearing rapidly. She saw the line of a shoulder, an arm, a face, never a complete body. Then there was a blur of many arms, many faces, like a crowd jostling for her attention.

"Cait, I think there's someone coming," called Danny from behind her. "We have to go now."

Ignoring him, she clutched the necklace her gran had given her and held the green stone to her eye.

There were so many of them. A crowd of children stood in a quiet circle around her, watching, etched there onto the night in grey lines, faintly glowing orange or amber as they moved. Their clothes were strange, like something from a history book. Many wore just tatters and it was impossible to tell what were strips of clothing and what were bandages. Standing nearest to her was a girl nearly Cait's own height, clutching a tatty rag doll to her chest. She edged closer toward Cait's outstretched hand.

Cait sat down on the ground, not wanting to tower over them. Were these ghosts? Actual ghosts? How long had they been here? What had happened to them, whenever it was they'd lived? And was this what Manchester was built on? Buried under the ground, concreted over, deep down below the smart office-blocks and houses? Was this what she'd been walking on all her life?

She hadn't really paid attention in history lessons, but she knew about the mills and the industrial revolution, of course. It had always seemed distant, a different world. Now it felt very close. This could have been her if she'd been born a century or two earlier. What must their lives have been like?

The girl touched Cait's hand with the tip of one of her fingers. It was a breath of frosty air, gentle but cold as stone. Cait smiled. Other wraiths edged closer too, reaching out to touch her, seeking her warmth. Soon they thronged around her, gently stroking her back, her hair, her face. They made no sound. Some, she could see now, were badly hurt. Missing fingers or limbs. One young boy, seven or eight perhaps, stick-thin, had lost an eye and some of his face.

Things were better these days. She thought about *Bling Thing*, the shabby office at the back. That was better wasn't it? She thought about her dad and what had happened to him. That didn't happen to children any more, at least. Yet she felt such an affinity for these faint, fading creatures. Felt the strong urge to help them, to make amends.

"Cait, what are you doing?" shouted Danny. He sounded far away, now, but frightened for some reason.

She let the ghosts continue to touch her. It was the least she could do. She wanted to find out who was responsible for what had been done to them. Make them pay. But how? It was all so long ago. She smiled at the lost faces. One day, she promised, she would help them. How, she had no idea, but she would.

"Cait! Look out!"

She heard the panic in Danny's voice even as she was grabbed from behind. A strong hand on her shoulder pulled her over, sent her sprawling backward. The green stone fell from her eye and the night closed in. She was on the floor, a leather boot next to her face. One of the riders.

The rider grabbed her arm and hauled her to her feet, the pain of having her shoulder wrenched making her cry out. He was huge, nearly twice her size. He still wore his motorcycle helmet. He said nothing but stomped back to the fence, dragging Cait with him.

She could kick him, slow him down while she worked some magic, knock him flat as she had the mugger in the tunnel.

She lifted her foot but the rider stopped, released her unexpectedly. He spun around, his arms flailing as if he were being attacked by a swarm of night-time bees.

Cait found the green stone and returned it to her eye. The ghosts, the echoes, whatever they were, were a whirlwind whipping around the rider. They'd changed, become something altogether different to the fragile waifs she'd seen. Now they glowed with fury, lines of red rather than grey. They swarmed over the rider, clawing at his body, burying him under the weight of their numbers. He tried to fight, lashing out with his fists, but couldn't connect. They became a blur, flying around his head, flying *through* his head, the helmet no barrier. What were they doing? He yelled as he fell to one knee, arms up to protect himself. The fear was clear in his voice.

One of the figures didn't take part in the attack. The girl with the doll stood apart, looking on. She turned to Cait with a sad smile. She stretched her arm out toward Cait's face, hesitated once, then touched Cait lightly on the forehead. The sensation was different this time. The contact was as cold as before but this time the chill spread rapidly over her face, down her neck and into her stomach, as if frost crept through her veins.

For a moment she was alarmed. Was she being attacked, too? But the cold didn't harm her. Her body welcomed it. It wasn't the ice of the frozen ground. It was the cool of an evening after a day of heat. It was the cold of snow when the world is transformed into something beautiful.

A presence was there within her. An echo of the dead girl, like a patina of frost on a window. A form. A spirit. A power, too. The girl's strength added to Cait's own, given as a gift. Power as cold as ice. Power she could use.

Distantly, Cait heard the rider scream once more.

She held the girl's hand for a moment, bewildered, thanking her silently. Who was she? Would she have been a witch too if she'd been allowed to grow up? She looked less solid now, the edges of the tower block visible through her, as if the effort of what she'd done had diminished her.

"Come on. Let's get out of here." Danny appeared beside her. All the children were fading away, their fury subsiding. They were a crowd of tattered scraps, just lines slowly dissipating. The girl with the doll was the last to go, a smile on her face. Then there was only the rider, lying on the ground behind them, unmoving.

Cait turned away from the scene, walking then jogging alongside Danny.

"What just happened?" he asked.

"They attacked him. Turned on him. Such fury."

"Who did? There was no one there. He just stopped and went mental."

"The children. There were so many of them. They hated him, really hated him, I could feel it. But they wouldn't have harmed us."

They stopped. They were near the other fence. The factory stood on the other side. In the distant shadows, back between the tower-blocks, the floored rider lay still.

"I didn't see anything," said Danny.

"Come on," said Cait. "Let's do what we came to do."

There were no gaps in this fence but it was lower than the other. They climbed over and onto the pavement of another road. Opposite them, a few metres away, was the factory where her dad had worked. She knew it well; she'd waited outside often enough and he'd taken her in once to show her what he did all day. She could recall only great noise and heat, the huge machines crowding around her.

A high fence of metal spikes protected the long, low building. With its blazing windows and bright security lights it resembled some great ship moored in the middle of the city. A chimney stack reached into the night, its top lost except for another red beacon, flashing high in the sky. A deep rumbling filled the air. She tasted the tang of smoke as she breathed.

She was ready. She could do this.

"OK," said Danny. "Let's try and blag our way in."

A figure stepped from the shadows of the factory gatehouse. "Cait Weerd. I believe you have a book of mine."

Nox grinned, as if he were an old friend.

16 – RETURNING

The handsome man in the black leather jacket stood in the middle of the road, his hand held out for the book. Four riders stood behind him, not moving.

Without a word to each other, Cait and Danny ran. It was useless, she knew. They had no chance of escaping. Where would they run to? They raced along the pavement anyway, away from the man. But it was playing for time. They had to turn and fight. They were out in the open, caught in the light, the chase over.

Footsteps pursued them. The riders. She slowed down. Enough running. She reached for the magic lying coiled and cold within her.

And what should she do? Play tricks with their minds, make them see monsters attacking? But perhaps that wouldn't work on such mindless beings. Turn their blood black or make it boil in their veins? Tell their bones to twist and writhe out of their sockets so they collapsed screaming to the floor? She might be able to do that.

But what would her gran think? Cait had stopped, Danny running ahead of her. She saw her gran's face in her mind's eyes: the familiar, fond smile. Her gran tolerated anything Cait said or did, but could make her true feelings clear with the briefest glance. What would her gran think if she learned Cait had done such things?

She turned to face her pursuers. They surrounded her, deploying with military precision. Underneath their black riot gear they looked like ordinary men and women. If she harmed them in some terrible way, wasn't she being corrupted by the magic, too? Where would that lead her? Where would she stop?

She made the decision in an instant, as if it were a matter of little consequence. She would never allow herself to become like that thing in the library. She would never have to see a look of disgust flashing across her gran's features.

Danny had stopped too, reluctant to leave her. The riders formed a ring around them then edged forward, wary for any attack or attempt to flee. The man strolled toward them, clearly enjoying himself, as if the whole thing was a playground game.

Cait clutched the book to her chest. The presence of the dead girl from the tower blocks stirred. She heard the girl's voice, gentle but clear.

Use your magic like this.

The voice breathed as quiet as cold air. It was old and wise. It knew how to use witchcraft. Cait held her arms forward, palms facing outward, and worked the magic she'd been shown.

An icy wind roared from her hand. It was easy enough to form: a mere channelling of the cold inside her. Even so there was a sharp pain in her chest as she worked the magic, as if something twisted in her heart.

She hit a rider squarely in the stomach. He stopped in his tracks, then toppled over, clutching his arms about himself. Frost covered him as if he'd been lying in ice all night. He didn't move.

Had she killed him? Had the girl's voice tricked her? She searched into the rider. The flame of life inside him flickered low but it burned still, deep inside his torpor. He was alive as much as ever.

The other riders acted immediately, their training sending them diving and rolling as if under fire. They darted at her from every angle, moving simultaneously so the odds were in favour of at least one reaching her.

Cait extended her senses farther, forming a picture of the whole scene in her mind. She could see herself and Danny, and then the remaining three riders throwing themselves at her. Wider still she could see the man who commanded them, unmoving, his mind hard to discern.

Everything moved in slow motion, like some movie combat sequence. Her own mind sharpened, her thoughts bright and clear. She whirled round, forming an arc of ice about her and Danny like a great blade. It struck the first rider in the head, knocking him backward. The second stooped to roll underneath, but by rotating her hands she caught him squarely with the blast. Without a sound the rider slumped to the ground. The final attacker lunged at them from behind, closer than the others. Cait, knowing precisely where he was, directed the flow of magic backward, halting him dead in his tracks. In a moment, all thee riders lay on the ground, unmoving, frost on their faces. The pain in her chest stabbed as she breathed. But she had done it: stopped them without really harming anyone.

The man still stood a short way off. "I should have trodden on you when I had the chance, little girl."

Cait said nothing. Danny breathed hard behind her, his mind all panic. Calmly, she reached into the magic that lay within her like a mountain pool, deep and wide. Wincing involuntarily at the stab in her chest she sprayed more ice at the man, putting all her strength into it, not caring now if she knocked him out or killed him. He was no victim. The world would be a better place without him.

But the spell never reached him. A halo, a shroud of indistinct images appeared around him. The magic struck it and stopped, absorbed. She caught a glimpse of distant faces screaming and writhing in pain within the shroud, as if it was made from spirits like those at the tower blocks. Then it faded away, leaving the man untouched. Some magic from the other world, some sorcery. Now what could she do?

Danny stepped forward as if he planned to fight the man. She grabbed his arm and tried to pull him back. "Danny, no. You've got no chance."

The man pulled a gun from inside his jacket. "You're all so boring, you know that? I'm going to kill you both just to shut you up."

Cait put herself in front of Danny. "But you can't shoot me, can you? You can't risk harming me."

"Actually, yes. I can."

"But in the library with that thing. And when you were shooting from the motorway. You were very careful not to harm *me*."

The man laughed. "You really haven't a clue about anything do you? We do want you alive, that's true. But *barely* alive will do fine."

He aimed at Cait.

She tensed involuntarily, her mind floundering as she tried to create some barrier, some shield between her body and the barrel of the gun. But panic drowned out the magic, the voice within her. All her new-found confidence fled. The muscles in her stomach tensed, ready for the impact.

She didn't see the bird flying through the darkness until it crashed into the man's arm, knocking him off his aim. She heard the bullet strike the ground with a sharp *crack* somewhere beside her. A small crow, a patch of grey on its head like a cap, stood on the ground in front of the man. It stared intently up at him, its head cocked.

The crow attacked, flying at the man's hand, pecking and scrabbling. The man fired again, the bullet whistling through the air. The bird struck. The man swore, dropping the weapon to the floor.

The bird fell in a flurry of feathers. Cait expected it to land in a heap, or right itself and fly away. But instead it changed shape rapidly, growing toward the ground and expanding at the same time. Wings became arms, feathers clothes, until it was a person crouching there on the floor, not a bird. The person stood up, brushing dust off legs and arms.

Cait would have recognized that old grey skirt and shapeless black cardigan anywhere.

"Mum?"

"Cait, love." She looked at Danny. "I'm afraid I can't remember the name of your friend."

"It's Danny," said Cait.

"Of course. Hello, Danny."

"Uh, hi."

Cait walked up to her mum. Behind her, the man scooped up the gun from the ground, aimed and fired. The bullet ricocheted harmlessly off a faint, shimmering wall that appeared in the air between them.

"You mean you …" said Cait.

"Oh, I'm your gran's daughter all right."

"But how …?"

"Actually, you can thank *him*. He came to see me. It shocked me out of my skin. I suddenly realised what I'd become. You needed me, all this time, but especially now. I knew I'd find you if I followed him. I'm sorry I … well, about everything really."

"So … it was you? That cat?"

"Oh yes."

"Oh, mum," said Cait. She was crying. Three times in the same day. It was pathetic.

Her mum kissed her hair, then turned around to face the man. She sighed, the sound of someone facing an unpleasant duty. She waved her hand, dissipating the shimmering wall.

"Let's get this over with," she said.

"Yes, let's," said the man. "Now you're here I can save time and shoot the two of you together. Then it's just your mother to deal with. I believe she was the old woman who scuttled off through the sewers?"

"Yes, you keep making these mistakes, don't you?" Her mum's voice was fearless. It barely sounded like her. "I wonder what your masters back in Angere will make of that,

Nox?"

The man's expression didn't change but Cait noticed the briefest pause, as if her mother's words had struck home.

"Oh, just *shut up.*"

He aimed and pulled the trigger once more. Cait winced, expecting the bang, imagining the bullet slamming into her mother's body. But there was nothing except a muffled click from the gun. He tried again and again, but the gun refused to fire.

"My turn," said her mum.

She held her hand toward Nox, palm forward just as Cait had done earlier. But instead of an icy blast she sent forward a pearly, white light: hazy like the sky at sunrise. As before, the grey shroud with its trapped, screaming faces became visible, forming a barrier around Nox. Cait could see people there now: men, women and children staring at her, shouting wordlessly as if trapped under ice. Could her mother break through?

Then Cait realised that wasn't her mother's intention. The light from her hand became dimmer, little more than a shimmer in the air, a silver thread. The writhing forms in the shroud began to travel along it, drawn out toward her mother's outstretched hand. They formed an elongated cone like some gauzy grey cloth in mid-air, pulled farther and farther away from the man. Nox lost his self-assured smile.

As the cone extended down the thread to touch her mother's hand, she kneeled and put her other hand to the road. A set of rails was embedded in the ground, leading nowhere, a remnant of the days when trains ran to the factories. Around them, patches of cobblestone peered through the modern tarmac like the bones of the old city.

The grey forms flowed over her mother's hand, up one arm, across her neck and face, then down the other arm to touch the earth. There they disappeared, like water soaking gratefully into parched ground. Within moments the grey shroud drained away. Nox stood unmoving, watching in horror.

Her mother stood, her shoulders heaving up and down. Cait could only guess what the cost of working such magic had been.

"There," her mother said, her voice wavering. "They're all at rest now."

Nox finally moved. He touched the silver stud in his ear and spoke quietly. Summoning help. Her mother turned to her and Danny.

"Cait, take the book and destroy it as you planned," said her mother. "You too, Danny. I'll keep Nox out of your way. Go on, be quick."

"Mum, be careful. There'll be others. There's an undain somewhere in the city, too."

"I'll be fine, love. Don't worry about this one, he isn't going anywhere for a bit."

Cait smiled, happy to see her mother restored, terrified she might not see her again after this.

"Go on," said her mother, almost whispering.

Cait turned to Danny, nodded and ran. Together, they fled toward the factory gates where Nox and the riders had waited for them.

The man inside the guardhouse sat slumped over his desk. He was alive, she could tell, but whether he was injured or unconscious they didn't stop to find out. They ducked under the red and white barrier.

A set of double doors surrounded by safety notices warned of the dangers of fire within. The thrumming noise in the air intensified. Cait glanced back to where her mother faced Nox. The two of them stood in the road as if chatting.

"Hey, you kids! What are you doing in here?" A man in a set of blue overalls, singed and stained all over, a yellow hard-hat on his head, strode along the side of the building. He held a cigarette in one hand. He looked angry at the sight of them. "You can't come in here. I'll call the police."

It was Danny that replied, using the polite voice he reserved for teachers and other old people. "No, it's OK.

This is Cait Weerd. Her father was killed in the fire here two years ago. The guard on the gate said we could come in and look around. Cait needs to … come to terms with what happened."

It was a huge gamble. The man might not have worked here back then. And the lie about the guard would be easy to disprove. But the man looked unsure of himself. They might get away with it. Cait glanced at Danny. He was doing his best to wear a forlorn expression. She tried to copy it.

"Wait here," said the man. "Don't move a muscle. I'm fetching the foreman."

They stood with their backs to a large yellow skip, piled high with broken machinery and coils of electrical cable. The longer they waited, the more nervous Cait felt. Had the man really called the police? And if he had, would it be Nox's private soldiers that turned up? She and Danny exchanged worried glances. Both of them, she knew, were inventing unrealistic plans to run into the factory, evade capture, and somehow throw the book into the blast furnace raging inside.

The man returned, accompanied by an older worker wearing similar blue overalls but a blue hard hat. Perhaps some designation of rank. The first man was scowling but the second, although weary-looking, smiled. His face was deeply lined, like crumpled paper.

"So you're Mike Weerd's little girl eh? Last time we met you were a sleeping babe. You've changed a bit."

She smiled and said nothing, trying to play the role of the sorrowful daughter. In truth, it wasn't hard. Coming here it was as though her dad was still around, as if she would find him working away inside.

"No harm in letting you look," the foreman said. "Make sure you stick close to me and we'll be fine. Just don't tell anyone, OK?"

"OK."

They walked through the large double doors to be hit by a wall of noise and heat. It was bright inside the factory, making it hard to take in all the detail straight away.

Her memory of her previous visit was of this terrible cacophony and great walls of spiked metal that threatened to snag you if you went too close. Also, she recalled her dad's hand in hers, cool and calm, telling her it was all right. Even so, she'd been glad to get outside into the fresh air.

Now, the machines didn't seem so terrible. They were big and noisy, running in lines down the open space of the factory floor, but they didn't reach to the ceiling and they didn't look as though they'd grab her as she walked past.

The foreman held out two pairs of oversized wooden shoes and two pairs of yellow ear-defenders, like ridiculous headphones. "Here, put these on. You'll need the clogs in case any molten metal gets spilled." With the ear-defenders on the noise became instantly muffled, making Cait feel curiously distanced from reality. She shouted out a *thank you* but the sound went nowhere, swallowed up by the crashing, roaring din. The clogs were heavy weights on her feet as she clomped forward.

The man guided them along a safe pathway painted on the floor in diagonal yellow stripes. As they passed, the men working at the machines glanced at her and Danny, some grinning, some not. How many of them had known her dad?

She thought of him working here, long hours, day after day to make a living for them all. It was ugly and dirty, a huge room full of inhuman machines whose function she could only guess at, so far removed from the comfort of their own home. He had been a gentle man, quietly spoken, rarely angry. What had it cost him to come here each day? He'd never complained, not to her ears anyway, and was always ready to play with her, talk to her when he came home at night. With hindsight, she could see he must have been exhausted a lot of the time. She missed him, then, with an acute pain, as sharp as the one in her chest when she'd worked the magic.

The foreman shepherded them through another set of double doors into a rest room. Scruffy chairs were set around the walls, each peppered with cigarette burns. Little tables held scattered newspapers and car magazines. It was quieter in here. A little. The foreman took his ear-defenders off, gesticulating at them to do the same.

"You look a lot like your dad, you know."

"Did you know him well?"

"Aye. We worked together. Used to talk all the time. He were quite the joker, Mike."

"How could you talk in all that noise?"

"I mean sign-language. You learn it quickly here. Mind you, we made up quite a few of our own signs." He grinned at that, remembering. "He were a good lad. Terrible what happened."

"Were you here?"

"No. I were away that week. Came back to find the place half burned down and your dad and the others dead. Last thing I said to him was *enjoy your week at work*, all cocky like."

"We have this book," said Danny. "Cait made it. It has ... memories and things of her dad. We wondered if we could throw it in the furnace. The one that went out of control."

It sounded ridiculous as he said it. Surely the man wouldn't allow it. Surely he would at least ask to look at the book. But he didn't even glance at it. He was full of sympathy, sadness of his own. He would have done more or less anything for her.

"It's against the rules, of course, but all those rules didn't save your dad, did they? The hell with them."

What they were doing was wrong: tricking this man, taking advantage of him. But they had little choice; they had to do it. And, she thought, coming here *would* help her, give her a glimpse of the man her dad had been. The place wasn't the factory she saw in her nightmares.

The foreman put his ear-defenders on and led them onto the machine-floor. They walked the entire length of the room. At the far end there were more doors, but these were larger, made of thick metal. More signs warned of further dangers: danger of explosion, danger of death.

Cait began to feel uneasy. It was fire, indeed it was *this* fire, raging in this enclosed space, that woke her up sweating at night. The room they were about to enter was where it had all happened. Those great doors would be shut behind them, and they would be trapped. Right here, at the end of their crazy journey across the city, she had doubts that she could do it after all.

Danny took her hand. His fingers were hot, not cool, but there was reassurance there, understanding. Danny moved forward, leading her gently. Her heart thumping, she let herself be led.

The heat inside the small room was tremendous, alarming to feel. One entire wall was taken up by the curving arc of the metal blast furnace, gleaming black, right up to the ceiling and presumably beyond. Its door was shut but even so it dried and cracked the skin of her face to be so near it. The air in the room was hazy with smoke, making details indistinct. It brought with it a sickly, acrid smell.

Another man stood near the furnace, watching an array of dials. He was clad head-to-toe in heavy protective gear, like armour. His entire head was covered by a curved visor made of some dark material. Dim reflections of the three of them reflected in it as he turned to see who had come in.

The foreman waved him over. Faint coils of smoke drifted off him. He had to stoop as the foreman shouted into his ear and indicated Cait and Danny.

The furnaceman nodded once. Her dad's friend turned to them and grinned. "Big Billy here will commit the book to the flames for you." He had to shout to make himself heard. "You make sure you stay well back, OK? Here, put these on."

From a rack near the double doors he took two pairs of eye-protectors, like oversized sunglasses, and gave one to each of them. "I'll leave you in peace for a few minutes then come and get you. Then you'll have to go, I'm afraid."

Cait smiled at him and nodded. He put his hand on her

shoulder for a moment and left, a roar from the factory floor greeting him as he slipped through the double doors.

Cait put her glasses on. Everything went crimson, like looking at the world through red liquid. Details became more indistinct. The scene shimmered and shifted because of the glasses and the terrible heat. She could see the shape of the furnaceman as he picked something up off the floor. A pair of long, metal tongs. He came toward them, holding out one of his gauntleted hands.

He said something unclear, muffled by his mask. Distantly, Cait could see her own distorted features reflected in his visor.

She handed him the book, which he placed into the jaws of the tongs. With a practiced motion he heaved on a lever, throwing the furnace door open.

The blast of heat was incredible. Cait stepped backward involuntarily, hard against the far wall. Danny was next to her. The searing blaze, bright even through the glasses, felt as if it was right in front of her face. She wanted to be outside, somewhere cool, where there was water and fresh air. She had to resist the urge to run.

The furnaceman pushed the book deep into the furnace.

Exhaustion finally overwhelmed her. It had been a long, long day. The chase, the magic she had worked and now the terrible heat of the fire had drained her utterly. But they'd done what they set out to do. Whatever else was going to happen, the terrible book was destroyed.

The furnaceman stumbled backward, then seemed to trip. Puzzled, Cait took her glasses off to see what was happening. Squinting through narrowed eyes she saw him lying on the floor, not moving. His visor still covered his face.

But something in the flames did move. A trick of the heat, perhaps. It was impossible to be sure, the fire too intense to look at directly.

"What was that?" she said, her parched voice cracked.

"What?" said Danny.

She saw it again. This time it was clear, a flash of black within the roaring fury of the furnace. "There."

She took a step closer. Walking toward the fire was a huge effort, like climbing a steep hill.

A flame shot out, a slash of orange-red. Not a flame: an arm. Then another, then a larger molten mass. Stepping slowly out of the furnace, an entire creature emerged. Its shape shifted and twisted as if it was trying to decide what form it should adopt. Finally, burning red, there stood the creature from the library basement. Smoke and flame coiled off its incandescent body. Its huge head was, as before, completely featureless.

It opened its mouth, splitting its empty face from side to side. Behind the white needle-teeth, like a great tongue, she could see the book. Undamaged.

She thought desperately of magic she could work. But there was no time. And she was spent. Her mind was all heat and fire, her thoughts wavering and unclear. The voice of the dead girl was there, but too remote to hear properly, a voice shouting from the grave.

The creature shambled toward her, in no hurry. Danny leaped at it but it brushed him aside, sending him flying across the room with a simple flick of a limb.

Then it had her, a grip like iron on her arm, burning her. She sensed magic. There was a rush of movement like falling and then they were no longer in the factory.

Darkness consumed her, save for the burning glow of the monster.

"Now," it said.

17 – AETHERNAL

The Aether

"So," said the archaeon, "would it be fair to say things are not quite going to plan, little witch?"

Fer had resisted talking to the archaeon for as long as she could. Partly because she didn't want to be the one to tell it they were trapped, partly because she didn't want to face the mocking look in its eye. But they could think of nothing else to try.

"That would be a fair thing to say," she replied.

They'd slept under the trees in the Tanglewood. Impossible to say for how long, but she at least felt rested. Ran and Johnny had been awake for hours while she slumbered, unable to do anything but scavenge for firewood without losing sight of their camp.

They'd talked about their options. Johnny had suggested she try to speak to the archaeon. When she'd explained she already had, they'd ended up shouting at each other. As if she'd arranged everything just to annoy him.

He was worried, of course. And perhaps she should have told them what she'd done. But then the undain might have found out about the book she carried and, one way or another, that could be important.

Once they'd calmed down, she'd consented to try the

archaeon again. This time she'd found the tunnel quickly. And it was easier to push through the veils of cobwebs that tickled her face as she worked her way into the underground chamber. Soon she stood before the wyrm's huge head, waiting for it to open its eyes. All part of its tiresome act. It must know she was there.

"So, let me see," it said, with relish in its voice. "How badly could it have gone? You are still alive so that is something. But perhaps others have been killed, hmm? Yes, I think so. But there is more. Let me see."

It was hot down here, as if fire burned within the wyrm's body, heating the air around them. The whole chamber resonated with the deep boom of its voice. Fer refused to be impressed. The creature played this little game just to awe her. She had the impression it had already guessed what had happened.

"Ah. I have it! We must be trapped in the Tanglewood. Some terrible calamity has befallen us and now we are unable to return to An and unable to reach the other world, too. Yes? Is that about it?"

"Yes. That's about it."

"So, tell me, little witch, who has been killed and who is still with us? Are you and I the only brave survivors?"

"A young witch was killed. Seleena. Still alive are a troubadour, Johnny Electric, originally from the other world and Ran, a dragonrider."

"Dragonrider? Interesting. Tell me, what colour are his tattoos?"

"What? They're blue."

"Does he have any of a different hue anywhere on his body? A black dragon, perhaps. Somewhere … not obvious?"

"How should I know, archaeon! What do you think I am?"

"I thought you were a witch. That you sought knowledge and understanding. Still, there we are. Times change. If you ever do have the opportunity, try and remember to check for me would you?"

"I may and I may not. It's none of your business, wyrm! Enough of these games. Can you help or not?"

"Perhaps. Let me think. Trapped between the worlds are we? There hasn't been a great deal written about *this* particular predicament. But now that I think about it, there was a brief mention of something similar in an obscure tract by an astromancer called Anson some six hundred years ago. Very difficult to read, let alone comprehend but I believe I followed it. Tell me, how are your summoning spells?"

"I don't have any. I mean, I don't dabble in anything so unnatural. I'm a witch, remember?"

"Yes, of course. An admirable calling. The problem is this. You're going to have to set aside your ethical stance and dabble in the mantic arts if we are to have any chance of escaping."

Fer sighed. An evil act for the greater good. It wasn't an approach that had ever convinced her. Could anything but trouble come from such a thing?

"Tell me what it is you're suggesting," she said.

The archaeon actually grinned, displaying its great teeth. They glinted in a light that wasn't really there. It was enjoying this.

"We are fortunate that this place is itself crafted, highly magical. There is power for you to draw upon. You need to use it to attract the attentions of an aethernal."

"What is that? I've never heard of such a thing."

"No. But fortunately, I have. A spirit of the aether; a dweller of the void, able to slip through the cracks between the worlds. Rare, but they exist. At least they did six centuries ago."

"There is no way into this wood. It's sealed now."

"Didn't I just say? An aethernal does not need doorways or portals. It goes where it will; it can pass through the walls between the worlds. Although it can only do so for a short time before it must return to the aether. Occasionally they are glimpsed in An, which accounts for most ghost stories, you might like to know."

"You are suggesting that such a creature would help us? Why? Are they benign?"

"Another meaningless question. Sometimes they are and sometimes not. Rather like humans, in fact." The archaeon shut its eyes for a moment, pleased with its observation. "But, although they are denizens of the void, they crave the life, the sensation, the *colour* they can glimpse when they visit one of the worlds. So Anson said. It is their doom that they can never stay for long. Material worlds leech them dry."

"I see."

"Do you? I doubt it. This Tanglewood is unique. It is a part of the aether but at the same time it is material. It is possible, likely even, that an aethernal could stay here permanently. After the emptiness of the void this place would be paradise for them."

"So, in return for giving one this wood to inhabit, it might help us reach the other world?"

"Ah, you have it at last! I knew you could work it out."

"It sounds dangerous."

"Yes."

"And sooner or later one will find us anyway won't it?"

"Eventually. Although the size of the aether makes that unlikely by chance for many of your lifetimes. It is limitless in extent, you know."

She didn't like it. To use summoning magic was bad enough, but who knew *what* this creature would really do? What imbalances she'd be setting up by giving one a permanent home in the aether. Could they even trust it to do what it said? On the other hand, what choice did they have? And she was sick of being manipulated by Hellen, by the archaeon, by all of them. She'd do what she thought best and that was that.

"If I summon one here we'll have nothing left to bargain with," she pointed out. "I mean, it'll already be inside the wood."

"You really do know nothing of summoning magic do you?" replied the archaeon. "What is summoned and held in the circle may be banished."

"So we hold it in a circle of power while we bargain?"

"Brilliant thinking! Yes, if you are able to learn the spell. And if we are able to attract the attentions of one. It will take time, depending upon how good you are at the magic."

"I can learn the spell. I assume that you, oh ancient and wise archaeon, would be able to teach me the words?"

"I think I might."

"Very well. And how do we converse with this being? Even wood and water spirits in Andar speak their own language. An inhabitant of the aether surely will, too."

"Well, well, you are thinking at last. Fortunately I can save the day again. I can translate. Didn't I mention that I know all languages?"

"How very fortunate we are to have you," said Fer.

"Indeed, so," said the wyrm.

The spell took time to learn. The words the archaeon told her felt rough in her mouth. There was power, too: jagged and hard-edged, like a knife slashing the air.

Ran and Johnny watched in silence as she worked. She soon had a headache from the effort, but she persevered, refusing to admit defeat. In truth, the pain made her feel a little better about everything. She could understand magic you had to pay the price for. Really, there wasn't *enough* discomfort involved for her liking. Although that thought struck her as odd. She didn't enjoy the pain, of course. What did it say about her that she welcomed it? Felt the need for more?

She shook her head, trying to set aside such troubling questions. That was the argument of a mancer. She was doing what had to be done.

Eventually, she was ready.

They cleared a patch of ground between the trunks of towering pine trees. Fer marked a circle in the soil, her stomach churning as she did so. She found herself wondering what Hellen would have said. Although the thought that the old witch might not approve made her feel a little better about the whole thing.

She went round the circle three times, making sure there were no gaps, no way that the aethernal could escape. Then she stepped inside and drew the five-pointed star that would be the focus. Finally, when all was ready, she told Ran and Johnny to stay back. Ran, uselessly, drew his sword.

She walked three times around the circle, sealing it. Then she sat cross-legged on the ground, shut her eyes and began the incantation.

She stayed like that for a long time, hours it seemed, chanting the raw words of the summoning, channelling the magic from the woods. Her throat became dry and sore but she persevered. With her mind she reached farther and farther into the infinite, grey reaches of the aether, trying to find a tiny mote of life.

Eventually, she had to stop for a drink. Nobody spoke. Johnny sat some way off, practising his juggling with five, fist-sized pine cones. Ran looked around warily, always on guard.

She wanted to stop, give it up until tomorrow, but time was short. Who knew what the undain was doing in the other world? She forced herself to resume. Chanting the words was like chewing on spiked metal. More time passed where nothing happened. Her fatigue grew. She had to concentrate to stop herself from slurring the words. Did the archaeon have the summoning spell correct? Was some vital ingredient missing? If so, there was no hope. They were trapped forever.

She was half-asleep, or half in a daze, when she finally caught a glimpse of something. A tiny speck floating in a limitless volume of grey. It was like glimpsing something deep in a vast body of water. Or high, high in the air. Or both at once. She bent her mind toward it, willing more power into her words.

Slowly it grew, allowing itself to be drawn in. She sensed

curiosity. It was little more than ragged tatters of grey. It changed shape constantly, as if billowing in a wind.

Closer it came, and clearer. Soon she saw it for real, there inside the summoning circle. It became more like a person in form, with distinct arms and legs, as if it had observed Fer and the others and shaped itself to fit. Perhaps that was what it always did that when it slipped into a world.

The aethernal's mind was vast but foggy. She sensed intelligence there, certainly, a bright core in the mist. It was intrigued. There was also a need, a great longing for sensation, for life. Wily, it kept that hidden. Fer's pleasure at her success faded, to be replaced by alarm, when she grasped the intensity of that hunger.

The aethernal spoke. At least, there were sounds: a low, slow moaning, like the winter wind through bare trees.

It wants to know who we are. What we are. The archaeon's voice spoke clearly in Fer's mind. As she'd suspected, the business with the tunnel and the cave was a charade. The archaeon was perfectly capable of conversing normally when it wished.

Tell it what we want and what we offer in return, instructed Fer.

The conversation lasted for some time. Finally, the archaeon reported back to Fer.

It says it will help us. In return for this wood, it will help. It says we can still reach the other side because we are partly through already. The door has gone but the doorway remains, it keeps saying. But once we do leave, the doorway between the worlds will be closed to us forever.

Fer turned to Johnny and Ran. Johnny looked worried, afraid of what he might hear. The dragonrider remained as impassive as ever.

"We have a choice to make," she said. "We must decide where to go. Back to Andar or on to the other world. Whichever we choose, we cannot use the portal again."

"I will follow you," said Ran. It was what she'd expected. As much as she disliked his devotion, his subservience, she found it reassuring just then. Two of them at least, three including the archaeon, would go where they had to go: on into the other world.

"If we go back to Andar," she said, talking mainly to Johnny, "then we are lost. We could only sit and await destruction. We must go on."

"There is a third way," said Johnny. He looked uncomfortable as he spoke.

"What?" said Fer.

"We could stay here."

"No," said Fer.

"All I'm saying is, being here, it could be worse."

"How? How could it be worse? We're trapped."

"Yeah, I know. I spotted that. But there's an upside. I mean, I don't like being trapped either, but if the An does freeze over, if the undain army does cross and Andar is destroyed, then at least we'll be safe here, yes? We can't get out, but nothing can get in."

"Others need us," said Fer. "Andar needs us."

"All I'm saying is, we could, OK? It's an option. We could, I don't know, build houses if we wanted. Must be plenty to eat. I mean, this is a rich woodland in perpetual summer. There may be animals to hunt, too. We've seen a rook already."

"That rook," said Fer, "was the undain watching us."

"It was? Oh. OK. Still, all I'm saying is, we should consider all the possibilities, yeah?"

"And what of *Smoke on the Water*? What of your travels? What about the people you've left behind, in both worlds?" She was cross, too tired to bother restraining herself.

He was quiet for a moment. Then he smiled, his good humour returning like a light in the dark.

"All good points, Fer, all good points. OK, cool. I'm in. But this spooky thing here, can we trust it? How do we know it won't cast us into outer darkness when we unleash it?"

"It can't. All it can do is open a door for us."

"And since you're obviously leaving I'd have to share this place with it if I stayed, yes?"

"Yes."

"Then what are we waiting for? We've gotta get out of this place."

Fer faced the aethernal.

Tell it we accept, she said to the archaeon. *Tell it we wish to travel on to the other world. Ran and Johnny are to go through the door first. I will then free it and follow them.*

Another long, slow conversation. She began to fear it had changed its mind, or wanted more from them. But then the archaeon spoke.

It understands. It will open the doorway now.

A circle of blackness appeared in the air near to the ruined oak tree. The aethernal appeared to expend no effort its creation.

Without a word, Ran strode toward it. Johnny followed, shouting to Ran to put his sword away before they reached the other world. Ran ignored him and, stepping into the disc, disappeared. Johnny turned, shrugged and followed.

Fer walked backward until she stood by the doorway. She watched the aethernal for a moment longer, trying to sense its next move, whether it had some ulterior motive. But she could feel nothing. Perhaps it was even a mistake to think of it in such terms. This was not a person but a being of infinite voids, its mind unfathomable. Where would it have learned duplicity?

Still, she was uneasy at what she had done. She thought about stepping through the doorway without unleashing the creature. Was it good to do the wrong thing for the right reasons? Just now, she had no time to consider the dilemma.

She said the words that unsealed the summoning circle.

The voracious longing in the aethernal swelled. The creature grew in size rapidly, expanding to fill the clearing, the grey mists of its body billowing toward her. How long had it been out here, craving sensation? It was as if it intended to consume the entire Tanglewood and everything within it.

With a shudder, Fer followed Ran and Johnny into the

other world.

18 – WITCH-MARKS

Manchester, England

Fer stepped into a large, dimly lit room. It resembled a cave but was clearly unnatural, the stones of its walls cut into squares. Johnny walked beside her. In front of them, Ran stood within a ring of bodies. Each of the dead was dressed in strange, black armour. Sword wounds punctured each of them: thin, clean cuts like little mouths dribbling blood.

"Only four," said Ran. "I expected more." He wiped his blade clean on one of the bodies. He wasn't even out of breath.

"More will come now," said Johnny. "Count on it. They aren't gonna mess around."

"Are these creatures magical, then?" asked Fer. "Would they have summoned their comrades before they died?" Under their armour they looked like normal people. Nearest to her, the lower face of a woman was visible beneath her helmet, her lip bleeding where she'd bitten it.

"No need," said Johnny. He pointed at the ceiling. "CCTV. They'll already be on their way."

"I don't understand," said Fer.

"No time to explain. Just trust me, OK? We have to leave right now."

Fer cast her gaze around, trying to decide what to do.

Books littered the floor: books wrenched apart and set on fire. Were the remains of the Grimoire among them? She doubted it. Scorch marks stained the walls. There was death here, recent death, but she couldn't tell who or what had died. It was hard to concentrate. Distant but incessant, the buzz of a great many people filled her mind. How big was this city?

"We must find steps to the surface," she said.

"Or a lift?" said Johnny.

"A lift?"

Johnny sighed. "Never mind. Good job I'm here to translate for you. Come on, the sign says the exit is this way." He pointed to a green square on the wall that showed someone walking toward a doorway.

"They will come that way," said Ran.

"OK, so zap us up to street-level with magic," said Johnny. "Use some of those weird words and spirit us outta here."

They both looked at her. Was this how some people became leaders and some followers? Was this what created covens and priests and rulers? To Islagray and then, eventually, to Angere and the Witch King? The trivial matter of one person making the decisions, other people becoming used to following them? The whole thing made her uncomfortable; she had no desire to lead just as she had no desire to be led. But she could see no alternative.

"You've spent too much time in the north with those mancers," she said.

He looked genuinely disappointed. "You mean you can't do it?"

She ignored him and walked over to the green sign. There were more marks on the wall below it. They'd moved, she was sure of it, but when she looked directly at them they weren't there. She tilted her head. She saw them again, a flick of movement in the corner of her eye. She could discern four or five lines drawn in a great hurry. They suggested a hare running at full speed across a field, all ears and powerful haunches. It was stylised, almost like runes: the mere idea of a hare. But there were words too, hard for the ear to catch.

It was a witch-mark, no doubt about it. She breathed deeply to relax, touching the wall and coaxing the marks to life. The leaping hare became clearer, bucking and running *away* from the exit. She thought she could understand the voice, too. The accent was strange, a speaker not used to the language, but there was a single word there, repeated several times. *Follow*, it said. *Follow, follow.*

Could the undain have crafted such a thing? She doubted it. This was too weak and insignificant a piece of magic. It would work death and fire, not harmless charms. It probably wouldn't even have noticed the mark. The undain lost much by gaining their terrible power.

"This way," she said.

"That way?" said Johnny. "Why that way?"

"The weird words told me," she called over her shoulder.

Ran said nothing, but overtook her to lead the way, sword held forward, glancing warily from side-to-side.

At a crossroads ahead there was another mark. Her senses were settling down. She made out the second mark quite clearly, even from a distance. This one was rougher, drawn in more of a hurry, as if the witch who wrote it were being chased. Who could it have been? Jaiin? Had she fled with the book?

"This way," she said, not stopping to allow any discussion. Johnny sighed, muttering something about women. Ran, as ever, said nothing.

As they walked, she felt the archaeon drift into her thoughts. Urgency, even anger, was clear in its voice.

What are you doing? The books! Leave me here in the books!

She felt its desperation to explore the universe of new worlds the library represented. In its desperation it appeared to have forgotten its arrogance.

Can't you see? said Fer, angry. She had enough other

things to worry about. *Can't you see what has happened to your books?*

See little witch? Of course I can't see. Didn't Hellen explain it to you? I don't live in your dull little world. I exist in a world of ideas, not things. Mere pieces of paper do not concern me.

But you can talk to me. Can't you read in my mind what has happened?

A little. I am out of practice with people. I can see … shreds of paper. Mountains of them. It is hard to make out through your fear and worry. But I do understand that you are leaving.

The books here have been destroyed, she said, more kindly. She hadn't thought about the loss it would represent to the bookwyrm. Haughty as it was she should be more considerate. *Torn to shreds and burned. The thoughts held in them have gone. I'm sorry.*

Then let us find another part of the library.

No. We must escape now or everything will be lost. Whatever happens if they capture us, it won't involve a large book collection.

But you promised me little witch! New books; new ideas uncounted!

And I'll keep my promise. But there is no time now. When we are safe we will talk again.

Witches' promises. When were they ever to be trusted? Hellen Meggenwar taught you well.

It withdrew from her mind, full of burning indignation. She nearly shouted, raged at the unfairness of its accusations. What was she supposed to do? How was any of it her fault? Instead she made herself put the creature out of her mind. They had more pressing problems.

They came to a metal grille in the ground. The nearest mark showed they should go that way. But a great padlock held it fast to the ground. Whoever had chased the witch down here had made sure she couldn't come back up.

"Can you open this?" she said to Ran.

"I could help too, you know," said Johnny.

She sighed to herself. "Of course. Can anyone think of a way of opening it? We have to go this way."

Ran tried to lever up the grille with the pommel of his

sword but the padlock held. Johnny took out a small set of knives from a pocket, all cleverly folded together for carrying, and tried to saw through one of the clasps.

"That will take too long," said Fer. "They're coming for us, from above." She could feel them, a large number of them, all moving together. "They are travelling quickly; they must be in this *lift* you mentioned."

"Then our only hope is some magic after all," said Johnny. Ran dropped the instrument-case he carried and walked a short way down the corridor to protect them if attack came. He held his sword forward, ready to strike.

"Then I'll see what I can do," said Fer.

She kneeled down at the grille, looking for a weak point, some way to crack the metal or the stone surrounding it. The hinges opposite the lock were a little rusty; she might be able to do something with those.

She closed her eyes, steeling herself against the pain. She reached for the burning flame within her. This was how she visualised her magical power. Sometimes it raged like a pyre in a gale, sometimes it flickered like a candle. Either way, it could burn her badly if she wasn't careful.

She began to work on the hinges. She tried to spread the rust by drawing on the dampness in the surrounding stone and pushing it into veins of weakness within the metal. A sharp stitch shot through her side, hot as if someone had pressed a brand to her. She tried to hold her body so it didn't tug too much and pressed on. She had no time for subtlety.

Soon one of the hinges snapped. Metal flaked off like tiny autumn leaves. She told Johnny to finish the job of breaking it while she set to work on the other. Distantly, she heard bangs and clangs. The sound of soldiers arriving.

She had two stitches now, one on each side. They spread a band of scalding pain across her lower back. She gritted her teeth and continued. This was such a small piece of craft. She hated being so weak, so useless. She refused to fail.

In a few more moments, she was spent, gasping for air as she kneeled on the floor next to the grille. It would have to do.

"Ran!" she called. "It will break now!"

The dragonrider hustled to her side and levered the trapdoor again with his sword. With a crisp *clang* it came free. The padlock stopped it from opening fully, but there was enough of a gap for them to squeeze through.

"You first," she said to Johnny.

He grinned, then lowered himself through the gap.

"There's a ladder," he said. "I can feel it with my feet. And it's dark."

"Go down," said Fer, trying not to breathe too heavily against the pains in her back. "I will follow and work a light."

After the burning heat of the magic she welcomed the cold metal of the rungs on her hands. She descended as quickly as she could, each step pulling at her sides. Ran came last. He waited until she and Johnny were some way down the ladder then slid through after them. Footsteps toward them. They had only moments.

She lit a small werelight, pale and wavering, and sent it floating upward to the grille. The light was so dim it was hard to see much, the shadows it cast jumping around. She tried to concentrate on the light, keep it steady. She could see the red stone of the walls and the ironwork of the grille above Ran's head as he descended.

"Ran, your sword. Use it to hold the grille," she called, her voice echoing through the shaft.

Ran pulled the grille into place over his head. An iron hoop on the underside fitted through a latch attached to the wall. He wedged the quillion of his sword - the outstretched neck and roaring head of a dragon - through the hoop, locking the grille into place.

Booms reverberated through the air as the soldiers above tried to force their way after them. They would get through sooner or later. Fer frowned in the darkness as they climbed down the shaft. They said a dragonrider's sword took a year and a day to craft. Yet on an instruction from her he had given it up. She would have felt better if he'd objected.

They stood together at the bottom for a few moments. She kept the tiny werelight bobbing around them. It showed a round, stone tunnel leading into the darkness, a trickle of icy water flowing down it. The air smelled foul.

"I'll lead the way," she said. She had to duck in the confined space as she walked. In truth, she didn't really need the flame. She sensed the line of witch-marks on the wall ahead like a string of lights. She didn't even need to stop as she came to each one. *Follow,* they said again and again. *Follow! Follow!*

Before too long, and with no further sounds of pursuit, they reached a metal grid. The marks told her this was the way out. Fer crouched in a low tunnel, square rather than round. Sounds echoed from the surface: great rumbling and booming noises. What was above their heads? What terrible creatures walked the streets of this place?

The grid was heavy as she set her shoulders against it and heaved. It budged a little. Ran, sidling awkwardly, came to help and they lifted together. The grid hinged around and onto the ground with a dull *clang.*

The three of them climbed into the fresh air of the city. It was late afternoon or early evening, warm still, with a light but persistent rain making every surface gleam. Late summer, she thought, slightly behind the turn of the seasons in Andar. Although it was difficult to be sure; she could feel little tree or animal-life.

She saw no terrible monsters. But there were people: many people. A few glanced over as Fer, Ran and Johnny hauled themselves up from the darkness of the shallow tunnel. But no one said anything or seemed particularly surprised.

The city around them rose huge into the sky. Hellen had said it was by no means the biggest city in this world, but it looked vast to Fer. Great towers reached upward, all stone and glass, crowding around them like walls. She'd never been as far up the An as Guilden, although she'd heard many stories. But this city was built on a different scale.

Metal machines moved around on wheels. None of the people seemed alarmed. Instead they sauntered off and on as the machines stopped. The people looked, apart from their unusual clothes, like people from Andar. Yet, she had to remind herself, Angere was here. No great river kept the undain at bay. She still couldn't understand how such a thing was possible.

Sheets of paper blew around their feet, sticking to the stone floor where they landed. The sheets were large, white and covered in black writing and pictures.

Johnny snagged one. "It's the Manchester Evening News. Hey, says here there was a terrorist incident at the library yesterday. Police called, bombs suspected. Interesting."

Fer examined the words but they meant nothing to her, of course. She thought about telling the archaeon what they'd found, but decided against it. She had promised it a great library and it might be more than a little upset if she offered it this scrap of paper.

"What's interesting?" she asked.

"It also says they're looking for some people who were there. A woman and a girl. What do you think? Could they be with us?"

"Maybe." She thought for a moment, trying to decide what to do. "I don't understand everything you say, but if they are being chased these two must have something Angere needs. The book, perhaps. Maybe there is hope yet."

She spotted one final witch-mark, bigger, made in less of a hurry, drawn on the nearest wall among some colourful writing. She'd felt its presence as soon as they'd emerged from the tunnels. She stepped up to the wall, a great stretch of smooth, brown-grey stone that towered above them. She touched the mark, stroking it, coaxing it into life. This one didn't move but there were several words there. It depicted some sort of scuttling creature, an insect or reptile perhaps.

Words coiled around the line of its body. *The Lizard King,* she heard. And then, *The Golden Palace.* The sign faded as she caught the words.

"Johnny," she said, turning away from the wall. "Do you know who the *Lizard King* might be? In a *Golden Palace?*"

"Huh? Why?"

"It's where we have to go."

"You're sure?"

"You'll have to trust me."

"OK, well, things may have changed since I was last here, but the Golden Palace I know. We need to get to Rusholme."

"Is that far?"

"An hour's walk, max. Or we could take a bus," said Johnny, indicating one of the large wheeled machines. "Be there in a few minutes, then."

"Let's walk," she said.

"Can we spare the time?" asked Ran.

"A walk will help me find my feet." She didn't say it, but she was afraid of entering one of the rumbling, thrumming machines. There was something alarming in the way they waited, doors open like jaws.

Johnny shrugged and set off. A silent line of people stood blocking his way, presumably waiting for one of the machines. Johnny pushed through them, then turned to call back.

"Come on then! I could do with a curry."

The walk took over an hour. Fer moved slowly, the burning pains in her body taking time to subside. She hated being so weak. Still, it felt good to be outside, even though there was so much stone and metal, so little green. Occasional trees in the hard path along which they walked looked stranded and forlorn. Once she saw a wood by the side of the road, dark and quiet, into which she longed to walk.

They made their way down an impossibly long road, more buildings lining each side: houses and shops and taverns and some whose function she couldn't even begin to guess. Everything was noise and bright lights and movement. Ran walked behind her, warily watching for signs of pursuit, while Johnny strode off in front, stopping repeatedly to let them catch up. He, at least, seemed to be enjoying himself. Fer had to struggle to contain her alarm.

The noise was constant: a stream of the metal vehicles sweeping past them, each like the onward rush of some terrible beast narrowly missing her. How was it they didn't crash into each other? Occasionally she caught a glimpse of the people sitting inside: bored, blank faces. Once a large red vehicle came roaring down the road, forcing its way through the crush, wailing in savage alarm. Her heart pounded as it approached. She was sure it was Angere, coming for them. But the machine sped past and no one else paid much attention.

The breath of the machines, the smoke, made her cough and wheeze. The smell of burning and dust smothered everything. She tried to keep her breathing as shallow as possible, to let in as little of the bad air as she had to. The sky grew darker and soon became invisible beyond the orange glow from the tall metal lanterns that lined the road. There were no stars. More and more lights shone from the buildings and cars, blinding her. She slowed more, dazzled by it all, wary of stepping the wrong way and being struck. There had been no more rain, but the hard ground was still slick with a film of water. The orange lights reflected back at her in a broken swirl, adding to her sense of confusion, making it hard to see what was solid.

"Where are they all going in such a hurry?" she asked. They stood at the edge of a crossing, cars roaring by in front of her in a blaze of bright lights. The road looked as uncrossable as the An. She had to raise her voice to be heard.

"Rush hour. They're all mad to get home," said Johnny.

She felt so much anguish from the people in the cars. It hung over them like a fog. They weren't undain, that was clear, but they were still, somehow, diminished. She'd seen lovers, for sure, walking along in their bubble of private bliss. And children, too, irrepressible even here, brimming with delight as they played games of catch and chase. Games any child in Andar could have joined. But dissatisfaction consumed the adults. Where was their spirit? Their passion? Where was beauty or joy?

"They all seem so *broken*," said Fer.

"Yeah," said Johnny. "Working all day can do that."

"Then, why do they do it?"

"Why else? So they can afford to eat. And buy stuff. You know, things they want, houses and cars and whatever. Just like people in Andar."

"People labour there, of course, but not with this ... desperation. I feel an emptiness within them. Not all of them, but most. It's as if something has been taken from them, something so huge they don't realise what it is."

Fer stood as three of the large buses whooshed by on the road, a finger's width from her face. Was it all to do with Angere? The people seemed free; she could see no chains. Yet they were subtly enslaved, the bindings inside their minds. How was such a thing done? Some sort of necromancy?

Staring across at the buildings on the other side of the road, she suddenly saw how short-sighted she'd been. She'd raged against Hellen and her games, against the archaeon, against all of them, but her anger was childish. The undain were the enemy, the killers, the destroyers, not the witches of Andar, not even the mancers. Her differences with Islagray meant little; fighting the undain was all that mattered. She'd known that, of course, but seeing the people of this world she properly understood it. The conviction burned within her. She'd been right to come here, right to do everything she could in the struggle against Angere. Even if it meant complying with Hellen's schemes.

"Come on," said Johnny, grabbing her by the arm. "We can cross now."

Rusholme, at least, was more to her liking. It felt more like a market in some large Andar town. There were shops selling fruits and vegetables, stalls flowing onto the street to tempt the passer-by. Many were familiar: gleaming red fire-fingers, large lime-yellow waterheads, mountains of oranges. Also some unknown to her: boxes and boxes of succulent fruit stacked in small pyramids, red and purple and green. Other windows blazed with gold jewellery, sparkling in the bright lights. Or clothing in an array of brilliant colours: peacock, water-blue, rose-red, purple, each decorated with delicate gold stitching. From the eating-houses, delicious smells scented the air. She couldn't identify what the spices were. Something like bittersweet or fireseed, perhaps. They made her stomach rumble.

The normal rules that kept people off the road didn't apply here. Cars were parked everywhere, sometimes side-by-side, blocking the road. People crossed among them barely bothering to look, forcing the machines to stop. Everyone was less weighed down with resentment. Their minds rang with the lighter tang of anticipation, their troubles forgotten for a time. She saw several groups of people: families or gaggles of young men and women. It was wonderful to see smiles on their faces.

There didn't appear to be anything that could be called a *palace*, however. Behind the bright lights the buildings looked drab and scruffy, the square stones from which they were built crumbling and sagging. Some appeared to be held together by sheets of paper pasted across them, covered in colourful writing. Did Johnny really know where he was taking them? After the vast buildings of the centre she'd expected something dazzling.

Johnny stopped outside one of the eating houses. Inside, many people sat at tables, eating from silver dishes, while others hurried to-and-fro bringing them food. The door opened as two young women emerged, engulfing Fer in a warm, delicious blast of air.

Johnny turned to them in triumph. "See, it's still here!

We made it. Behold, The Golden Palace, the finest restaurant in Rusholme!"

19 – THE GOLDEN PALACE

"You're telling me *this* is the Golden Palace?" asked Fer.

"Only one you're gonna find in this city," said Johnny. "Come on, let's eat."

"But … won't they expect payment for giving us food?"

"Sure." He pulled a small, colourful card from a pocket. "But money, at least is not a problem. See? Still six months on the expiry."

"That means?"

"That means we can eat. Come on."

It was warm and bright inside the eating-house. By the door, a cooking area filled a corner of the room, giving off a powerful heat. Servings of colourful, spicy food sizzled in large, shallow dishes atop some sort of oven. Next to them stood a pair of deep, urn-shaped ovens. A man worked behind them, expertly twirling circles of dough in one hand, stretching them into huge discs before slapping them inside the ovens. Miraculously, he remained unburned. Tattoos covered his arms. He glanced at them as he worked.

Another man, dressed in white, bustled up to them. She couldn't understand his words, of course, but he seemed welcoming. Johnny replied, and they were shown to a table at the back of the restaurant. Above them, a fan circled sluggishly, although she couldn't see what made it work.

Johnny studied a square of stiff paper that presumably listed dishes the eating-house offered. The man brought them a jug of water then stood waiting, holding a pen and pad of paper.

"I'll order for us all, shall I?" said Johnny.

She nodded. He was clearly enjoying himself. Ran said nothing, but looked uncomfortable. It was like having some big cat next to you. A cat that knew it was cornered.

Johnny gave the order, a long list of things over which he took enormous care, repeatedly asking questions as he went along. Finally, they were left alone to sip water.

"I see no *Lizard King*," she said.

Johnny shrugged. "Worth coming anyway, I reckon."

The tattooed man weaved his way over to them, carrying a large, silver plate piled with some of the round breads.

"You wanted me," he said, placing the plate in the middle of the table.

"Fresh nan," said Johnny, his face all delight. "There's nothing like it. Trust me." He was right, the bread did smell delicious. Fer felt immediately ravenous.

Then, as the man rearranged glasses and plates on the table, she saw the tattoos on the backs of his hands more clearly. One of them moved. A purple and green chameleon, its eyes shut, wound its long tail around the man's thumb. Its iridescent skin sparkled. It was only then she realised she'd understood the man's words.

She studied him. He was old enough for brush-strokes of grey to be shading his black hair. His skin glistened with sweat. The lizard tattoos extended up to his neck, the horned snout of some large red iguana peeping out from the collar of his white shirt. Its eye swivelled as it studied Fer and the others.

He was a witch. A wise man. A warlock. They were rare enough in Andar; she hadn't expected to find any in this world. Here was the Lizard King.

"Yes," she replied. "A witch-mark told us to find you."

"Hares?"

"Hares. You know the witch?"

"I do."

The warlock's eyes were deep brown, intense, focusing on things Fer couldn't see. He paused as they conversed, as if the spirits of other witches spoke to him.

"We came to take the book back to Andar," she prompted.

"I saw what happened in the Library," he said. "The one they killed and the one badly injured. And also the girl, Cait, who took the book and ran."

"What happened?"

"She tried to burn it but it wouldn't burn. She tried twice, but Genera have it now."

"Genera?"

"Angere."

"What happened to her?"

For a moment, the man's eyes softened, looked directly into Fer's.

"They took her, too," he said. "I could only look on, powerless."

Fer nodded. Was there any hope, then? Her hunger vanished. The book was in the hands of the enemy. What chance did they have of retrieving it? What chance did they have of helping this Cait? They were lost. She felt, more than anything, suddenly tired.

"Were there no others to help?" she asked. "Other witches?"

"One or two," he replied, almost whispering. "Here and there. Not enough."

"Where?" said Ran. "Where did they take the book?"

Ran, at least, had not given up. The dragonriders did not know how to give up. Driven by their endless guilt, it didn't occur to them to stop fighting. She found it unsettling, inhuman. But, just now, welcome. By comparison she felt so powerless, so helpless. Her burning rage at Angere seemed futile.

"They took the girl and the book to a refinery," said the

Lizard King. "A place called the Leviathan Refinery. I didn't recognize it. Not in Manchester."

"And tell me, do you see … what will come to pass?" She was afraid to ask but couldn't help herself.

"No. Only what is happening right now."

"Can you still see her? Is she alive?"

"I think so. It's very faint, as if she's far away. Or she may be asleep. I'm sorry. I wish I could help more."

With that the man turned and left. Soon another waiter arrived with their plates and an array of silver dishes containing bubbling sauces and mountains of yellow rice. The waiter placed them upon little stands within which candles burned to keep the dishes hot.

"Might as well eat," said Johnny. "Enjoy it while we can, eh?"

He tore off a handful of the bread and used it to scoop up one of the sizzling sauces. Fer thought about the Tanglewood. Perhaps they shouldn't have left. They were safe there, as Johnny had pointed out.

She ate. Slowly at first, picking, but then with more gusto as her body took over. It was good food, spicy and warming, bringing comfort as well as satisfying her hunger. Ran ate methodically, trying a small amount of each dish as if testing them for poison. For a time they were too busy to talk.

When they'd finished, the waiter removed their plates and dishes, piling them up precariously onto one arm as if performing a balancing act.

Johnny stood. "There's more to come. Be back in a minute."

He walked out of the eating house. He crossed the road and entered one of the shops, its window filled with a baffling array of small machines and lights.

By the time he returned, the waiter had brought more dishes, sweets and something cold, like ice but tasting of fruit. Johnny was engrossed in the small metal object he held. He was clearly delighted with it. He looked like any child with a present. The people of this world, she thought, were treated like kings when they had money to spend but like slaves when they had to earn that money. It made no sense.

"This is cool, look," said Johnny. "They've improved loads while I've been away. Wireless, net access, everything."

"What is it?" asked Fer.

"It's a phone. It lets you talk to people who are far away. It could be useful. We can look up that place the lizard guy mentioned."

"How so?"

A part of the little machine had tiny symbols upon it. Johnny pressed them, making writing and pictures appear.

"The whole world is on here," he said. "You can find out *anything*."

She watched as his fingers moved rapidly.

"You mean like ... a library?"

"Kinda. It can talk to millions of other computers the world over. Neat, huh?"

A glimmer of hope returned to her. Whether it was the food, or Ran's determination, or Johnny's light-heartedness, she couldn't say. But they had to act. They had no choice but to act. She damn well *refused* to be beaten.

"Can you find out where we have to go?" asked Fer.

Johnny pressed more buttons. "Here we are. Leviathan. Large refinery in Runcorn, Cheshire. Not far." On the machine's piece of glass, she could see a small picture, presumably of this *refinery*.

"Amazing," she said. "But I don't see how it works. There's clearly no magic to it."

"For someone so down on materialism you've sure taken to technolust pretty quickly."

As so often, she didn't really understand his words, but she thought she knew what he meant. "Nothing in life is black and white. There are only shades of grey."

"Sounds like you're starting to understand how this world works after all."

She looked up sharply into his grinning face. But he wasn't mocking her. He meant it.

"Maybe so," she said.

A plan occurred to her. It was a small thing, perhaps, and wouldn't do anything to save them from Angere. But it would mean a promise kept, the right thing done. And that would make her feel a little better about herself. Perhaps, somehow, it would balance out what she'd done in the Tanglewood.

She closed her eyes and sought the archaeon. There was resistance to her, a wall of lurking resentment, but it didn't shut itself off completely. She soon found it sulking in its great cave, eyes shut once more.

"I have found your great library, bookwyrm," she said.

The creature opened one eye, slowly, as if barely bothering to wake. "You have travelled to another of their libraries?"

"No. But there is a machine. I do not understand, but it is linked to many, many other machines. Somehow, all their knowledge is available to it. It isn't a book, but perhaps … perhaps you only need learn a new language to use it? Just as you are able to inhabit the thoughts inside my mind?"

The creature stirred, lifted its head, both eyes wide open. "Interesting."

"The machine is yours to explore, archaeon."

The creature snorted a puff of smoke, tinged with flame. "Very well, then. Let us see this great library." It was full of anticipation, impatient to explore the new worlds.

"I will let you move across."

"I thank you for this, little witch. And what of you? Where will you go?"

"The *Leviathan Refinery*. Runcorn."

"The portal?"

"You know of it?"

"It is described in Hellen's book. The largest and most stable portal on this world."

Fer floated up the tunnel, the archaeon and its caves

fading away. "Does the book say where this portal leads?" She was almost shouting, afraid the bookwyrm would be gone before it could reply. But its words came echoing from the cave, even as she found herself in the eating-house.

"To Angere. To the very heart of the White City. The portal leads straight to the halls of the Witch King."

Johnny was looking at her with a puzzled expression as if he'd been trying to speak to her.

"What is it?" he said. "You look ill. What's happened?"

"It is nothing," she said, trying to stop her voice wavering. The thought of a portal to the heart of Angere filled her with dread. "May I borrow your machine for a moment?"

"Sure."

She took the book from her backpack and placed it alongside, just as she'd seen Hellen do in the cave beneath Islagray. Her hand shook as she leafed through it. She found the archaeon, twined around the large, first letter of the beginning of a chapter. Its body was purple and vermilion, vivid as if freshly painted. The gilded outline of its body moved as it breathed.

She touched it as lightly as she could. The creature stirred. It untangled itself from the letter and began to walk, winding its way between paragraphs to the edge of the page. It sniffed at the machine with its snout. Perhaps her idea was impossible. But then, tentatively, as if stepping into cold waters, the bookwyrm worked its way across. In a moment she could see its image there on the machine's glass, the words and pictures flowing around it.

The bookwyrm turned around several times, as if trying to find its way, or get comfortable. Finally it began to shrink, receding into the page, into the *whatever it was* that allowed the machine to talk to the rest of the world. In a moment it disappeared.

"Cool," said Johnny. "Now that's what I call a *worm*. It uploaded itself to the internet?"

"I gave it a choice and it accepted," said Fer. She put the

book into her backpack. "So. Now we need to get to this Runcorn. How do we do that?"

"You're serious?" asked Johnny.

"I am."

"Hire a car, I guess. Shoot down the M56, be there in an hour or so. But it sounds like a pretty insane thing to do"

"I'm going to do what I can. Rescue this Cait. I'm not going to sit here shaking in fear. I'm going to take them on. But you, Johnny, you don't have to come. This is your world; you could leave us, return to your old life." Ran, she knew, would not be persuaded. Johnny might be.

He looked around the room, as if assessing whether this really was still his world. "Nah. You wouldn't stand a chance without me. And I do wanna sail *Smoke on the Water* down the An. Find the ocean it empties into. It'll take more than an army of superzombies to stop me."

"Thank you," she said, touching his arm.

The warlock looked directly at her as they left, his eyes bright and full of meaning, even as he twirled more bread dough around in the air. *Good luck*, he was saying. *Be careful.* He would see of course. He would see what happened to them but couldn't do anything about it. She almost felt sorry for him.

It took Johnny some time to sort out the car. They sat in the small, drab room of a shop where he said they'd be able to hire one. The wooden chairs were uncomfortable, the air stale, and she longed to be outside. Johnny bartered and argued, all something to do with pieces of paper. In the end, the small, colourful card he said was money resolved everything. They were taken through a back door to a large silver machine. She climbed in warily. It smelled strange, as if filled with sickly flowers she couldn't see, but its black leather seats were comfortable. It was surprisingly large inside too, with enough room to stretch out her legs.

"They had a nice Jag," said Johnny. "But only a two-seater. So I had to go for the Merc."

She nodded, as if she understood.

Johnny moved off, clearly enjoying himself. Alarm thumped through Fer as they surged forward. She shut her eyes; they were surely going to crash at any moment. They shot down a wide road, great lines of the cars moving at speed around them. They turned corners, stopped at lights, weaved between other cars and then they were on an even bigger road, bridges passing high above them.

After a time she relaxed. Once you got used to being powerless to do anything, being in the car became quite peaceful. Johnny pressed some buttons and music came on: raucous, discordant, rhythmic. The sound emerged from all around her so that it seemed to come from inside her head.

"Hah!" she heard Johnny say to himself, as if he recognized the music. He pressed more buttons and it became quieter. Johnny sang along with it. She hadn't heard him sing before. His voice was melodious, gentle yet rich. He seemed to know all the words.

The singing, the warmth, the low throb of the machine, the large meal she'd eaten, all had their effect. She succumbed to sleep, letting it take her, while Johnny drove on, transporting them at this great speed toward the Angere portal.

She awoke when the car stopped. Johnny and Ran had opened their doors to get out and Fer, once she found the correct lever on the door, followed. After the comfort of the car she shivered.

She tried to take in the scene. She'd never imagined anything could be so ugly, so brutal. The refinery was vast and monstrous, all metal pipes and spikes and misshapen blocks, all of it dirty grey and brown. Red flames flared from its metal chimneys. The air smelled bad, filled with acrid smoke, dusty in her mouth. She was reminded of standing before the archaeon in its underground lair. But this was much, much worse.

"Leviathan Industries," Johnny read from a sign attached to the high, spiked fence surrounding the place. "A division of Genera, Inc."

She looked at Ran. The dragonrider was sizing up the fence, as if thinking about trying to climb it. That seemed hopeless; the building had to be well guarded. She watched as one of the large moving vehicles stopped at some metal gates. Perhaps they could sneak inside in one of those? A team of uniformed security guards swarmed around the wheeled machine, checking the driver's papers, peering inside and underneath the vehicle before they opened the gates. No. They would surely be found if they tried.

"We have to find a way inside," she said.

"There's a path around the edge," said Ran. He set off, away from the gates, almost at a jog. Fer glanced at Johnny, who simply shrugged. They strode after the dragonrider.

The refinery consisted of countless buildings, all connected with huge pipes of tarnished, stained metal. They worked their way around for long minutes, the spiked fence always to their right, more grim ugliness revealed with each step. But there was beauty to be seen, too. The land beyond was pleasant in many ways: rolling hills, small copses of trees visible in the distance. In the glow of the sunset, scattered birds flapped westward, as if trying to flee the fall of night. It must have been pleasant here, once, before they built the refinery. Had they deliberately chosen somewhere beautiful to spoil? Or was all this because of the portal?

The path sloped upward. It led around a rocky outcrop and over the top of a hill. Refinery buildings had been placed here, engulfing the hillside like some terrible blight creeping over the land. She could see no possible way inside.

"Someone coming," Ran said. He stood a few paces ahead, poised, ready to charge into combat. He would fight any attackers with his bare hands. He might even defeat some of them.

The rising path curved behind a mound of scrubby bushes, their rampant summer growth making them large enough for a number of people to hide behind. The newcomers might be people out for a walk, although she couldn't imagine anyone coming here for the pleasure of it.

More likely they were soldiers like those from the library, guards from the refinery on patrol, come to capture them.

She reached with her mind, trying to see who lay in wait. The overwhelming sense was, unexpectedly, of something familiar. Yet she was sure she'd never met any of them. She felt their anxiety. They were alarmed about who she, Johnny and Ran were, too.

"They're friends," she said. "Ran, it's OK. They're not from Angere."

Ran said nothing, but he remained tense, preferring to trust his own eyes.

"Johnny, call out to them. I think they know we're here. Call to them and say we mean no harm."

Johnny shouted some words in the language of this world. There was a pause, then he shouted some more, laughing at something. It seemed to do the trick.

Three figures appeared. A young man and two older women. The strangers' faces were clear in the harsh light from the refinery. The women were dressed in warm-looking woollen clothes, black or grey, but the young man wore only a thin shirt, a garish picture emblazoned across it, and blue trousers like Johnny's. As they came nearer, a look of astonishment lit up their faces. The young man, little more than a boy, still growing into his gangling height, stared at Johnny, amazed at the sight of him. The meaning of his words was clear even to Fer.

"You? No!"

The two women were certainly witches, probably mother and daughter. They stared directly at Fer as if they, too, were unable to believe what they saw. The older one spoke, a disbelieving hope in her voice. It sounded like she uttered someone's name.

"Cait?"

20 – EXTRACTION ENGINE NMBR 1

Genera, Inc.

Cait awoke, feeling in her bones the deep hum reverberating through the walls. She'd been lost in disturbed dreams, lying inside some great machine. Trapped in a cavity between roaring cogs, unable to crawl out without being crushed.

She tried again to find the well of calm cold within where the magic lay. If she brought it to life, bent it to her will, then perhaps she could escape this terrible place.

But it was unreachable. In her mind she glimpsed a mountain lake covered in ice. She recognized it from a holiday hill-walk taken with her mother and father, years ago. A memory that had become, for some reason, the way she envisioned the magic inside her. The deep waters of that lonely lake the well of her power. It called to her. But her legs refused to work, like in a dream. She shouted to the cold presence of the dead witch-girl, imagining her floating there beneath that steel-grey surface. No reply.

Had they drugged her? Cut the magic out of her somehow? It was the same with the seeing stone. Last night, desperate, she'd tried it, hoping to spot some way to escape her prison. But it was dead glass. It was useless. She was useless.

She heard the door being unlocked. She didn't want to face the world, but knew she had to. She opened her eyes. Her bare cell seemed even smaller than she recalled. The light from the fluorescent tube in the ceiling lit the brown walls with a distracting, flickering light. She'd slept fitfully, writhing in nightmares of fire, the ceiling-light the glow of the flames. There was no switch to turn it off. In the middle of the night she'd tried to remove the bulb by standing on the bed, but couldn't reach. She'd thrown a shoe to smash it and let the welcome darkness into the room. But she'd missed again and again, each attempt more desperate, more angry. When, finally, she scored a direct hit, the tube was completely undamaged. She'd returned to bed, curled into a ball, put the pillow over her head and cried herself to sleep.

She forced herself to stand and face whoever was coming. More than anything she longed for a shower, fresh clothes, a brush for her hair. The meal-tray they'd given her last night when they'd bundled her into the room, sandwiches embalmed in cling-film, lay on the floor untouched.

Nox kicked it aside as he strode into the room. Behind him came a woman, her black business suit in sharp contrast to Nox's relaxed casualness. She wore her blond hair pinned up. Her makeup was immaculate, the colour and shading as good as anything in a magazine. It made Cait's own efforts seem crude and artless. The woman regarded Cait with a neutral expression, as she might some unimportant report. Two men in white coats followed her, one of them holding a small leather box.

Finally, a small, ugly creature waddled into the room. At first Cait thought it must be the undain from the furnace. Her arm still burned where it had grasped her. But surely that creature would have assumed the shape of something more vicious than this hideous little goblin? She wondered how it had got here. It was the size of a dog, its skin mottled green and its belly hugely distended. It walked awkwardly on stumpy legs, its bloated stomach brushing the floor with each step.

She forced her eyes from it. "You have the book," she said, her voice hollow in the confined space. "There's nothing I can do to stop you, now. Let me go. Let me out of here. Please." She couldn't help a sob from catching in the last of her words.

"You really are as stupid as they said, aren't you?" said Nox. "You haven't understood any of it."

"Understood what?"

Nox ignored her question. He indicated the woman next to him.

"This is Ms. Sweetley, my second-in-command. After we have completed our tests, she will give you the guided tour. You need to at least try and understand your role in what is to come."

"Tests? What tests?" Her mind was a fog, thoughts and questions slipping from her as she tried to hold on to them. What *role* did she have to play? She'd meant to ask him about her mother and Danny, but somehow she'd forgotten. Were they dead? Or had they managed to escape?

Before she could speak, the two men in the white coats stepped forward. One took a needle-tipped syringe from the black leather box. The other seized hold of her arms, pinning them behind her as she struggled. She was too weak to fight. She let her legs buckle, trying to use her own weight to drop to the floor, but the man held her up, keeping her steady.

The other white-coated man brought the needle toward her arm. Desperately, she reached for the well of magic within her, tried to lash out as she had the evening before. She felt only numbness within.

"What have you done to me?" she said, wincing as the needle slid through her skin into the crook of her left elbow. The thought of never being able to work magic again was terrible.

"Ms. Sweetley will explain all about *Spiritual Refraction*," said Nox. "Slowly, so you can understand it."

The man in the white coat drew back on the syringe, sucking dark, viscous blood from her arm. Hadn't she read somewhere that if this was done wrong and air bubbles were injected into the vein it would kill you instantly?

"Never heard of it," she said to Nox, trying to sound defiant.

"Of course you haven't," said Ms. Sweetley, then. "It wouldn't be much of a two-hundred year global conspiracy if we told everyone about it, now would it?" The woman looked cross at having to waste her valuable time speaking to Cait.

"A conspiracy? Great. Now you sound like Danny," said Cait. "*Just* what I need."

"The greatest conspiracy of them all, in fact," continued Ms. Sweetley. "The truth is we invent half the crazy theories out there to distract attention from it. It's quite amazing what people will believe. They don't like to think for themselves, you see."

The man withdrew the needle, placing a small wad of cotton wool over the puncture in her arm. He motioned to her to hold it in place.

The goblin-like creature waddled forward. It licked its lips with a long, fat slug of a tongue and stood with its mouth gaping wide open, stumpy arms crossed and resting on its spherical stomach.

The man squirted the blood from the syringe into the creature's upturned mouth. Cait's stomach lurched. The goblin tasted her blood, eyes closed, swilling it around its mouth as if savouring some thick, red wine. A dribble ran down its chin. After a few moments it swallowed and opened its eyes. It nodded its head at Nox.

"Excellent!" said Nox. "So you really are of the blood. Now we are finally ready for our visitor." He looked triumphant.

"Visitor? What visitor?" she said.

Nox ignored her again. "You caused me some difficulty, Cait. You and the others. It's time you paid the price for that." He turned to Ms. Sweetley. "Show her everything now, Emma. Make her understand how pathetic they were to fight us." He was enjoying himself, enjoying her alarm. "I want her to see there is no hope. No hope at all."

The woman nodded. She took out her phone and made a few entries on it with her thumbs.

"My mother," said Cait. "And Danny. What happened to them?"

"Won't it be terrible never knowing?" said Nox. "Off you go, now."

Ms. Sweetley marched out of the room, heels clacking on the hard floor. Cait, glad to have the chance to get out of the room, followed.

She was led down long corridors busy with hurrying people. Two guards strode behind them, marching in step. She couldn't tell for sure but guessed they were more of the human machines that had pursued them across the city. Briefly, she toyed with making a dash for freedom, but soon abandoned the idea. It seemed pointless.

They went through a guarded door into an air-conditioned room whose floor was taken up entirely with a mosaic of monitor screens. A hundred or more of them, each showing a different scene. Two men in business suits stood in the middle of the room, gazing down at one of the screens, discussing something in urgent tones.

Ms. Sweetley strode across the monitor floor to a window in the far wall. As Cait followed she glanced at the images. Footage of a flood, people dressed in rags, huddling on the roof of a shack. Pictures from a city somewhere in Asia, its streets crowded with people wearing masks over their mouths. A scene of some war-torn town, children playing among the rubble. Walking from scene to scene, she crossed the room to join Ms. Sweetley at the window.

They overlooked a hall almost filled by a machine. It was hard to grasp the scale of the device at first. It was surely larger than her house, larger than her school. It looked like something she might have been taught about in history lessons, a steam engine, all gleaming black steel. Wheels and cogs whirred while pistons shining with oil pumped in and out of cylinders. A confusing network of pipes crept over it. On its top stood a tall chimney from which smoke or steam escaped, sucked up by modern silver piping and carried away. She could feel the roar and thrum of it even at this distance.

A great number of people worked on the machine: polishing it, making adjustments, reading dials and consulting sheets of paper. They were dwarfed by it; they looked like toy figures working around some beast they'd captured, its limbs still flailing uselessly.

"Beautiful isn't it?" said Ms. Sweetley. "You've heard people talking about *the machine* perhaps. It's fair to say *this* is actually it. The Engine doesn't normally operate these days, of course. It's a museum-piece, maintained for historical interest. But we're getting it running for our visitor. The last time he graced us with his presence, a hundred years ago, it was out of commission."

Ms. Sweetley was effusive now, as excited by the prospect of this *visitor* as Nox had been. At least it showed she was human, that a scowl wasn't her only expression. But quite why the machine excited her, why she found it beautiful, Cait couldn't understand. It was impressive, yeah, must have taken great skill to make. But it was only a machine.

"So what does it do?" she asked. "I mean, what did it do?"

Ms. Sweetley stepped up to the window. "Do you see the nameplate on the side of the main inversion tank? There." She pointed at a cavernous horizontal cylinder at the heart of the machine, polished black.

Cait peered down. Painted in red letters was the name *Extraction Engine Nmbr 1* as well as a year: *1826.*

"It extracted something?" she asked.

"Ah yes. Indeed it did," replied Ms. Sweetley. "With this machine we began the extraction of raw Spirit from the population of the entire north-west of England. Its range was huge: Manchester, Liverpool, across into Yorkshire, down toward the Potteries. We don't make them anywhere near so powerful these days."

"*Spirit?* I don't understand," said Cait.

Ms. Sweetley smiled, clearly enjoying herself. She reminded Cait of a teacher gently explaining the wonders of life.

"You could use many words. Life force? Chi? Psychic energy? Soul? Choose the religious or philosophical term you prefer. You would probably perceive it as magical strength. But we call it Spirit. We suck it out of people, refine it, then pipe it off through the Portal. Millions of barrels of it every year."

Another portal. She should have realised. It explained what they were doing here, wherever *here* was. It explained the goblin. Another portal and not one going anywhere good, that was clear.

"The machine ... sucked out people's souls?"

"It did. A percentage of their souls, anyway. These days we have perfected the technology. Miniaturised and fine-tuned it. Now there are billions of tiny Extraction Engines embedded in electronic devices the world over. You're in range of any number of them wherever you go. People are even good enough to carry them around, in phones and the like."

"It's ... incredible."

"Oh, in fact, the hard part isn't the extraction, but the storage and collection. There is always a certain amount of wastage, regrettably. We have a global network of tankers and pipelines that brings all the precious Spirit here. The whole thing is miraculous, beautiful to see. If you know it's there. Such a shame we can't tell everyone about it."

"But why?" said Cait, "Why would you do such things? I mean, how is it even possible?"

"Why? Isn't it obvious? It's the reason your magic won't work here, why you're probably feeling helpless and hopeless. We, of course, have immunity technology shielding us, but you, and nearly everyone else on the planet, are fully exposed. You are currently having a very finely calculated portion of your Spirit refracted out of you."

"But why?" said Cait again. She was finding it hard to concentrate, let alone to form a reasoned response. Faintly, she saw her reflection in the glass in front of her. A puzzled, lost look was visible on her features, projected onto the great machine.

Ms. Sweetley glanced at her watch, frowned, then turned to leave the room, passing between the two guards who parted to let her through. "Follow. I will show you why."

They trooped out of the control room and down another long corridor, this one smelling of floor-polish and disinfectant. It was like primary school or a hospital, drab and frightening at the same time, Cait the helpless child in a scary world. The two guards followed silently.

Ms. Sweetley strode briskly and Cait had to hurry to keep up. They clanged down a long flight of metal steps then came to another door, identical to all the others. A number and some letters were stencilled onto it in blue paint.

"Now for the greatest sight of all," said Ms. Sweetley, holding the handle for a moment as if the door was the entranceway to some fairy-tale land. She touched the card she wore on a chain around her neck to an electronic pad, waited for the green light, then pushed the door open.

A roaring sound engulfed them. They stood on the floor of another great chamber. One end of it was a bare rock-face, the building encompassing an entire hillside. A waterfall ran off the rocks and down to the chamber floor in a billowing curtain. Droplets sprayed Cait's face even from this distance. Above the cascade, carved into the rock face, she could make out the words *The Gates of Hell.*

A fat pipe, surely tall enough to walk inside, travelled the full length of the room. It was fed by numerous smaller tubes emerging from the walls. It led directly through the cascade. Next to the pipe, a slow-moving conveyor-belt carried a long line of metal containers. They were the sort you saw articulated lorries hauling, all different colours, with writing in languages familiar and unknown. They, too, went into the waterfall. As they did so, they punched a square hole through the sheet of water so it looked like the cataract was opening its mouth to swallow them. The water pelted each container angrily, a great drumming sound added to the cacophony.

"Here we are," said Ms. Sweetley, shouting above the roaring white noise. "There's the central pipeline that carries all the refined Spirit."

"To the other world?"

"To Angere. The Spirit we produce goes a long way toward fuelling the Undying Land. We serve our masters well. It's fair to say they would find it hard to manage without us now."

"What do they do with it all?"

"It gives them life. It sustains them. It is life-blood for the undain nobility, for the Revenant Army, for all who live in Angere. Do you see now, Cait? Do you understand the beauty of it?"

"And the containers?"

This was the woman's final secret, told with clear delight as she spoke closely in Cait's ear. "Bone. They are each of them full of human bone. Bone from the whole world over."

"What ... what for?" asked Cait.

"They use it to build. A strong and malleable material in the hands of the sorcerers of Angere. They construct their cities with it. They have very ambitious plans for expansion and a constant supply is vitally important. One day I hope to see them all: the Cathedral of the Moon, The Six Palaces, the shining towers of the White City itself."

"You ... suck the life out of some people and take the bones of others?" She should have felt horrified, angry. In fact there was little inside her other than a dull numbness. Incomprehension at what she was being told.

"We do. A very fine balance to strike it is, too. The more Spirit we extract, the more cruel and angry people become. So Bone yields go up. But extract too much and long-term rates decline. I studied it for my PhD. The correlation between Spirit extraction rates and Bone yields. It turns out there's a clear formula: an optimal extraction rate that sustains what we take from the herd."

"The ... herd?"

"Don't you see, Cait? We farm humanity. That's what this world is: one great farm we manage to optimise our production of Spirit and Bone. A farm you've lived in your whole life without even realising. It can be a delicate operation at times, and there are always unanticipated events to deal with. But extraction rates and gross tonnages have risen steadily for over a century now. By carefully manipulating events, managing the herd if you like, we've achieved stunning results."

"And this visitor who's coming," said Cait. "Who is it?"

She turned to face Ms. Sweetley. There was a look of awe on that beautiful face. There was something else too, there in her eyes, in the curve of her bright red lips. She was envious of Cait.

"Menhroth and his entourage are coming through the Portal," said Ms. Sweetley. "Menhroth the First and Last. Menhroth the Great, Lord of all Lords, divine ruler of Angere. It is the Witch King himself who is coming. By this time tomorrow he will be here."

Cait struggled to understand, to take it all in. "And me?" She'd guessed what the answer would be. She hoped she had it wrong.

"You, Cait Weerd, along with the Grimoire, will be our gift to him." said Ms. Sweetley in triumph.

"And ... when he returns to the other world?"

"Then he'll take you with him, of course."

21 – SCREAMING MACHINERY

Cait stood near the water once more. In her mind's eye, in her dream, she was in the hills, the lake one of those tarns that nestle unexpectedly in hidden valleys between high peaks. The water was mirror-still, the reflections of the mountain-tops appearing solid. For a moment she had the dizzying illusion of looking through a gaping hole in the ground.

She stood nearer to the water than before; she could feel the cold coming off it. Light slanting through heavy clouds painted the scene in vivid purples and yellows, illuminating clumps of heather and gorse.

Come to the water, said a voice on the wind. *Come.* Cait tried to move. Each step took effort. Her limbs were clumsy and the wind resisted. *Come.* Step by step, the waters grew nearer. But the strength required to move increased, too. It was tempting to give up the struggle. But she refused, thinking of the smile on Ms. Sweetley's face.

Suddenly, the resistance overcome, she arrived at the lake's edge. She stood panting on a soft lip of moss, the stone waters lapping at her feet. A little way out, ripples ruffled the reflected mountain peaks. Something moved below the surface.

She kneeled to touch the water, sending out small, semi-circular waves. The chill on her fingers was welcome, sharpening her senses. The coldness spread through her hand, up her arm into her body, dissolving some of her indolence. She cupped her hand and drew water to sip. It tasted of ice.

The disturbance in the water increased. Cait reached with her mind, searching for the presence, trying to coax it from the depths. There were splashes as if a struggle was taking place beneath the surface. Then the witch-girl broke the surface, floating face upward, her arms and legs outstretched. Her eyes were shut, her lips blue. The rags of her clothes spread around her like a halo and her doll floated nearby, just its head visible.

I'm here, Cait tried to say, not at all sure if she was doing it properly. The girl didn't respond, although she drifted closer, carried by some current toward the shore. Cait tried to reach for her. Rocked on gentle waves, the lifeless girl bobbed nearer. Finally, leaning out so far she was sure she would fall in, Cait managed to touch her.

The girl's eyes opened wide and she gasped at the air. She splashed around desperately, searching for her doll. When she had it, she reached out a hand to Cait, who took it and hauled her into the shallows. The dead witch-girl stood, feet still in the water, droplets streaming off her as if she was part of the lake and could not leave.

"I thought you'd gone," said Cait.

"I slept," replied the girl. Her voice was ice and fog, sounding far away. "But now the Masters' machines have stopped. The screaming in your head that stops you from feeling."

"But I'm trapped," said Cait. "When I wake up, I'll still be imprisoned."

The witch-girl shook her head. "They tried to bury *us* under stone. Such heavy stone, for so many years. But we escaped, didn't we? And so can you. I'll show you the way."

"I don't have the strength," said Cait.

"I'll show you," repeated the girl, as if it was the easiest thing in the world.

"Even between us, we won't be strong enough."

The girl smiled, looking suddenly very young. "Then we'll ask *them* to help us."

She nodded to the sky over Cait's shoulder. Cait turned to look. Clear above the peaks shone three moons. One was full, a perfect circle, solid and bright. One was waning, little more than a sharp-edged crescent slicing through ragged clouds. The third was waxing, gibbous, only a few days past the half-moon. Between the three of them, they lit an area of the sky brightly. But they were more than mere illumination. There was a depth to them. It was like staring into a hole in the sky.

"What are they?" asked Cait.

"They are lights to show you the way. But we have to help them."

"I don't understand."

"Wake up, now. Hurry."

"But …"

The lake and the mountains faded. The girl's cold hand was still in hers. She could feel its icy touch, even as everything dissolved into fog. Then the fingers slipped through her hand and the touch was lost. Cait opened her eyes to see the blank walls of her cell once more.

She lay on her bed for a moment, disorientated. Had she simply dreamed the whole thing? Imagined it in her desperation? The glaring strip-light was still there, filling the room with its harsh light. Nothing had changed.

But, closing her eyes, reaching inside herself, she felt the touch. A cold contact with that deep pool, clear and cool. What had happened to the machines? Why were they no longer leeching her magic? Was it all some trick? Some new torment?

There was little point in trying to understand it. All she could do was seize the opportunity, try and make the most of it.

Like this, said the cold voice inside her. *Walk to the lights.* Without being able to see them, Cait found she was aware of the three points of illumination. They were a warm presence on the other side of a wall. But it was hard to focus on them with the fluorescent glare filling her eyes.

This time she used her magic. She could think only of smashing the glowing tubes. The guards had given her two bottles of water with last night's food. She'd drunk one, the tepid liquid tasting of plastic. The other was sealed. She put her trainers on, then crossed to pick up the other bottle. She held it before her, closed her eyes and reached down for the magic, drinking in the cold power. She let it build within her then sent it through her hand into the bottle. The stabbing pains in her chest were sharp but brief. To feel them again was almost welcome.

The water in the bottle froze, crackling in her grasp as she turned it into a solid block of ice. She tossed it from hand to hand as it stuck to her palms. Holding it by its neck, she lined up the shot, then hurled it upward at the fluorescent tube. As the bottle flew toward the light, she followed it with her mind, directing it onto the right line.

Darkness engulfed her even as she heard the shattering glass. A thousand shards of crystal tinkled to the floor. Some fell in her hair, which she shook out.

She took a deep breath in the darkness. Better. Much better.

Now. Like this, said the witch-girl's voice, urgent now. *Reach out like this!*

Between them they felt into the darkness, searching for the three moons, trying to draw them closer. The pain in Cait's chest mounted. There was no sharp stabbing this time but a growing hurt, as if someone was tugging on her muscles, stretching them tauter and tauter. She gritted her teeth, pushing herself on through the darkness.

She saw them. Three lights a long way off, little more than stars. Three points of illumination in the whole universe. She worked her way toward them, the pain alarming, sharp as if her body were pinned to a fixed point that she was striving to pull away from. She cried out in the darkness.

The three lights grew brighter, noticeably bigger. Now they were circles rather than points. She could sense the effort, the yearning in them as they, in turn, desperately tried to reach her. It was impossible to know who was actually moving, she or the lights.

With a scream through her locked teeth she threw all her strength into the effort. The pain of it filled her. The lights swam forward, moving around her until she stood, finally, among them. Her body rang with agony. But between the lights, a pathway led into the darkness, like a series of stepping stones across a shadowed river. Only a film of the thinnest material lay between her and them.

She reached out a hand and, with her long fingernails, sliced through, three cuts like a cat's claw on skin.

There was a crack of something breaking, a hard stab of pain in her chest, then pressure on her ears as the air roared around her. The forced slammed her backward onto the floor. Someone screamed. It might have been her. She lay stunned for a moment, not knowing what to do.

Then she heard laughter. Gleeful laughter. *We did it! We did it! We did it!* The witch-girl was singing.

Cait looked for the lights. They were gone; everything was utterly dark again. The floor was cold beneath her. She held her arms around her pained body and tried to work out what had happened. It was no use; it was too dark to see anything. Yet she was sure the pathway had opened, the sense of release had been quite clear. She waited for a moment, panting heavily, while the pain subsided a little and her thudding heart slowed.

The seeing stone. She felt it cold against her skin. Perhaps it, too, would work now. She held it to her eye. At first, there was nothing. But then, as she grew accustomed to peering through it the right way, her surroundings appeared in dim colours.

A circle of deeper blackness was on the wall opposite her, large enough to walk through at a stoop. A grey pathway led through the circle into impenetrable darkness. She had done it. They, whoever they were, had done it.

There was someone coming down the pathway. Surely it would be her mother, or her gran come to save her? Her rescuer stood on the threshold for a moment, wary, peering into the room. Then they stepped lightly in, crunching shards of glass underfoot. At that moment, an alarm sounded, wailing loudly. Cait jumped, letting go of the stone. The alarm shut off abruptly, but red emergency lights came on in the room, revealing the other person in scarlet and blood.

It wasn't her mum or her gran, but a man she'd never seen before. He looked fierce, stripped to the waist and powerfully built. Dark tattoos covered his whole body, winding in sinewy lines around his muscles, suggesting the lines of magnetic force she'd failed to learn about in physics. His hair was long and bound in a pony-tail. He carried a sheath-knife in his hand, blade at the ready.

At first she thought he must be something to do with Angere. Apart from his alarming appearance, he had no aura she could detect. Was he some sort of human machine like the riders and the guards? His expression was fixed, like steel.

He spoke to her with clear urgency in his voice. A single word, pronounced oddly, as though he'd just been taught it. "Go!" He indicated the grey pathway through which he'd stepped. "Go!" he said again, as if it was the only word he knew.

He turned from her and walked toward the locked door of the room. He moved with a feline grace, like a padding tiger, capable of bursting into violence at any moment. He stopped and waited, knife poised to face whoever came through the door.

He was guarding her escape route. Another alarm sounded, close by. Once again, it was cut off. She heard slamming doors, running feet. The tattooed man didn't flinch, standing with his back to her.

Cait ran to the dark circle, hesitated for a moment, then leaped into the void. Behind her, even as she stepped into it, she heard the door being opened. Then shouts and a single scream.

She ran. The pathway was indistinct, a forest trail in the moonlight. All around was limitless dark. If she stepped off the path, she knew instinctively, she'd be lost for ever. The important thing was not to stop. She kept running, eyes fixed ahead of her. It wasn't far. She could do this.

The ground beneath her feet suddenly vanished. She pitched forward and sprawled on her hands and knees. But it was wet grass she'd landed on. She was outside, the air cool and fresh. The oppression of the walls was gone.

She looked around. She sat in a circle of three figures, as still as standing stones, each lost in deep concentration as they worked their magic. Between them, they held open the pathway down which she'd run. One was her mother, her face fully lit, a frown furrowing her forehead. Next was her gran, most of her face in shadow, just the curve of her cheek visible. The third was a girl, surely not much older than Cait was, someone she didn't know. Yet who also looked familiar. Some cousin, perhaps, her mum and gran had called upon?

The mystery would have to wait. She dared not break their concentration. Somewhere inside the building was the man who'd come through for her, who was perhaps even now fleeing back to them.

Beyond stood a vast fairy palace. Countless twinkling lights shone like the stars on a clear winter's night, dazzlingly beautiful. Gold and white sparks lit glowing halos in the air. It made no sense. She looked again. Now she saw the outlines of large, square buildings in the spaces between the lights. This was where she'd been held. The refinery. Strange how beautiful it looked in the dark.

"Cait!"

It was Danny, nearby, in the shadows beyond the witch's circle, trying to whisper and shout at the same time. She rose to her feet and ran toward him, between her mum and gran. She embraced him. A sharp pain across her shoulders made her gasp as he squeezed her.

"What is it? Are you hurt?" He held her at arm's length, looking at her anxiously.

"I'm fine," said Cait. "Could do with a bath."

"But your neck. How did that happen?" He looked horrified.

"It's OK, they didn't touch me." She pulled her tee-shirt off her shoulder and tried to look down. A huge bruise, livid purple, spread across her shoulder beneath her bra-strap. It throbbed heavily, at its core the sharp pain she'd felt when they'd broken through the membrane and opened the pathway.

"It was the magic," she said. "When we opened the pathway so I could get out."

Danny was shaking his head, looking at her shoulder. "Your gran was right. That stuff is scary. You'll kill yourself with it if you're not careful."

"We had no choice. This is better than what would have happened to me. They were going to take me through to the other world, Danny. I was going to be some sort of gift for their king."

Danny hugged her again, more carefully this time. "You're safe now. I ..."

Surprising herself as much as him, Cait kissed him on the mouth, smothering the rest of his words. It was wonderful to be with him. To be free, outside, with friends. They kissed until they needed to breathe.

"But what about you?" she asked him. "That thing threw you so hard against the wall."

"I was winded, that's all. No damage done. Apart from, you know, not looking very cool."

"You shouldn't have started going out with me, you know," she said. "This is all too much. You should have stayed with Lil. At least no one would have tried to actually *kill* you then."

"Ah, so it's official then? We're going out?"

She laughed. "Well, here we are, out together. I mean, it's maybe not a dream date or anything. But, well, yeah. I guess so."

"And you're a witch."

"Looks like it. Is that a problem?"

"Oh, I think the goth look suits you. But does this mean you'll have to get a broomstick?"

"Never seen Mum or Gran with one. Only a hoover. I guess modern witches don't use them. I don't think they'd be very comfortable to ride, somehow."

"Come on," he said, smiling. "We have to get out of here. The getaway car is waiting with its motor running." He put his arm around her waist and led her along a path beside the factory fence until they came to a road. As promised, a car was waiting: a large, powerful-looking executive car with its engine purring and its doors open.

"We'll have to squeeze into the front-seat together," said Danny.

"OK. So, who's driving?"

"Johnny Electric."

"Very funny."

She looked inside at the man in the driver's seat. The long-lost, presumed dead, ex-guitarist of Screaming Machinery grinned at her. "Hi Cait. So, you OK?"

There was another moment when she wondered if this, all of this, really was a dream. This made no sense. It was too much to take in. Then came shouts from nearby: her mum calling to them to be ready.

"Yeah," said Cait. "Yeah, just ... fine."

She climbed in next to Johnny, Danny squeezing in after her. In the wing-mirror she could see her mum, her gran and the young witch fleeing toward them, exhaustion and pain clear in their movements. The alarming man with the tattoos followed, knife still in his hand. At first she thought he was chasing them. But no, he was deliberately running slower so he didn't overtake the three women. He glanced backward repeatedly, alert for any dangers. Numerous cuts decorated his body. Blood flowed freely from a gash on one arm.

An alarm blared from the refinery. More lights flickered on, as bright as daylight. Engines roared to life behind the fence, motor-bikes and cars. There were shouts too, then gun-shots and more shouting.

"Better strap yourselves in," said Johnny.

The young witch hurled herself into the back of the car to be followed, more slowly, by her gran and then her mother. The warrior came last. He only had one foot in the car when Johnny hit the accelerator. The car leaped forward, engine screaming, tyres scrabbling for grip. They surged away from the refinery, picking up speed. The warrior was still not in properly, one leg flailing in the air. Finally he got himself onboard, hauled in by the others. They slammed the doors shut. The man was in a heap at his mum's feet, panting heavily. The car engine growled as Johnny climbed rapidly through the gears.

"So," said her gran after a few moments. "I don't suppose anyone brought a flask of tea with them did they?"

They sped down the M56 toward Manchester, Johnny keeping to the outside lane as they touched 100 miles per hour. Behind them three cars and at least six motorcycles veered in pursuit. In the sky, a helicopter tracked them.

"Why the hurry?" asked Cait. "We can't outrun them. They can just wait till we run out of petrol or something."

"We need to get back to Manchester, love," said her mum, her eyes barely open. She was physically exhausted. All three of them were. The effort they'd put into forming the pathway must have been enormous. Her gran was already asleep. The young witch, introduced to her as Fer, slumped against the car door, one hand on her forehead as if she had a migraine. Silver jewellery in her eyebrow was visible beneath her clutched fingers.

Cait reached back to squeeze her mum's hand. Hopefully there would be time later to talk to her, to all of them, properly. There was much to be said. For now, it was enough to be away from that place. Through the car's rear window she could see their pursuers, lights blazing, easily keeping pace with them. They weren't free yet. Would they ever be? Could they ever hope to fight these people?

She glanced at the man sitting in the rear foot well. He said nothing, cleaning the wound on his upper arm with antiseptic from a first-aid kit her gran had given him. Who was he? And, come to that, who was Fer? They must be related; they looked alike. But how could that be? There was so much she didn't understand.

"Why Manchester?" she said, more to Danny and Johnny. "What's going to happen there?"

"We're going to another portal." The voice came not from any of the people in the car but from the dashboard.

"You ... have a talking car as well?" she asked.

"Nah, it's a creature from the other world," said Danny. "It's speaking to us through the phone there." A mobile was docked into a cradle in the car's fascia.

"What sort of creature? An undain?"

"Certainly not!" said the voice from the phone. "I am an archaeon. And it is thanks to me you were able to escape from that place."

Danny rolled his eyes but said nothing.

The screen of the mobile showed a colourful line-drawing, like something from an illuminated manuscript. It was a creature, a small dragon perhaps. It was beautiful, if pixellated, the colours shifting as it moved. It walked around the screen, occasionally turning its head toward them.

"Then, thank you," said Cait, feeling a little foolish. "Um, what exactly did you do?"

"I switched off the Spirit collectors in the refinery, of course. Did you think your magic started working because you'd miraculously become all-powerful, little witch? Then I deactivated the alarms and sent confusing images around their security systems. Actually, that was all very easy. Breaking into their systems was the hard part. I had to tunnel through three different firewalls. A password had me stumped for a while but I was able to dictionary-attack it by roping in several million zombies."

"Zombies?" said Cait.

"It means computers," said Danny. "Computers on the net it was able to control through some back-door exploit."

"They have computers in the other world?"

"No," said Danny. "As far as I can gather, it lived inside books there but discovered the internet when it got here."

"It's a bookwyrm," said Johnny. "Kind of like a small dragon thing but not really in the same world as us. It spends its whole life feeding on the words, the ideas, in books."

"It uploaded itself," said Danny. "It seems very pleased with it all. It keeps going on about all the new stuff it's finding out. Says it's replicated itself and sent copies into computers the whole world over."

"Cool," said Cait.

"Best to humour it," said Danny.

"It's just a good job they hadn't activated the old steam-powered engine," continued the archaeon. "Even I would have had no control over that. Fortunately, we were able to free you in time."

"And this portal we're driving to. It goes to this other world?" asked Cait.

"No, no. It is only a Lesser Portal," said the voice from the mobile. "It leads elsewhere within this world, not through to another. It is transient, too. It opens for only three seconds. That is why we have to hurry. We have to be there in thirty-two minutes, twenty-six seconds. I doubt Genera will even know it exists. It's the sort of thing only an archaeon would know. If we enter the portal at precisely the right moment, we'll go through and it will close behind us. Then it won't open again for another one thousand, four hundred and forty-four minutes. So it will give us, give you that is, some time to escape."

"This is all assuming we get there in time," said Danny. "If there are traffic-jams or something, or we have an accident because of the insane speed we're going, we'll miss the portal and be trapped."

"No worries," said Johnny, once again cutting into the middle-lane to flash past a BMW. "It's all under control."

"There are no traffic jams ahead," said the archaeon. "I have, of course, checked. And I've calculated your journey precisely. If you maintain a steady one hundred and one miles per hour on this motorway, then take the M66 clockwise and the M602 for the city centre, you will be on time. Almost certainly."

The neon lights along the motorway stretched before them like a tunnel in the night. Up ahead, the sky was beginning to brighten. A clock on the dashboard told her it was just gone five o'clock in the morning. Cait let herself relax a little. The drone of the engine calmed her. For a brief time she was safe, inside a bubble between the horrors she'd escaped and whatever lay ahead. The thing to do was to make the most of it, take pleasure in the moment. She rested her head on Danny's shoulder.

Johnny tapped out a rhythm on the steering-wheel as he drove, humming some song. He glanced across at her and grinned. So, he must have been in the other world, too? How had that happened?

"I was really into Screaming Machinery for those first two albums," she said. "I mean, the stuff without you on is good, too. But your guitar made all the difference."

"So there are new albums now?"

"Two more. And a live one."

"Who plays guitar?"

"They take turns. Singh and Sarah. To be honest, they've gone a bit electro. A bit, you know, *sonic landscapes*."

"No!"

"They still rock though."

Johnny thought about that for a few moments, staring fixedly ahead at the road as he steered with one hand. He chuckled to himself. "So, what did you hear about my disappearance?" he asked. "Big mystery, yeah?"

"Yeah. There were loads of stories going around. You'd jumped off a bridge, you'd gone crazy, you'd changed your identity. People reported seeing you all over the place, on a beach in India, backpacking in the Amazon. Some said you'd been abducted by aliens, crazy stuff like that."

"What did you think?"

"You disappeared on Glastonbury Tor, a few hours after performing on the Pyramid Stage. They found your guitar but nothing else. There was no note or clue. The other members of the band insisted they knew nothing about it. So I guess I thought ... I hoped ... you'd gone off-planet for a bit. I mean, not literally. Just got out of the spotlight, gone into hiding."

"Actually, that's not far from the truth. Although it was weirder than that. And, at least at first, it wasn't intentional."

"So what happened?"

"Well, OK, I'll tell you the story. Haven't been able to tell anyone else these past couple of years. After the show, I went up the Tor like you said. Took my guitar and walked there. It took a few hours, but it was a warm summer night and I wasn't tired. The moon was this smudge of yellow in a hazy sky, I remember. It seemed like it was, you know, lighting my way. The sounds of the festival died away behind me. I wasn't too sure of the way but I was pretty sure I'd get there if I followed the road.

"I wanted to clear my head, yeah? The gig had gone really well, like you say. The band were on top form. We'd rehearsed hard. But I felt like I'd played enough for a bit. Everything had become so intense. Sometimes, it wasn't much fun any more. The cycle of touring and recording, you know? You live out of a van and, if you get lucky - as we did - you get to live out of a tour-bus instead."

He smiled as he drove. "It sounds lame, I know. It's not like doing a real job or anything. But still, I wanted to think about what I was doing, where I was going. So I sat up there for a long time, looking out over the world, just me and Mr. Shankly. My guitar. As the sky lightened in the east it was beautiful, strands of mist drifting across the fields, glowing as if the light itself had paused to rest. There was this stillness, breathless expectation. And I began to strum this tune. Playing has always helped me think. It's like walking, yeah?"

"Yeah," said Cait.

"OK, so after a while I find this tune. Or it finds me. But it's good, really good. It comes from nowhere, no effort, like all the best stuff does. I get into it more and more, forgetting why I'm up there, who I am even. I can't really do it full justice on the guitar; it needs *orchestras*. But still, I'm caught up in it. It shifts and moves, never repeating the same theme but clearly the same music. Like, *variations* I guess. I'm chasing it with my fingers, reaching for it.

"What happens next I'm not too clear about. I recall feeling like I'm *inside* it, like I'm riding it. I know I lost consciousness at some point 'cos there's a blank there in my mind. There was also, I distinctly remember, a clear moment of choice. I hadn't lost control; I could tell what was happening. But I accepted it, welcomed it."

"What? What did you accept?"

"I let the music take me. Leave everything behind. When I woke up I was in this other world. In Andar. I didn't have a clue where I was or what was happening. And it felt bloody great. It felt like ... being reborn."

"Can you remember the tune?" asked Danny.

"I couldn't capture it again. I think maybe I could only do it on Mr. Shankly, because that was the guitar I grew up with, learned to play on. If there's one thing I've missed from this world, it's my guitar. Strange huh? Oh, but I did hear the music again, though. Just recently."

"Where?"

"In Andar. Place called the Witch's Isle. They have this song they sing without ever stopping. And what *I'd* played was clearly a theme, a riff, from that: the Song of Andar."

"You were at a Half Portal," said the archaeon. "Possibly where there was once a Greater Portal that had sealed up.

There are places where the worlds are close without touching. It is well documented. The music you played resonated with that of the other world and it brought you together, took you there."

"Ah, OK," said Johnny. "Thought it must be something like that."

"If you'd asked I would have explained it all to you," said the archaeon.

They were on the M66 now, the ring road. They flashed underneath the bridge where she and Danny had been shot at. There was no sign of the pile-up. Had anyone died here amid the carnage? It already seemed such a long time ago, although it was only a day and a bit. She was lost in thought, going over and over everything that had happened to her, trying to make sense of it all. Was the undain somewhere nearby, pursuing them in one of the cars? Was Nox? More than anything, she decided, she wanted to close her eyes and sleep.

"The end of the motorway is one mile away," she heard the archaeon say. "Now you must follow the route I'm displaying on the SatNav very carefully."

"Sure," said Johnny, grinning. "Got it."

They neared the end of the M602: the short, straight motorway that arrowed into the heart of Manchester. Where were they going to go from here? Their speed was suddenly alarming as buildings and vehicles gathered around them. Traffic-lights ahead showed an array of greens and reds, making it unclear whether they should stop or not.

"Ah, excellent, the Police are setting up roadblocks," said the voice from the dashboard. "Yes ... closing off roads to channel us and laying stingers to burst the tyres."

"That's a good thing?" asked Cait.

"It's an expected thing. It follows their agreed protocol. My plan depends upon them doing so."

Cait glanced into the rear of the car. Everyone was awake, peering anxiously ahead as the car slowed into the denser traffic of the city. Through the rear window she could see their pursuers, flashing blue lights among them. Her mum smiled reassurance at her.

"Not long now 'till we escape, love," she said. Cait smiled back, trying not to look worried.

"They're funnelling you up onto the Mancunian Way," said the archaeon. "They will stop others from going on so the road is clear. Then they'll try to stop you up there, out of sight on the overpass."

Johnny glanced between the SatNav and the road. He had both hands on the wheel, his knuckles white. He was concentrating hard. They weaved through the traffic, veering more and more violently. Horns blared after them as they forced their way through.

"The stingers. How far along the flyover are they?" asked Johnny.

"They do not say," said the archaeon. "That is the unknown variable in the equation."

"Unknown? I thought you knew everything, wyrm!" said Johnny.

"Oh no, I merely know more than all of you put together. You have to hope you get far enough along before you hit them. And go faster! You have only sixty-six seconds left before the portal opens."

The road took them through a short underpass before rising. Up ahead, the ramp climbed onto the Mancunian Way, the short stretch of elevated road that crossed the city centre. All other routes were blocked by vehicles parked sideways across the road junctions. Vehicles around them slowed to a halt, instructed by messages flashing on displays across the tops of the police cars. Only Johnny ignored them. They had to swerve to avoid collisions. Cait's shoulder was repeatedly pressed hard against Danny's, making her gasp.

They hit the ramp at speed, jarring the car with a sickening thump.

"Hold on!" shouted Johnny.

"Thirty seconds," said the archaeon. "Go faster."

They hit the main carriageway of the Mancunian Way and accelerated. There were no other vehicles in sight now apart from, in the distance, the flashing blue lights of a line of police cars. Where could this possibly take them? They'd been directed up here for a good reason: they were trapped. There was nowhere to go. There was no sign of any portal, surely no chance of escape.

"Twenty seconds," said the archaeon.

"Stingers!" shouted Johnny.

Up ahead, a strip of upturned spikes had been laid across the carriageway to burst their tyres. The idea was they would slow down to avoid them or, failing that, lose control and crash.

"The junction we want is just beyond," said the archaeon. "You'll have to go over the stingers and try to keep control. Don't slow down, go faster! Then at least we'll have the momentum to carry us forward."

Cait glanced through the side window down at the ground, at the street-lights, buildings and roads flashing by. She felt very exposed. Small groups of people had gathered at the road-blocks, upturned faces watching them as they sped by. What must they be thinking? Dangerous criminals? Terrorists?

"There is no junction!" shouted Johnny. The car's engine was screaming as he pushed it faster toward the line of stingers. "Where do I go? Where do I go?"

"The junction is there," said the archaeon. There's no sign. There should be a line of cones in the wall. Aim for them."

"Where does this junction go?"

"Nowhere. They never completed it. It runs for a few metres then stops in mid-air."

"*What?*"

"You need to drive off the end! Now! The portal is part-way to the ground. Just do it, human!"

There was a loud bang as they hit the stingers, the car lurching as the tyres blew out, adding a rumbling, flapping sound to the roar of the engine. The car carried on forward but drifted sideways too, as if it was a boat being pushed off course by a strong wind.

"I'm losing it!" said Johnny. His teeth were gritted, a look of alarm on his face.

They nearly missed the line of bollards, but Johnny managed to swerve on line at the last moment. There was an explosion of orange plastic cones, then they were snaking along the slipway, lurching left and right as Johnny struggled to control the car. They were still travelling at over 70 miles per hour.

"Through the barrier and off the end," said the archaeon.

"Here we go!" shouted Johnny.

There was no way they could survive this. They'd all be killed, mangled in the wreckage on the floor twenty metres below them. It was insane. Cait screamed as they hit the barrier.

They were jarred forward, the seat-belt biting into her, sending another stab of pain through her chest. They left the ground and flew.

For a moment, everything went quiet. The car tilted gently forward. Then the ground rushed up toward them, a road and a roundabout, cars stopped and people standing with upturned faces, open-mouthed.

There was more screaming. Cait closed her eyes and clasped Danny's hand as they plummeted toward the ground.

22 – HEDGE WITCH

The Forest of Dean, on the border between England and Wales

Cait and Danny stood among tall trees. A wooded valley lay before them, the rolling hills a sea of green. Frost gilded the ground but the sky was brightening. Early sunlight flooded the scene with a hazy glow, making the world seem like it had emerged then and there from the mist. Toward the top of the opposite slope, in a clearing, stood a huge chair fashioned from tree-trunks, as if some giant was in the habit of sitting there to survey his lands.

"Are you sure we aren't in Andar now?" asked Cait.

"Sure," said Danny. "The wyrm said we'd end up here. That's a sculpture. There's loads in the woods round here."

"Come on, let's get back to the others."

They headed into the thicker woods. The layer of fallen needles underfoot was soft: a thick, foamy carpet of spikes.

"It's weird this thing with Fer," said Cait as they walked. "I mean it's all weird, obviously. But the way she looks just like me."

"Yeah."

"What do you think of her?"

"Oh, I think she's pretty hot."

"You!"

She slapped him and he ran off, laughing. She chased after him. They soon came to the small clearing where the others sat or stood around the car. Johnny grinned at the sight of them arriving together, out of breath.

The car had slammed into the ground after falling through the portal. The impact jarring through Cait's body had made her bite her tongue. It still stung. The car was pretty wrecked, its tyres flat, wheels leaning at odd angles, bodywork mangled. Still, they might have tried to get it started if it wasn't for the trees packed around it. There was no way the car could fit between them.

She wondered what people would make of it when they found it. Would they think it was another sculpture? And how would they imagine it had got there, this modern car trapped among trees that were decades old? She would never know.

Her mum and gran sat against a tree, debating something. They glanced up as she approached, and Cait knew they were talking about her. Fer slept on the ground in the shadows of the trees. They were all exhausted but from what Cait could gather, Fer was already weak, recovering from some recent ordeal.

Johnny sat on the driver's seat of the car, the door hanging open. He fiddled with his mobile, pressing buttons and putting it to his ear. There was no sign of Ran anywhere. Johnny noticed her looking puzzled and motioned upward with a nod of his head. There was Ran, high in the branches of a conifer, watching over them. He'd been badly bruised and shaken up by their landing. They all had. But somehow he'd managed to climb the sheer trunk of the tree and reach his vantage point.

"Got it!" said Johnny, standing abruptly. "Been trying to get this thing onto speakerphone. Now the dragon thingy can talk to us."

The archaeon's voice came from the mobile, tinnier, distorting slightly through the small speaker.

"Listen to me," it said. "You must get away from here.

Nox is searching for you and it's too easy to spot the car from the air."

"I thought you said they didn't know about the portal," said Danny, walking up to Johnny.

"In all probability, they do not," continued the archaeon. "Right now they have no idea where you are. But rest assured they will be looking. Looking hard. Sooner or later they will find you."

"But where will we go?" Cait asked. "We need to rest. We need to eat. And where is there to run anyway?"

"We'll worry about that later," said her mum. "First we'll head deeper into these woods. We'll find somewhere secluded and decide what to do. And before all *that*, we'll get some breakfast."

"Then eat quickly," said the archaeon. "And make sure you don't leave this machine I'm speaking from switched on, either. I've obviously made sure they can't trace it but it's on battery now. Preserve the power for when you really need me."

"You said there was some sort of shop nearby?" asked her mum. "Somewhere we could buy food?"

"There's a lodge half a mile away on the opposite side of the valley. You can't miss it," said the archaeon.

"Very well," said her mum. "Johnny, do please switch our esteemed friend off for now."

Johnny did as she asked.

"Thank goodness for that," said her gran. "I think it's rather enjoying this whole thing isn't it?"

"It's having a wonderful time," said her mum. "But it's not the one in danger is it? This is all just a game for it. An interesting experience."

"So," said Cait. "We eat breakfast then hike into the woods?"

Her mum glanced at the prone figure of Fer, still fast asleep under the trees. "Oh, I think we can afford to rest a couple of hours first." She looked at Danny and Johnny, standing together by the car. "Will you two boys go and find this lodge? Buy some supplies? Once we've all had some food we can set out. Things always look better after a rest and a meal."

"OK, Mrs. W," said Danny. "Do we have money?"

"No problem," said Johnny, standing up. "As long as they take plastic."

"Good," said her mum. "And don't do anything to attract anyone's attention, yes?"

"We won't."

Her mum glanced at her gran. "And make sure you bring back at least one cup of tea. It'll be cold by the time you get back but I think I can manage a bit of magic to warm it up again."

"We will."

Cait watched as the two of them set off through the trees. "Will they be able to find us again?"

"I'll make sure they do," said her mum. "I believe you've already seen a werelight in action? I'll send something like that to bring them to us if they manage to get lost."

"Good," said Cait. She sat down between her mum and gran, resting against the tree. It was good to be with them again, but she wanted Danny to be there, too. She felt lonely without him.

"Cait, I'm sorry about all of this," said her mother. "I'm sorry for not telling you about ... what you really are. And I'm sorry you're involved and all these terrible things have happened. I hoped you wouldn't have the craft, I really did. I wanted you to be a normal teenage girl. Have unsuitable boyfriends and listen to noisy music. But not this. I would give anything to protect you from this."

Cait laid her head against her mother's shoulder. "It's OK, Mum. You don't need to keep saying sorry. It isn't your fault I'm involved is it? Just as it wasn't Gran's fault you are. We'll just have to get by." They were her mother's own words, used often enough over the years.

Her mum laughed lightly and took Cait's hand. "We should get some sleep while they're away. Let's lie down next to Fer. We'll be safe enough with Ran up there."

"What if Danny and Johnny get lost?"

"Don't worry. If they do I'll know about it. Come on, let's sleep now. All these old needles are soft enough to lie on."

Cait was tired enough to sleep on concrete. She crawled across to Fer, who slumbered so deeply she was barely breathing. Her mum and gran followed. For the first time in many years, Cait went to sleep with her mother's arm around her.

It was several hours later when her gran woke her by stroking her face. The sun was high in the sky. Cait peered at her watch through bleary eyes. 10:30. Danny and Johnny were arriving, laden with white plastic bags.

"Did you get lost?" she called, standing and hurrying to them.

"Nah," said Danny. "Had to wait for it to open."

"Did you see anyone suspicious?" asked her gran, coming up to stand next to Cait. "Anyone taking too much interest in you?"

"There was no one," said Johnny. "A few cars on the road, some cyclists and walkers."

"Come on," said Danny. "Let's eat. We've got cheese sandwiches, ham sandwiches, water and lots of chocolate."

"And cold cups of tea," said Johnny.

They sat down to eat next to the car. Her gran shouted to Ran, using words from the language she'd heard Fer use. Presumably Jane had taught her. Saying nothing, the dragonrider half-climbed, half-slid down the tree. They left Fer to sleep. She had still barely moved.

They ate hungrily, in silence apart from the *oohs* of satisfaction as her gran sipped at the magically reheated tea.

"Better be leaving then," said Danny after they'd finished.

"I'd like her to sleep as long as possible," said her mum, nodding her head toward Fer. "She needs it and she'll be able to go more quickly if she's rested."

"What happened to her exactly?" asked Cait.

"She killed one of the undain."

"One of those monsters? How did she do that?"

"No one knows. Even she doesn't know. Witchcraft presumably."

"But the wyrm," persisted Danny. "It said they'd be looking for us. Shouldn't we leave now?"

"Let's give it another hour," said her mum. "You two boys can sleep for a bit too, then."

"Suits me!" said Johnny. He stretched on the ground and shut his eyes. After a few moments Danny, shrugging, did the same.

They finally left after midday. Her mum led the way, followed by her gran. Danny, Johnny and Cait took turns to walk alongside Fer, offering her an arm for support. The Andar witch said little apart from murmuring thanks - one of the few words she'd picked up - whenever someone helped. She walked with her head down, breathing heavily, each step an effort. Ran came last, always wary, peering into the woods.

They worked their way across the side of the hill. A road ran nearby for a time, cars and lorries roaring past. They made sure they stayed out of sight. A twinge of anxiety thrummed through Cait each time she heard a vehicle approach.

They soon left the forest of conifers and began to walk among more scattered trunks of broadleaf trees. There were many old oaks, their bark lined and rough like the hides of elephants, branches stretching out to hold acorns over the ground on delicate twigs. Sunlight shone through the canopy of leaves. The greens of the unfurling ferns glowed. Small birds, robins and little brown ones Cait couldn't identify, twittered and flitted from bush to bush, feasting on berries redder than droplets of blood.

For a time they followed clear lanes through the woods, some wide enough for a vehicle to drive down, some mere paths. They met no one else. They took to smaller paths cutting through the undergrowth, perhaps the tracks of woodland animals.

As she walked, Cait thought about everything that had happened. She'd been so elated at her rescue, at being among friends. Now all she could think about was how hopeless their chances were. They'd be hunted down sooner or later. There seemed no way out of the nightmare. What could they do? They couldn't save the world; they couldn't even save themselves. Not her mum, with all her witchcraft, not the strong, silent Ran, none of them.

And the worst of it was, *she* was responsible. She'd been asked to destroy the book and she'd failed. Failed badly. Despite all the help given her, the sacrifices of Jane, Danny, her mum and gran. Despite the awakening of her magic and the gift of the dead witch-girl. Despite all that, she'd failed. She'd given them the book. And by doing so she'd doomed everyone.

She ambled along, lost in these thoughts, telling herself how useless she was. The sun drifted higher in the branches, the air warming. They passed a small lake, rippled by a welcome breeze that made the reflections of the trees dance. Cait barely noticed. But Fer, her arm hooked through Cait's, spoke, the sounds of her language liquid where Gran's attempt had been faltering.

"What did she say?" asked Cait, turning to Johnny who walked behind them.

"She said she didn't think our world would be this beautiful."

They stopped at the lake, the scene framed by trees growing upon its banks. Four ducks sailed for the far shore, where the woods met the water. Cait studied Fer. She had so many questions she wanted to ask the girl from the other world, but before she could put anything into words, Fer spoke again.

Johnny translated. "She says you're a hedge witch, like her."

"What's a hedge witch?"

"It's a solitary witch, I think," said Johnny. "One who does her own thing, goes her own way. Doesn't take orders."

Cait nodded at Fer. Was that what she was? There was so much she didn't understand.

She was about to reply when a roar echoed through the trees. An engine starting, momentarily loud before settling to a purr. They stopped, looking for the source of the sound.

"Is that a motorbike?" whispered Cait.

There was silence for a time.

"Chainsaw, I think," said Danny. "Just some trees being felled." He didn't sound completely convinced.

"Come on," said her mum. "Let's keep going."

They left the sound behind them as they pressed on, moving as quickly as they could. The effort of it was clear on Fer's face. The ground rose as they climbed away from the road. Danny took Fer's arm and Cait quickened her pace to catch up with her mother.

"How do you know which way to go?" she asked.

Her mum nodded into the trees. "I'm following her."

Cait peered into the shadows but could see no one. "Who?"

"Look more closely, love. Not just with your eyes."

"Or use the stone," said her gran.

The trees grew closely together, their leaves a million shades of green. There was a bird high in the sky, its cry piercing. But it was circling, soaring on thermals. They couldn't be following that.

Cait was about to lift the green stone to her eye when she caught a blur of white ghosting between tree-trunks. She pushed out with her mind, feeling the lurching sensation of flying from her own body.

She saw the white shape again, more clearly this time. A bird, gliding from branch to branch a little way ahead of them. It moved in complete silence as it swooped through the trees. She knew she wasn't seeing it with her eyes. It was too far off.

"An owl?"

"Very good," said her mum. "A Barn Owl. She is kindly showing us the way to a grove where we can stop and talk."

"I told you," said her gran to her mum, but loud enough for Cait to hear. "She's going to be another like you. She's had no guidance from anyone but look what she's capable of. That spell outside the factory. And then again when she opened the pathway. In the end there, we couldn't have done it without her. She's only come into her magic for a few days and look at her."

Cait said nothing. But that wasn't right. Part of it, a large part of it, was down to the witch-girl within her. At some point she would tell them. But for now she preferred to keep that to herself. She had so much to make sense of that she couldn't face their questions. Not yet.

"A grove like the one gran was in? That roundabout back home?"

"Yes," said her mum. "Wild creatures often live close to them. Owls, especially. Perhaps that's why people think they're so wise."

"So is she? Are you talking to her?"

"No, nothing like that. She knows these woods, knows each tree like you know the streets back home. I'm just … giving her the feel of the place where we want to go and she's flying there. She thinks we're her chicks, perhaps."

"How long 'till we get there?"

"Don't know, love. Owls aren't very good at telling the time."

In the end it was only another half hour or so. They walked through deep forest, the trees' outstretched branches touching each other, growing through each other, as though linking arms. There had been no path for some time. Instead, they picked their way between mountainous brambles, their distant peaks unreachable.

Occasionally they plucked blackberries the size of Cait's thumb from the bushes. Fer, especially, seemed to relish these and Cait gave half of hers to the other girl. The berries stained her skin an inky purple, peppering her fingers with tiny thorns. She stretched as high as she could, but there were always larger and juicier berries out of reach.

The grove, when they came to it, was shielded by a rampart of the bushes. There was a clear gap in the leaf-canopy, the afternoon sun shining through, but there was no path.

Cait was about to suggest walking around to find a way in when Johnny said, "Follow me! I reckon we can get through here." He slid sideways between bushes, clearly enjoying himself, suddenly a boy again.

They stepped after him in single-file, contorting their bodies through the thicket to avoid being snagged. Even so, they were all scratched again and again. Vicious spikes armoured the bramble stalks. Danny swore under his breath as another raked his arm. Was there really a grove here? Perhaps they were simply hacking their way into the largest blackberry bush in England.

Johnny shouted from ahead. "We're there! I see the clearing!"

One by one, they staggered into it, bleeding from tiny cuts, hair wild as if they'd hiked for a day through the jungle. The blackberry bush was vast, surrounding the grove. The tops of it touched the lowest branches of the trees. It encircled them like a green wall.

"We'll rest for an hour or two," said her mum. "Then it will be time to talk. Time to decide what to do."

No one else spoke. Were they safe here? She was too weary to worry for the moment. They collapsed on the ground. Except Ran, who walked around the edge of the clearing, peering warily into the brush.

Cait watched him circle two, three, four times before her eyes closed and she fell into a fitful sleep. Confused dreams came to her for a time, startling her awake again and again. She imagined hearing a murmur of voices from the trees, and then, indistinctly, she glimpsed the figure of a naked man with a full set of antlers upon his head. Only they weren't any sort of hat; they were growing from his skull. He was badly injured, blood running freely from a wound in his side. He beckoned to Cait, calling her into the shadows, mouthing words she couldn't hear.

She woke up with a start. There was no one there. Of course. Her exhausted mind was seeing phantoms. She slipped back into sleep, and this time there were no horned men to trouble her slumbers.

23 – A PARLIAMENT OF OWLS

"So, what's to be done?" asked her gran.

They sat in a circle, the last of the sandwiches laid out on plastic bags. Cait rested between Fer and Danny. Next to Danny lay Johnny, apparently still asleep. Then came her mum, her gran and Ran. The dragonrider had continued patrolling, but her mum had made him join them, assuring him she'd know if anyone came near.

"I've been thinking," said Danny. "Maybe we could try and get back into the refinery and destroy the pipeline. You know, stop any more Spirit being sent through. That would cripple them in a single blow. We could use magic. Or maybe just, I don't know, blow it up. I mean, do we know if Spirit is explosive? Does it burn?"

"I don't think we'd get back in there," said her gran.

"It wouldn't work anyway," said her mum. "Even if we could damage the pipeline, or the whole refinery, we couldn't hope to keep it out of action for long. They'd get it working again, put it all back together."

"Yeah, I suppose," said Danny.

"And who knows if people would get hurt?" added Cait. "Not just us, I mean them, too. Those who work there. You know, ordinary people."

"True," said her mum.

"Why did they test me, though?" Cait asked. "Nox said

I was *of the blood.* What does that mean?"

"Another thing we can thank the necromancer for. He used his own blood in the ascension ritual he performed on Menhroth."

"But Ilminion died ages ago," said Cait. "What have I got to do with that?" Even as she asked the question the answer struck her.

"Yes, love," said her mother. "I'm afraid so. There's no doubt about it. You, me, and your gran: we're all descended from him. We all carry that blood. He must have had children."

"But our family's from Chorley, not Andar!" said Cait.

"On your grandfather's side, we are. But your great great great great grandmother crossed through the Manchester portal from Andar in 1819."

"Why?"

"That's another story. A long story."

"And Fer? She looks so much like me. We're related aren't we?"

"We are," said her mum. "She's from the side of the family that stayed in Andar. But hers is the blood, too. A distant cousin, no doubt about it."

"So that's why the monster in the library wouldn't attack me."

"That's right."

"But it struck you, gran. It sent you flying. Why?"

"I don't think it recognized me," said her gran. "I'm not as strong as you."

"And that man outside the library," continued Cait. "The beggar. He knew didn't he?"

"Yes," said her gran. "Tom has a few threads of the craft. He had a moment of clarity and recognized you. It must have been quite a shock."

Cait gazed up to the branches of the trees surrounding them. It was a grim thought that she was descended from this necromancer. That she was tainted with his legacy. Could she be trusted with magic?

"There is something else we could do," she said, still not looking at anyone. "We should consider it at least."

"What's that, love?" said her gran quietly.

She hadn't really thought about what she was about to say, the idea only coming to her as she spoke. "They need the book and they need our blood, yes? They have the book now. But we could at least stop them getting the blood."

"What are you saying?" asked her mum.

"The four of us are too dangerous. If we were … no longer around then the book would be useless."

"Cait, no! I'll hear no more of that talk," said her gran. She'd never heard her gran sound shocked before. Nothing *ever* fazed her gran.

"Oh, Cait," said her mum, gently, reaching across the circle to place a hand on Cait's arm, "Nothing good could come from that. Put it out of your mind. We're not going to give in and we're certainly not going to do their work for them."

"Besides," said Johnny, sitting up, "There must be others of the blood. Here and in Andar. You'd be endangering them."

"I suppose," said Cait.

"And the way I understand it," continued Johnny, "they won't go away if they can't get your blood. Ritual of the Seven Whatevers or not, when the winter comes in Andar they'll still cross, yeah? It'll take them longer maybe. Years of war and horror rather than days. But sooner or later they'll get us. Our only hope is somehow, dunno how, stop them."

Danny put an arm around her shoulders. "Plus, I wouldn't let you anyway."

"Well," said Cait. "That's good. Thank you. But that means I don't know what we should do either."

"I'll switch on the archaeon," said Johnny, taking out his mobile and pressing buttons. "Maybe it's got some bright ideas."

"Is there a signal here?" asked Danny.

"Let's see. It didn't work when we walked through that valley but we're quite high now."

"Well, it seems to me," said her gran, "that this news about the Spirit pipeline is important. I think we should tell Hellen. One way or another it could be vital."

"Why?" asked Danny.

"It shows that Angere has a weakness," said her gran. "From what Cait's said they're dependent on vast amounts of human Spirit being piped through. Quite why, I don't know. Perhaps they're addicted."

"So you *do* think we should try and blow up the pipeline?" asked Danny.

"No. But maybe Hellen can use the information. If this is Angere's only supply of Spirit, it makes them vulnerable."

"I don't see what Hellen can do, sitting on the other bank of the An, waiting to be invaded," said Cait.

"Well, neither do I," replied her gran. "But *she* might."

"I don't know, are we sure this whole Spirit thing is real?" asked Cait. "It seems incredible. Is it even possible? I mean, people have always behaved badly. They've been cruel all through history, fighting wars and that, way before Genera started those machines."

"Oh, it is completely real," said the archaeon from Johnny's mobile, its voice clipped and distorted because of the weak signal. "They've kept it well hidden, of course, but the facts are there if you know how to find them. The science behind Spiritual Refraction. Micro-collectors in electronic devices including, you might like to know, the one I'm speaking from. The global network of extractors and pipelines, all leading to that refinery. No doubt about it."

"OK," said Cait. "So we need to tell Andar. Can't we just, you know, reach out like in the library?"

"The aether is disturbed at the moment," said her mum. "I've tried to find Hellen several times and been unable to."

"You mean, you normally *do* talk to her?" asked Cait. Her mum seemed to have no end of surprises. Which was wonderful, but it also meant more had been concealed from her.

"Off and on, over the years, yes."

"The only sure way to give her the message is for someone to take it," said her gran.

"From what Johnny said, the portal in the library is sealed now," said Danny.

"True. So we'll have to find another way," said her mum.

"There are no other portals into Andar," said Cait. "That's kept them safe all this time."

"But there is a half portal. The one at Glastonbury," said her mum. "What do you think, Johnny? If we could find your guitar and get you to the Tor, could you do it again? Get back into Andar?"

"Dunno. Maybe."

"But you'd go back if you could? You said something about a boat?"

"Well, yeah, before I got sidetracked, I was travelling. Down the An. Me and *Smoke on the Water*."

"And you'd like to resume that journey." It was a statement, not a question.

"Yeah," said Johnny. "One day. Ideally I'd like to be sure massed ranks of zombies aren't pursuing me first, mind."

"So will you try?"

"I guess so," said Johnny. "But I will need Mr. Shankly. I couldn't do it with any old guitar." He looked at Cait and Danny. "Do we even know what happened to it?"

"It was auctioned off as part of the Live 8 thing," said Cait. "Went for quite a bit. Don't recall who bought it."

"Well," said Johnny, "at least there's a chance they'll look after it, whoever they are." He laughed. "I wonder what the legal situation is if I turn up and ask for it?"

"Here," said Danny, holding out a small, black plastic triangle he'd fished from the pocket of his jeans. "This is a start. It's one of yours. You threw it out into the audience at the end of a gig at the G-Mex. I caught it."

Johnny grinned and took the guitar pick. "Thanks." He turned to face her mum. "OK, count me in. Find the guitar, get to Glastonbury, play my way back into Andar. It's a crazy plan but I'll give it a go."

"Excellent," said her mum. "But I don't think you should go alone. Genera will be chasing you and it'll be dangerous.

"Oh, no doubt," said Johnny, lying back again.

"Noble archaeon," said her mum, raising her voice, her tone only slightly mocking, "May we still call on your services in our quest for Johnny's guitar?"

"I suppose I could manage that," the wyrm replied. "Since I am able to divide my consciousness between multiple avatars I can spare you some time. And you do venture to interesting places."

"Thank you. And I think two others should go with you, Johnny."

"Which two?" asked Cait.

"Fer and your gran. Fer because I don't think she's up to coming with the rest of us right now. And your gran because she'll be able to look after everyone."

"And I still think I should go with Cait and you should go with Johnny," said her gran. This was clearly the latest round of a long-running debate.

"But where are the rest of us going?" asked Cait.

"Well," said her mum, "I plan to cross into Angere and retrieve both parts of the book."

"*What?*" said Cait and Danny simultaneously.

"And I think it should be me that goes, not you," said her gran. "Jane taught me a lot about both Andar and Angere. I'll have more chance there than you."

"I'm younger and stronger," said her mum. "It's a simple fact. Johnny will need your help and I should go to Angere."

"And if I put my foot down and tell you I'm going and you're not?"

Her mum smiled fondly at her gran. "Then I'll disobey you."

Her gran sniffed. "You always were a wilful child."

"And the rest of us?" asked Cait. It seemed her mum and

her gran had worked everything out already. Dire as their situation was she still felt annoyed.

Her mum turned to Ran and spoke in the Andar language Cait had heard previously. She watched as Ran paused for a moment. She wondered if he was going to refuse. But then he nodded his head in assent. He would go to Angere, too.

"Your accent was very poor," said her gran. "If you'd heard it spoken as much as I have you'd never have pronounced *inlaind* like that."

"I'll get by. And besides, you won't be able to find a cup of tea anywhere in Angere."

Her gran made a *hmphing* noise, clearly not convinced.

Her mum turned to look at Cait. "And as for you, my love …"

"Yes? And where have you decided I should go?" asked Cait.

Her mum sighed. "I think you should come to Angere with me. I would do anything for you not to have to. And of course it's up to you. But it seems to me this is where everything is leading. It can't be coincidence that you've come into your magic these past few days. I think you have a role to play. If I thought it were safe here I'd never let you go, but it's not. For any of us. Unless we can beat them. And that is another reason why I will go. To protect you."

"But what chance will we have?" asked Cait. "From what I've heard we won't survive long in Angere. And even if, somehow, we did manage to find the two halves of the book, what would we do then? How would we be able to get to Andar and safety? I mean, you can't. That's the whole point. The river is in the way."

"I don't know," said her mum. "I don't know the answer to any of those questions. But what else can we do? Maybe it's hopeless, but the alternative is not to try. To lie down and die. Sometimes all you can do is have a go, do your best. We'll probably fail, but at least we tried, yes? And, who knows, perhaps we'll find a way."

"And if you *do* escape, I reckon you'll at least be sorting Nox out," said Danny.

"How so?" asked Cait.

"You said yourself the Witch King is coming through the portal today. He must know the descendent of the necromancer guy has finally been caught. When he finds out you've escaped and can't be found in this world, he's gonna be seriously unhappy. He'll probably assume you've gone to Andar. Nox will be in *major* trouble."

Danny was right. By evading Genera they'd be condemning Nox to some terrible retribution at the hands of the undain. That, alone, made leaving worthwhile. Maybe they couldn't save Andar but at least they could put an end to Nox.

"If I agree, you'll stop treating me like a child?" Cait said to her mum. "You'll tell me the full truth about all this?"

"I will," said her mum. "So far as I know it, love. I promise."

Cait glanced at Danny, then back to her mum. "OK. I'll go. But I don't think I'll be much use. Look what a mess I made of destroying the book."

"Actually, little witch," said the archaeon, "You managed to do the one thing that gave you some chance of surviving. Unintentionally, I'm sure."

"But I gave them the book!"

"True. And that is unfortunate. But the main thing is you didn't destroy it. If you had succeeded then all really would have been lost."

"Why?"

"It should be perfectly obvious to everyone. You have to use the book, break the necromancy by turning it against them. Fight fire with fire. There is no other power great enough to defeat the undain. It is their weak spot, the fact that they used this magic to become what they are. That undain lord has saved you all by plucking the book from the flames."

"But gran said we had to destroy the book," said Cait.

"Then it is a good job you didn't listen," said the archaeon. "If you had asked *me* I would have explained it to you."

"But wait a minute, what about me?" asked Danny. "You haven't mentioned what I'm gonna do."

"I think you should go back home to your family," said her mum.

"No."

"It's too dangerous."

"You said yourself nowhere is safe now. And I want to go with Cait." He glanced at her. "Plus, you know, it might get me out of doing my exams."

Her mum sighed once more. "I don't like it. You're a nice lad, but you're just a boy."

"I'm two months older than Cait."

"And what would your parents say if I let you do this? What right do I have to draw you in?"

"It's too late for that."

Her mum thought for a moment, studying Danny. "We'll discuss it on the way, OK? That's the best I can offer."

"What do you think, Cait?" said Danny.

In truth she was torn. Yes, she wanted him to come, didn't want to have to say good bye to him. But was she just being selfish? And what dangers would she be leading him into? She couldn't ask him to do that.

"I think … I think it has to be up to you, Danny," said Cait.

Her mum looked hard at her, eyes narrowed. She sighed. "Very well."

"So, we do have to go back to the refinery after all?" asked Cait.

"We could hide inside one of those bone containers," said Johnny

"If we have to," said her mum. "I'm not sure yet."

"There again, you should have asked me," said the archaeon. "Didn't I mention that I know more than all of you put together? There is another portal that leads from this world into Angere. Actually there are several, but only one you have a chance of getting to. It opens on that side of the An, but a long way from the river and the White City. If you're lucky, they may not know about it and you'll be able to get through without being discovered."

"Is this end of it near?" asked her mum.

"No. It isn't even in this country. But it would be possible to get there by hopping between Lesser Portals, if you happen to be learned enough to know where they all are. I've plotted a route that will take three jumps. Fortunately for you, it is pouring in Manchester."

"What does that have to do with it?" asked Cait.

"If you get that far, you'll find out," said the archaeon.

"Very well," said her mum. "And how far is it to the first portal?"

"Around half a mile according to the GPS in this mobile. This whole area is a nexus. The one you need is a disused mine shaft named Hobbe's Adit. It leads to a natural cave the miners reached last century, exposing the portal. There are many superstitions about the mine, no doubt because of everything that has come through the portal over the years."

"Is the mine shaft sealed now?"

"There is a fence around it and there should be a locked metal gate covering the entrance itself."

"Excellent. Then we will go there first thing tomorrow and follow your route across to the Angere portal," said her mum. "I think it's best if we travel together for at least the first hop."

"The Portal into Angere itself, though," said the archaeon. "You might not like it."

"Why? Is it dangerous?" asked Cait.

"No. It is perfectly safe. But you do have to leap into the flames of a lava pit."

From the corner of her eye, Cait saw both her mum and her gran glance at her, worried, each aware of how she felt about fire. Deliberately, she kept her expression calm, although there was a knot of alarm inside her. To actually jump into the flames ...

"A lava pit?" she asked.

"It is in Iceland, in the mountains, an area of volcanic activity. There is a cave and inside a small but permanent lava pit: a pool of red hot, molten rock. You jump into it and end up in Angere."

"Out of the frying pan," said Johnny, quietly.

"Well, so we'll need to get warm clothes as well as some food on the way, then," said her mum.

"There's another thing," said the archaeon, who sounded as if it was enjoying being the bearer of bad news. "This portal only connects the two worlds once every *sixmoon*, which I take to mean every half a year. So you'll have to jump in together. At any other time it is a Lesser Portal and you'll end up somewhere on this world."

"But how do we know someone hasn't already used it in the past six months?" asked Cait.

"Ah, true, little witch. You spotted that. Well, either you hope they haven't or you spend that long sitting in a cave in the Icelandic mountains to check. Those are your only choices."

"That's fine," said her mum. "Thank you for the information. That's what we'll do. If we can get to Iceland, we can at least escape Genera. And that will mean Nox having to explain to Menhroth how he managed to lose the descendent of Ilminion. The Witch King won't give him another chance. Now let's try and get some sleep. It doesn't look like rain and we can light a fire in this clearing to keep warm. We'll set out for this mine in the morning."

A roar swept through the woods even as they lay down. It was distant but clear: an engine of some sort. Everyone went quiet, listening intently, all except for Ran, who sprang to his feet. Another engine-sound joined it, nearer, coming from a different direction. Distantly, Cait could sense owls taking wing and swooping away, animals of the woods scurrying for cover.

"More chainsaws?" she asked.

"They're moving," said Danny. "Coming closer."

"Motorcycles!" said Johnny.

"How can that be? How can they possibly have found us?" said Cait, fear thudding through her stomach.

"Bookwyrm!" said Danny, shouting into the mobile. "How did they find us? Only you could have told them!"

"Nonsense," said the archaeon, its voice calm and measured. "Why would I do such a thing? It must have been something you've done."

"We've done nothing!" said Danny.

"Then tell me," said the archaeon. "The food you're eating. How did you pay for it?"

"I used my card," said Johnny. Even as he said it, realisation flooded across his features. "Oh. Damn. You think they noticed? They spotted the transaction?"

"Of course they did," said the archaeon. "Didn't I explain things to you? They would have known within seconds. They would have come straight here. They must have been combing these woods ever since. Really, it is a miracle you have survived this long. Did you not consider it odd your card still worked when you have been missing, presumed dead, for so long? They obviously left it active in case you ever returned."

"I didn't think," said Johnny.

"None of us did," said her mum.

"Can we fight them?" said Danny, jumping to his feet. "We have four witches and a dragonrider. I bet we could take them."

"No. We run for the portal," said her mum, getting to her feet and helping her gran up. "This is not the time to fight. Archaeon, which way is this mine?"

"Due north. But hurry. The amount of electronic chatter is increasing. They're closing in on you."

"OK. Come on!"

"But I haven't told you how to open the portal yet," said the archaeon. "Listen to me before you lose the signal or they cut me off."

"Speak quickly," said her gran.

"Get inside the mine and head downward. Always downward. You need to pass through the cut passageways into the natural caverns. From there, look for an eye-shaped hole in the ground. That's the portal. The bottomless pit they call it. Jump in. But according to the book you must carry bloodstone with you. Bloodstone is the key. Without that, you will simply fall onto the jagged rocks."

"Right," shouted her mum. "Now let's go." She set off at a run toward the tall ferns that were the only easy way out of the glade. It was already dark under the trees. She raised a hand above her head as she ran and a faint, glowing globe appeared for them to follow.

Danny, Johnny, Fer, Cait, her gran and, at the back, Ran raced after the light. The sound of the engines grew louder. There were three or four of them, impossible to tell how close they were or which direction they came from.

They sprinted through the ferns, fronds slapping their faces, following the bobbing light. They had to weave between tree trunks to avoid low-hanging branches. The uneven ground was treacherous in the half-light. Cait fell and Danny stopped to haul her up. A few paces later he tripped. They ran as quickly as they could but the engines grew louder, roaring like wild creatures that didn't have to pause for breath.

Fer's breathing was rapid and panicky. Would she be able to make it? Cait slowed to lend the Andar witch an arm. Danny moved ahead. Johnny was behind with her gran, who was muttering something about her age. Ran was somewhere behind them all, no doubt ready to leap to their defence.

"How do we know which way is north?" shouted Cait between breaths.

"Follow your mum," said her gran. "She'll find the way."

"What does the archaeon say, Johnny?"

"It's gone," he panted. "No signal."

They careered on, seemingly for much more than half a mile, blundering through the darkness. Cait was completely disorientated, unsure about which way they were heading and which way they'd come. She tried to calm herself, reach out with her mind to see a picture of the woods and their position within. She couldn't do it. Fear clouded her mind. She saw only darkness, with flashes of light here and there: wildlife fleeing, perhaps, or a brief glimpse of one of their pursuers.

She was about to shout that they were lost when the werelight stopped bobbing.

"The fence!" called her mum.

They caught her up, all except Ran panting heavily. Her mum worked at pushing over a wooden post that supported the fence.

"They're right behind us," said Johnny. The sound of motorbike engines was all around, like a swarm of insects descending upon them.

Cait and Danny moved to help with the fence. The post gave way, its base rotten where it was embedded in the ground. The fence sagged enough to allow them to clamber over.

"Wait a moment," said her mum. "They know where we are now, anyway." The light which still guttered near her head shot into the sky. After a few moments it exploded like a distress flare, lighting the whole scene with a bright blue-white glow. Up ahead lay a mound, presumably the entrance to the mine.

"Come on!" said her mum. They took off, over the fence and up to the entrance.

As the archaeon had said, a metal door was set into the ground. Icy air breathed around its edges. The door was rusty but a large, silver padlock kept it clasped shut.

"What do we do?" said Cait. "It looks strong."

Her mum held her hands to the metal of the door. Cait could sense her working magic. Ice radiated from her mother's hands, frosting the door. The metal pinged and cracked. Ice, thought Cait. Was that how magic worked for her mother, too? Did she have her own deep pool of cold?

Cait reached for the quiet place within herself. There was a flutter in her stomach: a whisper of the witch-girl as she helped Cait work the spell. Then cold was pouring out of her hands, too. The pain in her shoulder and down through the muscles in her chest sharpened.

"Enough," said her mum. "It should be brittle now. Stand back."

Cait didn't dare turn around. The riders were right on top of them. Her mum raised both hands and an icy blue light shot out, something like Cait's outside the factory. Her mum grunted then the door shattered, broken into shards of frozen metal.

They were going to escape. They were free.

"Inside!" shouted her mum.

Cait glanced to make sure the others were ready. The light wasn't only coming from the flare. A semi-circle of motorcycle headlamps had them trapped, pinning them to the mine entrance. Danny, her gran and Johnny were standing still, silhouettes against the light, hands held up in surrender.

Only Ran was moving. He bobbed from side to side, deciding which rider to bring down first.

24 – SHADOW PATHS

"Into the mine!" Cait's gran shouted.

Her mum paused to scoop up several shards of cold metal from the ground, cradling them in the upturned hem of her black cardigan. She stepped through the doorway. The blue light above them shot past their heads and through the doorway.

"Get in quick," said her gran. "And watch your heads. Especially you, Johnny."

"But, Ran!" shouted Cait. "We can't leave him."

"No choice," said her gran. "He's buying us time. We have to go."

They pressed inside. Cait followed the light, Danny grasping her hand. It was still inside the cave, the air old and settled. The shaft sloped sharply down. Shouts from outside became distant as they felt their way forward. The rushing sound of their breathing was loud in the enclosed space. A fat drop of water splattered to the ground with a *tap*.

The mine shaft ran in a straight line. Here and there, rusting rails were embedded in the ground. It wasn't as cold as Cait had expected. The worst danger was the ceiling, which was uneven and very hard. A couple of times she scraped the top of her head on a low-hanging spike. From the cries of the others, so did they.

"Down here, I think," said her mum. The shaft

continued but a small tunnel burrowed steeply into the darkness on their left. In the bobbing blue light it was clearly natural. It would be a tight fit. Cait didn't mind enclosed spaces; it was crowds that stressed her out. But this would make Danny uncomfortable. She squeezed his hand.

Running footsteps pounded toward them. Cait turned in alarm, expecting attack, trying to ready some spell. But it was Ran who emerged into the blue light, out of breath, his face cut and bleeding. He didn't speak. He nodded, then turned to stand guard while the rest of them took turns to worm their way into the side-tunnel.

They scrambled down a steep slope. She banged her head again and again, making it throb. She spat out grit that found its way into her mouth. The thick air was a weight in her lungs. Danny said nothing. His breathing was rapid.

She was about to say something when they emerged into a large, square cavern with a sloping floor. It was perhaps only the size of their living-room back home, but felt much larger after the confines of the tunnel. In the lower corner of the room, a trickle of water drained into a small almond-shaped hole.

"Here," said her mum. "I think we need to go through here."

Ran arrived last, sliding down the tunnel to land beside them.

"The archaeon said we needed *bloodstone*," said Cait. "How do we get that?"

"The archaeon thinks we're all fools. But witches know all about iron and I think it's the iron in the bloodstone that opens the portal. The steel from these pieces of the gate should do just as well." She handed each of them a shard of the metal she'd been carrying in her cardigan. "Careful, don't cut yourself."

Danny kneeled to peer through the eye-shaped hole. He picked up a rock the size of his fist and dropped it through. After five or six seconds it crashed and clattered onto rocks far below.

"What if you're wrong?" asked Cait. "What if it has to be actual bloodstone, whatever that is?"

"I'll go first," said her mum. "If I'm right you won't hear me hit the rocks and you can follow. If I'm wrong, well, you'll need to think of another plan." She lay on the floor to wriggle through the small gap.

"See you on the other side!" she said, and she was gone. For a moment they were cast into utter darkness. Each of them, Cait knew, was counting to themselves, listening for the sound of a body landing on rocks. But there was nothing.

A faint light came from behind as her gran held aloft a guttering flame. Shifting shadows danced around the walls of the cave. At the same moment, calls and footsteps echoed down the tunnel. There was another noise, too, like the snuffling of large animals.

"Let's go," said her gran. "Hopefully they won't know about the iron."

Cait lay down to squeeze through next. She clutched the shard of cold steel in her hand, held her breath and launched herself into the darkness. There was a dizzying moment as she tumbled through empty space.

Then she found herself sprawled on freshly mowed grass. Her mother stood next to her. Trees and bushes swayed around them. No one else was in sight.

"Well then," said her mum. "That worked."

Danny appeared next, then Fer, each tumbling to the ground, shock on their faces. Next came Johnny then Gran. There was a pause while they waited for Ran. Had he become involved in a fight? Had they captured him? Danny helped her gran up. Then Ran appeared, unharmed, rolling over and onto his feet in one liquid movement.

"Let's go," said her mum. "In case they do know about the iron."

Cait stood, realising the piece of metal she'd carried was gone, eaten by the portal. "Where are we anyway?" she asked.

"Dublin," said the archaeon's voice from Johnny's mobile. "St. Stephen's Green."

"Ooh, lovely," said her gran. "Haven't been here since my honeymoon."

They hurried away. Cait glanced nervously backward, expecting to see riders in black leather materialising. In the distance, the delighted shouts of children and the squeak of swings filled the air. Beyond that was the rumble of traffic.

"Where is the next portal?" asked her mum.

"You will have to search. It moves around," said the archaeon.

"OK, so what does it look like?" asked her mum.

"The book said you have to find a blind minstrel that sings of death and reward his work with gold."

"And that means what?" asked Danny.

"It means you must find a blind minstrel that sings of death and reward his work with gold," said the archaeon.

"OK, so, a singer," said Johnny. "Plenty of those in Dublin."

"They will be on the streets," said the archaeon. "In a doorway of some sort. That is the portal. Hear the song, pay the gold and you will be allowed passage."

"But how can the book know this singer would be here tonight?" said Danny.

"The minstrel is always here. They are a part of this place, much older than the city, in fact."

They'd reached the entrance to the park: a grand, wrought iron gateway that led onto a busy road. Across the road was a pedestrianised shopping area, bright lights shining through the gloom.

They crossed. There were one or two buskers about, generally ignored by the crowds. An artist painted head-to-toe in silver, pretending to be a statue. A string quartet and a man playing the bagpipes. No one who could be considered a blind minstrel.

They stopped outside a bookshop, its window filled with a display of colourful fantasy books. Cait wished for a moment she was a character in one of them. In real life such adventures were much too painful and distressing.

"We need supplies," said her mum. "Food, waterproofs, backpacks, everything like that. Johnny, can you use your card again and stock up for us? Take Danny. I think the rest of us should separate. Try and find this minstrel. Let's all meet back here in half an hour."

"They'll see the transaction," said Johnny. "They'll find us again."

"I know. I'm hoping we can be away from here by then. It might throw them off our scent for a bit."

Johnny shrugged. "OK. I'll do my best."

He and Danny headed up the street toward a large department store. Fer found a space on a bench and sat down, her shoulders sagging. Cait's mum glanced at Ran and indicated Fer with her head. The dragonrider nodded his head and stepped to the side of the street to watch over Fer.

Her mum and her gran set off in opposite directions and Cait, after a moment, followed, heading for a side street that seemed less crowded. She came across a few buskers, but none that were blind or singing about death. She felt more and more uncomfortable, more and more alone. Everyone seemed to be watching her. She probably did look quite a state by now. She stopped to study her reflection in the window of a pizzeria and saw the dim image of a wild-haired girl superimposed onto the seated diners. Her clothes were badly stained from crawling through the cave. Quickly, she hurried on.

She returned after twenty-five minutes having found no sign of the minstrel. Fer was still there, looking a little better. She smiled as Cait approached. Ran, unmoving, continued his vigil.

Her mum strode up a few moments later, a look of anxiety on her face. "No sign. When Johnny gets back let's interrogate that bookwyrm a little more."

Right on cue, Johnny and Danny raced toward them, barging through the crowds. They were laden with bulky carrier-bags, making it awkward for them to run.

Johnny shouted something. "Come on! We've been spotted. Security fascists in one of the stores!"

"Maybe they thought you were robbing the place?" asked Cait.

"It was after I used the card."

In the distance, a siren wailed. Perhaps it was coincidence.

"We'd better go," said her mum.

"You found the minstrel, yeah?" asked Danny.

"No," said her mum. "We didn't. But it's too dangerous to wait."

"Where's Gran?" asked Cait.

There was no sign of her in the crowds. Danny dropped his bags and stepped onto the bench were Fer sat, looking out across the sea of people.

"I see her," he said after a few moments. "She's coming this way. Quite slowly."

"Let's go."

Cait helped Fer up and Ran joined them. They pushed their way through the crowds to meet her gran.

"I found him!" she said as they drew near, a wide grin on her face. "Not far, down this way."

"We think we're being followed," said her mum. "Best hurry."

"I am hurrying!"

She led them down a quiet side-street, no shop windows, just brick walls, the sides and backs of shops, then onto another large road. They threaded their way through the traffic as it waited for the lights, hurrying down a street lined with bars and pubs. A burst of noise and warm, beery air came from each as they passed. Cait glanced backward, watching for pursuit. Ran did the same. She wondered what he made of this strange world. She felt out of place herself.

They heard the minstrel before they saw him. The tune was eerie, winding its way up the street, sounding both mournful and exuberant at the same time. His voice flowed from one syllable to another as if he was simply making sound. It took Cait a few moments to grasp he was singing in English. Something about loss and longing.

He sat on a tattered rug in the doorway of a crumbling office building. Dark, square windows filled its stone façade. The minstrel plucked at a small guitar-like instrument through fingerless gloves, singing apparently to himself. His milky eyes stared into the distance. He had a grin on his face, as if whatever he saw amused him, and he wore a grey greatcoat, stained and frayed, that could have been made at any time in the previous hundred years.

"Let's pay him then," said Cait.

"No. We have to let him sing his song first," said her mum.

"But there isn't time!"

"It's what we have to do. Reward him for his work. We can't give him payment if he hasn't earned it. That's the way it works."

They stood in a circle around the man for anxious minutes, listening to the music. Cait glanced up and down the street, expecting to see people running after them. The man, meanwhile, seemed oblivious. He knew they were there but paid them no attention. His song continued, sometimes striking off into new melodies, sometimes returning to familiar themes. Cait couldn't decide if he sang a single melody or several, or whether he improvised music without end. His words were still hard to understand, but the theme was clear. They were all *lost upon that distant shore* and *you walk upon the land no more*.

At long last there was silence. The minstrel stared into nowhere, unmoving, like a machine that had run down.

"Fantastic," said Johnny, with clear delight.

Her mum twisted the ring off her finger and kneeled to place it on the man's rug.

"But mum, that's your wedding ring!" said Cait.

Her mum shrugged. "It's the only gold I have. Plastic won't do here. And it's just a piece of shiny metal, love. It's not important really."

"But you and Dad … what would he say?"

"Oh, I think he'd understand."

The only indication from the man that he'd noticed was the slightest nod. He shuffled to one side to let them pass, indicating the shadowy archway behind him with a tilt of his head.

The sound of more sirens came to them, nearby but hard to locate, their calls echoing off the buildings. There were shouts from somewhere, the words impossible to discern.

Johnny picked up the carrier bags and walked into the dark archway. He disappeared.

"Quick now," said her mum. "Best we're not seen."

Fer went next, then Danny and her gran. Cait thought she'd smack into a stone wall when she followed, but instead she found herself stepping into a large, low-ceilinged space. She turned to see her mum and then Ran pass through a solid metal door with the words *Authorized Personnel Only* stencilled in red letters. She wondered if all the doors she'd ever seen with that were really portals.

"Hey, I know this place," said Danny. "This is the car park under the G-Mex centre. We're back in Manchester."

Cait looked around. He was right. Gleaming rows of expensive cars stretched into the distance, parked between the massive pillars that supported the building. No doubt about it. Which meant they weren't far from Central Library, back where everything had started. The thought didn't do anything to calm the fizzing in her stomach.

"Manchester is a nexus," said her gran. "Many portals lead to and from here."

"So, which way to the last jump?" asked Danny.

"No signal down here," said Johnny. "Let's go up to ground-level."

"Wait," said her mum, a note of concern in her voice.

"What is it?" asked Cait.

"There are undain here. Many, many of them. Hundreds. On the streets, all around us. Manchester is full of them."

"Must have come through from Angere," said her gran. "Sent to look for us."

"But I can't see them!" said Cait. In truth, she felt too panicky to focus her mind's eye properly.

"Look for the gaps, the spaces that move. The deeper chill in the night."

"So," said Johnny. "I'm thinking if you can see them, chances are they can see us, right?"

"Probably," said her mum.

"Then let's not get trapped down here," said Johnny. "Let's get outside at least, yeah? If the archaeon can tell us where to go, maybe we can get there before they jump us."

"We can try," said her mum. "Stick together everyone, OK?"

They went up a short flight of concrete steps to emerge by the side of the great barrow-bulk of the G-Mex centre. It was fully dark now. Rain teemed down, as the archaeon had predicted. It looked like it had been raining for hours judging by the puddles. Cait was soaked instantly.

Several people walked by, but she couldn't pick out any undain. She had the idea of using the seeing stone. With it in front of her left eye, Manchester became an indistinct green haze, the buildings ethereal, shifting around. She could see the sparks that represented people, but she couldn't identify any of the gaps where there should be light.

Open both eyes said the hushed voice of the witch-girl inside her. *Look with both eyes.* Cait reopened her right eye. Now she had both views of the city. A woman drove past, the flickering yellow light of her aura visible at the same time. It was awkward, but it worked.

Now she could see, by concentrating on first one view and then the other, which people were normal and which weren't. Her mum was right. The undain were *everywhere*. A bus thundered by that was nearly full of them. They looked like normal people but they were dead and empty where they should have glowed with life. Was it always like this? Had she walked among them, oblivious, all her life? It made sense they were in Manchester, so near the library, but how many were there everywhere else? Back in the forest, in Dublin, in the other places they might have gone? Nox must be directing thousands of them, the world over. What chance did they have against such an enemy?

She looked into the sky. On the top of the hotel opposite, a large CCTV camera perched like a cyborg bird-of-prey. It pointed directly at them. Was Nox watching through that, thinking he'd won? A gull fell from the darkness to land next to the camera. It, too, was one of them.

"Do you see them?" asked her mum.

Cait nodded. "We have to get going. I don't think we have long."

She turned to Johnny. "Have you got the archaeon? Does it say where we need to go?"

"It hasn't shown up yet," he said. "I've got a signal now, but no sign of the wyrm."

All her fears thudded through her. Had the archaeon betrayed them? Had it simply led them into this trap? The thought filled her with anger. She stepped up to Johnny and shouted into the mobile.

"Are you there, bookwyrm?"

After a moment, the archaeon's voice came through. "Yes, yes, I am here little witch. At your beck and call."

"The last portal, where is it? There are undain everywhere."

"Interesting. Well, let me see. The entry is cryptic but I believe I have deciphered it correctly. Where Oxford road meets St. Peter's Square, a puddle will have formed, wide enough to cover half the road. Leap into the middle and you will be carried away."

They half-walked, half-ran up Mosley Street. They'd be at St. Peter's Square in a minute or two, assuming they weren't intercepted. Did the undain know where they were going? Did they know about this portal?

"What's to stop them following us through?" asked Cait.

"Ah, did you think I wouldn't have considered that?" asked the archaeon. "This water portal behaves like the fire portal in Iceland. It ebbs and flows. In this case, it will only work once, each time the heavy rains come and the puddle forms. If you leap in together, you will be safe."

"But someone else may already have ..."

"Yes, yes. But that's unlikely in my judgement. You have to leap right into the centre."

"Well, it's us that's in danger here, not you. Perhaps you should tell us next time you make these judgements," said Cait, still cross.

"Wait a minute," said Johnny. "What about me and the others? We're supposed to fetch my guitar. Not whizzing off to Iceland."

"We've no choice," said her mum. "You'll have to come with us. It's not safe here. The archaeon said the lava pit becomes a Lesser Portal when it doesn't lead to Angere. You'll have to take your chances with it once we've gone through."

"One other thing," said the bookwyrm. "There will be no signal when you get to Iceland. You will be on your own."

"Well," said her gran. "We'll just have to try and manage, won't we?"

"Then I shall wish you luck," said the archaeon. "Thank you for a most interesting time. I suppose it is possible I will talk to some of you again, some day."

"Perhaps you will," said her mum.

"He's gone," said Johnny, pressing buttons on his phone. "Screen's blank."

"Then let's find this puddle," said her mum.

St. Peter's Square was in sight, traffic-lights pinning the waiting cars, a tram trundling by. More and more people thronged the pavements. Three young men with long, lank hair and lurid heavy-metal tee-shirts strode toward them. Cait lifted the stone to her eye. They were undain, all three of them, no doubt about it. She caught a glimpse of a different body, a different face. Their true selves. It was like looking at one of those paintings where you saw the same face from two different angles. *There* was the boyish grin and *there*, at the same time, the hungry snarl of the monster.

"Across the road!" shouted Cait, weaving between the stopped cars. The others followed. Ran, who seemed to be able to spot the creatures too, walked backward so he could keep a close eye on the three.

The undain followed them. Cait had the distinct impression of being herded. There was no urgency to the creatures' actions. Why didn't they attack?

They reached the corner of St. Peter's Square. There was Central Library. She'd come full circle. Strange how events had led her back here. The undain were everywhere, on the streets, on the roofs. She was seeing them clearly now, even without the stone. There was a sense of emptiness, of wrongness when you looked at them. Each turned to watch as Cait and the others arrived, like an audience when the actors appear on stage. One of them, standing like a statue on top of the war memorial, leaped. It didn't break stride as it landed across the road and marched toward them. It was in the shape of a woman about her mum's age, but Cait could see another form flickering in and out of existence. A misshapen, winged creature with an overlarge head full of clashing teeth.

No, said the voice of the witch-girl suddenly, sounding very faint. *Not here again, please.* Cait tried to speak to her, find out what she meant, but there was no response.

To their right, a short way away, was the huge puddle the archaeon had described. It had to be the one. It was so deep that cars crept around it rather than driving through. Pedestrians tip-toed on the pavement, hugging the walls of the buildings.

The urge to run rose within Cait. The water looked deep and dark, the orange lights of the city shimmering on its surface. What if someone had jumped in already? Someone messing around or drunk? She had a vision of the seven of them standing knee-deep in the puddle while a hundred Angere monsters surrounded them. They'd have no chance and, what's more, they'd look pretty stupid. Or what if they *had* walked into a trap, if the archaeon really was their enemy? It was quite clear: if this large, unlikely-looking puddle wasn't a doorway out of Manchester, they were doomed.

One of the monsters landed from the skies in front of them. A man in his forties wearing a smart business-suit. He carried a leather brief-case, but it was a clawed talon rather than fingers that curled around the handle. He must have leaped off the high building to their right. With a snarl, he charged, suddenly all mouth and teeth. For the briefest moment she heard a chorus of terrible screams and wails coming from the monster, as if a thousand lost souls were imprisoned within it. She found herself wondering how many people had died to fuel its unnatural life. Had they been killed recently? Were they people she'd actually met? Or were these ancient crimes, hundreds of years old?

Danny jumped between them, colliding with the undain. The creature roared and whipped around, lashing out at Danny, knocking him to the wet ground.

"Run!" shouted her mum. They were only a few paces from the edge of the puddle. A car drove past, sending a fan of water over it.

"Danny!" shouted Cait. "We have to help him! Mum, Gran, do something!"

She stopped. There were so many undain crowding them she lost sight of Danny. The monsters were within touching distance. Some didn't bother to maintain their human aspects any more. They merged into one laughing, snarling mass. An acrid smell of burning metal and decay filled the air, making her feel sick and weak.

Distantly she heard Danny's muffled shouts. "Get away! Get away!"

"No!" she shouted, pushing toward him and the undain. Ran stood next to her, fighting to protect her.

Her mum seized hold of her arm. "We must go! It's us they want, not him."

At the same moment, something grabbed Cait's ankle. A pale claw reached out of a drainage grid, fingers clamping tightly onto her. Revulsion at the creature's touch filled her. Instinctively she lashed out, sending a jolt of icy magic into the creature without even stopping to think what she was doing. The sharp pain hit her a moment later but she ignored it. The iron grasp on her ankle lessened and Cait kicked and kicked to shake herself free.

She turned to the puddle and her gran took her other hand. The undain surrounded them now, their hot breath filling the air. But they still moved slowly, almost casually, enjoying a game they thought they'd won.

"After three," said her mother. "One, two, three …"

They jumped together, hurling themselves into the middle of the pool of water.

25 – NIGHT FALL

Mount Öræfajökull, Iceland

Fer expected to land in water, but a bitter cold seized hold of her. For a moment she thought they were stranded in the aether, the limitless void sucking their life away. But light blinded her. It took a few moments to adjust to the dazzling brilliance of the scene before her. They stood part way up a mountain, a precarious ledge far above ground level.

Before them lay a landscape of rock and snow, breathtakingly beautiful. She couldn't grasp the scale of it; she felt tiny and huge at the same time. Snow and rock reached all the way to the edges of the world. At the same time, she felt she could reach out and touch the tips of those far mountains. The sky glowed blue. The sun hung low in the west, but it was bright still, warming the ice to the colour of honey. It was quiet. Nothing moved.

She looked at her companions, making sure everyone had come through safely. Strange how protective she felt about them, how she was beginning to see Cait and Cait's mother and grandmother as her family. Her coven. She had no hope, now, of saving Andar from what was coming. But if she could help destroy the man who controlled Angere in this world, she'd be happy. A battle won. Angere itself was a fight for another day.

Odd, though, how it had taken coming to this world to feel she *belonged.* Perhaps it was because the witches here were so powerless, so hunted. She'd worked with Fiona and Catherine to rescue Cait from that vast, metal building without even stopping to think about it. In Andar, if Hellen or anyone else had suggested such a thing, she'd probably have refused, resenting the intrusion. Here, she'd consented without a thought. Having seen what this world did to people, she'd do *anything* in the fight against Genera.

If she'd stayed in Andar, if that undain had never flown across the An, perhaps she'd have ended up at Islagray after all. Perhaps she would have been another Hellen. A strange thought. She would never know, now.

She hooked her arm through Cait's. Her cousin, her sister from another world.

Tears blurred Cait's eyes. What was happening to Danny? She wanted to step back through the portal, try and save him. Was this what it had been like for him, when the undain had taken her at the furnace? The pang of loss was sharp inside her. Her shoulder throbbed and she couldn't tell whether this was the backlash from the magic or the pain of his absence.

Fer, standing next to her, slid her arm through Cait's. Cait had often offered Fer an arm in their long chase but now it was the other way round. Fer gave her support. Cait smiled at the girl from Andar. She wished they'd known each other all their lives. It felt like discovering a sister you never knew you had. And no time, now, to talk.

"We'll try and find him," said her gran, standing next to Cait. "Wherever we end up once we jump through the portal, we'll try and rescue him, love." She placed fleeces from Johnny and Danny's shopping spree around her and

Fer's shoulders. "The archaeon may know something. Or the Lizard King."

Cait nodded but didn't reply. They didn't even know if Danny would be kept in this world. They might take him through the Runcorn portal for some terrible purpose. Or he might be dead already.

She turned to gaze at the bulk of the mountain towering over them. They should go. Nox would be desperate; he'd stop at nothing to capture them. They had to find this portal before Genera came. Otherwise Nox had won and Danny's loss was for nothing.

"Look." It was Ran's voice. He stood a few metres up the slope, examining something in the thin snow that covered the ground. Beyond him, a steep path wound up into a cave entrance, like a long tongue protruding from the mountain's mouth. It was inaccessible to anyone not using the portals.

Ran looked at them and said more words that Cait didn't understand.

"Footprints," said Johnny, translating. "He says there are fresh footprints."

No one speaking, they went to see. The footprints in the snow were quite clear, leading up into the cave. Ran spoke again and Johnny translated. "A man. He walked into the cave recently. Within the last hour."

They glanced at each other, alarm clear on everyone's face. Cait wiped her eyes with the sleeve of her fleece. She saw who this must be, who had preceded them into the cave. And so they had failed after all. *She* had failed and *he* had won.

"But that means we're cut off from Angere," said Johnny. "And we can't wait here for six months. The next time it rains in Manchester they'll come through and get us. And that's not gonna be very long is it?"

"No," said Cait. "You're wrong, Johnny. The portal's still open. He's waiting for us."

"What do you mean? Who is?" said Johnny.

"Come on," said Cait. She turned to climb, using her hands to steady herself as she scrambled up. She would face him now, before she stopped to think about what she was doing. Ran followed, silent, ready as ever to protect her.

"Cait?" called her mum.

"Come on," said Cait. "He'll be waiting."

The wind at her back was welcome; it seemed to keep her pinned to the side of the mountain. She concentrated on the ground. Heights didn't worry her, but the scale of the panorama was dizzying. She felt light-headed from the altitude. She had the perverse desire to step off and see if she could fly. Perhaps she could. Her mum had done it. But now wasn't the time to try.

The snow beneath her feet thinned, the ground becoming scattered stone shards. Distant heat warmed her face. Her skin was already cracked and dry from the wind. She longed for moisturiser.

She stood at the cave entrance. It was larger than she'd thought, tall enough to walk through without stooping. A red glow tinged the blackness. The glow from the lava pit. She glanced at the others following in a line. She was surprised how steep the path was.

She stepped inside. From the red glow the cave looked small, a tear-shaped room with a floor that angled to its centre. The lava pit was a rough circle of fire in the middle, colouring the walls of the cave, the heat coming off it intense.

And there, a mere silhouette in front of it, was a man waiting for them.

"Hello, Nox," she said.

Ran and the others arrived one by one at her shoulder. Her mum lit another hazy ball of light and set it bobbing over their heads.

Nox seemed calm, as if waiting for a meeting to start. Something in his face looked odd, though. The arrogant grin was there but with less of an edge. Perhaps it was just the light. He wore sensible walking gear: boots, waterproof trousers, a fleece. He had come prepared. He was alone, though. Why was he alone? He had a rucksack on his back but in his hand, oddly, he carried a black leather brief case.

"Hello again, Cait," he said.

"Get out of our way, Nox," said her mum. "You won't stop us using the portal. I'll kill you first."

Cait could tell her mum was working on some magic. She could feel the power gathering, like a livid storm on the horizon, glimpsed in the corner of her eye. The bobbing blue light above them dimmed as she concentrated her strength. It didn't make sense, though. Nox was never alone. He always had his riders, his guards with him. And now here he was.

"Wait!" shouted Cait. "Don't kill him. He's not here to stop us." A picture slotted together in her mind. Things became clear. She'd been wrong. They hadn't lost, not yet.

"Of course he wants to stop us," said her gran. Her voice quavered as she spoke.

"No," said Cait. "Tell us, Nox. Tell us what they did."

For an instant, his self-assurance slipped. A frown, an expression of pain moved across his face. He stared at the ground, pausing before replying. "They threw me out," he said.

"Speak up," said Cait.

"They promised me eternal life!" He was suddenly shouting, his calm demeanour lost. "Promised power and riches beyond my dreams. Then they took it away. All because you escaped. Because you slipped through my hands three times. Do you see? But I left before they could take me. And now I'll get revenge."

"On Genera?"

"Genera, Angere. The undead lords and ladies. The Holy Court. The Witch King himself. All of them. They thought they could toss me aside but they were wrong. Attention to detail, you see? I made plans even for this eventuality, unlikely as it was."

"You knew about this portal?"

"I've always made it my business to gather useful information. I've been aware of this place for years. Once I knew what you were planning and that you'd escaped the forest, I came here to wait for you."

"The archaeon," said Cait. "Did it help you?"

He looked baffled for a moment. "I have no idea what an archaeon is. Is that how you navigated the portal web so skilfully?"

Cait ignored his question. "But how are you going to get your revenge? How is coming with us going to help?"

"Because of this," said Nox. He opened his briefcase and took out something wrapped in a sheaf of cloth. He pulled aside the cloth to reveal a large book. Cait recognized the red leather. The etched diagrams of skeletons and the strange symbols. The stains.

"You took it from them?" asked Cait.

"While people still obeyed me. I did more, too. Certain secure messages transmitted to our installations, the right keys used. As we speak, operations the world over are shutting down. Genera, and therefore Angere, are crippled."

"And you'll give the book to us?" asked her mum. "Just like that?"

"There is a carrot and a stick," said Nox. "The book is the carrot. If you'll take me, I will give it you. I have no use for it."

"And the stick?" asked Johnny.

"I know how this portal works. I need only take a step backward and I will reach Angere. Bad for me. But you will be stranded here. And they *will* find you."

"You're not asking us to believe this are you?" said Johnny. "You seriously want us to trust you?"

"I will give you the book if you let me come with you. What more can I offer? Sooner or later they'll catch up with me. I have nothing to lose. And I can help you. I've picked up a lot about Angere, how it works, what goes on there. I can speak the language."

"I don't trust him," said Johnny.

"I do," said Cait quietly. "At least, I think he's telling the truth."

"No!" said Johnny. "He's Mr. Evil! He's the Man!"

"Yes," said Cait. "He is. But I still believe him. Don't you see? We broke him after all. And now he has to ask us for our help. We should take him."

"Cait," said her mum. "You're sure of this?"

"Yes," said Cait. "This is doing what we have to do."

She stepped toward Nox. "Give me the book."

Nox didn't move. For a moment she thought it was a trick after all, that he would hurl it into the pit. But instead he held it out. Cait took it and turned to her gran.

"Will you take it with you? To Andar?"

"I will," said her gran, quietly.

Cait hugged her gran hard for long moments. "Take care."

"I will, love," whispered her gran. "And you make sure you stay out of trouble."

Johnny, standing beside her gran, took his turn to hug her next. "I never played for you, Cait. But I will. For you and Danny, a gig all of your own. I promise. Hell, you might even get your own album after this."

They were being brave for her, pretending it was all going to be OK. She smiled at them both, continuing the deception.

She turned to Fer. There was much she wanted to say to the young witch. Much she wanted to hear from her. But right now she couldn't think where to start. It was a bit like looking into a mirror and being embarrassed by your own reflection.

Fer spoke instead, her words gentle and flowing, like a river.

"She says she'll be with you," translated Johnny. "In her thoughts."

"She'll be in mine, too," said Cait, hugging Fer close.

Cait let go and turned to Nox.

"Watch him, love," said her gran from behind her.

"Watch him every second. I don't trust him as far as I could spit him out. Maybe he's telling the truth and maybe he's not. But he's angry and resentful. He may blame you for what's happened. Watch him like a hawk."

"I will," said Cait.

She peered into the lava pit. The heat was intense. It felt like her skin would crack open just standing there. The pit was deep: a natural tube with straight sides. At its bottom lay a bubbling, heaving pool of molten rock. It moved constantly, flicking off tiny plumes of lava.

The sight of it filled her with dread. Fire terrified her, everyone knew that. Her insides lurched. But with the fear came a cold determination, too. She wouldn't be beaten. She could do this. This had to be done.

"I'm ready," she said.

She took Ran's hand. Nox took his other. Cait held her free hand out to her mother who stood in the shadows, deep in whispered conversation with her gran.

"Mum?" said Cait.

She would never know precisely what happened next. In everything that was to come, through all the horrors she was to meet in Angere, she thought about it often. But she never could decide which of them jumped first.

Together, Cait, Ran and Nox fell into the searing flame.

The travels of Cait and Fer continue in *Wyrm Lord* and conclude in *Witch King*.

Wyrm Lord – The Cloven Land Trilogy, Book 2

Lost in the land of the nightmares...

Cait Weerd has reached Angere in the company of Ran, Nox and the dead witch-girl she carries within her. Now all she has to do is cross the land of the undain without being captured, steal the Grimoire from the Witch King himself, and then, somehow, make it across the famously uncrossable river An.

Oh, and it would be quite nice if she could rescue Danny, too.

Meanwhile, in our world, Fer and her companions have to track down Johnny's lost guitar and use it to reach the safety of Andar. But Genera and the undain are closing in, and not everyone will survive the battle.

https://simonkewin.co.uk/wyrm-lord

Witch King – The Cloven Land Trilogy, Book 3

The war for Andar begins...

The mighty river An freezes from shore to shore, and the army of horrors from Angere marches across to devour peaceful and beautiful Andar. Cait, Hellen and the others head north, hoping to slow the invasion. At Islagray, Ashen battles to make sense of the reunited Shadow Grimoire, seeking a way to turn the undain's necromancy against itself. Fighting dark magic with dark magic is a grim and dangerous road.

Meanwhile, in our world, Fer evades Genera and the undain as she undertakes a desperate mission to sever the supply of Spirit fuelling the armies of Angere.

Unlikely friends rise to the skies, and hidden enemies wait to betray Cait and Fer. With every defeat, Andar fades. And at Islagray, the heart of the land, the last free place, the Song can barely be heard over the rising tide of war.

https://simonkewin.co.uk/witch-king

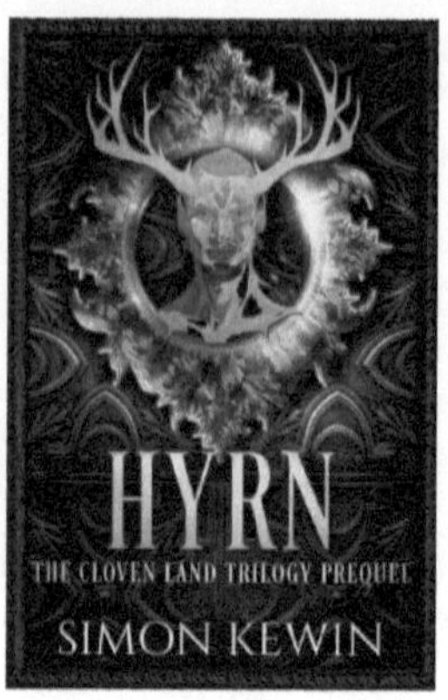

Hyrn – a Cloven Land Trilogy prequel

Some wounds are too wide to heal...

The world changes one bright morning in spring. The ageing king of Angere turns to necromancy to prolong his existence, and the price of dark magic is paid in innocent lives. The land descends into chaos as loyalties are tested and friends become bitter foes.

For Black Meg, eldest witch of Angere, time is desperately short. She receives a vision from Hyrn, the horned man of the woods. The future is worse than anything she could have imagined. But Hyrn also shows her an answer, a way out.

It's a terrible and desperate path. But the free people of Angere have no choice but to take it.

Free to download.

https://simonkewin.co.uk/hyrn

ABOUT THE AUTHOR

Simon Kewin was born on the misty Isle of Man but now lives deep in the English countryside. He writes fantasy, science fiction and some things that can't make their minds up. He is the author of over 100 published short stories as well as a growing number of novels.

To find out about his other books, go to:

www.simonkewin.co.uk

Sign up for his newsletter and you'll be the first to know when he has new books out. There are some fine sci/fi and fantasy books to download for free as thanks